A
BRIDE *of*
CONVENIENCE

Books by Jody Hedlund

The Preacher's Bride
The Doctor's Lady
Unending Devotion
A Noble Groom
Rebellious Heart
Captured by Love

BEACONS OF HOPE

Out of the Storm: A BEACONS OF HOPE Novella
Love Unexpected
Hearts Made Whole
Undaunted Hope

ORPHAN TRAIN

An Awakened Heart: An ORPHAN TRAIN Novella
With You Always
Together Forever
Searching for You

THE BRIDE SHIPS

A Reluctant Bride
The Runaway Bride
A Bride of Convenience

A BRIDE *of* CONVENIENCE

JODY HEDLUND

BETHANYHOUSE

a division of Baker Publishing Group
Minneapolis, Minnesota

© 2020 by Jody Hedlund

Published by Bethany House Publishers
11400 Hampshire Avenue South
Bloomington, Minnesota 55438
www.bethanyhouse.com

Bethany House Publishers is a division of
Baker Publishing Group, Grand Rapids, Michigan

Printed in the United States of America

Library of Congress Cataloging-in-Publication Data
Names: Hedlund, Jody, author.
Title: A bride of convenience / Jody Hedlund.
Description: Minneapolis, Minnesota : Bethany House Publishers, [2020] | Series:
    The bride ships ; 3
Identifiers: LCCN 2019059333 | ISBN 9780764232978 (trade paperback) | ISBN
    9780764236341 (cloth) | ISBN 9781493425211 (ebook)
Subjects: GSAFD: Historical fiction.
Classification: LCC PS3608.E333 B75 2020 | DDC 813/.6—dc23
LC record available at https://lccn.loc.gov/2019059333

Scripture quotations are from the King James Version of the Bible.

Marriage vows and prayer in chapter 8 are adapted from the *Book of Common Prayer*, which is in the public domain.

Cover design by Jennifer Parker
Cover photography by Mike Habermann Photography, LLC

Author is represented by Natasha Kern Literary Agency, Inc.

20 21 22 23 24 25 26   7 6 5 4 3 2

*Now unto him that is
able to do exceeding
abundantly above all that we ask
or think, according to the power
that worketh in us, unto him be
glory in the church by Christ
Jesus throughout all ages,
world without end.
Amen.*

Ephesians 3:20–21

one

VANCOUVER ISLAND
JANUARY 12, 1863

"I ain't gonna make it, Zoe."

"Don't say such nonsense." Zoe Hart clutched her friend's hand tighter as if by doing so she could keep Jane from leaving her.

The beginning of a cough slipped from Jane's lips, and the young woman cupped a rag over her mouth. While Jane might be able to muffle the deep hack, there was no hiding the bright crimson that seeped through the linen.

Zoe wound an arm behind her friend, holding her up, trying to ignore the outline of bony ribs. Not that Jane needed her support, since she was strong enough. It was just that staying on their feet was difficult against the rocking of the steamship in the choppy water surrounding Vancouver Island.

"Once we get to land, you'll be much better," Zoe said loudly enough for Dr. Ash to hear from where he stood across the deck. "You're needing solid ground again is all."

Scratching at his long gray beard, the ship's surgeon was speaking in low, almost urgent tones to the HMS *Grappler*'s commander, Captain Verney, and gave no indication he'd heard Zoe.

'Course, she'd said her piece to Dr. Ash earlier in the day and would say it again if she needed to. She wasn't letting him take Jane away. They hadn't been apart during the entire voyage— not since they'd left Manchester in September and boarded the *Robert Lowe* in Gravesend. And there was no need to separate now, not when Jane just needed to get off the cramped ship and have a few days to recuperate.

After 114 days at sea, they *all* needed a few days to recuperate. Aye, their journey from England across the Atlantic, around South America, and up the Pacific to Vancouver Island had been uneventful—and easy, according to the sailors. But still, the voyage had taken a toll, especially because so many of them, like Zoe, had already been near to starving before setting foot on the ship.

Even when the *Robert Lowe*'s supplies had dipped dangerously low over the past week, so that each passenger had been given strict rations, the gurgling and grumbling in Zoe's stomach couldn't compare to what it had been like during the last awful months in Manchester when starvation had plagued them.

Captain Verney nodded gravely at Dr. Ash before pulling back and straightening his blue jacket with its many golden stripes and trimmings. The middle-aged man swept his gaze over the women gathered on the deck, all thirty-eight of the brides. He didn't have to say anything for Zoe to sense his disapproval. The downward slant of his brows and the pinch of his lips spoke loudly enough.

The *Tynemouth*, the other Columbia Mission Society bride ship that had sailed to Vancouver Island several months earlier, had apparently contained a mixture of poor laborers from London along with an equal number of wealthy middle-class gentlewomen.

If that's what Captain Verney had been expecting again, then no wonder he was disappointed in getting a shipment of unemployed cotton-mill workers. They were already drab, but their months at sea had made them duller and dingier.

Perhaps the captain was worried none of the men in the colony would want them for brides, that they weren't appealing enough. Maybe he'd decided to send them back to England.

Zoe tucked a strand of her dark hair under her knitted head-scarf and swiped at her cheeks, hoping she didn't look quite as grimy as her companions but guessing she did. They needed the opportunity to clean up before meeting any men, and that would help their chances. Maybe she'd suggest that to the *Grappler*'s captain.

"May I have your attention, please?" Captain Verney's voice was commanding.

The women stopped their chattering and turned to look at him. The rumble of the steam engine beneath their feet filled the silence along with the splashing of waves against the hull. Overhead, smoke from the funnel billowed into the sky, making the low blanket of clouds a dirty gray.

Since they'd sailed through the Strait of Juan de Fuca two days ago, a chilled rain had fallen off and on, keeping the passengers mostly to their cabins when all they'd wanted was to be outside on the decks taking in the view of their stunning new home. Even now, Zoe let her gaze stray to the mountains on the mainland. Their peaks were snow covered, and they were dressed in thick, dark green pine.

The mountains. The Fraser River Valley. And hopefully Zeke.

Before he'd run away over a year ago, her brother had said he was heading to the goldfields of British Columbia and the Fraser River Valley. What if he'd never made it or had given up his prospecting and gone elsewhere? All she could do was pray she'd be able to find him so she could give him the news that would finally set him free. And maybe—just maybe—he'd forgive her for her part in all that had happened that had forced him to leave home.

She pressed her hand against her pocket beneath her skirt, assuring herself that Zeke's pendant was still with her and had been since he'd thrown it down at her feet before running off.

"We shall be arriving in James Bay shortly," Captain Verney said. "However, after speaking with Dr. Ash about the illness in your midst, I have decided we shall delay disembarking until after the afflicted are taken over to the hospital in West Bay."

"We're all suffering from one thing or another, Captain," Zoe said before she could stop herself. "Does that mean you're gonna take us all to the hospital?"

"Zoe, please try to understand." Dr. Ash tugged at his beard again, his weathered face lined with deep grooves. "If we don't quarantine Jane and Dora, the rest of you won't be able to go ashore. At least not without causing a panic."

"No telling who else has it," Zoe insisted. Mill fever was common among mill workers, and they couldn't put life on hold because of it. They had to keep going and fighting and hoping for the better. If they worried every time something went wrong or they had a slight cough, they'd have given up a long time ago.

"Miss, I am sorely tempted to quarantine all of you." Captain Verney leveled a stern look at Zoe. "But if I arrive in Victoria without any women, the waiting men will riot, especially since they were already fighting each other this morning when the *Emily Harris* delivered the other passengers."

After resting aboard the *Robert Lowe* on Sunday in Esquimalt Harbor, everyone had been anxious on Monday morning to disembark. The *Emily Harris* had arrived early to ferry newcomers the short distance to Victoria's inner harbor. Zoe and the other women had watched with both frustration and longing as the steamer had chugged away, leaving them behind.

Now that they had boarded the *Grappler* and were so close to being on land, Zoe didn't want to be the cause of any further delays. Yet how could she allow them to take Jane away?

"I'll go." Jane broke away from Zoe.

Zoe grabbed Jane's arm, but her friend shot a warning glare, one filled with more life and energy than Zoe had seen in recent days.

"I'll be able to rest in the hospital just as well as anywhere." Jane closed her fingers around the bloody rag as if to hide it.

Zoe hesitated, unable to let her friend walk away. Everyone knew hospitals were where people went to die.

"I'll make a point of looking after the women," Dr. Ash said as though reading Zoe's mind.

"Royal Hospital is a fine one," the captain added, "and shall provide them the best care possible."

Zoe examined Jane's dear face, noting the pallor, sunken eyes, and sharp angles. Gone was the robust young woman Zoe had met the first day she'd started at the factory when she'd filled in for her mum in the cardroom.

Jane hadn't questioned Zoe's presence or given away her true identity and as a result had won Zoe's gratitude. When Jane had quietly shown her each step of the carding process of combing and cleaning the cotton fibers, she'd won Zoe's admiration. And when Jane had pretended not to notice Zoe's tears when her mum had died, she'd won Zoe's everlasting devotion. The overlooker hadn't realized Zoe had replaced her mum until weeks later. By then she'd learned to do the job so efficiently that he'd kept her on.

Zoe swallowed a sudden lump in her throat. Jane's body might be a shell of what it used to be, but her friend's sweet spirit hadn't changed.

"Don't be thinking you can get rid of me so easily." Zoe wrapped Jane's rainbow scarf around her neck. Zoe had knitted

11

the colorful creation during the voyage using cast-off yarn. If only she'd had more material to knit Jane a thick sweater. "I'll be visiting you every chance I get."

"Nah," Jane said with a wavering smile, "you'll be busy fightin' away all the men who want you."

Zoe forced a return smile. "I'll be sure to save one for you."

Jane nodded but then began coughing. She stumbled and would have fallen if Dr. Ash hadn't caught her. Gently, he led her away while their chaperone, Mr. Reece, and his wife guided Dora, the other ill woman, toward starboard.

The lump lodged in Zoe's throat again, and her mind flashed with images of her father leading Mum down the street to visit the dispensary. Her mum's shoulders had been hunched with coughing. It was the last time Zoe had seen her alive.

Several of the other women patted Zoe's arm or offered a kind word. But their eyes held a resignation that only made Zoe angry. Jane was going to be just fine. After everything they'd been through over the months of unemployment and then during the months at sea, Zoe would make certain Jane had the chance at having something good happen.

When the *Grappler* began to turn the last bend leading into James Bay, the captain ordered the women to go belowdecks to wait until Jane and Dora were taken away by a Royal Navy tender. Zoe supposed the captain wanted to give the appearance that the ill women had been kept separate from the rest. But the truth was, they'd all lived together in cramped third-class cabins for the duration of the trip. They'd already been exposed to the illness, and there was no changing that now.

The steamship's engine finally silenced, and Zoe was surprised along with the other women to hear cheers and whistling.

"Are them the men a-waiting for us?" asked one of the women, her wide eyes revealing both excitement and fear.

"Heard Capt'n Verney saying there's hundreds of fellas on the shore," said another.

"All I need is one," Zoe chimed in. "The right one."

"Handsome?"

"Aye, a handsome fella and a good kisser."

The women giggled at Zoe's brash declaration.

"How you gonna tell if he's a good kisser?"

"I'll have to test him out."

Her comment earned more laughter.

She grinned. "'Course, he's gotta be rich. And willing to take me up into the mountains so I can find Zeke."

"You planning to put up a sign with your requirements?" teased someone.

"I might," she teased back. At nineteen, Zoe wasn't the youngest woman in the group, but neither was she the oldest. With her long raven hair and bright green eyes, everyone had always said she looked just like her mum, who'd been considered one of the prettiest women in Manchester. Even wasting away on her deathbed, Mum had still been beautiful.

Zoe supposed that's why Father had taken Mum's death so hard. His wife had been his source of beauty amid the bleakness and hardships of life. Truthfully, she'd been the beauty for all of them, both in body and spirit. And when she'd gone, they'd lost the goodness that had been holding them together. Without her, their family had frayed into a thousand threads.

"You'll find a handsome fella in no time," said Kate from her spot next to Zoe on the bottom step of the deck as they waited to go above.

"You will too." Zoe tugged the girl's long blond braid, which earned her a smile. A year younger, Kate Millington had grown up with Zoe in the same neighborhood and had always been like a little sister. It was hard to believe the pretty young woman was old enough to take a husband.

"Too bad Jeremiah wasn't richer and better looking," Kate continued. "You could have married him, and then you wouldn't have had to leave home."

Kate's older brother Jeremiah had been a good man, one of Zeke's best friends. But Zoe had never paid him or any other man much heed. At first she'd been too busy working at the mill. Then after she'd been let go with all the other women, she'd filled her days taking care of Eve, her sister Meg's babe, and trying to survive the hunger along with her father's drunken rages.

"Time to go ashore!" came a call from above deck. Within minutes, the women congregated at the main railing, taking in the scene before them—the small but sprawling town of Victoria along the harbor with more of the thick forests of stately pines that seemed to cover everything that hadn't been cleared to make room for the new colony.

Zoe's gaze frantically searched the boats and ships that filled the busy harbor until she found a Royal Navy tender rowing away toward the east with two women inside, both with heads bent and shoulders slouched.

"Jane," she called, even though her friend wouldn't be able to hear her amid the clamor of the people lining the shore.

A dull ache throbbed in one of Zoe's temples. She took a deep breath and started kneading the spot. She didn't have time for a headache. Not today. Not when she had to find a way to get to the hospital and do her best to save her friend. She couldn't lose Jane. Not when she'd already lost so much.

two

$\mathcal{A}$be Merivale wasn't a blushing man, but a hot flush had worked its way up his body, into his neck, and all the way to the roots of his fair hair. He averted his attention away from Pete kissing his new bride and focused instead on the layered chocolate cake sitting atop the center worktable.

Little good it did to look away. Abe could still picture Pete's hand splayed across Arabella's lower back, crushing her body into his. And he could still hear the eager melding of their lips and their heavy breathing.

At a soft moan from one of them, a fresh dose of heat shot through Abe along with keen desire for Lizzy. How long had it been since he'd seen her?

He mentally tallied the years he'd been ministering in British Columbia, from 1860 to the present. Had he really been away from Lizzy for close to three years?

The time had gone quickly, and most oft he was too busy to think about Lizzy, much less physically desire her. But here. Now. With Pete and Arabella's passion radiating through the bakeshop with more heat than the ovens, Abe tugged at his collar and tried not to think of how much he wanted Lizzy.

Only two years left, he chided himself. Only two until he finished his commitment in the colonies and returned home to Yorkshire and Lizzy. He was over half-finished. Before he knew it, they would be married, and he'd be able to kiss her every day for the rest of his life.

Against his will, his gaze strayed to Pete, to the hand still pressed possessively against Arabella's back and the other hand gently cupping her cheek. As Pete's kisses dropped to Arabella's jawline, Abe tore his attention away again and cleared his throat.

Pete broke away from his wife, looked at Abe, and chuckled. "That's how it's done, my friend. In case you were wondering."

"I wasn't." Abe tried to keep his tone dry.

"Then you don't know what you're missing." Pete stole another kiss from Arabella, this one quicker, but nonetheless passionate enough that Abe's body betrayed him with urges he'd been trying to ignore. If only he'd never had that encounter with Wanda. . . . If only he'd never gone to her house. . . .

Abe lifted a silent prayer of repentance, as he did almost daily, and asked God to deliver him from temptation so he wouldn't compromise his integrity any further. No, he and Lizzy weren't officially engaged, but they'd been friends since childhood, and he'd always known she was the perfect woman for him.

When the Society of the Propagation of the Gospel had offered him the five-year position establishing churches in British Columbia, he'd asked Lizzy if she would wait for him, and of course she'd agreed. She'd understood his devastation at the riots and resulting deaths of the laborers in his Sheffield parish. She'd understood his need to take a break from the heartache and gain a new perspective. She'd always understood him better than anyone else had.

From her faithful correspondence, he knew she was keeping busy giving music lessons as well as doing charity work.

Lately her letters were so full of all her activities he'd begun to wonder if she missed him. Whenever he doubted her affection, he reminded himself that his letters touted his activities too. With his work in Yale and among the mining camps, he'd had little time to pine away for her. Even though he replied to her regularly, he could admit that sometimes his letters were abysmally short and hurried.

Even so, Lizzy was the love of his life. She was refined, poised, elegant, and soft-spoken. When he sailed home and took another rector position, she would fit into his life seamlessly and would be the kind of helpmate he'd always dreamed of having. Their parents heartily approved of their relationship, and Lizzy's mother had been planning their wedding for years.

Though he and Lizzy had always been close, he'd never kissed her except for the morning he left England—if the peck on her forehead could really be called a kiss. In hindsight, he wished he'd demonstrated more ardor. Maybe not the way Pete kissed Arabella. Or the way Wanda had kissed him. But surely he could have managed something a little more impassioned.

Abe's gaze drifted to Arabella's delicate face, the rosy color in her cheeks, and the delight radiating from her eyes as she peered up at Pete.

Would he and Lizzy look at each other that way, with such longing? Would he hold Lizzy and press her body against his? Would he kiss her senseless?

At such brazen thoughts, heat simmered up his torso and into his neck again again. He and Lizzy were too timid and refined for such displays, and he suspected their affection would one day be contained to kisses under covers in the dark. Even so, he couldn't deny his urges were intensifying.

As though sensing the direction of Abe's thoughts—or seeing the flush in his face—Pete arched a brow. "Get on down to the wharf and pick out a bride."

Arabella had come on the *Tynemouth*, the bride ship that had arrived in September. Even though Pete had claimed her the first day he'd seen her, it had taken him weeks to win her heart. Now that he'd found marital bliss, he assumed everyone ought to have a woman from a bride ship.

The local newspaper, the *British Colonist*, had been full of reports of the latest bride ship that was arriving today, lauding the newest batch of women sent by Miss Rye and the Columbia Mission Society as exemplary in character.

Even so, Abe wasn't interested. "I am doing just fine for now."

"Someone wise once told me that God said it wasn't good for man to live alone."

Abe rued the day he'd spouted the verse to Pete. His friend never failed to remind him of it. "I'm not alone. God's presence is with me wherever I go. Besides, I have Lizzy."

Pete's grin turned mischievous. "Then what are you waiting for? Tell Lizzy to get on the next ship and come marry you."

Abe straightened to his full six feet, seven inches, his muscles tensing. He didn't want to admit he'd already invited Lizzy, that he'd sent her a letter last autumn asking her to come and marry him. Then he'd have to explain his indiscretion with Wanda and the desperation that had led him to quickly pen the correspondence to Lizzy.

Once a fair amount of time had passed, he'd regretted his rash letter and wished he'd remained true to his resolution to wait for marriage. After all, he didn't want Lizzy to experience the dangers of the long voyage. Didn't want to expose her to the harshness of the mountain wilderness. Didn't want her to face the deprivations of his humble existence.

But perhaps he'd been wrong to think they needed to wait until he finished his five years of service. If she desired him enough, wouldn't she be willing to brave the discomforts to be with him? Although he couldn't picture a woman like Lizzy ministering with him, what if she was willing nonetheless?

With thoughts of Lizzy racing through his head, he said good-bye to Pete and Arabella. Pulling his thick cloak tighter about him, he hunkered down against the winter chill as he slogged down the muddy street. Although he tried to avoid getting splattered with mud from the passing horses and wagons, by the time he reached the end of Humboldt Street, his freshly laundered trousers were hopelessly dirty.

How would Lizzy fare here? What would she think of the mud? It was worse in the mining camps up in the river valley. And what would she think of his tiny log cabin? Or of the rugged town of Yale that served as his home base?

Surely at the prospect of being together she'd overlook the negatives. Besides, in spite of the austere living conditions, the beauty was unlike anything else. He lifted his sights to the distant mountain peaks and began to whistle one of his favorite hymns, "God, Who Made the Earth and Heaven."

As he turned a corner and the harbor spread out before him, his whistle faded, and he stopped short at the sight of the crowds lining the shore. Men stood on wharfs, waited in moored boats, and perched on fences.

"Lord have mercy." Abe's jaw slackened. There had to be at least a thousand men swarming the waterfront. Did every single one of them hope to find a bride? Or were some mere spectators?

As a cheer went up, his attention shifted to two tenders pulling up alongside a wharf that had been cordoned off by constables. A few minutes later, the women climbed out of the boats, and Abe watched with fascination, unable to tear himself away. He hadn't been in Victoria when the *Tynemouth* had arrived and had only heard embellished secondhand stories—or at least he'd assumed the tales had been embellished.

Maybe the miners hadn't been exaggerating after all.

When the women began to make their way down a roped-off path, he half held his breath, wondering if anyone would be brave enough to propose like Pioneer had when the *Tynemouth* women came ashore.

From what Abe had heard, the young miner had singled out a pretty lass from the group, stepped right up to her, and offered two thousand pounds if she agreed to marry him. Sophia had hesitated only a moment before saying yes. And less than a week later, Abe had performed the wedding ceremony.

Of course, Abe hadn't approved of the hasty arrangements. He'd had a long talk with Pioneer the morning of the wedding, encouraging him to consider postponing until he had the chance to get to know Sophia. But Pioneer had insisted she was the one.

The last Abe had heard of Pioneer and Sophia, they were living in Johnson's Creek, where Pioneer had his profitable claim. As far as Abe knew, the couple was getting along well enough, but he wouldn't know for certain until the spring thaw when he began his circuit riding.

"Get on down to the wharf and pick out a bride." Pete's teasing from earlier resounded in Abe's head and kicked him in the gut with the same longing as before. Though he needed to continue on his way to Christ Church Cathedral and his meeting with Bishop Hills, he couldn't make his feet move and instead studied the bride-ship women.

They wore the plain skirts and cloaks of the poor working class. In fact, their garments were unkempt, making the women appear almost shabby. In addition, the women were pale and thin from their months at sea. Even so, their faces held an innocence and appeal that made them different from the prostitutes who lived in Victoria and the mining towns.

An interaction near the end of the wharf drew Abe's attention. Someone had stopped one of the brides. From his hilltop position, Abe glimpsed a pretty face with especially fetching eyes. As she smiled at the man talking with her, dimples made a quick appearance in her cheeks.

When the man reached out and tugged off her headscarf, her long dark hair fell forward and framed her face, making her even more beautiful. She batted his hand, and her expression turned feisty. Her reaction must have made her more appealing to the man ogling her, because he yanked off her cloak, giving full view of her womanly figure.

Her dark brows furrowed and formed storm clouds as she jerked her cloak back around herself. She said something to the man, but over the distance and commotion, Abe couldn't make out the words.

The man tipped his head back and laughed, clearly pleased with the woman's spunk. As the man exchanged a grin with one of his companions, Abe recognized the swarthy young face— Dexter Dawson. Or Dex as he was known up in the mining towns.

Dex and his men caused trouble wherever they went, carousing, brawling, and stirring up dissension. They never stayed in one spot long enough to strike it rich, but somehow they always seemed to have plenty of gold. Abe couldn't be certain, but he guessed Dex and his men stole from caravans loaded with gold that were heading out of the mountains back down to New Westminster and Victoria.

With a surge of alarm, Abe watched the pretty woman stride away. Dexter Dawson surely wasn't thinking about marrying one of the bride-ship women, was he? Dex was handsome and charming and popular among saloon women. But he had no business interfering with these newly arrived brides. They certainly hadn't come halfway around the world to get tangled up with the likes of him.

Abe lifted his broad shoulders and pressed his lips together. Maybe he needed to seek out the chaperones or speak to one of the members of the welcoming committee and warn them about Dex so that they could encourage the new arrivals to stay away from him.

With so many other God-fearing and upright fellows in the colony looking for wives, the women would have plenty of suitable options. He just prayed they would take their time and choose wisely.

three

Zoe blinked back a wave of dizziness. Her headache wasn't completely gone, and the jarring of the carriage ride over to the hospital hadn't helped, but at least the blinding pain had diminished. She'd been able to keep down toast and tea at breakfast, the first meal she'd eaten since setting foot in Victoria two days ago.

"Maybe I shouldn't leave you here by yourself," Mrs. Moresby said as the weight of the stairs creaked under her hefty frame. "I don't think you're entirely well yet."

"I'll be just fine, ma'am." Zoe paused and gripped the rail. "You needn't fret about me."

Mrs. Moresby from the welcoming committee had been a godsend from the moment the brides had arrived at the Marine Barracks. The matron had informed them that the large house would be their living quarters until they found employment or a husband—whichever came first.

She'd also shown them around, provided additional clothing, and patiently answered all their questions. She'd even been there when the ache in Zoe's temple had finally become so unbearable that she'd collapsed from the pain. Mrs. Moresby had been the one to accompany Zoe to her room, help her don a clean nightgown, and tuck her into bed.

The kind matron had tended her throughout the day yesterday, bringing her tea and warm compresses. When Mrs. Moresby arrived this morning, Zoe forced herself to get up and act normal, desperate to go to the hospital and discover how Jane was doing. No one else had visited the patients, and Mrs. Moresby hadn't needed much persuading to allow Zoe to go. She'd even arranged to deliver Zoe in her own carriage.

"Maybe while you're here, we'll have one of the doctors take a look at you." She was a giant of a woman with her wide shoulders, thick arms, and broad girth. Her hooped skirts brushed against the narrow stairwell, and the tall, colorful feathers on her hat dusted the low ceiling.

"The headaches just come and go, ma'am," Zoe said, as she had already a dozen times. "My mum, bless her soul, tried everything she could to ease the pressure, but nothing worked except the passing of time."

"Yes, but we have such good doctors here in Victoria. They might be able to discover what ails you and find a treatment."

"I'm more concerned about my friend, ma'am." Zoe had only needed to step one foot inside the hospital for dread to pound out its ugly rhythm. The dark, damp entryway had greeted her with the stench of death. The silence, the chill in the air, and even the somberness of an attendant on duty had only made Zoe all the more anxious to find Jane and Dora and haul them back to the Marine Barracks. Surely she could coax Mrs. Moresby to take her side. Maybe, with a little charm, she could even convince the woman to arrange the transportation.

At the second floor, she followed Mrs. Moresby down the hallway. They stopped in front of the closed door the attendant had indicated belonged to the quarantined women. In the room across the hallway, a man rested in a bed with a bloodied bandage around his head. At the sound of their footsteps, he opened his eyes and took them in.

"Why, hello there, beautiful," he said with a weak smile.

"Hello yourself." Mrs. Moresby paused with her hand on the doorknob and glared down her prominent nose at the man.

"I meant the compliment to the young lady." He averted his gaze. "But you're a fine-looking lady too, that you are."

Mrs. Moresby glared at the man a moment longer before she swung open the door and bustled away in a flurry of swishing skirts and rustling feathers.

Zoe repaid the man's compliment with a nod and smile before following Mrs. Moresby. At the sight of Jane, pale and motionless on the bed closest to the door, Zoe rushed to her friend, her heartbeat picking up pace. "Jane, I'm here."

Jane's eyelids fluttered, but she didn't open them.

Zoe dropped to the edge of the bed and took her friend's hand. It was cold and waxy . . . the same way baby Eve's had been that last morning Zoe had held her. With mounting panic, she shook her friend. "Wake up, Jane. It's time to be going."

A breath slipped from Jane's lips before they curled up just slightly into a smile. "Did you find me a husband, then?"

"Aye." Zoe kept her voice lighthearted even though the anxiety inside twisted tighter than thread around a spindle. "Found you the handsomest fella in all the colony."

"Good."

Zoe's mind went back to coming ashore two days ago and the fellas she'd seen during the walk to the Marine Barracks. Thankfully, the men hadn't seemed deterred by the dirty, disheveled state of the women and were now apparently lining up at the door to come calling on the brides.

She'd gladly give them all to Jane. "You're coming back with me, and I'll introduce you to your new man today."

Jane wheezed, coughed weakly, then grew still.

Zoe picked up Jane's colorful scarf where it had fallen on the floor and gently began to wrap it around the young woman again. Her dear friend was worse. Much worse. How had she deteriorated so quickly in just two days?

"Miss Hart," Mrs. Moresby said from beside Dora's bed.

Something in the older woman's tone drew Zoe's attention. Dora's body was frozen in place without even the slightest rise and fall of her chest. Zoe lifted her eyes to Mrs. Moresby's to find somber resignation.

"I'm sorry," Mrs. Moresby whispered.

Zoe clutched Jane's hand harder. "We need to be getting Jane over to the Marine Barracks right away."

With heavy footsteps echoing ominously, Mrs. Moresby crossed the room, stood next to the bed, and stared down at Jane.

Zoe tugged at Jane and forced a smile. "Or maybe we should go right to the church and have the wedding today."

Again, Jane's lips curved, but barely.

"That's my girl." Zoe leaned in and brushed a kiss across Jane's forehead. It was just as cold and waxy as the rest of her, as cold and waxy as the face of her precious niece when Zoe had found her dead in her crib.

Eve had been only six weeks old. Had been so full of life and energy. Had filled Zoe's heart with such love. And had given her purpose when she'd had none.

The babe had been too young to die. . . .

A sharp pang reverberated in Zoe's chest, and she took a deep breath to force the pain away. She couldn't think of Eve right now. This situation was different. Jane was still breathing and talking. With the right kind of care, Jane would regain her strength and be as good as new.

As Zoe sat back up, she caught Mrs. Moresby studying her, the woman's eyes saying everything Zoe didn't want to hear.

Zoe smoothed back her friend's limp hair. "I'm sure your driver would help us carry her out."

Mrs. Moresby shook her head.

"Please." This time Zoe reached for Mrs. Moresby's hand. She would have gotten on her knees and begged the woman, except Mrs. Moresby placed her other hand on Zoe's shoulder and pinned her in place.

"If we move her," Mrs. Morseby said softly, "we'll kill her."

Zoe's throat constricted.

"She has to stay here."

Mrs. Moresby was right. "Then I'll be staying here and helping her is all." She jutted her chin and dared Mrs. Moresby to stop her.

"Of course you will." The matron's expression was tender. "I wouldn't expect anything else."

At the sight of a woman sitting on the edge of the bed, Abe halted abruptly, his frame filling the hospital room doorway. Mrs. Moresby hadn't indicated anyone else would be present when she'd sought out a reverend earlier to perform last rites for the dying bride-ship woman.

Apparently, one of the women had already died and the second would soon join her companion in the afterlife.

Abe took in the unmoving form of the patient lying on the bed. She was so silent and still that Abe guessed he was too late, that she'd already passed. At least she'd had someone present with her during her last moments.

He shifted his attention to the friend. Holding the woman's hands along with a colorful scarf, she was bent over with head bowed. Half of her dark hair had come loose from the knot at the base of her neck, and long wavy strands fell over her shoulders in disarray.

Hearing the muffled sniffles and seeing the slight shaking

of her thin shoulders, Abe stepped into the room, compassion stirring within him. Even though he'd encountered plenty of death during his years as a minister, he hadn't ever learned how to remain detached the way some of his friends had, not even with complete strangers.

Trying not to disturb the grieving woman, he treaded lightly and circled to the other side of the bed. Towering above the patient, he couldn't see any evidence of life in her pale features or any movement in her chest to indicate breathing.

He wouldn't be able to offer up any prayers on her behalf, but he could pray for this grieving one she'd left behind. He bowed his head. *Bring her comfort, Lord. Let her know you love her and that she's not alone.*

At a sharp intake of breath, he lifted his head to find that she was sitting up, averting her head, and rapidly swiping her cheeks. "I didn't know I wasn't alone."

"I'm sorry. I didn't mean to disturb you—" Words fled as she shifted and gave him full view of her face, her beautiful face, the same face of the bride-ship woman he'd noticed coming ashore the other day.

Up close, she was even prettier in spite of her tousled appearance. Her eyes were a dark green, made darker by the long lashes that framed them. Her high cheekbones were elegant, her lips a deep rose, and her chin gently rounded.

Even though she'd tried to dry the evidence of her crying, tears still clung to her lashes and streaked her cheeks. Dark half circles under her eyes testified to sleeplessness. And the hopelessness in her expression spoke of previous pains that made this parting even worse.

Nevertheless, her beauty was mesmerizing, her body willowy, like a forest nymph from a Greek tale, with a tiny waist and gentle curves. He shifted on his feet, suddenly realizing he was much too conscious of her appearance.

This was neither the time nor place to concern himself with the beauty of one of the bride-ship women. Actually, he didn't *ever* need to concern himself over the beauty of one of the newly arrived women. He was present to offer spiritual guidance. That was all.

"I am very sorry for your loss, Miss . . . ?" He attempted to speak in his kindest, gentlest tone, the one that never failed to put people at ease.

"Zoe Hart." She glanced down at the bed and blinked back more tears.

He smoothed a hand over the cover of his Bible, drawing comfort from its solid presence in so difficult a situation. "People around here call me Pastor Abe."

Her stunning green eyes shot back to him. "You're a reverend?"

"I am." He was accustomed to surprising people, especially since he no longer wore his suit or clerical collar, which, of course, was another of the grievances Bishop Hills had listed during their recent meeting. Shortly after arriving in the colonies, Abe had decided to shed the formal attire in favor of the corduroy trousers and flannel shirts the miners wore. Not only were the simple garments sturdier and warmer, but he felt as though the miners accepted him more readily as one of their own when he didn't emphasize the differences in their status. If only Bishop Hills saw the benefit of the apparel.

"You don't look like a reverend," Miss Hart said.

"I didn't know reverends were supposed to look a particular way." He smiled with what he hoped was his most sincere, pastor-like smile.

She studied him openly. He was tempted to brush a hand over his hatless head and make sure his unruly locks were in place, but he resisted the urge. "Guess I always thought reverends were old and ugly. I've never met any who were young and handsome."

Handsome?

Her gaze was direct and unabashedly curious, so much that he dropped his attention to his Bible.

She thought he was handsome. Part of him wanted to stand a little taller. At the same time, he was tempted to duck his head in embarrassment. After three years of living among miners, he was clearly out of practice at interacting with single young women.

And *clearly*, he was an oaf for focusing on himself at a time like this. What was wrong with him?

He shifted his attention to the lifeless woman on the bed. "May I read a few words of Scripture and pray with you? I know it won't bring back . . . " He paused, hoping she'd supply the woman's name.

"Jane."

He wasn't accustomed to using a woman's given name, but he couldn't correct Miss Hart. Not in the wake of her loss. "Nothing I can say will bring back . . . Jane . . . but God's Word and His presence can bring you comfort as you grieve."

Miss Hart glanced at her friend's pale face. Tears rapidly formed in her eyes and glistened. After a moment, she nodded.

Abe opened his Bible and read several verses. Then he prayed aloud for Miss Hart that Christ's love would soothe her and be with her in the days to come.

"Finally, Lord, I pray you would bring along a husband for Miss Hart. She's traveled here to the colony in search of a help-mate, and so we ask that you would direct her choices, give her wisdom, and make clear to her the right man. In the name of Jesus our Savior, amen."

As he lifted his head, he was surprised to find Miss Hart staring at him. Framed by those dark lashes, her eyes were as wide and rich as the mountain forests. For a few seconds, he allowed himself to get lost there.

"My mum used to pray like that," she said.

"Like what?"

"Like God is right here with us, listening."

She was offering him the perfect opportunity to speak of God's love. As a minister, he was always on the lookout for such openings. But somehow, today, around her, his brain was sluggish, and he couldn't formulate a response.

"Do you really think God cares who I pick for a husband?" She tilted her head so that more locks of her thick hair fell loose and tumbled over her shoulder, making her look vulnerable, almost desperate.

A protective urge rose up within him. "He cares very much and will direct you if you let Him." Sometimes grief led people to do things they normally wouldn't consider, things they later regretted. He prayed this woman wouldn't do anything rash in her sorrow.

"Pastor Abe?" A timid voice came from the doorway.

Abe started, guilt rushing through him, though he didn't know why he should feel guilty. All he'd been doing was speaking words of comfort to this grieving woman. There was nothing wrong with that, was there?

A shabby miner stood in the doorway, holding a valise. With the hair falling into the man's eyes and with his overgrown mustache and beard, Abe struggled to see past the scruffiness and identify him. His clothes were ragged and stained with mud and tobacco juice. And his body was as thin as a plank, the outline of his shoulder bones jutting through his coat.

"It's me, Herman Cox. The nurse downstairs told me you were here."

Abe sized up the newcomer again, this time noting the blood-shot eyes and the hollowness of his cheeks. This was Herman

Cox? The robust miner from Richfield who'd married a native woman and recently had a baby? When his wife was having trouble with her labor, Herman had brought her down to Victoria for help. A young ship's surgeon, Lord Colville, who had arrived with the *Tynemouth* brides, had been kind enough to help the couple when no one else had wanted anything to do with the native woman due to the smallpox scare.

"Good to see you, Herman." Abe crossed to the man and reached out for a handshake, another mannerism for which Bishop Hills criticized him, labeling the greeting as too familiar.

Herman returned the clasp, but his grip was weak. A waft of the man's body odor hit Abe, causing him to breathe through his mouth instead of his nose. During his circuit riding between camps, he'd grown accustomed to all manner of stench. But Herman was especially ripe, and the bag he carried was worse.

"I came to find Lord Colville. He was kind enough to help me once. Figured he could again, but the nurse said he ain't in Victoria anymore."

"That's right. He and his bride left a couple of months ago."

Herman's shoulders slumped, and he moved his bag to his opposite hand as if the weight had suddenly become too much to bear.

"If your wife and child need attention, I'll speak to one of the other doctors. I'll do my best to convince them to offer assistance." Now that the worst of the smallpox scare was over, surely Herman could bring his family into Victoria without causing any trouble.

"Rose didn't make it." Herman's lips trembled as he spoke. "The smallpox took her."

Genuine sorrow speared Abe's heart. "I'm so sorry, Herman. So sorry. I know you loved Rose very much."

Tears pooled in the man's eyes, and he blinked rapidly, struggling to compose himself.

Abe didn't approve of the way miners invited native women into their shanties, using and discarding them at will. So when Herman had asked him to officiate a wedding ceremony for him and Rose, Abe had been more than willing, especially because he'd witnessed Herman's kindness and gentleness to the native woman.

"She's got no family left," Herman said through a wavering breath. "I tried to find them, but they're all dead."

Abe wasn't surprised. Last year a smallpox epidemic had ravaged the tribes on Vancouver Island and had spread to the mainland, killing thousands upon thousands of Indians who seemed more susceptible to the disease than European immigrants did. Abe had recently learned how to administer vaccinations and had done his best to inoculate the natives living around Yale. But like many doctors and missionaries, his attempts to protect the Indians had come too late.

"Is there anything I can do?" Abe asked.

"Aye, Pastor." Herman's face contorted with heartache and desperation.

Abe's chest squeezed with a need to ease the man's burden.

At a wail rising from the valise, Herman held out the bag. "Find a home for my baby."

four

A babe?

Zoe jumped up from Jane's bed and started across the hospital room, her focus upon the battered leather bag the miner was holding.

Another muffled cry came from inside, this one angrier than the last.

"I can't take care of her no more, Pastor." Herman extended the bag toward Pastor Abe, but the young minister took a step away, confusion—and fear—rounding his blue eyes. Even though Zoe had just met Pastor Abe, she suspected he'd never held a babe and wouldn't know the first thing about looking after one.

"Are you sure you can't care for her, Herman?" With stiff arms, Pastor Abe shoved his hands into his pockets, clearly having no intention of accepting the bag.

"I ain't fit to be her father."

"You can be," Pastor Abe said gently. "God will give you the strength you need."

"She needs a mother and father," Herman insisted. "I was hoping Lord Colville could find a place that would take her. But with all your connections, I bet you can find her a new family."

"What's her name?" Zoe asked as she approached.

"Violet." Herman's outstretched arm shook. "Rose wanted me to give her the name of a flower, same as her." His jitters and bloodshot eyes were the same symptoms Zoe had seen in her father countless times, which meant he was in need of his next drink.

When her fingers closed around the handles, Herman offered no protest and relinquished the burden. He stank of rum, tobacco, and urine. But the bag smelled even worse. When was the last time the man had changed the babe's napkin?

Zoe placed the valise on the floor and knelt beside it. "How long ago did she eat?"

Herman lowered his head, but not before she caught sight of his shame. "Think it were last eve."

"Last eve?" Indignation rose in Zoe, but she bit back her angry retort. After Zeke was no longer around to protect her, she'd earned the back of her father's hand across her mouth one too many times for speaking her mind, especially when he was drunk or in need of his next binge. As a result, she'd learned to control her temper when necessary.

Instead of giving Herman the tongue-lashing he deserved, she made quick work of unbuckling the strap and pulling the bag open. The stench was enough to wrinkle even the stoutest of noses.

Yet, the second Zoe laid eyes upon the wee infant inside, she forgot all about the urge to gag, especially when the babe peered up at her, then reached out tiny fingers and grabbed a handful of Zoe's hair.

In that instant, Zoe fell in love.

She scooped up the child in spite of the foul odor and damp blankets. She cuddled the wee one in her arms, unable to tear her gaze away. "Oh you precious, sweet babe."

The infant stared back, as though trying to figure out who

Zoe was. Dark brown, innocent eyes, a smattering of downy hair, rounded cheeks.

An ache swelled inside Zoe with a need so deep she couldn't begin to explain it, even if she'd tried. With the small bundle warm and wiggling against her chest, pain came rushing back along with memories. Memories of holding Eve in just the same way, of blowing bubbly kisses against her belly, of snuggling her close and singing lullabies.

If only Meg had been home that fateful morning. If only Meg had paid the infant more attention. If only Meg had been more responsible. Instead, Meg had been out all night and hadn't returned. And Zoe, as usual, had been watching over Eve.

The ache in Zoe's chest squeezed into her throat. She'd cared for the babe as best she could, and she'd loved the babe when no one else would. All she'd done was lay Eve down for a morning nap like she always did. She'd made sure the child was asleep before starting on the laundry.

But for a reason Zoe still didn't understand, Eve had never woken. When Zoe had checked a short while later, she discovered Eve wasn't breathing or moving. Though she rushed to the nearest dispensary, the infant never cried another cry or breathed another breath.

No one, not even the doctor, could determine what had caused Eve's death. After all the months that had passed, Zoe still blamed herself, figured she'd done something wrong. Meg hadn't passed any judgment, had acted almost relieved not to have an illegitimate child anymore. Or maybe she'd been relieved she no longer had to listen to Zoe's scolding and ranting about her need to be like their mum.

Whatever the case, Zoe hadn't been able to save Eve, but she could help this child here and now, couldn't she?

The babe began to suck her thumb noisily, making angry

grunts in the process. She was tiny and delicate, and yet she didn't have the look of a newborn.

"How old is Violet?"

"Four months." Herman slanted a glance toward the door. No doubt he was wondering how much longer he had to stay before he could slip away and drown himself in drink.

Violet slurped at her thumb but apparently realized she wasn't getting any nourishment from the sucking. Her lips wobbled and her eyes squinted as she released another wail, a demand for something to fill her stomach.

"Do you have a bottle for her?" Zoe directed the question at Herman, who shook his head and focused on the floor.

"We'll need bottles and pap or milk—maybe both." She bounced Violet in an effort to calm her.

Neither of the men moved.

Zoe glanced first at Herman then at Pastor Abe. "Right away."

Pastor Abe jerked his hands out of his pockets and straightened. "Of course. Bottles and milk." He started toward the door but then paused before exiting, looking back at her with the kindest eyes Zoe had ever seen. "Will she need anything else?"

"I'm sure the attendant can provide me with a few rags for making a clean napkin." And warm water for bathing the child. No telling what kind of rash the babe had from lying in her own filth for so long.

Pastor Abe nodded and then glanced at Herman. "We'll talk more when I get back, okay?"

"Sure, Pastor." Herman spoke with forced cheer but didn't meet Pastor Abe's gaze. Zoe was well acquainted with the tactic of avoidance, the one that meant the need for drink was more important than anyone or anything.

Pastor Abe, however, seemed satisfied with Herman's assurance. He continued on his way, his footfalls in the hallway and on the stairs loud and urgent. When the hospital door gave a resounding thump of closure, Zoe straightened and faced Herman.

"I'll take care of Violet this afternoon," she said as nonchalantly as she could manage. "You needn't worry about her." The truth was, she wouldn't hand the babe back over to Herman, not even if he threatened to beat her. The man didn't deserve to have the child—not now, not in his current condition. But she'd learned that some people—like her father—worked better if they thought they were in control.

"I'll take her back to the Marine Barracks with me," she continued, "and you can come and get her there later."

"Thank you, miss."

"I don't mind." She refused to look over at the bed where Jane lay motionless, having breathed her last over an hour ago. Zoe had been nearly mad with her grief when Pastor Abe had arrived, hadn't wanted to leave her friend's side, hadn't been sure she could go on.

Even now, the loss hurt so acutely that if she focused on it, she was sure she'd lose herself. Maybe she'd even end up like her father, drinking to escape the sorrow.

The babe released another wail. Zoe guided the girl's thumb to her mouth. It would have to sate her until Pastor Abe returned with real sustenance.

She expected Herman to leave, wanted him to leave. But he hesitated. "Rose was a good wife and mother." The words came out in a broken whisper. "I'd be obliged if Violet knew that someday."

Herman's words sounded final, almost like a good-bye. Zoe narrowed her eyes upon the miner, but he refused to meet her gaze. Maybe Herman had no intention of coming back for Violet later. If so, she wouldn't try to change his mind.

Pastor Abe might attempt to convince Herman Cox of his need to turn his life around and become the kind of father Violet needed. Pastor Abe might know how to offer the right Scriptures and prayers to comfort him. But Zoe had nothing to say.

"You'll take good care of her, won't you?" Herman's eyes brimmed with tears.

"'Course I will."

Blinking rapidly, he turned and hurried toward the door.

Zoe had seen too much heartache in her life to do anything but let this man go, if that's what he wanted. She bent and placed a tender kiss on the babe's forehead. Violet deserved better. And Zoe intended to see that she got it.

———

Pastor Abe returned to the hospital a short while later and was whistling a familiar hymn as he breezed into the first-floor examining room the attendant had allowed Zoe to use while bathing the babe.

He carried a crate. "My baker friend still had half a bottle of milk remaining from his baking projects."

Zoe stopped bouncing Violet only to have the babe release a wail that was becoming more pitiful—and uncontrollable—with hunger. "Were you able to find a baby bottle?"

"Pete's wife knew of a customer who just had a baby. And thankfully the family had an extra." Pastor Abe placed the crate on the table, then held up the typical clear glass, banjo-shaped bottle used for feeding infants. A tube was inserted through the stopper and dangled down into the bottle.

Bouncing Violet again, Zoe crossed to the table and stood opposite the reverend. "Did they give you a nipple?"

Pastor Abe fumbled in the crate before retrieving the small rubber piece that attached to the tube projecting from the top of the stopper. Looking everywhere but at the nipple, he held it out gingerly, almost as if the item were indecent, like a piece of women's undergarments.

Zoe reached for it but then stopped, humor tickling her, even if faintly. Pastor Abe had clearly never held a nipple. The word itself likely flustered him.

Biting back a smile, Zoe retracted her hand. "You'll need to get the bottle ready."

His gaze flitted to the offending object before darting away. "I'm afraid I'm woefully ignorant about nipples. . . ." At his declaration, his eyes widened as if he hoped the floor would open up and swallow him.

His innocence was a refreshing change from the fellas Zoe had known in her Manchester slum neighborhood who were rough and crude and lustful. If she'd been talking to one of them, she could only imagine the turn the conversation would have taken.

Pastor Abe cleared his throat, and then he dropped the nipple back into the crate, his coat stretching taut against his broad shoulders and muscular arms. She couldn't keep from studying him as she had earlier when he'd first walked into Jane's hospital room.

She was struck once again that he was much too good-looking to be a pastor. His jaw was square and sturdy, his nose and forehead in perfect proportion, and his mouth attractive. To top it off, he had sandy-blond hair and the bluest, kindest eyes she'd ever seen.

Violet's fussing turned louder, forcing her to stop gawking and return her attention to the infant. "Hush now, little one. Your belly will be full soon enough—as soon as Pastor Abe gets your bottle ready."

He held up his hands to deflect her request. "I really am ignorant about such matters."

"Then you'll need to be holding the babe while I ready the bottle." She extended Violet.

Pastor Abe recoiled, his features reflecting horror as if she'd asked him to swim naked in the ocean.

This time she couldn't hold back her smile. In fact, her smile changed into laughter.

Pastor Abe lowered his hands and then smiled. This smile was different from the one he'd given her earlier, which had been impersonal but full of compassion. This smile was wide, revealed his perfect teeth, and made him roguishly endearing.

As Violet's angry wails intensified, he reached again for the discarded nipple and picked it up cautiously. "Let's get this baby fed."

Over the noise, Zoe instructed him how to fill the bottle with milk and attach the nipple to the piece of rubber tubing. Once he finished and passed Zoe the container, Violet took to it greedily, grasping the glass with both hands, her cries now replaced with noisy sucking.

For a minute, Zoe watched the sweet babe eat and pictured Eve doing the very same thing. Swift tears stung Zoe's eyes, and grief rushed into her heart, nearly overwhelming her. Not only was Eve just a memory, but now Jane was dead. Her dearest friend was gone.

Several tears escaped and slid down Zoe's cheeks. She swiped at them, wishing the pain would go away and that the loss didn't have to hurt so much.

"Are you thinking of Jane?" Pastor Abe's voice was gentle. He still stood at the center table across from her.

"Aye." When she chanced a glance at him, the sympathy in his eyes unleashed her grief again. She had the sudden need to fall into his arms and sob. There was just something comforting about him, an air of understanding and compassion that she needed. She supposed that's what pastors were like. They probably practiced lowering their eyebrows sorrowfully and setting their mouths into grim lines.

"I'd love to hear about Jane and what she was like," he stated softly.

"You would?"

"Yes. She must have been a wonderful person if she had a friend as kind as you."

Kind? Zoe had never thought of herself as particularly kind. No, but she was determined, resourceful, and persistent. Those qualities had helped her survive when her world had crumbled, especially over the past couple of years when most of the cotton mills in Lancashire had closed. With the ongoing war in the United States, England lost the steady cotton supply that fueled the mills. As a result, the booming textile industry had come to a near halt. Thousands upon thousands had no work and therefore no means to pay rent or purchase food.

Like many others, Zoe had resorted to standing in long lines every day for food from different charity organizations that had come to Manchester in an effort to provide relief. She'd hated accepting the handouts, had only gone when she absolutely needed the food. She'd been waiting in one such charity line with Jane when Miss Rye of the Columbia Mission Society offered them an alternative.

"Jane *was* wonderful. And of the two of us, she was the one who deserved a better life."

"Were you friends growing up?" His expression contained genuine interest, as though he truly cared and wasn't asking because that was his job.

"I met her when I started working at the mill three years ago—"

"You began working three years ago? You must have been just a child."

Her mind flashed back to her first day of walking to the mill with the other workers, the darkness of predawn, the frigid air waking her up, the clomp of their clogs on the stone pavement, huddling under her shawl and head covering for warmth and to hide her identity.

"I was sixteen. Most of the others, including Jane, started a lot younger than that. But my mum wanted me to be attending ragged school as long as possible."

"I like your mother. She was not only a praying woman but a wise woman for valuing your education."

"Then you approve of girls going to school?"

"Absolutely. Why wouldn't I?"

Was he sincere? She hadn't met too many men who thought her schooling was worthwhile, least of all her father. He'd only agreed to it because he'd adored Mum and did whatever she wanted. "Some fellas don't want a wife who has more learning than they do."

"You needn't worry on that score. From everything I've witnessed about you, you'll have no trouble finding a husband. Fellows will line up at the door of the Marine Barracks, if they aren't already."

Once his words were out, he rapidly dropped his attention to the crate on the table and began fidgeting with the empty milk bottle. "So tell me more about Jane."

Zoe smothered her smile. Pastor Abe seemed to have about as much experience with women as he did with bottles. But in some indefinable way, his presence and his company were the distraction and the balm her aching heart needed.

five

*A*be stood in front of the sitting room fireplace of the Marine Barracks and held out his hands to warm them. From the hours spent combing Victoria's streets and taverns last night and all morning, not only was he weary to the bone, but the damp cold had seeped into his limbs as well.

Unfortunately, he wasn't any closer to finding Herman Cox today than he'd been yesterday after the man had disappeared from the hospital, leaving Violet in his care. Even so, he softly whistled the hymn he oft did when he felt discouraged, knowing that praising the Lord was one of the quickest ways to take his mind off his troubles. *"Rejoice, the Lord is King! Your Lord and King adore! Rejoice, give thanks, and sing, and triumph evermore—"*

"Pastor Abe?" Someone spoke behind him.

He spun to find Miss Hart standing in the doorway, holding Violet, who appeared to be sleeping contentedly, thank the Lord. After the bouts of crying yesterday, he'd been uncertain whether Violet would ever stop, even after Miss Hart assured him the baby would be fine once she had enough nourishment.

The young woman didn't step into the room but regarded

him warily. Except for the slight pinch of a frown between her brows, her face was flawless, even more beautiful than he remembered. Not that he'd been thinking of her. At least not oft, and only because she'd insisted on bringing Violet back to the Marine Barracks with her and taking care of the baby while he looked for Herman.

"How is Violet today?" he asked.

"She was fussy off and on throughout the night, but she's sleeping now." The dark circles under Miss Hart's eyes told him she'd gotten very little sleep herself.

"Is she still hungry? Do you need more milk?"

"We've plenty left from what you had sent over last eve." Miss Hart tucked in a corner of the infant's swaddled blanket. "She's sated now."

"Is she ill, then? Shall I call for a doctor?"

"She's got her nights and days mixed around is all." His expression must have shown his ignorance, because she offered an explanation. "Herman probably stayed up drinking at night and slept during the day, so Violet naturally thinks nights are the time to be awake and days are for sleeping."

"I see. That poses a problem."

"My niece was mixed around for a while too. But I eventually got her straightened out."

He was tempted to ask how one went about changing a baby's sleeping habits but decided he'd already shown enough of his lack of knowledge for one day. Instead, he leapt upon the chance to talk about something else. "Your niece? How old is she?"

"She was six weeks old when she died."

Miss Hart wavered slightly, a sign of her exhaustion. Perhaps her grief over her friend had also interrupted her sleep.

Whatever the case, Miss Hart needed to sit down before she collapsed. Though the room was sparsely furnished, Abe strode to Miss Hart, took her arm, and guided her to the closest sofa.

"Thank you," she whispered, her eyes glistening with sudden tears. "I'm just tired. Mum always said everything's worse when you're tired."

He crouched before her, wishing he could do something to ease her grief and heartache. He started to reach for her hand, but then drew back. He needed to be careful. As a pastor and a single man, he couldn't place himself in any compromising situations.

Yesterday's time alone with Miss Hart at the hospital had bordered on inappropriate, even with the examining room door open and an attendant nearby. He'd lost track of time while Miss Hart had shared about Jane, about their escapades at the mill together, their months of unemployment, and finally their voyage across the Atlantic to Victoria.

In the moment, he'd told himself he was simply fulfilling his pastoral duty of comforting the bereaved. He oft sat with grieving families as they poured out memories of their loved ones. The sharing was the beginning of the healing process.

Even so, she was a single woman. And he needed to exercise more caution so he could remain above reproach. He'd learned that lesson all too well when he'd been offering comfort to Wanda.

If only Miss Hart didn't look so forlorn. . . .

He hesitated in front of her. Her dark hair was pulled back today into a simple knot, but already a strand had come loose, as if it couldn't stand to be contained. Her lashes were wet, making them appear longer and darker as they framed her shimmering eyes.

"Did you find Herman?" she asked.

"Not yet—"

"Good." Her shoulders visibly relaxed, and she hugged Violet a little closer.

Unease nudged Abe, prodding him to stand and put some

distance between himself and so beautiful a woman. He crossed to the fireplace and stretched his hands toward it, though he was no longer cold.

He cleared his throat and stared at the flames rather than at Miss Hart. "I'll continue to look for Herman. And I will find him eventually." He had enough connections throughout Vancouver Island and on the mainland that Herman Cox wouldn't be able to avoid him for long.

"He doesn't want the babe back," Miss Hart said with too much confidence.

"Herman Cox is a good man. It would appear he's simply lost himself to grief since his wife passed away."

"That's no excuse for neglecting this babe."

Abe turned to face Miss Hart. Though tears still glittered in her eyes, now fire sparked there too. "You're right—"

"He doesn't deserve the child." She jutted her chin, daring him to contradict her. Her expression reflected all the hurt and injustice and pain she'd experienced so far in her life.

Although she'd shared some of her hardships, he suspected he didn't even know the half of what she'd suffered. Her hurts likely went deeper than he could begin to understand.

Even so, Herman Cox was the baby's father. Abe planned to find the man and point him to the only One who could truly carry his burdens. Once he was sober and right with God, Herman would be as good a father as he'd been a husband.

"Miss Hart," Abe started, uncertain how to communicate his thoughts.

"I've had the night to think about it. And I'm keeping the babe."

How had this situation become so complicated so quickly? "I understand your concerns." He was grateful for his practice using patience with the miners so that his tone didn't betray his mounting worry. "But even if I'm unable to find Herman, you cannot keep the baby, not as a single woman without any means of support."

"I'll get a job and place of my own."

"That's not so easy to do. And even if you can support yourself, who would take care of the baby while you worked?"

"Who will see to the babe when Herman works?"

She had a point. Without a woman to aid him, Herman would be in a difficult position. Even so, Miss Hart had to realize she would have an even harder time keeping an infant.

"If Herman will not have her, then she must be given up for adoption, hopefully to a real family." He honestly didn't know any English families who would be willing to adopt the child, especially since Violet was of mixed race. Perhaps that's why Herman had been looking for Rose's tribe—he'd been hoping to place her with a native family. But a tribe might not want Violet any more than the English. The sad truth was that the child likely wouldn't belong in either place and would be an outcast.

The other sad truth was that the smallpox epidemic among the natives had already left too many orphans and not enough people willing to care for them.

Pete and Arabella would take the child in if he asked them to. They had large and willing hearts. Already they'd adopted two native girls who'd lost their family. But now with Pete's parents having moved to Victoria, the small apartment above the bakeshop was overflowing. Of course, Pete was in the process of purchasing land and ordering supplies to build a house. However, the project was still months away from completion.

What about Sque-is? Would he and his wife be willing to give Violet a home? Abe hadn't seen or heard from his native friend since late autumn. Although he prayed for Sque-is and his tribe, that they'd been spared from smallpox, the longer he went without word, the more he suspected something had happened.

"Ultimately," Abe said, "the best place for Violet is with her family—her father."

"Absolutely not." Zoe stood, her body rigid. "It's the worst place."

"I'll talk to Herman and help him—"

"No one can help a drunk unless he first wants to help himself. Believe me, I know."

How did she know? Had she suffered at the hands of a drunk? Was that why she felt so strongly about protecting Violet?

"I don't know what you've experienced," he said gently, "but not everyone who drinks is hopelessly lost. I've seen many hardened men repent of their sins and turn to the Lord."

"Herman's not hardened. He's dead inside."

"Not dead. Not yet." Abe refused to give up on people. Nothing was impossible for the Lord. In fact, the Lord was in the business of bringing the dead back to life.

"Herman was obviously trying to give his child a better life, especially for the sake of his late wife." Zoe looked down at the sleeping infant and brushed a finger across her cheek. "Let him give his child this gift."

"There's no guarantee she'll be better off with someone else—"

"I can guarantee it. With me. Violet will be better off with me."

Abe swallowed a frustrated sigh.

"'Course, I'm planning to get married. If I can't keep Violet without getting married, then I'll hurry things along and find a husband right away."

"It's not wise to rush into marriage. Choosing a spouse is too important to be undertaken without a great deal of thought."

"And I am planning to think on it long and hard."

"You'll need to take your time and get to know the young man. Surely you see the importance of having shared values as well as shared affection?"

"All I need to know is that he'll take care of me and Violet.

And I also need him to take me up to the mining camps so I can find my brother."

"Your brother?"

"Aye. My twin."

Miss Hart had a twin brother living in the mining camps? Abe was sure his surprise showed on his face. "My circuit takes me among many of the mining camps and puts me into contact with many men. Perhaps I know your brother."

"Zeke Hart?" she asked hopefully. "Six feet tall, medium build, dark hair, and green eyes?"

Abe searched his mind for the fellows he'd come to know that resembled Miss Hart. But he'd never run across a Zeke Hart. And of course the description could fit any number of men.

With Miss Hart's expectant gaze upon him, he continued to mentally comb through the many people he'd met. "When did he arrive? And do you know approximately where he's located?"

"He left over a year ago, and all he said was that he was going to the Fraser River Valley."

"The Fraser River Valley spans hundreds of miles. And many of the miners have pushed farther inland into the Cariboo area. Has he written with a more specific address?"

She dropped her gaze. If she was hoping to hide her guilt, it was written into her expression as clear as daylight. "I haven't heard from him, but I was hoping once I got up into the Fraser River Valley and started asking around, people would be able to point me to him."

"It's possible." Especially if he'd made a name for himself by striking a vein of gold. But it was also possible she'd never locate him, that he could have been one of the many thousands of miners who'd hoped to make a fortune last spring or summer, only to leave more destitute than when they arrived.

"I really need to find him," she stated, the guilt still creasing her face. "And I need a man who can help me do that."

Since Abe had been born late in his mother's life and many years after his siblings, he'd never been close to his older brother and sister. He didn't have a relationship with them—certainly not the kind of bond that twins had. Even so, whatever Miss Hart's connection to her twin brother, her predicament didn't sit well with him. "I would still urge you to use a great deal of caution in choosing a spouse."

"Some nice fellas came calling last night. I'm sure it won't take too much longer to pick one of them." She met his gaze head on, as though daring him to stop her.

With a sinking feeling in his stomach, he realized he couldn't prevent her from a hasty marriage. But perhaps he could slow her down. "Violet is not yet yours, Miss Hart. Herman could very well show up later today and collect her. It would be best to refrain from any drastic measures until we know Herman's intentions."

She hesitated, the moment drawing out so that the sounds from within the house became more prominent—the footsteps overhead in the women's bedrooms, the chatter and laughter in the sitting room across the hallway, and the clinking of utensils and pans from the kitchen at the back of the house.

Finally, Miss Hart nodded. "I'll wait a few days until after Jane's funeral. But then I'll be ready to move on." Without sparing him another look, she crossed to the door and left.

Abe could only stare after her, worry nagging him. Although he was tired from the long hours of searching for Herman, he realized he wouldn't be able to rest anytime soon. Not until Violet was back where she belonged and Miss Hart was safe from the pressure of rushing into marriage.

six

Zoe stared at the plain wooden coffin as the men lowered it into the gaping hole. Slowly the ground swallowed her friend, taking her away forever. Though Zoe's chest ached with the need to sob, her eyes remained dry, probably because she'd already shed all the tears her body held. The past two sleepless nights with Violet had given her too much time to cry over the loss of Jane.

Violet grunted, and Zoe automatically began to rock the babe. She certainly didn't want the babe wailing now, not with all the other women around mourning for Dora and Jane. Most were already irritated enough that the babe woke them at night with her noises. They'd only complain all the louder if Violet disturbed them again.

If Zoe had ever entertained the idea of living at the Marine Barracks with Violet, she'd quickly tossed it aside. Not only were her bride-ship companions grumbling, but the ladies from the welcoming committee were too—all except Mrs. Moresby, who'd been kind enough to collect donations of baby clothing, infant napkins, blankets, and more.

Zoe had reassured everyone she'd soon be married and would take Violet away from the Marine Barracks.

Today. She'd find a man today. In fact, earlier, as she'd walked to the cemetery, she'd made a point of spreading the word that she was looking for a husband. Surely when she returned to the Marine Barracks she'd have a line of fellas waiting to meet her.

Zoe had tried not to let her gaze stray toward Pastor Abe during the ceremony. She had no doubt he'd overheard her announcement when she'd arrived. And she'd kept her attention on the coffins so she didn't have to chance seeing his disapproval.

He had no reason to be upset with her decision. She'd agreed to wait until after the funeral. He couldn't expect her to put off a wedding indefinitely, could he? Especially since he hadn't been able to locate Herman. He'd kept her up-to-date on his progress each evening when he came to check on Violet. He'd been kind enough to continue his visits and clearly took his responsibilities for the infant seriously.

Though he hadn't admonished Zoe again regarding her efforts to find a husband, she'd sensed his caution, and she understood the need to be careful about getting into a potentially bad marriage. She'd seen her fair share of unhappy situations in the slums.

Like Pastor Abe, the welcoming committee had assured the bride-ship women that they needn't hurry, that they could take time to be properly courted by their suitors. But people married for convenience all the time. Some people got lucky and developed affection for each other, and some people didn't. If love never came for her, she'd make the best of it.

Besides, did love really matter? All the people she'd loved had either left or died. Maybe she'd be better off if she didn't allow herself to love again. Maybe a marriage of convenience to a complete stranger was exactly what she needed to keep from giving her heart away only to have it crushed.

"In the name of the Father, the Son, and the Holy Ghost, amen," Pastor Abe concluded, making the motion of the cross. Even today, having changed out of his casual attire into a dark suit and clerical collar, he still didn't look like any reverend she'd ever seen. She couldn't figure out why, except that he was simply too handsome.

A murmuring of *amens* came from around the graveside followed by the thud of dirt hitting the coffins as the grave-digger and his apprentice shoveled from the waiting pile. The others took that as their cue to step back and give the men room to work. Even Pastor Abe began to walk away and was immediately flocked by several of the bride-ship women who'd made a point of noticing and speaking to him whenever he came to visit the Marine Barracks. After he left, they giggled and whispered over him like schoolgirls instead of grown women.

Zoe couldn't make her feet move. Instead, she stared at the dark opening as the damp scent of earth rose up. The weather was warmer and balmier, the cold nip gone. Though the sky was overcast with low gray clouds, the rain had held off during the funeral. And now it was sprinkling, finally shedding tears upon the departed.

Good-bye, Jane, she said silently. *You were a dear, heaven-sent friend when I most needed one. Thank you. I will never forget you.*

The clacking and whirring of the looms reverberated in Zoe's head, the noise that had been their constant companion every day from before dawn until after dusk. She could see the floating pieces of cotton in the dusty haze that filled the cardroom, the same dust that eventually filled Mum's lungs, and Jane's, and the lungs of countless other mill women, who were hired on for half the pay of men. The long hours, the stifling air, the dim lighting, the dangerous machinery that easily caught fingers and hair—at the time they'd considered themselves lucky to have work. But had it really been worth it?

Zoe stood for several more long moments, an ache pulsing through her. This wasn't how things were supposed to end for Jane. This wasn't what they'd dreamed about during the voyage over. They'd both wanted to find husbands with good jobs that didn't involve weaving or textiles. They'd planned to be neighbors and help each other when their babies came along. They wanted to have better lives here in this new land, free from the sickness that ran rampant in the Manchester slums.

"Miss?" said someone from close behind.

She turned to find a man holding his hat in his hands and watching her expectantly. Of medium build, he was stocky and rugged with his brown hair slicked back and beard neatly trimmed.

"Rumor has it you're wanting to find your brother. Man by the name of Zeke Hart."

Ever since the true culprits of the mill fire had been caught, she'd been bursting with the need to find Zeke and set him free from the guilt and heartache that had forced him to run away from Manchester. Everyone now knew he'd been accused of a crime he hadn't committed and that he wasn't responsible for the deaths of the mill workers. He was a free man. She wouldn't be able to rest until she told him the news. "Aye. He's my twin. Do you know him?"

"I know a fella who goes by Jeremiah Hart. You share a family resemblance."

Jeremiah Hart? Was it possible Zeke had changed his name as an extra precaution? It made sense. And it also made sense that he would have taken the name of his best friend—Jeremiah Millington.

The man perused her again, taking her in from her scarf-covered head down to her muddy boots. His gaze hesitated on

Violet before landing on Zoe's face, a slow smile forming. "Yep, just what I remembered. You're the pretty one."

He remembered her? From when she'd come ashore? She studied his face again. Aye, he was the cocky man who'd tugged at her scarf and cloak and made lewd comments about her body and how he wouldn't mind having her warm his bed this winter.

She scowled.

He tossed back his head and laughed. "Good. I see you remember me now too."

"Not willingly."

He laughed again. "I like you."

"What do you want?" The others were drifting farther away, and she needed to join them. Also, she needed to get Violet out of the drizzle.

"Heard you're looking to get married right away, and I'm here to tell you that I'm the man you want to marry."

Her sights narrowed on him. "And why would I want to marry you?"

"You did say you want a man who can take you to your brother, right?"

She could feel Zeke's pendant in her pocket weighing ever heavier with each passing day. "That's right. But how do I know this Jeremiah Hart is really my brother?"

"Like I said, you look alike—same black hair and green eyes."

"I'm sure that could apply to lots of fellas."

"It's obvious you're twins."

Aye, even though Zeke was bigger and broader and masculine in every sense of the word, they shared similar features, even down to having the same dimples. Was it possible she'd found Zeke? That this man could take her to him? For the first time since she'd arrived in Victoria, anticipation leapt to life inside her.

"Do you know where my brother is?"

"Yep. He's up in the Williamsville area doing real well for himself. I know the way up the canyon. Traveled the route more times than most miners."

"Then you're a miner?"

His grin inched higher, almost as if he thought the question was funny. "I've made a sizeable fortune so far."

A sizeable fortune? "Then you can support and take care of a wife and child?" She let her sights drop to Violet and stroked the babe's back.

"I don't want Herman Cox's half-breed."

Zoe's head snapped up. "Then I don't want you." She spun and started to stalk away.

"Hold on now." His footsteps pounded the earth behind her, and his hand closed around her upper arm, halting her.

She was tempted to jerk free and continue on. But this man knew Zeke's whereabouts and was willing to take her there.

He spun her around and gentled his hold. "I'll build you a house in Williamsville. A real big fancy one." His expression was earnest.

A real big fancy house? She'd always lived with her family in rented rooms in one tenement or another in Manchester. And the possibility of finally having a house—no matter the size—sent a thrill through her. It was just what she and Jane had talked about. But she also wanted Violet. "I'm obliged to take care of this little one."

"Let someone else be responsible for the babe."

"Herman gave her to me. And now I have the chance to do her some good and give her a better life."

The miner hesitated.

Would all the fellas feel the same way about Violet as this one? Zoe hadn't considered the possibility that having a babe would limit the number of men who might be willing to marry her. With so many wanting wives, she'd thought she'd have no trouble. But what if she couldn't find anyone to take her with the babe?

A sliver of anxiety worked its way under her skin. "I promise Violet won't be any trouble."

He stared at the outline of the babe within the bundle of blankets. "What if I find Rose's relatives? And what if they're willing to provide a home for the babe?"

"Herman said he already tried to find them and that they're all dead."

The man scoffed. "Herman's a lazy drunk. He wouldn't be able to find his face in a mirror."

"Then you think Violet might still have family somewhere?"

"I've got connections. If Rose still has family, I'll find them."

Zoe wasn't sure whether to be worried or happy about the prospect. 'Course, the babe deserved to have family raise her—especially if they were a loving family.

Yet Herman had all but given Violet to her, hadn't he? Perhaps God had even ordained their meeting. After all, she'd still been at the hospital when Herman had come. And Pastor Abe had been there at the right moment too. Besides, she was experienced with infants and knew just the kind of care Violet required. How many other women would have been willing or able to take the babe? It was almost as if God knew she needed the babe as much as the babe needed her. Just when she'd been experiencing loss, new life had been dropped into her lap.

Whatever the case, she wasn't planning to give Violet up. Not yet.

As if sensing her resolve, the miner released her and stepped back. "I'm giving you a good offer. Why don't you take some time today to think on it?"

"Why don't you think about the fact that if you want me, then you'll have to want the babe?"

He grinned. "I'll do that. You just might be worth it."

As he walked away, she exhaled slowly, releasing the tension. She watched him join a couple other men, exchange a few words, and then laugh as they ambled away.

Maybe he wasn't exactly handsome. But he was decent looking and could provide for her. Best of all, he could help her find Zeke. That's all she needed in a man. Wasn't it?

A clearing throat startled her.

She spun to find Pastor Abe holding his Bible and prayer book against his chest. A scowl marred his handsome face as he stared in the direction of the miner who'd been speaking with her. "What were you talking about with Dexter Dawson?"

Dexter Dawson? Her face flushed with the realization that she'd practically agreed to marry a man whose name she hadn't known. Was she really so desperate?

The truth was, she didn't care what his name was. It was irrelevant in the bigger scheme of things. More important was that he might be willing to take care of both her and Violet.

"He asked me to marry him."

"He what?" Pastor Abe seemed to choke on the words.

"He said he'd marry me and take me to my brother."

Pastor Abe stepped closer, his brow furrowing even deeper. "You can't marry Dexter Dawson."

"Why not? He promised to build me a house and said he had a sizeable fortune."

"Because he's a crook."

She scowled. "You're saying that to discourage me, because you don't think I should get married yet."

"I don't agree with hasty marriages—that's true. But it's also true that Dexter Dawson is not an honest, law-abiding man."

"He looks normal enough."

"He's not innocent or normal. He's dangerous and steals gold from the expressmen and caravans coming down out of the mountains."

She paused at the accusation and glanced at Dexter's retreating form. He had the confident swagger of a man who thought too much of himself. But he'd given her no reason to believe he was a dangerous crook. "If he's such a bad criminal, then why isn't he in jail?"

"Because he hasn't been caught in the act."

"So there's no solid proof he's doing the stealing?"

Pastor Abe drew in a breath, whispered something that sounded like a prayer, then spoke calmly. "Miss Hart, you must believe me that Dexter Dawson isn't the type of man you want for a husband."

Pastor Abe had gone out of his way to be helpful even when he had nothing to gain in return. Why would he lie to her about Dexter Dawson?

Violet stretched her legs and then released a squeak—one Zoe had learned signaled hunger. She hefted the babe, switching arms. Even though the wee one was just a wisp of a babe at four months of age, Zoe ached from holding her almost nonstop.

"I need to be going," Zoe said. "Violet is due for another feeding soon."

"Do you have enough milk? If not, I'll make sure to have more sent over."

"Aye, Pastor, she's getting her fill and is the happier for it."

Pastor Abe leaned in and peeked at Violet's face beneath the blanket. "She looks content. Much more so than the first day Herman brought her in."

Violet's lips puckered with another cry, and Zoe shifted the infant's hand to her mouth, helping her find her thumb to suck. "She's doing much better. And that's exactly why I'll be keeping her."

Pastor Abe released a long sigh. "You can't—"

"If Dexter's willing to have me with the babe, then I'll marry him. And if he doesn't want Violet, then I'll find a husband who does."

Without waiting for him to argue with her further, she strode away, her boots squishing in the wet grass. She half expected him to follow and continue trying to talk her out of her decision. But when she glanced back at him a moment later, he'd already turned and was walking away in the opposite direction.

A strange sense of disappointment slowed her steps. She wasn't sure why it should matter that Pastor Abe had given up so easily. That's what she'd wanted, wasn't it? For him to stop protesting and let her have her way with Violet?

'Course she wouldn't marry Dexter if he really was a criminal. That wouldn't give her or Violet the kind of life she wanted. But she'd find someone willing enough to have her and the babe. Surely in this land filled with marriage-hungry men she'd latch on to at least one ready to take a bride of convenience.

"Sorry, miss." The young fella rose from his chair, buttoning his coat. "I'd marry you today—tonight—but I'm not interested in getting a child in the bargain."

Zoe swallowed her discouragement. He was the last of the callers, and his response had been typical of all the rest.

He put on his hat and tipped up the brim, his eyes still eager. "If you change your mind, let me know, and I'll be back here putting a ring on your finger before you can blink." He paused as though giving her the chance to change her mind right then and there.

She considered telling him he could take his ring and shove it in a pig's snout. But she'd already spoken enough choice words for one day. And she was weary.

When she didn't respond, the young man gave a polite nod and then exited. A moment later, the front door of the Marine

Barracks closed firmly. The quiet in the hallway confirmed he'd been the final suitor. Zoe stood in the center of the room unable to move, unable to think, unable to do anything but stare at the open doorway.

The darkening sky hinted at evening. The day was coming to a close. And she was still woefully unattached.

Had she been mistaken to insist on keeping Violet?

"She's awake." Mrs. Moresby appeared in the doorway, holding the babe and smiling down at her.

With wide eyes, Violet stared at the giant silk butterflies that adorned Mrs. Moresby's hat. She reached up as though to grab one, and Mrs. Moresby used the opportunity to kiss the babe's outstretched hand.

"Guess I need a hat like yours." Zoe shook herself out of her melancholy. "Seems to be working wonders for Violet."

"I'm the wonder-worker." The giant of a woman made eyes at the babe.

Zoe smiled in spite of herself. "You've been a godsend, Mrs. Moresby—"

"Velva."

Zoe couldn't get used to the familiarity of calling the gentlewoman by her given name. It didn't seem right, even after Mrs. Moresby had shared about her humble past when she'd been a maidservant for a wealthy Victoria family.

Mrs. Moresby seated herself in the chair the young man had just occupied, all the while cooing at Violet.

"Thank you for watching Violet during my meetings."

"From the sounds of things, you didn't have any takers?"

"None."

"That's a shame. A man couldn't ask for two prettier girls than you and Violet."

Zoe lowered herself to the chair opposite Mrs. Moresby and sat on the edge. She reached for the ball of soft white lamb's wool yarn and her knitting needles that sat in the basket she'd brought with her into the sitting room. She was halfway done with the baby blanket. Was it really worth her effort? Maybe she should have continued knitting mittens for her friends instead.

"Am I making a mistake in keeping Violet?" She voiced the question that had been clamoring louder with each passing rejection.

All her friends at the Marine Barracks had told her to give the babe back to Pastor Abe and let him find a home for the child. They didn't understand why she wanted Violet. At times, Zoe didn't understand either, especially when the infant awoke crying at night.

Now with the difficulty in finding a man who would be willing to marry her with Violet, maybe she was asking for the impossible.

Mrs. Moresby sat up and leveled a look at Zoe. "Do you want my honest opinion?"

"'Course." Zoe braced herself for one more person telling her she needed to let go of the native babe.

"There are a lot of abandoned and unwanted children in this world. And not enough people willing to love and care for them."

Zoe agreed. She'd experienced that firsthand with her sister's abandoning Eve.

"If God places within you a desire to take care of helpless and unwanted orphans, then I'd say you can't ignore His calling."

"His calling?"

"The good Lord calls us all to serve Him in one way or another. Most of the time we're too focused on what we want to pay attention to what He's asking of us."

Zoe was guilty of that. She'd always believed callings were for ministers or missionaries. But what if God had something special for everyone to do?

"Sometimes we want to know the whole plan and how it will

work out before we agree to start," Mrs. Moresby continued. "But all we can do is take one step at a time, one day at a time, as He leads us along."

"Then you're saying I should keep Violet?"

"I'm saying that since you have such deep compassion for this orphan, then you best take care of her for as long as God leads you to do so."

Zoe reclined in her chair, a strange sense of peace settling over her and chasing away her tension. Aye, she loved babies. And she had deep compassion for orphans. Was it possible God had plans to use her not only for Violet, but for others?

The very thought seemed presumptuous. After all, she was a poor, simple mill worker. She had no way to take care of herself, much less this babe or any other. But maybe Mrs. Moresby was right. Maybe all God required was a willing heart and the trust that He'd work out the rest of the details in His timing and in His way.

A thumping on the front door startled Zoe, and she dropped the half-finished baby blanket into her lap.

Violet released a cry, and Mrs. Moresby's brows rose. "Are you expecting someone else tonight?"

"That was it. Unless Pastor Abe's coming to check on Violet."

Mrs. Moresby sat up straighter. "That Pastor Abe is quite the handsome man."

"Aye." Zoe pictured him as he'd looked solemnly reciting from the book of prayers at the funeral. "I can't argue with you there."

"Too bad he's practically engaged to a woman from his home back in Yorkshire."

Zoe hadn't realized he was engaged. Part of her fought against the same disappointment she'd experienced when he'd walked away from her after the funeral. But at the same time, she had no reason to feel anything. They'd been thrust together in their quest to save Violet. That was all.

Footsteps in the hallway drew nearer. A knock on the door was followed by Kate holding out a folded note. "A message came for you, Zoe."

Zoe rose and crossed to the pretty young woman, eyeing the slip of paper. Who was sending her a message? As she took the sheet and opened it to a note, all she saw was Dexter Dawson's name scrawled at the bottom. She didn't need to read his message to know what he'd decided.

He'd agreed to marry her in spite of his reservations about Violet.

The question was, did she want to marry him? After Pastor Abe's warning, she'd tried to gather more information. From the little she was able to discover, Dexter seemed harmless enough and well liked. The constable at the gate wasn't familiar with the name and said not to let one rumor stop her, since the miners liked to exaggerate their tales.

She smoothed out the sheet and traced Dexter's name with her finger. What if he was one more step in God's plans for her? If marrying him would allow her to carry out God's calling to care for Violet, then how could she turn down his offer?

seven

$\mathscr{H}$is duties finished for the day, Abe entered the side door of Christ Church Cathedral, letting his whistle fade to silence out of reverence for God's house.

Over the past few hectic days in Victoria, he'd allowed himself to get too busy so that he'd neglected his prayer time and casting his cares on the Lord. Now the burdens were weighing him down and churning through him, especially since speaking with Zoe Hart after the funeral service. Even hours later, every time he pictured her talking with Dexter Dawson, his body tensed with the urge to break up their conversation.

He hadn't noticed Dex after the funeral, hadn't seen him speaking with Miss Hart until it was too late. But the moment he'd spotted the man, he'd rushed over to her as fast as he could. By the time he'd reached her, Dex had already walked away. Although Abe wasn't a fighting man, he'd wanted to stride after Dex, shove him, and yell at him to stay away from Miss Hart.

"Exactly why I need to be in your presence, Lord," he whispered as he moved into the dimly lit side aisle. "I'm weak and sinful and in desperate need of your strength."

At the sight of a parishioner speaking with Bishop Hills in

the narthex, Abe tread quietly so he wouldn't disturb them. Though he had many prayer spots, this church was one of his favorites. The peace of the cathedral always embraced him, and the quiet reverence soothed his soul.

The colorful stained glass, grand pillars, and high arches brought back memories of his home church in Yorkshire and reminded him of God's calling, that he hadn't taken up service to the church merely because he was a younger son without an estate to manage or inheritance to claim. No, he'd taken it up because he'd truly wanted to make a difference in the world, wanted to share God's love with those who'd lost hope.

"There he is." Bishop Hills's articulate voice carried across the nave. "Mr. Merivale, we have just been speaking of you. As a matter of fact, the constable came here hoping to find you."

The constable? Abe's stride lengthened, and he veered through the transept toward the two. Did the constable have news of Herman Cox's whereabouts? Abe had gone to the police headquarters the day Herman had abandoned the baby. He'd returned every day for updates, except for today since he'd been so busy with the funeral and his committee meetings.

"Officer Green." Abe nodded at the constable. "How is your wife?"

"Weak, but on the mend." The constable bobbed his head. "The medicine and prayers have been helpful."

"Then I'll keep praying."

"Thank you, Reverend. You're mighty kind, sir."

Abe avoided Bishop Hills's gaze. His superior would admonish Abe once again to focus on his own parishioners in the mountain towns and to stay out of matters that weren't his concern. He hadn't approved of Abe asking Doctor Helmcken to visit the ailing Mrs. Green, but as a result of the visit, the kindly doctor had diagnosed and treated her severe influenza. Bishop Hills was of the mind that God had appointed pastors to address spiritual issues, and that Abe was spending too much energy and time on physical needs.

"We are not a charity organization, Mr. Merivale," Bishop Hills had said at their last meeting. "We are here in the colonies to spread the gospel and build churches. Only the gospel has the power to truly change lives, and it must remain our central focus and priority."

Abe understood and agreed in the power of the gospel. But he lived with a lingering regret that he hadn't done more for the file grinders of his Sheffield parish. The hard work of smoothing and shaping and polishing metal was fraught with injuries and illness. If he'd stepped in and addressed the file grinders' complaints sooner, could he have prevented the tragedy?

Maybe if he'd validated their concerns regarding the poor working conditions and low wages, he might have been able to bring about a peaceful resolution to the tension. Instead, the workers' discontentment festered, culminating in violence. They'd blown up a house, killing one of their supervisors, his wife, their two children.

The lost lives weighed on him. Since leaving Sheffield, Abe had resolved not to sit back and ignore the tribulations of the people he met. If only Bishop Hills could try to understand. . . .

Someday, when Abe became a bishop, he'd work to understand the men under him better. And he'd certainly advocate for more changes in church policies when needed.

"Officer Green tells me you're involved in finding the father of an abandoned native baby." Bishop Hills's tone was laced with fresh disapproval.

"The miner is one I've met riding my circuit, Your Grace," Abe said hastily. "His wife recently died, and he's beside himself with grief."

"But it's not among your job duties to find homes for unwanted children." Hands crossed behind his back, Bishop Hills rocked back and forth on the balls of his feet. Shorter than Abe by at least a foot, the bishop still had a way of looking down upon Abe and making him feel like a child.

"My intentions are to minister to the baby's father so that he will put his hope in the Lord and in so doing be able to provide care for his daughter."

The constable cleared his throat. "I'm sorry to say Herman Cox won't be able to do any of that."

"I'd at least like the chance to talk and pray with him—"

"He's dead." Officer Green's eyes were grave. "I came as soon as we got the news at headquarters. Figured you'd want to know right away."

"I appreciate that, Constable." A disquieting worry expanded within Abe's chest.

"Found cold as ice in his hotel bed over in New Westminster."

"Does anyone know the cause?"

"Deputy Farthing over in New Westminster ruled out murder. He said there was no evidence of any struggle."

"What about suicide?" Even as Abe spoke the word, a weight of sadness and fresh guilt fell upon his shoulders so that he slumped deeper into his coat. He should have done more for Herman, should have gone to visit him after his marriage to Rose, shouldn't have left the hospital the other day without first praying with him.

"Deputy Farthing didn't rule out suicide," Officer Green replied. "But he couldn't find any proof. From all appearances, the man died in his sleep."

"Looks like his baby is truly an orphan after all."

Bishop Hills laid a cautioning hand on Abe's arm. "We are not equipped to handle orphans, Mr. Merivale. You must allow Officer Green to take the infant and do his part."

"Oh no." The constable stepped rapidly away. "I can't take

a babe back to headquarters. We aren't equipped for such a situation either. Not in the least."

The bishop scowled. "Then surely you can find someone among our community willing to house and care for the infant until a permanent solution is found."

"We're not an orphanage."

"Neither are we." Bishop Hills waved his hand toward the nave as if to make his point.

Abe's mind whirled with a hundred thoughts in a hundred directions. He didn't know what to do any more than the constable or bishop. But he did know he had to try to help the child. "Herman wanted me to find a good home for the baby. Perhaps if I spread the word around town, someone will come forward."

"Mr. Merivale," the bishop said, "in addition to not being an orphanage, we are also *not* a foundling placing agency. I forbid you to waste your time and energy any further on this matter, especially since we both know how futile such efforts will be."

Because the child had a native mother? Abe was sorely tempted to blurt his question. But he bowed his head and silently prayed for the grace to be submissive to his superior as well as for wisdom in how to handle the matter.

"The best solution is for the baby to live within the native community," the bishop continued. "Officer Green, I suggest you take the child out to the Northerner's Encampment and leave it there."

"He cannot simply leave Violet at the Northerner's Encampment." Abe's objection came out more forcefully than he'd intended.

Bishop Hills lifted his brows, his eyes full of censure.

Abe reined in his mounting frustration and continued more calmly. "The Encampment isn't what it used to be. So few natives are left, and fewer are coming to trade, especially this time of year. Taking the child there would be the same as delivering her to a grave."

"No need for theatrics, Mr. Merivale. I'm sure someone at the camp will have pity on the orphan."

"One of the bride-ship women is looking after the child." For the first time since Zoe Hart had insisted upon caring for Violet, Abe was grateful she'd taken the baby into her charge. "She's mentioned wanting to keep the child—"

"The child should be placed with someone of its kind. Besides, a single woman isn't fit to take on the responsibility of raising a child."

"My sentiments too, sir," Officer Green said.

"She is seeking a husband," Abe admitted even as he rejected the idea of her marrying Dexter Dawson. "If she gets married, then she'll certainly be a fit mother from what I've witnessed."

"Even so," the bishop said, "such a placement should remain temporary with the end goal of returning the child to her people."

The constable and bishop spoke a few more minutes, voicing their concerns. By the time Officer Green took his leave, Abe's nerves were pulled taut, and he was in need of prayer even more than before.

As he started toward the apse, the bishop called after him. "A moment, Mr. Merivale. You received a letter from Elizabeth this morn."

A letter from Elizabeth? Abe's heart jumped within his chest. Although it was slightly early in the month for Lizzy's usual correspondence, he had a sudden keen need to hear from her. Perhaps she'd responded to the letter he'd sent last autumn with the marriage proposal. In the several months it took for his letter to reach her and then the months it would take for her letter to get to him, it was unlikely this was her answer. Yet it was still possible. . . .

Returning to the bishop, he took the outstretched envelope, which contained Lizzy's familiar, neat handwriting. Eagerly he retreated to the front pew and lowered himself. Then, exhaling, he opened the correspondence, held it to his nose, and tried to breathe in her sweet fragrance.

After the miles the letter had traveled to reach him, the only scent upon the paper was the mustiness of the cargo hold where it had lain while traveling from England to the Pacific Northwest.

Smoothing out the paper, he began to read. *My dearest Abraham, I have been delaying this letter for some time and realize I can no longer do so. In fact, by the time you receive this letter, I will likely already be married.*

Married? What did she mean? He scrambled to read the next sentence. *I am to marry Daniel Patterson of Rithet on Christmas Day.*

Abe's pulse leapt forward at double speed. She couldn't possibly be marrying someone else. Not when she'd promised to wait for him. Not when they were so right for each other. Not when marriage had entered his thoughts more and more lately.

Daniel and I have spent much time together over the past year, and we have grown in our affection for one another. I do believe I love him, Abraham. I pray you will understand and be happy for me.

Something hot and sharp stabbed Abe's chest so that he couldn't breathe. Lizzy loved another man. She loved another man and not him. While they'd never declared their love for one another, he'd assumed she loved him. She always had, hadn't she? And he'd certainly always loved her.

Why had she changed her mind? And how in the world could she expect him to be happy for her?

He skimmed the rest of the letter, hardly able to take in her words—how she and Daniel had gotten to know each other during their mutual volunteer work, how her parents had encouraged the match, and how she enjoyed spending time with him.

While no one can ever compare to you, Abraham, I have realized Daniel is a good man who will provide me with the stability and family I long for.

Was Lizzy implying he wouldn't be able to give her stability and a family? Surely she knew he would do so once he returned. After his time as a missionary, the church would assign him a sizeable parish. As a rector he'd give her a comfortable life with everything she could ever need or want. Hopefully one day he'd become a bishop, which would bring even more prestige.

Had she simply grown tired of waiting for his return? He let his mind sift back through the letters she'd written in recent months. She hadn't hinted she was weary of his absence. She hadn't hinted at discontent with their arrangement. And she certainly hadn't hinted she was falling in love with another man. At least, he didn't think she had.

Why hadn't she said anything? He would have sent for her earlier. She could have sailed to the colonies a year ago, and they could have been married by now. As it was, she probably hadn't received his proposal until she was engaged and planning the marriage to Daniel Patterson, much too late to change her mind.

He read over her letter again, this time his eyes burning and his chest throbbing. When he finished, he crumpled the sheet, let it drop to the floor, and then buried his face in his hands.

Lizzy was married. The woman he adored was no longer his. The woman who would have made a perfect wife and helpmate belonged to someone else.

Oh, Lizzy, what have you done? his heart cried with an ache that drove him off the pew and down to his knees.

He needed to pray, needed to cry out to the Lord, but he

couldn't find the words. All he could think was that Lizzy had left him for another man. She'd rejected and tossed him aside with no warning. Hadn't given him the chance to try harder. Hadn't explained her feelings until too late.

If she'd truly cared about him, she would have given him more warning, wouldn't she? How could she be so selfish to think only of herself and not of him in the least?

If that was the woman she'd become, then he was better off without her. He didn't need her. He'd find someone else and be a good husband and show Lizzy all she'd missed by not marrying him. Eventually she'd regret her choice. Then she'd come to him and tell him she'd made a mistake and missed him.

"Pastor Abe?" A woman spoke above him.

He didn't want to be disturbed right now. He wasn't in the frame of mind to speak calmly or kindly to anyone. All he wanted was to be left alone with his thoughts.

"Are you marrying me?"

He jerked his head up to find Zoe Hart standing beside him. Her long hair was free of its knot and hung in waves over her shoulders with strands at her temples pulled back into a pretty twist. If he'd thought she was beautiful before, she was stunning now with her hair spilling about her in a glorious dark canopy. She peered down at him with her green eyes framed by those lush lashes.

Had she just proposed marriage to him?

Her question was so startling and unusual, he couldn't make his mouth work to formulate a response. He could only stare and try to understand why she wanted to marry him. Of course, she was desperate to find a husband in order to keep Violet. She'd told him at the funeral earlier that she'd even consider marrying Dexter Dawson if she had to.

Maybe Dex had turned her down. Maybe she couldn't find any other man willing to marry her and take care of Violet.

And maybe she figured he might be willing, since she knew he felt responsible for Violet's care.

"Well?" Miss Hart glanced toward the narthex, which was empty. Thankfully, Bishop Hills had gone on his way and hadn't seen Abe's breakdown over Lizzy's letter.

At the merest thought of Lizzy, hurt shot through his veins. Since Lizzy was married, nothing was holding him back from taking a wife. He could get married and then write another letter to Lizzy and tell her he'd found someone else. At least she'd know he wasn't pining over her, that he'd moved on just as quickly as she had.

Miss Hart's brow furrowed. "Are you alright? You don't look so good."

He dropped his head, the reality of Lizzy's letter hitting him again. But just as quickly as the pain came, anger rushed in and chased it away. He pushed himself up until he was towering above Miss Hart.

"When do you want to get married?" he asked.

"I thought it was to be tonight at seven."

"Tonight?" He swallowed hard and looked around the empty nave. Could he really do this? An inner voice told him such a move was rash. After all, he was the one who'd been urging caution with the new brides, urging the men and women alike to take their time and not make impulsive decisions.

But after Bishop Hills and the constable's admonition to take the baby to the Northerner's Encampment, his worry over what would become of the child had doubled. He had to find a viable solution quickly.

"If you're not willing to do it," she said, "then maybe you can check if there's someone else—"

"I didn't say I wouldn't."

"Then you're planning on it?"

Why shouldn't he? Although his mind rapidly started to give

him a dozen reasons why he needed to be wary, he shoved the warnings aside.

Miss Hart watched his face expectantly. The lamplight from the sconces reflected in her eyes, deepening the green and turning her skin to a creamy porcelain. If he married Miss Hart, at least she was fair on the eyes. He'd never get tired of looking at her. Her beauty was untamed, almost exotic compared to Lizzy's no-nonsense looks.

"Very well," he heard himself saying even as his chest burned again with the pain of losing the woman he'd always wanted. "I shall marry you."

eight

Zoe studied Pastor Abe's face. Something was definitely amiss. She'd expected more resistance to her request that he do the marrying tonight. Surely he'd offer more protest if he realized she'd chosen Dexter Dawson. Maybe he thought she was marrying a different man.

She glanced at the door, and not for the first time wondered if she was really doing the right thing by agreeing to wed Dexter. When she'd arrived to discover she was early, she'd almost turned around and walked away.

"Bishop Hills might still be here," Pastor Abe said hesitantly. "But I'm not sure he'll be in agreement to the marriage."

"We don't need the bishop's permission, do we?"

"Not necessarily." He tugged at his clerical collar as though it were choking him. "I suppose we could go over to Justice Woodcock's house. He owes me a favor."

"As in a justice of the peace?" Pastor Abe wasn't making any sense. Since he'd just agreed to do the ceremony himself, why would they need to involve anyone else?

"Unless you had your heart set on a church wedding?"

Before she could answer, the side door opened. She expected

to see Dexter Dawson and was surprised instead at the sight of a young man attired like Pastor Abe in a dark suit and clerical collar.

"John, my man," Pastor Abe said, relief flooding his voice.

The young man smiled widely, revealing crooked front teeth but a kind-enough smile. He made a direct line to them, a waif of a man—short and thin and likely to be blown away at the slightest breeze. His face was dotted with various blemishes but radiated a youthful energy that reminded Zoe of her brother.

Pastor Abe and John exchanged a hug with some backslapping. "You're just in time."

"Time for what?" John peeked at Zoe shyly.

"In time for my wedding."

Zoe sucked in a rapid breath, her gaze darting to Pastor Abe. He was getting married too?

John's smile froze. "Your wedding?"

"Yes. I'm marrying Miss Hart tonight, and I'd like you to officiate."

The world around Zoe began to spin. What was happening? Why did Pastor Abe think he was getting married to her? She replayed everything she'd said and done since she'd arrived at the cathedral. Had she somehow given him the impression that she wanted to marry him? Or had he heard about all the rejections today and assumed he was her only option? Maybe he'd heard of her plans to marry Dexter and decided to offer himself instead?

John's smile fell away altogether. "I didn't know you'd ended things with Lizzy."

At the mention of the woman's name, Pastor Abe's expression hardened. "Lizzy is married to someone else now. I'm free to do as I please."

"She's married?" John squeaked.

"On Christmas Day, apparently."

The hurt in Pastor Abe's voice and the flash of pain in his eyes spoke all Zoe needed to know. Lizzy was the woman waiting for him back in England, the one Mrs. Moresby had mentioned. And she'd jilted Abe.

John cast another shy look at Zoe before leaning in toward Abe and muttering under his breath. "I didn't know you were close to anyone else."

"I've worked all week with Miss Hart saving a baby. While we're not close, I have gotten to know her and can attest to her good character."

John glanced back and forth between her and Pastor Abe as if somehow he could solve the mystery of their meeting and this hasty wedding. But Zoe was as confused as he was and could only shrug.

"We may as well begin," Pastor Abe said.

John lifted off his tall black hat, wiped his forehead, then resettled the hat. "You're certain?"

"As long as Miss Hart is certain." Pastor Abe finally looked at Zoe, the blue of his eyes revealing deep wounds she hadn't noticed there before. His jaw muscles worked up and down as though he was willing himself not to contradict his friend.

Was she certain? She'd come to the cathedral expecting to marry Dexter Dawson. But Pastor Abe was a better option by far. There was no question he was above reproach or that he'd accept and care for Violet—rather than simply tolerate the babe.

Truly the only other thing that mattered besides Violet was finding Zeke. Since Pastor Abe lived up in the mining region, no doubt he'd be able to help her find her brother, or at the very least he'd be kind enough to make inquiries.

"Herman Cox is dead," Pastor Abe blurted.

Her heartbeat halted abruptly. Part of her wanted to shout out in relief. But another part of her grieved for Violet's father and for the life he'd lost, especially because he'd never get to see his daughter grow up.

"Now my superior, Bishop Hills, has requested I take Violet to the Northerner's Encampment," Pastor Abe said as if that explained his willingness to marry her. "And he wants me to leave her there."

Zoe had never heard of the place, but the gravity of Pastor Abe's expression told her she needed to make sure Bishop Hills didn't get his way. "Will he force you to do it?"

"I don't see why he would if we're married and agree to care for the child."

She prayed he was right. "I was expecting to have to marry Dexter Dawson. But if you're willing to marry me, how can I say no?"

Pastor Abe glanced at a crumpled piece of paper on the floor, paused a moment, and then gave a curt nod. "Let us proceed."

She had the feeling if she didn't take advantage of this moment, if she waited even five more minutes, he'd come to his senses and walk away, that she'd lose the chance to marry him and end up stuck with Dexter.

Pastor Abe positioned himself in front of John expectantly. And Zoe took her place at his side.

Once again John looked from her to Abe and back, his brow furrowing above baffled eyes. "This is most unusual, to be sure." He slipped his hand into an inner pocket and retrieved his *Book of Common Prayer*.

"Unusual circumstances call for unusual measures." Pastor Abe didn't break the intensity of his stance.

"Very well, my friend." John opened the well-worn black book. "I trust you like I do no other and realize you wouldn't enter into so serious a commitment without a great deal of prayer and thought."

Pastor Abe flinched but didn't budge.

John flipped the thin pages until he found what he was looking for. He started to read the opening of the marriage ceremony.

"Perhaps just the vows?" Pastor Abe suggested in a tight voice.

John's eyes widened. He looked as though he might say something more, but after a second, he nodded and began to turn the pages ahead in the service.

"'Wilt thou have this woman to thy wedded wife, to live together after God's ordinance, in the holy estate of matrimony? Wilt thou love her, comfort her, honor, and keep her, in sickness and in health, and forsaking all other, keep thee only unto her, so long as ye both shall live?'"

Pastor Abe didn't respond.

Zoe peeked at him sideways. The muscles in his jaw were once again flexing, and his eyes were filled with distress. She didn't know what had happened to cause such anguish. In fact, she didn't know much about him at all. But compassion stirred in her nonetheless. She wanted to reach out and comfort him, to let him know he wasn't alone in his hardship, that she understood what it was like to feel such pain.

But she sensed that if she touched him, he'd only draw away, perhaps even leave the cathedral.

"Abraham?" John asked, his tone pleading with his friend to see reason.

"I will," Pastor Abe said quickly, decisively.

John watched his friend for a long second before turning his attention back to the open page of his book. "'Wilt thou have this man to thy wedded husband, to live together after God's ordinance, in the holy estate of matrimony? Wilt thou obey him, serve him, love, honor, and keep him in sickness and in health, and forsaking all other, keep thee only unto him, so long as ye both shall live?'"

"I will," she replied.

John then situated Pastor Abe's right hand together with hers as was the custom. Pastor Abe's fingers were cold and clammy, but unswerving. He repeated his vows without hesitation. When he finished, Zoe spoke hers.

"Do you have a ring?" John directed his question to Pastor Abe.

He shook his head. "I'll purchase one just as soon as I can arrange it."

"Very well. Then let us pray." John read a prayer and afterward placed their hands together again. "'Those whom God hath joined together, let no man put asunder. Forasmuch as you have consented together in holy wedlock, and have witnessed the same before God, and thereto have given and pledged your troth, I pronounce that you be man and wife together. In the name of the Father, and of the Son, and of the Holy Ghost. Amen.'"

Pastor Abe kept his head bowed. Zoe didn't want to interrupt his prayer—if he was still praying—so she remained quiet. John bowed his head too, stealing a look now and again at Pastor Abe. After several minutes of silence, John finally stared directly at his friend and cleared his throat.

Pastor Abe lifted his face, determination etching his features.

John clamped his friend on the shoulder. "Congratulations, Abraham. May God bless your union and bring you great happiness through it."

"Thank you, John."

John turned to her with his warm smile. "May God bless you too, Mrs. Merivale."

Mrs. Merivale. She was Mrs. Merivale. How strange.

"You have for yourself a very fine husband in Abraham," John continued. "No woman could ask for a better man."

"Apparently Lizzy could," Pastor Abe murmured.

John's smile faltered. "Ah well. 'Tis her loss entirely and Mrs. Merivale's gain."

The cathedral bell began to ring the top of the hour. Dexter Dawson was due at any moment. What would he say—or do—when he discovered she'd married someone else in his stead? Though she'd only encountered Dexter on a couple of occasions, she suspected he was the type of man who was accustomed to getting what he wanted and wouldn't take kindly to her rejection.

"I best be going," she said. "I don't want to be away from Violet for too long."

"Certainly," Pastor Abe replied. "I shall walk with you to the Marine Barracks."

And then what? She didn't voice her question aloud. Though she was bold, she wasn't quite so brazen.

The men spoke a few words of good-bye before Pastor Abe led the way toward the same side door that John had entered through. As they exited, she didn't see Dexter anywhere, but she hastened her stride anyway and kept her head down.

"You're in quite the hurry to return to Violet." Pastor Abe easily kept pace with her.

"Aye. The women were nice enough to watch over her. But she gets fussy easily and can try the patience of a saint."

Ahead, a raucous group turned onto the street, their laughter ringing out. The heavy darkness of the evening shrouded them, and the light from the sporadic streetlamps didn't illuminate anything well enough for Zoe to identify them. But just in case Dexter Dawson was among them, she veered off the plank sidewalk into the muddy street and crossed to the other side.

Pastor Abe followed, and she was thankful when he didn't attempt any more conversation. When they reached the front gate of the government complex, she stopped and hesitated.

He shifted and stuffed his hands into his pockets. "I shall go in with you and help you collect your belongings."

"I don't have much." What would the other women say when

they learned she was married? She hadn't told anyone except for Mrs. Moresby of her plans.

"You'll have Violet and her things."

"She doesn't have much either." But with all the donations Mrs. Moresby had collected, Violet had a fair share more than Zoe did.

"Nevertheless, Miss Hart, I'd like to help."

She wasn't Miss Hart anymore. Everything in her life had changed in an instant when she'd spoken her wedding vows—including her name.

As if realizing the same, he shifted again and looked everywhere but at her.

"You can call me Zoe," she offered softly.

"Very well . . . Zoe." As he spoke, his gaze collided with hers. Bright light from the front windows of the government building cast a glow, turning his eyes a warm, innocent blue. He didn't hold her gaze long before dropping it shyly. "You can address me as Abe."

"Not Abraham?" she teased.

"If you prefer."

"I like either one."

"Then you can choose." He toed a stone in the path until he knocked it loose.

Was he hesitant about having her lodge with him tonight? Where did he live while he was in Victoria? Maybe he didn't have space for her and Violet. Perhaps they could avoid the whole awkward wedding night scenario if she stayed at the Marine Barracks until he was ready to leave Victoria and return to the mountains.

"I realize the wedding came up at the last minute and that you might not be prepared for me and Violet to stay with you. We can remain at the Marine Barracks awhile longer if you want."

His arms were stiff with his hands still bunched in his pockets. "I have a place I stay whenever I'm in Victoria—one of the cabins on the bishop's property. He makes them available to the traveling preachers whenever we're in town."

"I don't want to impose."

"You won't." His voice cracked, and he cleared his throat. "There's plenty of room."

She waited for him to glance up and reassure her. But he remained silent, his focus on the rock he was pushing around.

"Violet might keep you awake—"

"I don't mind."

"Are you sure?"

"Zoe."

She liked the way he said her name, delicately and earnestly. And when he lifted his gaze again, she liked the kindness in his eyes.

"You're my wife now. I plan to take care of you and Violet."

His words sent warmth spiraling through her. How long had it been since anyone had taken care of her? Certainly not since Zeke had left. Maybe even before that.

"Thank you, Abe."

He nodded, his lips rising with the beginning of a smile, almost as if he were pleased at her use of his given name. "Shall we go collect Violet?"

"Aye."

He opened the gate and ushered her through. As they followed the path around the main government building to a center courtyard, her steps were much slower now. She couldn't keep from noticing that once again he matched her pace, and she was all too aware of him beside her, especially his strong, towering height, the thickness of his arms, and the broadness of his chest.

"Did you have the chance to speak with Herman before he died?" she asked, needing to focus on something besides him.

"No. Unfortunately. I wasn't able to locate him in time."

"I'm sorry. I know you wanted to."

He stopped, his head dropping in a posture of defeat. "I should have done more."

His self-censure took her by surprise. She grabbed his arm and turned him to face her. "Don't you be saying that. You did everything you could—more than anyone else. The truth was, Herman didn't want you to find him, and there was nothing to be done about it."

"I could have visited him more, and maybe I would have learned of Rose's death and his grief sooner." Abe's dejection again surprised Zoe. She hadn't realized pastors got discouraged or had regrets.

"I'm guessing his wife's death wasn't the first time Herman drowned his problems with drinking."

"No. But I could have prayed for him more fervently."

She lifted a hand to Abe's cheek and forced his head up. The pain in his eyes radiated into Zoe so that her chest expanded with compassion for this generous man who clearly cared about the people he met. "You couldn't help him, not when he didn't want it. But you've been given the opportunity to help his daughter."

He studied her face, the light from windows of the Marine Barracks illuminating the grassy yard where they stood. "You're right. I can't squander the chance to do for Violet what I couldn't do for her father."

She smiled her approval of his decision.

His return smile was easy and genuine—and very fine looking. She was suddenly conscious of the slight scruff on his cheek beneath her hand as well as the strength in his jaw along with the fact that he was her husband and she'd be living with him from now on.

Her heartbeat gave a strange lurch. She wasn't actually looking forward to living with him, was she? She dropped her hand and took a step back. "I guess we should get on inside."

As they moved up the stairs and he held open the door, she didn't allow herself to look at him again. Instead, she mentally chastised herself to remember she didn't want to care too deeply about a husband. Her heart ached too much already, and she didn't want to allow herself to love again only to lose.

No, she was a bride of convenience. And she planned to remain that way.

nine

Zoe stood in the open doorway of the dark cabin and waited as Abe rummaged inside. Violet rested contentedly in her arms, having fallen asleep almost the moment Zoe gathered her up after returning to the Marine Barracks.

Apparently Violet had cried inconsolably the entire time Zoe had been away. With Mrs. Moresby having gone home, the other bride-ship women had been near to crying with frustration themselves when Zoe had reclaimed the babe. None of them had been disappointed to hear Violet was leaving. And while they'd been surprised to learn of Zoe's marriage, especially to a reverend, they'd hugged her and wished her well, obviously relieved she was taking the babe away.

All the more reason Zoe knew she'd done the right thing in getting married.

At a thud within the cottage followed by Abe's grunt, Zoe squinted at his outline. "Are you okay?"

"Yes. Just bumped my head."

Zoe glanced at the mansion across the yard. Even in the dark, she counted six chimneys and three elegant turrets. A tall iron fence surrounded the property, as did holly trees. A winding garden path led from the main house to the cabins and a number of other outbuildings, including a two-story barn.

When she'd voiced her astonishment that Bishop Hills lived in such a large place, Abe had explained that one of Victoria's prominent families owned the home. They had returned to England and during their absence had given the bishop leave of their house.

Several windows on the ground level were lit, and she caught a glimpse of a woman. Bishop Hills's wife or a maidservant?

The other two cabins nearby were dark like Abe's. And so far, no one had come out to greet them or question why Abe had a woman and babe with him. She didn't want to cause a scandal. And she certainly didn't want anyone to assume she was a loose woman. But she guessed the rumors would fly until everyone learned they were married.

The scratch of a match was followed by the hiss of a flame, and an instant later, a lantern in the middle of the table glowed with amber light and brought the room to life. Abe hurried over to the double bed and yanked the coverlet up. Then he scooped up a shirt, socks, and even underdrawers from the floor. He wadded the garments and dumped them into an open wardrobe before shoving the door closed.

Though the cabin was only one room, it was bigger than she'd imagined.

"Sorry for the mess." He crossed and picked up a mug and plate from the pedestal table next to a wingback chair, both positioned near a cast-iron hob, which took up the final corner.

A round table with two chairs stood near a medium-sized window that overlooked the garden and main house. She guessed by daylight the view was pretty, especially when the flowers and trees were in bloom.

"It's a nice place." She stepped farther into the cabin and closed the door behind her. Abe had deposited her bag along with Violet's necessities in a haphazard heap near the table. She had pitifully few things and would be able to unpack everything in no time.

Abe swiped at the tabletop, brushing crumbs onto the floor. "I didn't realize I'd have visitors or I would have taken the time to clean up."

"Perhaps you need to be hiring a maid," she teased.

"I have considered it." He stepped over to the stove door, opened it, and stirred the coals. "Since I'm here so irregularly, I've opted instead to make use of the bishop's offer of a maidservant from time to time. Perhaps I ought to utilize her more oft."

"Perhaps," she teased again.

"Then I shall make mention of it to Bishop Hills and ask if he can spare one of his maidservants for the duration of our time in Victoria."

Was he jesting back? From the seriousness of his expression as he added another shovelful of coal into the oven, she guessed he had every intention of following through. Did he think she was incompetent? That she couldn't take care of his home?

"Don't you be worrying. I can manage just fine with cooking and cleaning."

Crouched in front of the stove, he paused and looked over his shoulder at her. "You'll be busy taking care of Violet."

Was he already having second thoughts about marrying her? "With my mum working at the mill, I've been cooking and cleaning my whole life."

He frowned before closing the stove door and standing. He dropped the shovel into a coal bucket with a clank, brushed his hands together, and then balled his fists deep in his pockets with his usual stiff arms. Something in his stance and in his eyes told her he was thinking about another time and another place and perhaps even another woman.

Lizzy? The woman who'd jilted him?

Zoe shifted Violet in her arms to reposition the babe's weight even as she fought against the feeling that Abe regretted marrying her. "I can do it all, Abe. I vow it."

"Forgive me." His brow furrowed. "I didn't mean to imply that you aren't capable. I only thought to ease your burdens with the assistance—"

"Would Lizzy want a maid?"

"Of course."

'Course. Zoe should have guessed Lizzy was a gentlewoman. Which meant Abraham Merivale was a gentleman, born into a well-to-do family, where he was accustomed to having servants pick up his clothing, wash his dishes, and tidy his bed. Apparently he was making do without the help here in the colonies. But no doubt, his preference was to have maids, not only for himself but for his wife.

She should have realized he, as a reverend, was in a class above hers. He had the air of someone well educated and had impeccable manners. Yet, except for today, he'd always worn the same casual attire as the working-class men. And he'd always been humble, without any of the snobbery of the upper class. Even so, she should have known better.

He may have overlooked her background tonight in a noble effort to give Violet a home. But how would he feel once he had time to fully comprehend what he'd done?

She shuddered and hugged Violet closer.

"I'm sorry for the chill." He gathered the coverlet from the bed and started toward her. "You and Violet can wrap up in this until the cabin is heated."

She didn't protest as he draped the blanket about her shoulders or when he guided her to the chair next to the stove. When she was situated with Violet, he stood awkwardly, glancing around the room as if unsure what to do with himself.

Should she offer him the cushioned wingback chair? It was his house, after all. She could easily sit in one of the simple wooden chairs at the table. However, she couldn't imagine he'd want to linger and talk for too long. The hour wasn't late, but surely he was eager to take her to bed.

Maybe if she didn't make eye contact. . . . She focused on Violet's sleeping face, her sweetly puckered lips, her dark lashes, her exquisite olive skin.

"Would you like something to eat or drink?" Abe asked, clanking the lid of the pot on a back burner. "Perhaps a cup of tea?"

"I can make it." She started to rise. It wasn't right for a man of his station to wait upon a woman like her, not even in marriage.

"Please." He motioned for her to remain in the chair and offered her a warm smile. "I shall do it, or you might threaten to make me hold the baby."

"Very true." She laughed, the tension easing from her body. "You must learn to hold her eventually."

"Oh, must I?" His voice hinted at laughter.

"Aye, and I'll bet you'll even like it."

"What will you wager?"

"Wager?" She gave a mock gasp. "You're scandalous, Pastor. I didn't think reverends were allowed to wager."

"I can be quite scandalous when I choose to be." He flashed a grin before turning back to the tea canister he was in the process of opening.

She wasn't exactly sure what he was referring to, but it didn't matter. His grin warmed her faster than any tea could.

Maybe the evening wouldn't be so unbearable and awkward after all. Maybe she'd even enjoy it.

"You married the mill girl simply to challenge my decision regarding the infant," the bishop said from his chair beside the fireplace. His dressing gown was tied shut across his bulging waist but only just barely covered his knees, revealing a stretch of hairy legs and red swollen ankles above the washbasin where he was soaking his feet.

"That's not true at all, Your Grace." Abe focused on the glowing embers upon the hearth and wished he'd waited until morning to pay a visit to the bishop with news of his marriage. "I told you I did it because of my letter from Lizzy—Elizabeth. After learning of her nuptials to another, I realized I was free to support Zoe and the baby and felt it my Christian duty to do so."

"I ought to send you back to England in disgrace," the bishop said, as he had at least half a dozen times since Abe had entered his study an hour ago.

Abe had no doubt the bishop would follow through on the threat if he gave his superior any further cause for concern. "My parishioners will see it as an act of goodwill. It can only serve to open more doors of ministry."

The bishop leaned his head back and closed his eyes for a moment, his lips pursed, his features taut with exasperation. "Now not only will you have the distraction of the infant, but also a wife."

"I guarantee my marriage will not interfere with my ability to focus on my ministry." Abe tried to quell his inner debate on the very same issue.

"I pray you are correct, but I fear you will be wrong." The bishop opened his eyes, giving Abe a rare glimpse of his turmoil. "You know I have left my wife and family behind for the duration of my time in the colonies in order to concentrate entirely on the task at hand. And you also know only single ministers were chosen for this work for that exact reason."

Abe nodded. Yes, he and John and the other ministers were all single. But they were also all at prime marriageable ages. What difference would it make if they married now or waited until returning to England?

Bishop Hills had supported the bride-ship endeavors, claiming that the mining towns would benefit from the influence of good Christian women and that families were the foundation of a stable society. If only Abe could convince the bishop that his new family could function in that role. Perhaps he'd simply have to prove it.

"You may have attempted to have your way," the bishop said testily. "But I shall not be thwarted. I shall give you until spring to return that infant to its people—"

"But, Your Grace, I can provide a good home to the child—"

"You are a representative of the greatest church and country on the earth. As such you must be above reproach in all things. You have already caused a scandal with your impetuous marriage. And I will not allow any further disgrace. Do I make myself clear?"

Abe couldn't respond. His insides were churning too fast.

"Furthermore, if you have any desire for my support in your future efforts to become a bishop, then you would do well to heed my instructions."

While bishops were elected to their positions, Abe was well aware he needed Bishop Hills's recommendation in order to have the slightest chance at being selected as a candidate. Even then, if he was chosen, he'd still have to go through another process of discernment before being approved to take part in the election. Bishop Hills's support was crucial in every aspect.

"Find an Indian family willing to take the infant by spring, Mr. Merivale. That is my final word."

What tribe would take in a strange baby? Not when they were already struggling to take care of their own. Besides, Zoe had married him in order to keep Violet. After going to such lengths, she'd never agree to give the child to a random family, especially if she sensed any hesitation on their part. For now, he'd have to keep the bishop's ultimatum to himself and pray he'd discern a viable solution by spring.

As a maid stepped into the study with another pitcher of steaming water, Abe excused himself and retreated from the bishop's home. When the rear door closed behind him, Abe allowed himself a full breath, the first one he'd taken since he'd knocked on the door. He hadn't expected the conversation to take so long, but he should have known better.

Bishop Hills hadn't been pleased to hear about his marriage, to say the least. John had mentioned it to their superior. So Abe's news hadn't taken the man completely unaware. Nevertheless, the past hour of the bishop's censure had exhausted Abe.

He started down the gravel pathway that led to the cabins, to the simple place he made home whenever he came to Victoria. The light was extinguished and the window dark, which hopefully meant he'd given Zoe plenty of time to take care of her personal needs.

They'd talked while sipping tea, and he'd learned more about her niece, about how Zoe had been the baby's primary caretaker because her sister hadn't wanted the child. He'd understood without her saying so that the baby's death had been difficult—perhaps almost as difficult as losing a child she'd borne herself.

He'd shared more about his work in the mining camps, his small cabin in Yale, and the church he was hoping to construct there in the spring. She'd asked him questions about what life was like in the mountains, and he'd explained how the gold rush had started in '58 when gold was discovered in the Fraser River Valley. As word got out to San Francisco, prospectors, speculators, land agents, and outfitters had flocked into Victoria, turning the town of a few hundred into a bustling city of over five thousand within days.

With so many men arriving in the colonies, the Church of England had sent over missionaries for the purpose of establishing churches. The church had always been on the forefront of crown colonies, helping to replicate the order of the motherland.

Abe was one of seven ministers who'd volunteered for the daunting task of transforming the fur-trade and gold-rush towns into civilized places. Like John and the other missionaries, he had no salary here and relied upon his savings and inheritance. The satisfaction of leading men to deeper faith was well worth the sacrifices he was making for the time being.

When Violet had awoken and started fussing, he'd helped Zoe get a bottle ready and watched the baby consume her meal. He'd lingered as Zoe changed the infant's napkin and dressed her in a flannel nightgown. Then he'd aided Zoe in lining a crate with blankets and making a bed for the baby, all the while discussing how he might be able to convince one of his parishioners, a carpenter turned miner, to craft a cradle, especially during the idle days that remained until the spring thaw opened the way for mining to resume.

Finally, with Violet tucked into her crate, Zoe had grown silent—almost shy. He didn't know much about womanly things, but he'd surmised she had needs of her own to attend to and would appreciate some privacy. So he'd gathered his coat and informed her he was stepping out to see the bishop.

Now with the half-moon overhead guiding him, Abe's footsteps crunched against the path, echoing a strange foreboding. Upon reaching the cabin, he hesitated. At the complete silence from within, he tried not to make any noise as he entered. The glow of coals within the stove illuminated the room enough that he could maneuver around without bumping into furniture.

When he reached the bed and took in Zoe's form underneath the coverlet, he froze. What was she doing in the bed?

For an instant, he was mortified, even scandalized. Then heat flooded his face. Of course she was in his bed. Where else was she supposed to sleep? The small cabin had only one bed.

With a sense of desperation, he scanned the darkness, looking for another spot for himself, any other option. He could sleep in the wingback chair. But with his large frame, he was never entirely comfortable in the chair. If he spent a whole night in it, he'd awaken with a sore back and kinked neck.

He glanced at the slight floor space near the stove. It was too small. He'd never fit. He could shove aside the table and chairs and possibly eke out enough floor space by the entry. Even as he considered the possibility, he put it from his mind. He might be able to make do for a night or two with such rudimentary sleeping arrangements. But could he do so night after night?

Closing his eyes, he tried to calm his racing heart. He'd been so focused on everything else that he hadn't considered the practical implications of living with a woman. Or the conjugal aspect.

Would Zoe expect him to consummate their marriage?

His eyes flew open to take in her form. Though the coverlet shielded her, he easily pictured her lovely curves, tiny waist, and willowy body. And he just as easily pictured himself gathering her into his arms, pressing against her, and kissing her.

Heat swirled low in his gut, an unfamiliar heat, but one that was certainly pleasurable, and pulsed into his blood.

He gave himself a sharp mental shake. He couldn't. She might be his wife, but they were practically strangers. Surely they needed to get to know each other before engaging in so intimate an act. Besides, if she'd been expecting him, wouldn't she roll over and acknowledge his presence? As it was, she had her back facing him and was already asleep.

No, tonight was not the time to bring up the intimacies of married life. He'd attempt to have a conversation about her expectations at a future date. That would give him time to figure out his first. Obviously, he'd always assumed he'd fulfill his marital duty. He was, after all, no saint. And he had normal manly desires. That had been plain enough lately with his growing needs.

But he'd never anticipated this kind of marriage arrangement or such a sudden wedding. He could afford to be patient, couldn't he? Even if his desires had become more prominent since his encounter with Wanda, surely he could wait a little longer, long enough to earn Zoe's trust and admiration and devotion.

He slipped out of his shoes, shrugged out of his coat, then pulled his clerical collar off, letting it fall to the floor. He unbuttoned his shirt and tossed it on the growing heap.

She made a tiny sound like the intake of breath.

He paused and watched her, hoping he hadn't woken her. When she didn't move or make any other noise, he tugged first one suspender from his shoulder then the other, and a second later his trousers slid down with a *swoosh*.

With a shiver of trepidation, he eyed the bed. It was a double, and she was as close to the opposite edge as she could go without falling off. Even so, he was accustomed to sprawling out on the entire mattress. How would he be able to share the bed without coming into contact with her?

Tentatively, he lowered himself until he was sitting on the edge. He glanced again to the spot on the floor by the door. Maybe that was the better option.

He shook his head. No, now that he was married he had to get used to sharing a bed. The sooner he shared, the easier it would get, wouldn't it?

Slowly expelling a breath, he swung his legs up, leaned back, and tugged the coverlet up.

Still she didn't stir.

He stared up at the ceiling and hardly dared to move lest he accidentally brush against her. After long moments of silence with only the slight whistle of wind in the chimney, he closed his eyes.

The first image to assault him was one of Lizzy in bed, not with him, but with another man. What had her experience been like? He hoped her first night was as awkward as his, that she was filled with regrets that she wasn't in his arms.

As soon as the thought entered his mind, shame followed on its heels. Even if he was angry and hurt, he didn't wish her ill. He only wanted her happiness. Truly he wanted the best for her. If only he'd been enough. . . .

Pain slashed through his chest again, this time constricting his airways.

He opened his eyes and stared at the ceiling again. All evening, since marrying Zoe, he'd kept distracted and busy so he didn't have to think about Lizzy. But now in the quiet of the night, he was alone with his thoughts, and they were clamoring louder with each passing second.

He had to reflect on something else—anything else—or he'd only sink deeper into despair. He needed to pray, but somehow, somewhere during the evening he'd lost his sense of God's presence, as if he'd fallen overboard and was drowning. The wind and the waves pounded against him so that he couldn't hear or see the Almighty.

Oh, God, he silently whispered through a haze that rapidly swelled and threatened to suck him down. *Please.*

A strand of hair tickled his cheek. He lifted his hand only to find that Zoe's long, thick hair spread out over her pillow and cascaded onto his. Gently he touched the strand.

When she didn't react, he glided his fingers in deeper. As he did so, the silkiness and the thickness and the warmth soothed him. He lightly twisted the strands. Then, expelling a deep breath, he closed his fingers about her hair and brought a thick fistful to his nose. He breathed it in, then pressed it against his cheek before sliding it to his lips.

The touch was exquisite and made him want to dig into her hair and breathe her in more fully. He held himself back. With the silk cascading through his fingers and against his face, he closed his eyes and let the sensations soothe his aching heart and help him forget about all he'd lost.

ten

*A*be awoke with a start.

"Hush now, wee one" came a whisper.

Gurgling and cooing rose up in the darkness. And for a moment, Abe couldn't make sense of the sounds.

"You've got to be going back to sleep," said the same voice.

He sat up and blinked hard, confusion hanging like a thick mist. Who was in his home and why?

At another soft squeak of a baby, realization crashed through him with the force of raging rapids. He'd gotten married last night. To a woman he barely knew.

Oh, Lord God Almighty, what had he done? And what had he been thinking?

He dropped his head into his hands and almost groaned. For a second he willed the silence to continue, for the woman and infant to disappear, for himself to wake up and discover he'd only been dreaming.

But the baby chirped a contented noise, and the woman once again murmured soft words in response. Zoe Hart and Violet Cox were in his wingback chair in front of the stove.

He buried his face deeper as the memories came back. He'd

gotten Lizzy's letter, had been shocked to discover she was married, and had been so overcome with pain and anger that he'd been blinded. Yes, blinded. There was no other explanation for why he'd so hastily married Zoe.

Instead of taking the time to present his heartache to the Lord and prayerfully consider what to do next, he'd forged ahead with his own plans in his own way.

Misery slithered around him like a draft of cold air, making him want to shudder down to his bones. What had he been thinking to rush into marriage like this? Hadn't he warned Zoe about the need to take her time in finding a husband?

Now he was a hypocrite—preaching one thing but doing another. Once the miners discovered what he'd done, they'd lose respect for him. They would surely think he was a desperate, lusting man who couldn't control his urges.

Oh, Lord, he silently prayed. *Help me.*

Was there any way he could change what had happened and make things right? For long moments, he sat with his head in his hands and tried to think, tried to find a way out of the mess in which he found himself. Was he stuck?

The bed beneath him seemed to sag lower. The bed. He lifted his head. Even though they'd shared the bed, they hadn't consummated their union, which meant they still had time to nullify the marriage and go their separate ways. Surely Zoe would understand and would keep quiet about the whole affair.

A glance out the window to the faintly lit sky told him dawn was close at hand. If he spoke with the bishop now, perhaps he'd find a way out of the situation. After the bishop's anger the previous evening, surely the older gentleman would be all too happy to give Abe an official annulment.

Abe swung his legs out of bed, his bare feet brushing against the cold floor.

"Good morning," Zoe said, her voice sweet and shy.

"Good morning." He earnestly prayed he hadn't touched her inappropriately during the night and flushed at the very thought.

He groped at his pile of clothing, hoping to make contact with his trousers. "Violet is up early this morning."

"She's still needing to learn what's day and what's night."

He fumbled to find a trouser leg. Even though the room was shrouded in darkness, he could see her outline in the chair. That meant she could see him partially too. And he was all too conscious that he was attired in his drawers and nothing else.

"I hope we didn't wake you."

"No, I'm a heavy sleeper." He flushed again. The revelation seemed too intimate. In fact, the entire predicament was too intimate. If only he could step into another room to finish dressing and grooming instead of fumbling around in front of her.

He stuffed his leg into his trousers only to find his foot wedged tightly. Standing on one leg, he jerked at the trousers and managed to get his other leg inside except that his other foot also stuck. With both feet trapped, he lost his balance and fell backward onto the bed.

"No need to be in the dark." She rose from her chair. "Since we're all awake."

"I'll be fine." He attempted to pull up his trousers again.

"It's no trouble." Before he could protest further, she lit the lantern on the pedestal table. Adjusting the wick, she stood with her back to him. Her hair was unbound and reached nearly to her waist. The rich ebony was a contrast to the pure white of her nightgown, and the thick waves shimmered as though beckoning to him.

His fingers twitched with the need to tangle there. Had he really touched her hair last night before he'd fallen asleep, or had he only dreamed it? The sensation of her thick strands in his hands and against his lips was all too real. And all too real was the pulsing urge to touch her hair again.

As she turned, he tried to send his thoughts in another direction, but long cascades fell over her shoulders, richer and finer than any luxurious pelt he'd ever seen. She had beautiful hair. There was no sense in denying it. In fact, he'd probably feel better if he acknowledged the facts.

"There. That's better, isn't it . . . ?" Her gaze connected with his bare chest. Her eyes widened, and pink infused her cheeks before she shifted her attention down. Her eyes rounded even more, and after a moment a smile twitched at her lips.

Embarrassment rushed through him. He was still bare chested, his shirt discarded in a heap with the rest of his garments on the floor. What did she expect? She should have heeded his admonition not to light the lantern. Now they were both in an extremely awkward situation.

He tugged at his trousers so he could at least cover his lower half.

A laugh escaped before she cupped her mouth. Even so, her eyes danced with merriment.

He gave another futile pull before glancing down to discover his legs each stuck in a shirtsleeve. With his feet and calves trapped in the shirt, his bare knees and thighs were exposed up to the edge of his light blue underdrawers. For a second, he was tempted to drag the coverlet over his body and bury himself in mortification.

But at another muffled laugh coming from behind her hand, he glanced at himself again. Even though he was mortified, he managed a grin. He looked ridiculous. It was no wonder she was laughing.

He allowed himself a chuckle.

She dropped her hand, giving him full view of her beautiful smile and her adorable dimples.

He laughed again, and when she joined in, somehow the

embarrassment dissipated. Their laughter grew louder until the cabin rang with it and she was wiping tears from her cheeks.

Finally, she crossed to him, set Violet on the bed, and reached for one of the shirtsleeves. "I think you'll be needing help if you have any hope of freeing yourself today. Unless you're hoping to set a new fashion trend."

"The only thing this will set is tongues to wagging."

"Aye." She gripped the wrist of the shirtsleeve and attempted to wiggle his foot free. "That it will." With her dark hair flowing over her shoulders, her lips puckered in concentration, and her long lashes framing her bright green eyes, he couldn't remember why he needed to protest their marriage. Why couldn't he stay married to this breathtaking beauty?

"There." She freed first one leg, then the other. "Now you needn't ruin a perfectly good shirt." Her nightgown pulled snug, drawing his attention downward. The scooped neckline was modest but emphasized her womanliness and reminded him of just how desirable she truly was. She finally glanced up at him and smiled, her expression so innocent, so trusting, so sweet.

This time he couldn't make himself smile back. Instead, heat spilled through his veins like low flames, blazing new trails and bringing him an awareness of the sharpness of his desire.

As though she sensed the direction of his thoughts, her smile faded. She visibly swallowed before picking Violet back up and situating her against her chest, almost as a shield. The baby reached out and clutched a fist of Zoe's hair, kicking her legs and cooing in obvious pleasure at being in Zoe's arms again.

Zoe's lips turned up in a tender smile, and she bent and kissed Violet's cheek.

It was Abe's turn to swallow hard. He didn't know why he was in such a hurry to leave the cabin when all he wanted to do was watch Zoe. Why had he considered running to the bishop and asking for an annulment? Yes, their marriage had been impetuous. But she and Violet needed him. And maybe, just maybe, he needed them too.

Zoe sneaked a peek in Abe's direction. He wiped the last of his shaving cream from his chin and tossed the towel onto the table. He peered at himself in the small wall mirror, smoothed back his unruly hair, and then turned toward her.

Attired in his suit and clerical collar from yesterday, he looked mighty fine. In fact, he'd looked mighty fine without them on too.

She cast her sights to Violet, who'd taken another bottle and gone back to sleep.

"So, I'll get more milk and a few simple food items," he whispered. "Do you need anything else?"

Images of his bare chest swam in her mind. With his broad shoulders and bulging arms, he reminded her of a picture she'd once seen of a medieval knight. She could just imagine Abe brandishing a sword and shield, his muscles rippling, as he towered above the enemy.

"Violet and I will be just fine." She couldn't meet his gaze lest he see the train of her thoughts and realize how fascinated she'd been watching his grooming. She wasn't sure why she should be so fascinated. It wasn't as if he were the first man she'd seen in a state of undress. In the close living quarters of the slums, she'd witnessed plenty of immorality, and she wasn't naïve about what happened between a man and woman.

Nevertheless, there was something different about Abe. Maybe his self-consciousness and modesty made her more aware of him. Or maybe he was so pure and different from all the men she'd known. Whatever the case, she was having a difficult time ignoring him.

Daylight now cascaded through the windows. She rose and turned off the lantern and then situated Violet in her crate bed.

Abe donned his hat and black broadcloth coat and crossed to the door. With his hand on the handle, he paused, his face troubled, as it had been from time to time since he'd awoken. Though his eyes were as kind as always, she could read the regrets there and guessed he was having second thoughts about marrying her.

She couldn't blame him. She probably wasn't the kind of wife he'd hoped to have. And maybe after a night of thinking about the marriage, he realized his mistake. Should she give him a way out? It seemed like the right thing to do.

He opened his mouth to say something, paused, then closed his lips firmly.

"I'd understand if you don't want me," she said.

Guilt clouded his eyes. "I'm sorry, Zoe. It all happened so fast, and I'm still trying to make sense of everything."

"I'll go. I can find someone else. You're not obligated to stay with me."

He shook his head. "No—"

"Dexter Dawson was expecting me to marry him."

"Absolutely not." Abe's brows dipped in a scowl. "I wouldn't give you over to Dex, not for all the gold in the Cariboo."

She liked so many things about Abraham Merivale and knew he'd be a good husband—probably the best she could find. But she couldn't abide trapping him into marriage. She had to release him from staying, if that's what he wanted. "One night together in this cabin doesn't bind us."

She liked that he'd been patient and restrained last night. 'Course, she'd been wide awake when he'd gotten into bed. She'd waited tensely for him to reach for her and had been more than a little surprised—and relieved—when he hadn't demanded anything. Instead, all he'd done was gently touch her hair.

Aye, he'd bumped into her numerous times throughout the

night—a leg or foot or elbow brushing up against her. One time, he'd even draped his arm across her. But he'd done so innocently in a deep sleep that hadn't been disturbed even when Violet had awoken crying.

"I blame only myself for our predicament." His voice was harsh and filled with self-censure, and he tipped the brim of his hat down, casting a shadow over his expressive eyes. "In a moment of weakness, I acted rashly and went against my own principles."

What moment of weakness? Abe always seemed so strong and sure of himself.

"I have no right to ask you to be patient with me as I sort through our options. But would you give me some time?"

A part of her wanted to gather her belongings, pack up Violet, and storm out of the cabin. He didn't want her and thought their marriage was a mistake. Though she didn't want to be hurt by that knowledge, it pricked her anyway, more sharply than she liked.

But when he lifted his eyes to hers, the churning blue radiated with apology, giving her no other option but to nod and accept his request.

"Thank you, Zoe," he whispered. Then he opened the door and was gone. Through the window, she watched him stride down the garden path, his shoulders slumped and head bent.

The pricking in her heart turned into a stab of remorse. She should have known she'd landed in a situation too good to be true.

With a loud exhalation, she pressed her hands against her hips and took in the disheveled state of the cabin. After a moment, she gathered her hair and began to tie it back into a loose knot. There was only one thing to do. Prove to Abe she'd be the kind of wife he wanted and needed. And she'd start by cleaning and organizing his house.

eleven

*A*be shifted and gave his fullest attention to his hat, which he was twisting in his hands.

The soft kissing noises between Pete and Arabella never failed to embarrass him—or to drive the temperature of his body to unbearable levels. He liked to blame the heat of the three brick ovens set into the outer wall. After hours of being heated by coals, the ovens reached temperatures hot enough to bake dozens of quartern loaves as well as rolls, which Pete, his father, and his assistants prepared every night.

Now, at the break of day, Pete's young assistant was finishing up the work of delivering the loaves and rolls while Pete cleaned up the bakeshop. Although the other workers had already left and were likely abed, Pete usually lingered until Arabella came down to begin baking cakes.

Abe had hoped to find Pete alone, but he'd walked in only to find the two locked in an embrace. He cleared his throat.

"Ten more minutes, Pastor Abe," Pete said between kisses. "Can you give me ten minutes with my wife?"

"Peter Kelly," Arabella said breathlessly as she slipped out of his grasp. "I am surely worth more than ten minutes of your time."

"You're worth an entire day." Pete lunged after her.

Laughing, she grabbed a baking pan and held it between them. Her eyes sparkled with love and desire and contentment.

Again, Abe dropped his gaze to his hat, and he smiled at the memory of his banter with Zoe from earlier when he'd put on his shirt in place of his trousers. He'd never laughed like that with anyone else. Certainly not with Lizzy. In fact, he was sure Lizzy would have been mortified if she'd been in Zoe's place and probably would have ignored him until he'd straightened himself out. And then she would have pretended the incident never happened.

Not so with Zoe. She'd made him feel as though he'd won a prize for making her laugh. And she'd come right over and helped him without any hesitation.

"Just one more kiss," Pete pleaded.

Arabella laughed softly. Abe glanced up in time to see her lean in and accept another kiss.

All he could think about was Zoe and how much he wanted to kiss one of her smiles—those smiles that lit up her eyes and made them irresistible.

Pete's eyes opened, and he caught Abe watching them.

Abe dropped his attention to a small mound of flour on the floor, but not before he saw Pete's lips curl into a devilish grin.

"You need to get yourself a wife. And soon."

"About that . . ." Abe said.

Pete stilled. "About what?"

"About getting a wife . . ." After leaving his cabin, Abe had decided it was too early to visit the bishop. So he'd headed over to the bakeshop. Usually Pete was the one asking him for advice and needing the rescuing, but this time, Abe desperately needed to talk with someone.

"You finally wrote and invited Lizzy to come?" Pete asked.

Abe wished there were a way to retract that letter he'd sent to Lizzy last autumn. She would surely think him pathetic once she got it. "Actually, I received a letter from Lizzy yesterday—"

"And she said she misses you so much that she's coming regardless of how you feel?"

"No—"

"Then she's demanding you return home?"

The anguish Abe had been trying to hold at bay returned with full force, barreling into him so that he slouched inside his coat. "She fell in love and married someone else."

The bakeshop turned suddenly silent, magnifying the clopping of a passing horse and carriage.

"I'm sorry," Pete started.

"I got married last night." Abe blurted the words before he lost his courage.

Again silence descended so that the thumping of footsteps in the overhead living quarters echoed around them.

Abe couldn't look his friend in the eyes. He didn't want to see the censure sure to be there. He stared instead at the misshapen brim of his hat.

"Married?" Pete found his voice, and it was laced with humor. "You're serious?"

Abe didn't find any humor in the situation. "Have I ever lied to you?"

Pete studied his face, his eyes widening, until a smile broke free. "You're married."

"Yes."

Pete crossed to him, slapped his back, and enveloped him in a hug. "Congratulations, my friend. It's past time."

How could Pete so easily accept the news and congratulate him without knowing any of the details? Surely if his friend knew more about the circumstances, he'd show some concern.

"After remaining celibate for so many years, it's no wonder you were in a hurry." Pete pulled back with a laugh. Arabella chastised Pete under her breath for his ribald comment even as Abe felt his ears turning hot and red.

"Can't believe you're up early this morn and out of bed." Pete's grin spread wider. "With Arabella, I couldn't bear to—"

Arabella snapped a towel at him and gave him a mortified and pleading look.

Pete's gaze softened into an apology.

Abe used the opening to get to the point of his visit. "I think the marriage was a mistake."

His friend's attention shifted to him again, and this time all humor disappeared. Abe relayed the events from meeting Zoe and their working together to care for Violet to Herman Cox's death and the unexpected arrival of Lizzy's letter last night.

"I wasn't in the right frame of mind," Abe said. "I actually don't know what I was thinking when I agreed to the marriage."

"If she's willing to help an orphan, then she sounds like a perfect woman to me." Pete winked at Arabella.

"She does sound positively kind and compassionate," Arabella added. "Especially if she's agreeable to caring for an infant. 'Tis surely no easy task she's taken on."

"I have no question regarding her compassion," Abe said. "She's most certainly kind and sweet and caring."

Pete's brows lifted. "If you like her, then what's the problem?"

Abe honestly didn't know what the problem was—except that Zoe wasn't Lizzy.

"Oh, I see." Pete scrutinized Abe's face. "You're not attracted to her."

Abe hesitated. How could any man not be attracted to Zoe? She was a ravishing beauty. He had only to think of how she'd looked this morning, sitting in the chair, trying not to watch him groom himself. Even with her wrapped in the blanket he'd insisted she use, he'd been intensely aware she was attired in only a nightgown. The few times he'd caught her looking at him, her eyes had been wide with a curiosity that only made him want to sit down and spend more time with her.

"Mayhap Arabella can give her some beauty tips," Pete suggested.

"It's not that. She's actually the loveliest woman I've ever met." It was the truth. But he couldn't base the marriage on physical attraction, could he? He'd counseled many men not to make intimacy the foundation of a relationship. There needed to be much more, including friendship, shared goals and interests, and a common faith in the Lord.

"It's clear you're already smitten." Pete clamped his arm.

"I barely know her."

"You like her. Otherwise you wouldn't have jumped at the chance to marry her."

"I didn't jump."

"You leapt." Pete's grin was playful. And infectious.

Abe smiled in return. "So you don't think I should get the marriage annulled?"

"Annulled? Absolutely not." Even though Pete's smile remained in place, his words took on a serious undertone. "Honor the commitment you made before God. You married her. You told her you'd love and cherish her until death. And now you need to follow through."

The words drove into Abe like a spike into stone, shattering his last resistance. Pete was right. He'd taken vows before God. He couldn't set aside those vows just because he'd woken up in the morning scared and uncertain.

No, whether for good or bad, he'd spoken binding words to Zoe. What was done was done, and he needed to accept it. He had to move forward with his choice.

"Thank you for your advice," Abe said. "You're right. I need to honor my marriage commitment."

"You're the wisest man I know, Pastor Abe." Pete began to untie his apron, which was coated with flour. "I have no doubt you'll figure this all out in a way that pleases God."

Abe prayed Pete was right. After leaving the Lord out of his planning last night and muddling things, he had to involve the Almighty moving forward.

Abe started toward the door. He was married. He was staying married. And now he needed to let Zoe know. She'd obviously sensed his confusion this morning, which hadn't been fair to her.

"Bring your wife by." Pete followed him, unwinding the long apron strings that wrapped around his waist. "Then I can tell her everything she'll have to put up with."

"She will indeed have to put up with a sinful man."

Pete socked Abe in the arm. "I'm only teasing. You're a good man, and she's blessed to have you."

"I know nothing about how to behave around her. She likely already thinks I'm an imbecile." His thoughts returned to the shirt incident.

"You need to woo her."

"Woo her?"

"Do things that will make her fall in love with you, just like I did with Arabella."

"Isn't it enough to provide for the needs of her and the baby?"

"Mayhap"—Pete's voice dripped with sarcasm—"if you were her father."

Abe paused at the door and squirmed at the notion of attempting to make Zoe fall in love with him. He wasn't a man given to the outward displays Pete relished. The closest he'd ever gotten to being romantic with Lizzy was copying a line of poetry from a book. He couldn't imagine Zoe wanting him to spout poetry. "What kinds of things should I do?"

"Spend time getting to know her. Find out what she likes. Be charming like me."

Arabella gave an unladylike snort as she cracked eggs into a mixing bowl.

"Admit it," Pete called to her. "You fell in love with me because of my looks and charm."

She tossed the eggshells into a wooden bucket at her feet. "I fell in love with you because you saw me the way no one else ever has—as a valuable woman."

"And because of my charm."

Abe opened the door and stepped outside, relishing the nip of cool morning air against his overheated cheeks.

"Well, if it isn't Holy Man, the wife stealer" came a voice from Abe's left. Before he could make sense of the comment, a fist pummeled into his cheek with a smack that sent him reeling backward. Pain clouded his vision, and he might have fallen except that Pete steadied him.

The attacker swung again.

"Hey!" Pete released Abe and blocked the hit. "What do you think you're doing?"

Abe grabbed Pete's shirt and yanked him out of the fray, blinking hard to regain his vision and see through the pain. But Pete broke free with both arms swinging, connecting first with the stomach and then nose of none other than Dexter Dawson.

Two of Dex's friends stepped out of the shadows of the nearby public bathhouse and began to cross over, hands on the pistols holstered at their belts.

Abe had seen too much violence in the mining camps to allow the fight to continue. He and Pete could very well end up dead, or at least injured. Steeling himself, he grabbed Pete again and hauled him away from Dex. "Hold on now. Let's solve our differences peacefully."

Pete's shoulders rippled, but thankfully he didn't attempt to go after Dex again. Rather, the two stared at each other, their eyes shooting anger.

"What's going on?" Abe winced at the throbbing in the side of his face.

"You stole my wife."

"Zoe?" Abe's question came out in a puff of white against the chill of the air.

"I told her to meet me at the church last night at seven. When I got there, the reverend said I was too late—that she'd married you."

"That's right. She asked me to marry her and I accepted." He replayed the events of last evening when Zoe had approached him in the sanctuary where he'd been kneeling. Why had she asked him to marry her if she'd come specifically to marry Dex? Maybe she'd been desperate for another option. Although she hadn't seemed desperate. . . .

"Or maybe you convinced her to change her mind." Dex's voice was a snarl, and he took a step toward Abe.

Pete stiffened, and Abe tightened his grip on his friend. If Pete let loose again, Dex's friends would surely let loose with their pistols.

"She proposed to me," Abe said again, but less certainly. *"Will you marry me?"* Hadn't those been her words—or something similar? What if she'd merely been asking him to perform the marriage ceremony between her and Dex? What if he'd been the one to mix everything up? It was certainly possible considering his state of mind.

"Everyone round here knew I planned to marry her." Dex's tone was unrelenting, his expression deadly. "And now everyone knows you stole her from me."

"I didn't steal her intentionally—"

"Pastor Abe couldn't steal something that wasn't yours to begin with." Pete's voice was as hard as Dex's.

The traffic on the street had halted, and the altercation was drawing the attention of passersby. Men stood in open doorways and peered out windows, likely expecting more fists flying, if not a gunfight.

Abe could only imagine Bishop Hills's reaction once he learned of the showdown. The bishop was already angry enough. This altercation would be just the excuse the bishop needed to send him back to England and put an end to his career aspirations.

He had to find a way to solve this problem with Dex peacefully. And immediately. "There are still plenty of other bride-ship women looking for husbands." He spoke as congenially as he could, although he couldn't in good conscience wish Dex upon any woman, bride-ship or not.

"I don't want anyone else." His words came out in a low growl. "I want Zoe Hart."

A flame sparked in Abe's gut—the same feeling he'd had the day of the funeral, when he'd seen Dex talking with her. "If she'd wanted you," Abe blurted before he could stop himself, "don't you think she would have waited for you to arrive?"

"Not with you putting on your airs and feeding her lies."

The burning in his gut swelled, as if needing release. This was a new sensation, one he didn't quite know how to handle.

"Give her back to me, Holy Man," Dex demanded.

Abe's muscles tightened with an unfamiliar need to swing out and hit the man. With Pete straining to break free from his grasp, Abe was tempted to release him and join his friend in the fight. But a whisper of warning rose in his soul, the warning that he needed to use God's strength and wisdom instead of giving in to the flesh.

With a silent prayer for help, Abe straightened his hat and then his clerical collar. "Zoe chose to marry me, not you," he said loudly and clearly enough that everyone around could hear him. "She's my wife now. And there's nothing you can do to change that."

He shoved Pete toward the bakeshop door, then spun and strode down the wooden sidewalk away from Dex and his men. He kept his spine rigid and his sights straight ahead, waiting for the blast of a gunshot, his body tensing in readiness of the pain that would follow.

But the only sound was the hard thump of his boots. He could feel not only Dex's eyes following him, but everyone else's too. He didn't let his stride falter. Or his resolve.

For the first time since leaving the church last evening, he was relieved he'd married Zoe—relieved she was with him and safely away from Dexter Dawson and others like him. The trouble was, Dex wasn't the kind of man who easily accepted defeat, and Abe had the feeling he hadn't heard the last from him.

twelve

Zoe reached for Jane's hand, smiling at her friend as they walked along the rocky shoreline, icy wind whipping their hair and tugging their skirts. As they laughed and breathed in the scent of pine that hung in the air, the setting sun glistened on the strait and poured its rays all the way to the snow-covered peaks of the mountains on the mainland.

"We can start over here and make our lives whatever we want them to be." Jane's voice was faint, far away.

When Zoe turned again, Jane had dropped behind. She'd stopped walking and was waving at Zoe, almost as if she were saying good-bye.

No! Zoe tried to shout at her friend, but the words wouldn't come out. *Stay with me! You can't give up yet!*

She startled at a gentle touch against her shoulder. Her eyes flew open to bright daylight and a strange room. Abe's cabin.

She calmed her thudding heart and listened for Violet. Silence met her and meant Violet was still sleeping. Zoe knew she needed to wake the babe and try to keep her occupied for greater lengths each day. But after the sleepless night next to

Abe, Zoe hadn't been able to resist lying down and resting while Violet napped.

At another gentle brush upon her shoulder, Zoe twisted her neck to find Abe sitting on the edge of the bed. As with last night, he'd taken the liberty of touching her hair, his fingers caressing a loose strand that had fallen across her shoulder. His touch was as soft as a summer breeze blowing through an open window.

She didn't know quite what to think of his caress. No one had ever touched her hair except Mum, who had stopped brushing her hair years ago.

Abe had propped an elbow on his knee and rested his forehead in his hand. His shoulders were slumped, his hair tousled, and his collar askew. He was the picture of dejection itself, which only sent a shiver deep into her body. He still regretted their marriage, and he must have made up his mind not to go through with it.

Maybe if he saw how she'd tidied the cabin, folded his clothing, made the bed, and swept the floor, he'd realize she was good for something. At the very least, he wouldn't have to hire a maid.

"Abe?" she whispered.

His head jerked up and his eyes opened. In the same moment, he drew his hand away from her hair as quickly as if it had burned him. "I hope I didn't wake you." He shifted enough that she glimpsed the opposite side of his face—the black and purple that rimmed his eye.

She gasped. "What happened?"

He angled his face away from her. "Nothing I want you to worry about."

Wrestling against the sagging mattress, she pushed herself up until she was sitting and could see his face more clearly. The area beneath his eye was swollen and discolored. She grazed his skin.

He winced and pulled back farther, making a motion to stand. But she tugged his arm to keep him in place. "No, sit. I'll get a cold rag to help with the swelling."

"I'll be fine," he murmured.

"Don't move," she insisted as she rose from the bed. She was surprised when he did as she said while she retrieved one of the soft cloths she used for bathing Violet and dipped it into the pail with the remains of the frigid water she'd drawn from the well. She wrung out the excess, the cold stinging her fingers, and then she returned to the bedside.

Without waiting for Abe's permission, she tilted up his chin so she could get a clear look at his injury. He'd taken a hard hit in the face. That much was clear.

"This might hurt a little." She pressed the cloth gently against his cheekbone.

He winced again.

She studied his face for any other injuries. "Who hit you? And why?"

"What makes you think someone hit me?" He avoided her gaze, looking instead past her to the window. "What if I ran into something?"

"The only thing you ran into was someone's fist."

His lips twitched with the beginning of a smile.

Satisfaction wafted through her. She liked that she could make him smile. "So will you tell me what happened, or am I gonna have to search Victoria for the man whose knuckles are as bruised as your face?"

"You won't have time to search," he said, much too serious again. "We're leaving Victoria today just as soon as we can."

Her heart skipped a beat. He'd said *we're* and *we*. "Does that mean you've decided to stay married to me?"

He reached up then and cupped his hand over hers. "I'm sorry for my indecisiveness earlier. I was wrong to consider other options. We were married in the sight of God and man, and I need to honor our vows and the commitment I made to you."

At the sweetness and sincerity of his words, her breath stuck in her chest. "Are you sure?"

"Yes. We'll make the best of the situation."

The best of the situation? Her breath deflated, her confidence slipping away with it. It appeared he still regretted their hasty marriage but was resigned to staying with her anyway. She ought to be happy about his decision. After all, this was exactly what she'd wanted in marrying a stranger—no feelings, no attachments, no worry about losing someone she cared about.

She shifted the cloth against his bruise.

He sucked in a breath.

"What happened?" By the light of day, his hair was lighter, almost blond. It was in disarray with a long strand falling over his forehead.

"Seems I made a wrong assumption last night."

"How so?" She was tempted to comb that stray strand back, but such a move seemed too forward with a man she'd known less than a week.

He shifted on the mattress, his sturdy square jaw flexing as though he didn't quite know how to formulate his answer. "I assumed you were proposing marriage to me," he finally said. "But apparently you were asking me to officiate your wedding to Dexter Dawson?"

She cast her eyes down, unable to meet his gaze. She'd known something wasn't quite right, but she hadn't corrected him. "I thought you were proposing to me to keep from having to take Violet away to wherever the bishop told you to."

"I suppose I was."

"I'm sorry I didn't clear up the misunderstanding."

"It's not your fault. I wasn't thinking clearly."

Because he'd been downhearted about his fiancée getting married to someone else?

"All that to say," he continued, "Dexter Dawson is not very happy this morning, to say the least."

Her gaze darted up. "He hit you?"

"He's claiming I stole you from him."

"He's an arrogant cur." She stepped back, letting the rag fall away from his bruise. "All he did was send me a note saying he'd marry me. If I was so important to him, why didn't he come tell me in person?"

"I'm glad he didn't." Abe reached for her, settling his hands on her hips and drawing her back.

The strength of his touch and the span of his fingers circling her waist sent warmth spiraling into her middle. His hold was decisively possessive, and she had the sudden urge to thread her fingers in his hair, pull him close, and let him rest his bruised face against her chest.

She'd witnessed her mum do that very thing to her father many times, standing while he buried his face against her body. Mum would hold him close, letting him shut out the problems and draw solace and strength from her.

"I think it's best if we get out of town and away from Dex as soon as possible." Abe tilted his head so his chiseled face was in perfect range of her hands. "I don't want to risk him finding you and thinking he can take you."

"He wouldn't. I'm not that important to him."

"You're very desirable." His voice and eyes radiated sincerity.

"Am I, now?" She tried to mask her pleasure at his compliment with a light, teasing tone.

"Of course Dex is attracted to you. What man in Victoria wouldn't be?" Once the words were out, he paused. Then, as if realizing the boldness of his confession as well as the intimacy of his hold, he released her and fumbled for a place to put his hands, crossing them, then folding them in his lap before crossing them again.

She bit back a smile.

"I'm afraid once Bishop Hills hears of my altercation with Dex, he'll decide he can no longer abide my propensity for scandal and will put me on the first ship back to England."

"Then he didn't take kindly to the news of our marriage?"

"To put it mildly."

"Are you in trouble because of it?"

Abe pushed himself up from the bed and crossed to the wardrobe. "The bishop and I have already been at odds over other issues, and this only adds to the tension already there." He yanked out a bag from the bottom of the wardrobe, knelt, and began to stuff his clothing items inside haphazardly.

She watched for only a moment before *tsk*ing and starting toward him. "You'd better let me pack if you don't want every stitch of your clothing to be hopelessly wrinkled."

He halted, one hand in the bag and the other in the items she'd carefully folded earlier. Before she could say anything further, a firm rap upon the door made them both jump.

Abe's gaze swung to the door. "The bishop." His whisper was drenched with dread.

Zoe's stomach twisted into a knot. She'd supposed she would have to meet the bishop at some point. But she hadn't expected him to visit today, especially at this moment.

"I can't let him see me with a bruised eye." Abe rose, his expression panicked. "What should I do?"

Zoe searched the cabin. Abe was too large to fit into the wardrobe or to hide under the bed. "Get in bed and pretend to be asleep."

"I don't want to speak an untruth."

"I'll be the one speaking the untruth."

"I don't want you speaking untruths either—" Another knock sounded at the door, this one louder.

"I'll tell him you're *resting*," she hissed.

Abe nodded, apparently satisfied with her answer. He dove onto the mattress, yanked the covers around him, and turned to face the wall. One of his boots stuck out, and Zoe tugged the blanket around it.

"Are you *resting*?" she asked.

He expelled an audible breath. A second one. Then a third. "I think so."

She almost smiled at his vain attempt to relax. Instead, she schooled her expression into what she hoped was severity. Surely the bishop would want Abe to marry someone serious. And polite. And perhaps gentle.

As she lifted the handle, she did her best to portray herself as respectable, although she suspected she looked as rigid and her smile as comical as one of the caricatures on the totem poles they'd seen from the ship as they'd neared Victoria.

Opening the door, she froze with the realization that she didn't know whether she ought to bow to the bishop or not. Maybe she needed to kiss his hand. Or his feet? With a growing sense of alarm, she started to shut the door and turn back to Abe for further advice when a woman's voice stopped her.

"There you are, my dear."

Zoe glanced through the crack to find Mrs. Moresby standing outside, a large basket dangling from each hand. "I had to come see for myself if the rumors were true."

Zoe opened the door wider and smiled at her friend. "Rumors are never completely true."

Mrs. Moresby eyed her from the tip of her head to her toes as if attempting to decipher a riddle. "If the rumor that you married Mr. Merivale isn't true, then why are you in his home?"

Zoe released a laugh of relief. "Aye, that rumor's true enough. I married him last night."

"I've also heard that miner who planned to marry you is quite livid."

"I've heard that as well."

Mrs. Moresby held up both baskets, the rows of ribbons on her cloak fluttering like a bird taking flight. "I've brought you a few wedding presents."

"Mrs. Moresby!" Zoe clapped her hands in delight. "How kind!"

The matron inched into the doorway. "It's nothing fancy, mind you. . . ." Her gaze snagged on Abe's stiff form under the coverlet, and she froze. She stared for a moment, her mouth hanging open.

Without the bishop making an appearance, Zoe had forgotten all about the need to hide Abe. Now she scrambled to find a way to explain why he was in bed at this hour of the morning. Mrs. Moresby's gaze swung from Abe to her and back before she finally snapped her mouth closed. Her eyes remained wide, and she slowly backed out of the cabin.

"My, my, my." She glanced at Zoe's hair.

Zoe rapidly smoothed the strands that had come loose during her recent nap, hoping Mrs. Moresby didn't think she'd just come from bed too.

"When you didn't answer the door right away, I should have realized." Mrs. Moresby's eyes began to light up with mirth. "I'm sorry for disturbing the two of you."

"You're not disturbing anything," Zoe rushed to explain. "Abe didn't sleep well last night. So I insisted he rest."

"Of course. Of course," she whispered almost conspiratorially. "You must be tired too."

Heat spread across Zoe's face.

"Would you like me to take Violet for a little while so that you can *rest* with your husband? I wouldn't mind in the least."

"You're very kind, Mrs. Moresby." Zoe stepped outside and attempted to close the door behind her, praying Abe hadn't heard any of the insinuations. "We'll likely be on our way soon. Abe's anxious to leave town."

Zoe directed their conversation to the baskets and the items inside, distracting the matron from talk of Abe. Thankfully, Mrs. Moresby was all too excited to show Zoe everything— more baby items for Violet, several new linens, including towels and a fancy embroidered tablecloth, matching pillowcases, and a silky but scanty new nightgown that made Zoe blush. The second basket contained an assortment of yarn in every color and thickness.

"To keep you busy during the long days of winter yet ahead," Mrs. Moresby said.

Zoe exclaimed over the yarn, thrilled by the bright skeins and imagining all the things she could make. But then she protested that she couldn't accept so many gifts. No one had ever bestowed so much on her before.

Mrs. Moresby waved off her concerns. "All I want in return is a visit when you come back to Victoria. And I wouldn't turn down a really colorful scarf if you happened to make me one."

A colorful scarf. "Wait just a moment, Mrs. Moresby." Zoe opened the cabin door. Abe had gotten out of bed and was kneeling in front of Violet's crate.

"Violet's awake," he said almost reverently, glancing at Zoe over his shoulder.

Zoe approached to find that Violet had clasped one of Abe's fingers within hers and was staring up at him with wide, wondering eyes.

"I think she might like me," he whispered, staring down at Violet with matching wonder.

Zoe couldn't keep from smiling at the sight of the towering, muscular man completely mesmerized by the wee babe. "Of course she likes you. Everybody likes you."

"Except for Bishop Hills and Dexter Dawson."

"They don't count."

"Let us pray so."

She rummaged in her bag until she found what she was looking for. She started back to the door only to realize Mrs. Moresby was peeking inside. As Zoe stepped out, the matron backed away and began to pump a fan in front of her face in spite of the cool January temperatures.

"I see Mr. Merivale is done resting," she said.

Zoe thrust the item out, hoping to keep the conversation from veering into dangerous territory again. "I'll still make you another one. But I want you to have this too."

Mrs. Moresby fingered the rainbow-colored scarf.

"I knit it for my friend Jane." Zoe's chest constricted with the ache of her friend's absence.

"I couldn't—"

"You stepped in and were a friend when I needed one most." Zoe pressed the scarf into Mrs. Moresby's hands. "She'd want you to have it every bit as much as I do."

Mrs. Moresby was silent, gently tracing the neatly stitched rows. When she looked up, tears shone in her eyes. "Thank you, Zoe. I know you're going to make a very fine reverend's wife."

Zoe hesitated to accept the compliment. She didn't know the first thing about being a reverend's wife or what Abe or the people he served would expect from her. What if she let everyone down?

"Remember," Mrs. Moresby said as she wrapped the scarf around her neck, "you don't have to be perfect or have your situation all figured out to be used by the good Lord. If you have a willing heart, that's all He needs."

A willing heart. Was that really all that was required? Zoe

wanted to believe Mrs. Moresby was right, that maybe eventually she could become the kind of wife Abe needed. But could she? Or would she be his downfall instead? After all, he'd said their marriage was a scandal. That the bishop might even send him back to England.

Though Abe had insisted he wanted to go through with their marriage, she didn't want to see him come to ruin as a result. Did she need to set him free from his commitment to her? Should she go to the bishop for an annulment before their marriage went any further?

A part of her admonished her to do the right thing for Abe. He was a good man and didn't deserve to suffer on account of her. But another part of her resisted. It was selfish of her, she knew. But now that she had him, she wasn't sure she could let go, not when she felt so safe—safer than she had in a long time.

With a final hug and the promise to visit next time she was in Victoria, Zoe watched Mrs. Moresby make her exit through a side gate. Then she turned back inside, determined to make the most of her new life but unable to keep her doubts battened down.

thirteen

here." Abe's cheerful whistle faded away. "New Westminster."

In the middle of the canoe, Zoe followed the direction of his pointed finger past the grassy delta to what appeared to be a town on the northern bank of the Fraser River.

So far the entrance to the Fraser River had been surrounded by low marshlands with sandbars and jagged rocks jutting up from the river. With the mountains in the background, the wild, untamed beauty of the land had taken her breath away. She'd been awed at the sight of harbor seals lounging on the bank, their bulky white bodies covered with black spots. Abe had also pointed out an eagle nesting in a cottonwood.

Without a sign of civilization since leaving Victoria and Vancouver Island, the town of New Westminster was a welcome sight even though it was small, with only a few people going about their business, mostly at the waterfront. A long wharf ran along the edge of the river, with low buildings nearby likely serving as storage facilities, as well as a host of shack-like homes that were gray and dingy.

On the hill that led up and away from the river, a few newer multistoried buildings stood out, larger, whiter, and cleaner than the rest—hotels, taverns, and a church. The rise was a dull brown of dead grass and brush and was dotted with the stumps of trees that had been cleared to make room for the town. At the top of the hill a section of evergreens still remained, almost as if a barber had given the rest of the area a trim but had forgotten to cut one section. Douglas pine. That's what Abe had called the majestic columns that rose tall above the others.

"They are solid, straight, and thick, which makes them ideal for ship masts," Abe had explained when she'd first pointed them out.

Zoe rose to her knees to get a better look at New Westminster, wondering which of the hotels had sheltered Herman Cox in his last moments. Now that he was dead and she didn't have to fear his coming to claim Violet, she could allow herself to feel some compassion for him.

"Has Herman Cox had a proper funeral?" Holding Violet, she shifted to watch Abe paddle as she'd done before, fascinated by the strength and swiftness with which he maneuvered the canoe with the help of Tcoosma, the old Indian he'd hired to help them cross the Strait of Georgia to the mainland.

At the front of the canoe, Tcoosma slumped over as he rowed, his wide-brimmed hat sagging low. He wasn't at all as fierce or imposing as Zoe had expected a native to be. Instead, he was short and wore a breechcloth and leggings, a leather shirt with strange stitching, and a wool cloak that looked like it had once belonged to an Englishman. Tcoosma had gathered his silvery-black hair into two thick braids that reached far down his back. Strangest of all, his earlobes were filled with shells, making them sag low.

When they'd met Tcoosma at a secluded stretch of Victoria shoreline, he'd greeted Abe warmly. He hadn't done more than nod at Zoe. And he hadn't given the babe a glance, even when Abe had explained who the child was. Zoe didn't know whether to be irritated that he had so little regard for Violet's life or to be relieved that he hadn't demanded she hand the infant over.

"I haven't heard the latest on Herman." Abe's coat pulled taut at his shoulders with each dip of his paddle. "Only the news of his death that the constable delivered last night."

Zoe pulled her cloak about her more firmly, forming a tent around Violet and against the cold breeze blowing off the gray, choppy water. Even though the trip from Victoria to New Westminster had taken only a few hours, she was still chilled, her toes and fingers frozen. Once they docked in New Westminster, she wanted a chance to go inside out of the cold for a little while and make sure Violet was warm.

On the other hand, didn't she owe it to Violet to find out what had become of her father? "Do we have the time to make inquiries? Perhaps even mark his grave so we know where to take Violet some day?"

Abe's paddle dug low for several strokes before he flipped the dripping beam to the other side, where he continued effortlessly. The cold air had turned his face ruddy, which only made his eyes a brighter blue. As he shifted his attention to her, something warm in his eyes made her feel as though sunshine had parted through the low clouds and fallen upon her.

"That's a fine idea. If Herman hasn't had a proper burial yet, I'll give him one."

She nodded her approval, sensing his in return. Even so, the glaring bruise under his eye reminded her that all she'd done was cause him trouble since the day they'd met. "I'm sorry that we had to rush out of Victoria like that."

He'd led her through back alleys and as far from crowds as possible. She hadn't been sure if he was embarrassed to be seen with her or was simply hoping to avoid Dexter and another black eye.

"Don't be sorry," he replied. "I finished most of my meetings yesterday—at least the ones that mattered. I have the bishop's blueprint for the new church, and now I need to head home and start gathering the supplies."

The previous night he'd told her a little bit about his work in Yale, the church services he currently held in taverns, and his hope to finally have a place for worship that didn't reek of beer. Since hearing his descriptions, she had to admit she was looking forward to seeing Yale and his home. Now that she had a wee babe and a husband, somehow her trip up into the mountains was turning into more than just a need to find Zeke.

"Bet when you planned this trip, you never expected you'd be leaving with a wife and child."

"Not in a million years." Though his words were spoken lightly, something hinted at regret, something that made her pivot and face the town that was growing larger with each stroke. Of course he felt regret. She'd practically tricked him into the marriage—or at least it seemed that way now. And he was too good-hearted, too honorable, and too responsible to do anything other than carry through with his part of the bargain.

The same nagging from earlier told her she should have let him go, that he was too good for her, and that she deserved someone more like Dexter Dawson. If she'd had an ounce of integrity, she would have given Abe his freedom before trapping him even deeper into a marriage that wasn't even supposed to happen.

"You still have the chance to change your mind." She forced the words. "I can stay in New Westminster or even go back to Victoria."

"No, Zoe." His reply was firm. "I cannot leave you behind. The more I've contemplated the matter, the more I've realized how selfish such a decision would be, especially after—well, after spending a night under the same roof."

"I'll tell everyone nothing happened."

He cleared his throat. "People will assume otherwise."

Just as Mrs. Moresby had.

"And I won't chance sullying either of our reputations."

She hadn't thought how this situation would affect his reputation, especially if he spent one night with her and then they parted ways. As a minister, he would probably run into criticism, not only from the bishop, but from many others as well.

Their marriage might cause a scandal, but leaving him had the potential to make things even worse for him.

"Can we agree to move forward with no more talk of splitting ways?" he asked.

"Aye, if you think it's best."

"I do." As if the matter were settled, he resumed his whistling of one hymn or another, which she realized was something he did quite often.

A short while later the canoe scraped the wharf of New Westminster. Abe helped her out and onto the dock. As she swayed, he steadied her, his large hands gently gripping her upper arms. He didn't linger or give her any indication that he desired her, as he had earlier. Rather, he was polite and respectful, treating her more like a sister than a wife.

Surely, she ought to be content with that.

Abe guided her to a nearby hotel, where she tended to Violet while he inquired after Herman Cox. They spent the afternoon making arrangements for Herman's burial. Finally, at dusk, Abe conducted a short funeral at the graveyard at the top of the hill on the outskirts of town. With only the gravedigger and constable joining them, Zoe was all the gladder they'd taken the time to give Herman Cox a final good-bye.

Since the steamers had made their last passages up the Fraser River for the day, the hotel proprietor urged Abe to stay for the night, giving him a room free of charge and providing supper. "For you and your bride," he'd said with a toothy grin as he'd placed steaming bowls of salmon chowder and warm bread in front of them at their table near the fire.

It hadn't taken Zoe long to realize Abe was well liked wherever he went. And it hadn't taken her long to understand why. Abe knew just about everyone. And when he didn't know someone, he remedied that by making introductions. He showed genuine interest in their lives, asking them about their families and work and well-being.

She found she loved watching him interact. His face lit up as he spoke, becoming more animated in conversation. His easy laughter warmed her. And his kindness engulfed not only her, but everyone around them.

Just when he'd hinted at retiring for the night, a distressed middle-aged man burst into the hotel and asked Abe if he would come and pray with his wife, who'd barred herself in a room and was talking about taking her life.

Abe jumped up and was almost out the door before he seemed to remember Zoe. She'd started putting on her cloak as well, intending to go with him, when he turned, his expression grave. "You and Violet head up to the room."

"We'll accompany you."

"It's late and you both need rest." He was out the door and gone before she could say anything more.

After the busy day, Violet fell into a deep sleep, and in turn Zoe slumbered longer than usual, waking before dawn only to realize Abe hadn't returned. As she fed and changed Violet, she worried over him, a hundred different thoughts racing through her mind, mainly that he'd been hurt. She'd almost worked herself up with the need to go looking for him when the door creaked open slowly, and he slipped inside.

At the realization that she was awake with Violet, he shared the details of all that had transpired. Apparently he'd prayed for a while before he'd convinced the suicidal woman to open the door and give the gun to her husband. Then he'd stayed and talked with them afterward for hours and had left hopeful.

Abe finally dropped into bed and slept for a few hours. Zoe did her best to keep Violet quiet and even dozed for a little while in the room's only chair. By the time Abe awoke, they had to rush to board one of the few paddle-wheel steamships in operation at that time of year.

The soot billowing out of the funnels and the low-lying clouds obscured the distant range out the window of the enclosed deck where Zoe had taken refuge, but anticipation surged through her as the steam engines rumbled to life beneath her feet.

By tonight she'd be up in the Fraser River Valley. She'd soon see Zeke. Her heart both thrilled and quavered at the thought. How would her brother react when he realized she was standing in front of him? Would he be able to forgive her for not defending him when he'd most needed it? Or would he want nothing to do with her?

She stuck her hand into her pocket and retrieved his pendant, the one he'd received at ragged school after he'd made his profession of faith. She traced the image of the engraved crucifix, the black lines against bronze.

"You should wear it on a chain." Abe's voice came from beside her. Since boarding, he'd been busy greeting and speaking with the captain, deckhands, and other passengers. She'd hovered near him for a while, but when Violet had protested the cold and wind, she'd retreated inside, where most of the other passengers were already sitting on benches or lined up at the windows.

Abe bent and examined the pendant more closely. "The details are incredible."

"It was my brother's."

He straightened, allowing her a view of his face, of his windswept hair, the color in his cheeks, the brightness of his eyes. After so little sleep, how did he have the energy to reach out and continue giving of himself to every person he met? Even now he regarded her with interest, as if he really cared about the pendant, her brother, and what she had to say.

"Our teacher, Mr. Lightness, not only taught us to read and write and do sums, but he encouraged us, like Mum always did, to make our belief in God personal and real, not just a tradition. When Zeke stood up in class and made a public profession of his desire to follow God, the next day Mr. Lightness gave Zeke the pendant to help remind him of his decision."

"Mr. Lightness sounds like he was a devoted man of God."

"Aye, and Zeke admired him." Their teacher had been a fatherly influence when their own father had struggled to be present and loving.

"But . . ." Abe gently prodded.

"But Zeke gave up his faith when he left home. He threw the pendant on the floor and said he didn't want anything to do with a God who could allow such heartache to happen to our family and to him."

She could still picture Zeke as he'd stood in their apartment, feet spread, shoulders stiff, his handsome face clouded with bitterness toward her and God. His impassioned words filled with such anger echoed in the dark corners of her heart. *"This is all your fault, Zoe. I don't need you or God anymore."*

Next to her Abe was quiet, contemplative, staring out the window at the rocky riverbanks thick with pine, hemlock, fir, and other evergreens. They'd left New Westminster behind, and now the paddle steamer was chugging eastward, upstream against the swiftly moving current.

She'd heard the captain tell Abe they were sailing at five knots at low tide, which would allow them to make good time to Fort Langley, where they would stop for refueling before moving on to Yale. Although the Fraser River continued north up into the mountains for hundreds of miles, the ships couldn't navigate the narrow gorges or shallow depths beyond Yale.

"I don't want to pry," Abe said, "but if you want to tell me more about what happened, I'm a good listener."

She'd already noticed he was a good listener, that he didn't just hear what people told him, but he engaged in the conversation. Even so, how could she share the truth about Zeke? Already she was inferior to Abe in so many ways. He'd think less of her if he learned her part in driving Zeke away.

At a shout and commotion behind them, they spun to find a young woman chasing after a toddler. The woman was wearing a scarlet gown that dipped low in the front and revealed cleavage that was bouncing enticingly. "Get back here, Lil' Man." She bunched her silk skirt as she attempted to maneuver around bags and the legs of other passengers.

The boy was indeed little, his footsteps unsteady, his hands outstretched for balance. From his chubby cheeks to his lurching walk, Zoe guessed he was over a year old, but not by much. Even so, he moved quickly and was headed straight for the door that led to the outer deck.

Zoe reacted without thinking. She leapt into his path so that he had no choice but to smack into her. He released a startled *oomph* before falling backward and landing on his backside.

For a moment he stared up at Zoe. Snotty goo ran in rivulets from his nose and over his top lip. His flushed cheeks were crusted with the discharge, and the scant fine hair on his head was matted. Even so, Zoe would have scooped him up if she hadn't been holding Violet.

"Hi there, Lil' Man." She smiled down at the child, hoping to put him at ease. "Where are you headed in such a hurry?"

As he peered at her, his bottom lip began to quiver. Meanwhile, Zoe had slowed him down enough that the woman in the scarlet dress caught up. She grasped the boy's arm and then dipped low so she was at his eye level, giving every man in the vicinity a peep show of her ample bosom and leaving little to the imagination.

"Lil' Man, you have to stay inside where it's safe and warm." Even as she finished speaking, she remained bent over, glancing around as if making sure she'd gained an audience.

At so wanton a display, mortification spread up Zoe's neck into her cheeks, and she hoped Abe wasn't joining the other fellas in ogling.

He'd stepped with her to the door and had, thankfully, trained his attention on the child. "Looks like Lyle's trying to make an escape. Aren't you, little fellow?"

"Hey there, Pastor Abe." The woman remained in her brazen position, smiling up at Abe and batting her lashes. "Ever since he learned to walk, he's been keeping me real busy."

"I can imagine."

"I see you've got yourself a handsome shiner. Makes you look like a real hero."

"I don't know about that," Abe replied, his focus still on the child.

Zoe wanted to yank the young woman up and in the process pull her bodice up several inches. How dare she flirt with Abe? Didn't she realize Abe was no longer available? That he was married? To her?

"I'm Abe's wife," Zoe said.

"Yes." Abe cleared his throat almost nervously. "Wanda, this is Zoe. Zoe, this is Wanda Washington."

The woman finally straightened, narrowing her eyes at Zoe. Her fair hair was coiled in perfect ringlets that hung down to her shoulders. Her cheeks and lips were red with rouge. Her long dangling earrings glittered with rubies. She was beautiful in a voluptuous way, and from the sensual smile curving her lips, she knew she had power over men.

"Wanda lives in Yale," Abe hurried to explain. "She was widowed last autumn for a second time."

"Why, Pastor Abe," Wanda practically purred as she walked

her fingers up his chest. "I didn't take you for the marrying type or I would have snatched you up for myself." She spoke the words and took in Abe's chiseled chest and thick arms as if she wanted to eat him up right there for her dinner.

Zoe had the urge to shove Wanda away and tell her to keep her hands to herself. Who was she, and why did she think she could touch Abe with such familiarity?

Thankfully, Abe broke the connection by stepping away. "Zoe came on the bride ship."

Wanda wrestled with her little boy, who was squirming and trying to break away. At Abe's news, she stilled and her attention flew to Zoe as though assessing her competition.

Zoe sidled closer to Abe. Surely the woman didn't really think she was competing with Zoe for Abe's affection. Abe had told her he'd honor their wedding vows. There was nothing Wanda could do to change that . . . was there?

"Well, Pastor Abe, you've broken my heart." Wanda lifted a fluttering hand to her chest and sighed deeply so that the mounds of her flesh rose and fell in an exaggerated motion, clearly another attempt to draw Abe's attention. Apparently Wanda wasn't the type of woman to let marriage stop her from getting what she wanted.

But Zoe wasn't the type of woman who would sit back and ignore such blatant overtures. Abe was hers now. And she wouldn't let anyone take him away.

Before she could stop herself, she reached for Abe and wrapped her arms around him as best she could, shifting Violet out of the way and pressing her body fully against his. "Sorry to disappoint you, but Abe doesn't need what you're offering. He's got plenty to keep him happy right here."

For a long instant, no one in the enclosed deck spoke or moved except for Wanda's little boy, who had begun to whine as he struggled to free himself. Everyone stared at Zoe, mouths agape and eyes wide. Even Abe was frozen in place, the shock in his expression almost comical.

The silence was finally broken by the guffaw of a man sitting nearby. "Well, lookee there. She put you in your place, Wanda."

"That's right," said another.

As the remarks rose up around them, Wanda closed her mouth, her pretty brows coming together in a scowl.

Zoe lifted her chin and glared back.

As the little boy threw himself onto the floor in a full-fledged temper tantrum, Wanda had no choice but to attend to him, dragging him away while he kicked and screamed his protest.

When she and the boy were at the opposite end of the deck, Zoe glanced down to find Violet's eyes open wide and watching her innocently. And at the same time, she realized she was plastered to Abe tighter than thread to a loom.

Mortification rushed through her, and she released him.

Slowly he stepped away, letting his hands hang awkwardly for a moment before shoving them deep into his pockets.

She stood unmoving and focused all her attention on Violet, who was still peering up at her with such trusting eyes.

Abe shifted and cleared his throat.

Zoe held herself stiffly. What had she been thinking to do something so brash in public?

"I think Violet is hungry," she said at last. "I'm gonna go sit down and feed her."

"Good idea." Abe's voice squeaked, and he cleared it again. "I think I shall go resume my conversation with the captain."

"Good idea." She forced her legs to walk to the nearest empty bench. As she collapsed onto it, all she could think about was Lizzy, Abe's lost love, and how much he must miss a gentlewoman like her.

fourteen

be trudged up the muddy path, each squelching step pulling at his legs and reminding him of how little sleep he'd gotten in recent nights. The two heavy packs of supplies upon his back as well as the two valises he carried, one over each arm, didn't make the trip any easier.

"Almost there." He held up the lantern, illuminating the sorry excuse for a street that led to his cabin. A glance over his shoulder told him Zoe was still on his heels, Violet bundled securely in her arms.

If the uphill hike through mud in the dark was taxing him, he could only imagine how difficult the trek was for Zoe. Nevertheless, she'd kept up without a single complaint.

When the steamer had docked in Yale, he'd hoped to find a horse he could borrow for the climb up to his cabin. But at the late hour, he hadn't located any readily available. With the cold mountain air settling around them, he'd opted to walk rather than wait any longer.

The town wasn't large anyway. His cabin was only a short distance from the river and was nestled with other homes on the hillside that rose above the bustling business district, which had been bright, lively, and noisy, even at the late hour.

At the height of the gold rush, the town had burgeoned with thousands of residents, mostly men camping in tents and panning gold on Hill's Bar and other bars in the Fraser River. But now that most of the gold had been mined from the region, the prospectors had moved north and east into the Fraser Canyon and Cariboo region.

Even so, Yale was still a busy stopping place, since it was the last steamer way station for those heading up into the canyon. The current population was around five thousand in the winter, when the cold and snow in the mountains forced the miners to halt their quest for riches and find warm lodging.

When he'd first arrived in Yale, he'd learned the town had been nicknamed "the wickedest little settlement in British Columbia" because of all the violence there.

After the past few years of ministering in the area, Abe liked to think he and his fellow missionaries had been able to shine God's light into the darkness. But the work wasn't finished. God still had much for him to do among the mountain community before he returned to England.

Having finally gained permission and funds from Bishop Hills to begin construction on a church in the spring, at least he could bring a tangible sign of God's presence to the town. He understood the bishop's caution in building churches. Too many of the mining communities that had sprung up overnight had subsequently dwindled away to almost nothing as residents and businesses moved farther inland chasing new deposits of gold.

But Yale had withstood the test of time and still had a stable population. Now with so many Royal Engineers constructing the Cariboo Wagon Road that started at Yale and would go up the Fraser Canyon to Lytton and beyond, the need for a church for his growing congregation had become inarguable.

While Abe had never complained about meeting in taverns and hotels, a special meetinghouse would certainly appeal to more people. The only problem was that Abe wanted to keep things simple, much simpler than the architectural plans Bishop Hills had sent along. The conflict over the church design was just one more among a growing list.

Hopefully, the bishop hadn't learned about the altercation with Dexter Dawson, although Abe suspected it was only a matter of time before rumors reached his superior. At least Abe had managed to sneak out of town without the bishop seeing his black eye.

"The town's a pretty place by daylight," Abe said over his shoulder, again gauging Zoe's progress.

"Is it always so muddy?" Her breath came in gasps, the only sign of her struggle to climb the hill.

"I'm sorry to say, the mud is quite a permanent fixture here, especially in the winter months." They passed by one of his neighbors' homes, the light from the window illuminating several nearby barren copper beech trees that had been left standing when the area had been cleared for the cabins. "The mud goes away when we get snow, but the melting makes the sludge worse than before."

"Does it snow often?"

"Off and on all winter, just like the rain." Several more steps up the path brought him to the front door of his cabin. In the lantern light, his home appeared to have been undisturbed during the time he'd been gone. His neighbors were kind enough to keep an eye on his place whenever he traveled, which during the summer months could be quite frequent as his circuit ride led from camp to camp.

While some of the original log cabins around had been torn down and replaced with sawn-lumber structures, Abe hadn't considered making the change, not when he'd only be in the area for two more years and not when he was gone for weeks at a time.

But now, as he lifted the door latch on the log building that had served as his home since he'd arrived in Yale, doubts swarmed him. What would Zoe think? Would it be big enough for her and Violet?

It was a plain seven-by-ten-foot rectangle with hand-hewn floorboards, a wood stove on one end, and a window on the other. When he'd first purchased the place from a miner who was returning to America, a piece of old calico had served as a covering in the window. Since then he'd purchased a glass pane, had the chinking replaced, and fixed the leaky cedar shakes that made up the roof. The place was sturdy but wasn't meant to be a permanent dwelling.

He supposed now that he had a wife and child, he'd do well to take up the bishop's offer to have a rectory built next to the new church. Yes, that's what he'd do. He'd inform the Royal Engineers not only of their new task in constructing the church but of a home to go with it.

Before entering, he kicked his boots against the sturdy doorframe and attempted to dislodge as much mud as possible. Then he stepped inside and hung the lantern from the nail in the wall above the table.

Unfortunately, the cabin was as disheveled as usual. The small table that served as his writing desk was piled with books and papers and inkpots. The bed, which filled up half the room, was unmade, the sheets and coverlet tangled and dirty. At least his clothing was heaped on the chest at the end of the bed instead of strewn about the floor.

Behind him, Zoe was still kicking her boots against the doorjamb just as he'd done. He didn't have time to tidy up, although he made a valiant effort to kick several old newspapers under the table and out of the way.

As she stepped inside, he placed their two valises on the bed and then carefully lowered the supply packs to the floor, trying to avoid her gaze, something he'd been attempting to do since the incident on the steamer when she'd pressed up against him.

Even now the very thought of the incident made his insides flame. At first he'd been too shocked to move. Then after his body had registered her nearness, he hadn't wanted to separate. But he shouldn't have lingered. Should have backed away sooner. Any polite man would have done so.

"I know the place isn't big or fancy," he said, trying to divert his mind for at least the hundredth time.

He heard her shut the door. "I like it. It's cozy."

Cozy. He fumbled with the valises. He couldn't share a bed with her. He just couldn't. Not after feeling her on the steamer. Even if he had good intentions to take some time to get to know her better, he was afraid of what he might accidentally do, that he'd be tempted to reach for her in a moment of weakness.

He'd sleep on the floor. He glanced at the narrow spot, relieved to find that it offered more room than the floor of the cabin in Victoria. Bedding down there would allow him to feed the stove during the night to keep Zoe and Violet warm. It would also give Violet room on the bed with Zoe, since he didn't have anywhere else to put the infant for the time being.

As a puff of his breath showed white in the air, he chastised himself for his insensitivity and crossed to the stove. He opened the door, grabbed the small shovel in the nearby pail, and began to remove the ashes.

Yes, Zoe was his wife. But they were still practically strangers. He'd be wise to do as Pete had instructed, to put an effort into winning Zoe's heart. Their marriage would fare much better if they built it upon a foundation of trust and friendship.

Surely he could do that, couldn't he?

As he worked to light the fire, Zoe settled the sleeping Violet on the bed, then busied herself by unpacking their belongings. She wasn't shy by any means and had no trouble making herself at home. By the time he'd stoked the stove to a blazing heat, she'd organized the cabin and had it more picked up than he ever had the entire time he'd lived there.

He swept up several pieces of bark in front of the stove and returned them to the kindling box, trying to do his part rather belatedly. He could admit housekeeping wasn't his strong suit. In fact, it fell quite low on his daily list of priorities.

"I realize the place is sparsely furnished." He swished the teakettle on the hob only to discover it was empty of water. "In the morning, we'll go to Allard's General Store, and you can pick out anything you want or need."

She took in the few pots and pans hanging from nails in the wall above the stove, the shabby calico he still had hanging in the window for a curtain, and the shelving unit overflowing with more of his books and his odd assortment of plates, cups, and silverware.

"Do you like to read?"

"I do." He crossed to the stack on the chair and began to shelve them since they'd have need of two chairs now. "Reading helps to pass the time on long winter nights when I'm home."

She picked up several tomes from the floor next to the chair, studying their titles before handing them to him. "I suppose they're also useful as a step stool for items that are too high to reach?"

He paused in his attempt to wedge a book into a tight spot. "I can't remember the last time I've needed to use a book as a step stool."

"That's true. You're more than tall enough. Then maybe they're useful in helping you to fall asleep."

"I don't need any help in that area either—"

The humorous twinkling in her eyes and the smile playing upon her lips told him she was teasing.

He wasn't accustomed to bantering but realized he liked the exchange and the way it seemed to ease the awkwardness between them. "Are you insinuating that my books are boring?"

She retrieved another thick volume and read the spine. "*John Calvin's Commentary on Isaiah.* It sounds very exciting. Maybe you can read it aloud to me and Violet."

At her growing smile, he couldn't contain one of his own. He pulled a book from his shelf and held it up. "How about this one? *Lectures on Systematic Theology.* You might like it better."

She laughed lightly. "With so many exciting books, how will I ever choose?"

"I guess I'll have to pick one and surprise you." He had a sudden picture of them sitting in chairs next to each other in front of the stove while he read aloud and she held Violet. The image filled him with warm pleasure and anticipation, something he'd never felt in regard to being in his cabin.

He supposed if he was honest with himself, he'd never truly liked being alone. In the past, he'd always tried to find ways to keep busy in the community, visiting neighbors and parishioners so he wouldn't have to sit by himself with nothing but books to keep him company. Now with Zoe and Violet, maybe he'd want to be home more often.

For a time, they chatted easily about his work in the community and the people who lived in the area. He shared the history of the town, how it had been founded by the Hudson's Bay Company as Fort Yale during the fur-trading years of the colony.

When Violet began to stir, he retrieved a pail of well water and started it boiling for tea. Zoe made quick work of changing the infant's napkin and preparing a bottle. Then he placed a chair for her close to the stove and positioned his nearby, and while Violet ate, he and Zoe sipped tea and talked again.

Once Violet finished, Zoe tickled and kissed the infant with such love that Abe concluded Zoe would make a good mother and should have many more children. The thought was unsettling. Although he'd believed he'd have children of his own one day, he certainly didn't want to have any now while he was in British Columbia. Especially not after Bishop Hills had expressed concerns about marriage and children distracting from his work.

Abe had guaranteed the bishop that his new family wouldn't interfere with his duties, and now he needed to prove that. All the more reason to keep his relationship with Zoe platonic. In fact, with two years left in the colonies, the slower they moved physically, the better.

The baby soon fell asleep, and not long after, Zoe began yawning. While he wanted to go on talking with her and enjoying the camaraderie, he finally stood and made an excuse for leaving the cabin to give her privacy to attend to her personal needs.

He went next door and visited with Little Joe, his neighbor, fielding questions about his marriage and black eye before returning to the cabin. At the sight of the darkened window, he let himself in as soundlessly as possible and was thankful to find Zoe in bed with Violet and that he didn't need to have an embarrassing conversation about their sleeping arrangements.

Using his only extra blanket, he lowered himself to the floor in front of the stove. Though the planks were cold and a draft crept under the door and across the floor, all he could think about was Zoe, the image of her face as she'd teased him about his books, and how much he'd enjoyed her company tonight.

For the first time since he'd gotten the letter from Lizzy, the pain in his heart didn't throb quite so hard.

fifteen

With daylight finally peeking in the cabin's window, Zoe draped the coverlet over Abe and then stepped back to watch him sleep. He'd sprawled out as best he could in the tight confines next to the stove. No doubt he'd wake up cold and stiff. The cabin floor was no place to sleep.

All the same, she had to admit she'd been relieved when he hadn't joined her in the bed last night. After sleeping with him in his cabin in Victoria, she'd been sure he'd climb in beside her, and she'd positioned Violet as a barrier.

As it turned out, the barrier had been as needless as her anxiety. For some reason, he'd decided not to share the comfort and warmth of the bed. Had his first night sleeping beside her been so terrible that he'd rather endure the discomforts of the floor than face her?

By the light of day, his expression was peaceful in slumber, his hair messy, the shadows on his face dark with unshaven stubble, which made him all the more ruggedly handsome. Not for the first time, guilt prodded her to wake him and invite him onto the bed, especially now that she and Violet were awake.

Neither Violet's crying nor baby noises had roused him in the night or even now, which Zoe supposed was a good thing.

She didn't want him growing irritated at Violet like the women at the Marine Barracks and regretting his marriage to her even more than he already did.

With a final hesitant look at his sleeping form, she decided against disturbing him even though she'd already finished dressing and grooming herself. She tiptoed instead to the bookshelf that took up the last of the wall space next to the table. Abe had placed a stack of books on the top shelf, but not before she'd glimpsed a portrait there.

Shifting the pile carefully, she located the gilded oval frame about the size of her hand, large enough to have special meaning and hold someone dear to Abe. She glanced at Abe again before lifting the frame and crossing to the window. She pushed aside the flimsy material and held the picture up into the daylight.

A young woman stared out of the frame. Poised on the edge of a chair, she was stiff and unsmiling. And yet she had an elegance and gentleness to her bearing. Her stylish clothing, the brooch at her neck, the dainty earrings, and the pearl circlet in her hair spoke of wealth and refinement.

Was this Lizzy? The woman Abe loved? The one he'd hoped to marry but who had rejected him?

Zoe felt a prick in her chest. Surely she wasn't envious of this woman, not now that Lizzy was married to someone else and Abe was securely hers.

She studied the daguerreotype. Lizzy was rather plain, not at all the beauty Zoe would have expected for a handsome man like Abe. If Lizzy wasn't pretty, then what about her had attracted Abe? Maybe she had all the qualities that made for a good minister's wife, all the qualities Zoe lacked. She certainly wouldn't have made her husband sleep on the cold floor her first night in their home. Most likely she would have welcomed him into the marriage bed with open arms.

At a rustling and groaning behind her, Zoe let the window

covering fall into place and hastily returned the picture to the bookshelf, sliding the stack of books in front of the frame once more. She guessed Abe hadn't hid the picture from her purposefully. He probably hadn't given a second thought to where he was piling his clutter.

Nevertheless, she didn't want Lizzy's picture sitting out. Did she dare attempt to stow it somewhere where neither of them would stumble across it?

Moaning again, Abe sat up and rubbed the back of his neck. As the cover fell away, she was relieved to discover he was fully dressed, unlike the other morning. In fact, from all appearances, he'd slept in his clothing from yesterday, including his coat.

Her relief was rapidly replaced with guilt. She was selfish. There was no other word to describe her. "This is your home," she blurted, "and if anyone should be sleeping on the floor, it should be me."

He sat up straighter, rolling his shoulders as though working out the aches. "No, Zoe. This is *our* home now—"

"I can't be sleeping on the bed while you're on the floor."

"I want you to have the bed." His voice turned softer with obvious embarrassment. "And Violet should sleep with you, at least until we're able to get a cradle for her."

"It's not fair to you—"

"I have to add fuel to the stove at night. Besides, I'm a sound sleeper." But even as he stretched his legs, he grimaced.

"It's not right for me to come in here and make life more difficult for you."

"Really, Zoe, it's no trouble."

She wanted to tell him there was enough room for both of them in the bed. But she couldn't make herself say the words. Instead, she silently vowed to show him that he hadn't made a mistake in marrying her and prove to him that he could be happy with her after all.

Allard's General Store was crammed full of every item a person could ever need in a dozen lifetimes. Zoe could only wander among the overflowing shelves and stare in wonder. Household items, ready-made clothing and shoes, penny candy, canned food, canvas for tents, lantern oil, and items Zoe couldn't name.

While she browsed with Violet, Abe talked with Mr. Allard, the store owner, a shaggy-looking fellow with long hair and an even longer beard. The conversation was nearly identical to the one Abe had with every other person they'd met on the walk to the store. After sizing Zoe up, each man had slapped Abe on the back, teased him, or offered ribald comments that made Abe's ears turn red. 'Course, they'd also wanted to hear all about his bruised face.

Abe had taken the time to speak with every person and had politely introduced her as "Mrs. Merivale." The walk to the store had taken so long, Zoe wasn't sure they'd ever reach it. At least she'd had plenty of time to take in the town of Yale by daylight. It was nestled against the foothills of the Cascade Mountains to the east and the Coast Mountains to the west. The view of the high rising peaks all around, with snow covering the jagged rocky areas above the tree line, was breathtaking. Winding through the valley, the Fraser River was broad with tree-covered sandbars in the middle. The water rushed a thick brown from all the rain and runoff.

The town itself was nothing fancy. And the streets were soggy with mud, just as they had been last night. Many of the houses and businesses had been built atop risers to avoid the mud. Thankfully, plank sidewalks lined the sides of the streets so that they could escape being splattered by the horses and wagons rumbling past.

She wasn't surprised by the lack of women about town. She

supposed that was why the bride ships had come to the colonies in the first place. As she and Abe passed by a native woman attired in a plain English gown, Zoe had held Violet a little closer, not wanting the woman to notice the babe or question Zoe's right to have her. But she needn't have worried, because the young woman kept her head and gaze down, not making eye contact with anyone.

Upon reaching the general store, Abe had ushered Zoe inside and had told her she could buy whatever she wanted or needed. But what kinds of items did he expect her to pick out? She'd never had a chance to shop in Victoria's stores and had only ever visited the slum shop in her Manchester neighborhood back in England.

Pausing in front of a shelf full of bolts of material in all colors and patterns, she fingered a particularly pretty light blue calico with white polka dots. Could she attempt to make new curtains in place of what was there? She'd learned to sew at school, but only practical things like clothing. Certainly, curtains for her home wouldn't require much more skill.

With mounting anticipation, she trailed her hand over the thread, a pincushion, and a packet of needles. Could she make a new coverlet for the bed? Or maybe use scraps of material to braid a rug?

"I've already asked Mr. Allard to add another blanket to my tab." Abe approached, his large frame dwarfing her in the narrow aisle. "Are you finding what you want?"

"Yes." She yanked her hand away from the material and shifted Violet to a more comfortable position in her arms. "I mean no. I don't know what you want."

"I want you to pick out what *you* want. As you've already seen, my home is woefully inadequate, other than a few essentials."

She didn't want to admit that her family had only ever had

the essentials too, that his home was already better than any she'd had. Clearly he assumed she'd want more. And clearly he wanted more too, perhaps hoped she'd create the kind of home he was accustomed to in England, the kind of home Lizzy would have made for him.

What exactly would that entail?

He reached for the bolt of material she'd been touching. "If you need new clothing, perhaps we can find a tailor—"

"Do you think I need new clothing?" Was he embarrassed by her garments? The few skirts and shirts she owned were plain and well worn, except for the items Mrs. Moresby had provided, which had been donated by Victoria's wealthy women. Maybe a minister's wife needed to wear nicer outfits. "If so, I can make my own. I know how."

"No. No need. I mean yes—you may if you want." He dropped his hands from the material and stuffed them into his pockets. His brow furrowed, and he opened his mouth to speak again, but then closed it.

She waited, suddenly painfully aware of their different backgrounds.

"If you ask me," Mr. Allard said, heading their way and waving at the shelf of sewing supplies, "I'd say Mrs. Merivale needs to have a variety of material for clothing as well as for making all the practicalities womenfolk like in the home—tablecloths, doilies, chair pillows, basket covers, afghans, quilts, and even samplers."

With each item Mr. Allard rattled off, Abe's eyes grew wider. "I had no idea. But you're entirely correct."

Zoe had no idea either. What were doilies and basket covers? And chair pillows? Why would anyone ever need a chair pillow?

Mr. Allard's smile was smooth and practiced. "If you'd like, I can assist Mrs. Merivale as she browses and make sure she gets everything she needs."

"Would you?" The relief on Abe's face made Zoe want to smile.

"Of course. I've been running general stores for most of my life and have a sixth sense about women's needs."

Zoe suspected the store owner had a sixth sense for helping women spend their husbands' hard-earned money. All the same, she couldn't turn down his assistance.

"Thank you, Mr. Allard." Abe took a step back but in his haste bumped a shelf. A pile of ready-made clothing items wobbled. As they toppled, Abe moved with exceptional speed, grabbing the clothing that was falling and propping the rest up with his shoulder.

"Please forgive me for my clumsiness."

"Not to worry, Reverend. Not to worry at all."

For a moment, Abe worked to steady the pile still left on the shelf. Then he held out the remaining pieces he'd kept from hitting the mud-caked floor. "I do apologize for making a mess."

Mr. Allard hesitated and then lifted his hand to cover a fit of sudden coughing.

Only then did Zoe realize Abe was holding a lacy corset along with a silky pair of women's underdrawers. It was her turn to cover her mouth to contain her laughter.

Abe's brows shot up, but as his gaze dropped to the items in his hands, he thrust the undergarments out farther, dangling them from the tips of his fingers as though they might explode at any second. "Lord have mercy."

"I'd be happy to set those aside for Mrs. Merivale," Mr. Allard said, finishing his cough and grinning.

"Well, if she has a need for the unmentionables . . ." Abe's voice squeaked on the last word, and he cleared his throat. "That is, if she'd like them . . ."

"Mrs. Merivale, would you like the pretty corset and drawers your husband has so kindly picked out for you?"

"I didn't pick them out." The tips of Abe's ears were turning red. "They fell, and I just happened upon them."

"Of course, Reverend. Of course." Somehow Mr. Allard managed to wipe the grin from his face and don a serious expression. But he couldn't hide the mirth in his eyes as he addressed Zoe again. "Mrs. Merivale, would you like the pretty corset and drawers that *just happened* to end up in your husband's hands?"

She couldn't keep from teasing Abe further. "He's so considerate. But I have other more urgent needs today."

Mr. Allard took the drawers from Abe and began folding them slowly and meticulously, making Abe dangle the corset a little longer. "Not to worry. The reverend can come back and browse through the undergarments anytime."

Zoe laughed, then cupped a hand over her mouth.

Finally Abe smiled. Just as soon as Mr. Allard relieved him of the corset, he practically ran out of the aisle and retreated to the counter, where he didn't budge the rest of the time they were in the store.

sixteen

oe stirred the bubbling soup, the waft of onions, carrots, cabbage, and beef making her stomach growl. With a rag cloth, she moved the pot to the warmer, scooped a scant amount onto the wooden spoon, then blew on the steaming broth before taking a taste.

As she turned, a face outside pressed against the window, making her jump and yelp at the same moment. Seeing her reaction, the person backed away, but not before she recognized the young boy, one she'd noticed earlier when she'd gone to the well. He'd been hiding in the brush near the privy, as ragged and skinny as a street urchin. He'd stared at Zoe then with as much fascination as now, almost as if he'd never seen a woman before.

"Wait!" She dashed to the door and threw it open. The daylight was fading fast, and darkness was bringing a chill that seemed colder than earlier.

She'd taken the faded piece of calico down from the window after returning from the store earlier in the day. And she'd spent part of the afternoon cutting and hemming new curtains from the material Abe had purchased for her. Though she'd hoped to have them finished by nightfall, she'd run out of time between tending Violet and making dinner. She'd have to put the old fabric up in the window again for another night, especially since they'd had a steady parade of visitors throughout the day who thought nothing of privacy or coming inside without knocking.

Abe hadn't seemed to mind. In fact, after they'd returned from the store, he'd left the door wide open, as if to let people know he was home and available. When the cold had become too much, Zoe said so, and Abe had apologetically closed the door and kept it that way the rest of the afternoon. That apparently hadn't stopped the entire town from swinging by to see the reverend, his black eye, and his new wife.

When Abe had left to visit several of his homebound parishioners, more fellas poked their heads inside. But without Abe around to talk to, none of them had lingered.

"Stop!" she called after the boy as he scampered away.

He glanced at her over his shoulder but darted faster, like one of the hares she'd seen on their trudge back up the hill after shopping.

She stepped onto the muddy stoop, debating whether to chase after him but knowing she couldn't leave Violet alone. She did the only thing she knew to do—offer him food. "Would you like some soup?"

His steps halted.

"And biscuits." She added to the temptation. "With butter."

Slowly, he turned to face her. His hair hung unkempt over a freckled face, and curious brown eyes regarded her through the strands. He wore trousers he'd long outgrown that showed the bare skin of his calves and the dilapidated condition of his boots.

Though he was thin, almost scrawny, she guessed his age to be ten, maybe twelve. He carried himself with a sense of wary experience that told her he'd been making his own way for a while now. She'd seen many boys like him back in Manchester, orphans who'd been forced too young to survive on the streets.

"Come on with you." She beckoned him with the wooden spoon. "You can warm yourself and fill your belly."

"Can't pay you none." He remained frozen in place, clearly wanting to take her offer, but ready to bolt all the same.

"The only payment I require is that you lick the bowl clean. Can you do that?"

"Aye. That I can."

"Good." She turned back into the house, leaving the door open, hoping he'd soon trail after her. As she approached the stove and removed the lid, she heard his slight footsteps at the stoop. She reached for one of the tin bowls she'd found among Abe's odd assortment of cooking ware and began to ladle soup into it.

When his footsteps moved inside the cabin, she nodded toward the table. "Go ahead. Have a seat."

In addition to starting on the curtains, she'd spent time organizing and cleaning so that the place was beginning to look and feel like home. The table and chairs were finally cleared and Abe's books now neatly shelved—except for the stack that she'd left in front of Lizzy's picture.

"What's your name?" she asked as she heard the chair scrape against the floor.

"Will."

"I'm Zoe."

"And your baby?"

She glanced at Violet napping in the middle of the bed, surrounded on all sides by pillows and blankets to keep her from rolling off. "Her name's Violet."

"That's sure pretty."

"It is, isn't it?" As she placed the soup and biscuit in front of Will, she waited for him to ask more questions about Violet as most of the others had. Thankfully, Abe's answer about Herman Cox's death seemed to satisfy everyone. But she still couldn't shake the feeling that someone was bound to tell her she had no right to the babe and to hand her over.

Will stuffed the biscuit into his mouth. As fast as he chewed and swallowed, he couldn't have had time to taste it. "You're sure pretty too," he said with his mouth still half-full.

"Thank you—"

"Never expected Pastor Abe to get himself a wife. Never figured him for the type."

"What type?"

"The marryin' type."

"And why is that?"

"Cuz he don't watch the Hurdy Gurdy girls like the other men."

Hurdy Gurdy girls? Zoe could only imagine what that was.

"And he never stares at Wanda the way everyone else does. Never even seen him look at her."

"Well, that's good to know."

"But I can see why he took a fancy to you, since you're such a good cook and all."

Zoe smothered a smile. "Aye, I'm sure it's my cooking."

Will slurped through his bowl of soup, telling Zoe everything she wanted to know—and then some—about Wanda Washington. Apparently the woman had come from San Francisco to Yale several years ago, working in the saloons as a madam. Since she was so pretty and popular, she'd earned numerous offers of marriage and had held out until the richest man in town had proposed. He'd died only a few months later in a steamboat accident, leaving her a fortune. Eventually, she'd married another rich man, Mr. Washington, who'd lived a mite longer, long enough for her to have a baby boy. Then he'd been shot and killed in a saloon brawl, leaving Wanda Washington even richer than before. Apparently she was a multimillionaire with more money than some of the richest gold miners.

"Wanda's got the biggest house in town," Will said, finally slowing down with his second helping of soup and biscuit. "I ain't never been inside, but heard it's got dozens of rooms."

"And now she's looking for a new husband?"

"Acourse she's lookin'. Wanda's always lookin'."

Zoe frowned, but before she could pry further, Violet woke up crying. Will hopped up onto the bed and entertained Violet by playing peekaboo while Zoe got her bottle ready. Then he watched as she fed the infant, seeming in no hurry to leave, telling Zoe all about himself—how he'd been born in California, how his pa had brought him along when he'd come to Yale to mine gold, how his pa had gotten sick and died two winters ago, and how he'd been living above the livery ever since and working in the stables for Mr. Barton.

From how independent Will was, she suspected he'd done more taking care of his pa than the other way around. In some ways the boy reminded her of Zeke, of how her brother had to grow up so quickly after their father had resorted to drinking and lost his mill job after being late too many times. Zeke had borne the weight of supporting their family, even after Zoe had taken over their mum's position in the cardroom.

If only Zeke hadn't had to bear such a heavy weight. Maybe then he wouldn't have gotten involved in the wrong crowd and in so much trouble. . . .

When Abe ducked inside as Violet finished her meal, Will offered to hold the babe so Zoe could serve Abe dinner. She settled the two on the bed and dished up a bowl of soup and a biscuit for Abe. She was surprised when he insisted that she sit down and eat with him, waiting to start until she'd taken the chair across from him. Even then he offered up a short prayer before digging into his meal with gusto.

She refilled Abe's soup three times, cleaning out the pot. His compliments over the meal warmed her every bit as much as the flow of conversation and the kindness he extended toward Will. Abe never once questioned the boy's presence in the house, accepting him there as if he belonged.

Abe pushed his empty bowl away and sat back in his chair, crossing his arms behind his head and stretching his long legs under the table so that they almost bumped hers. "I can't remember the last time I've had so fine a meal. Thank you, Zoe."

She reclined in her chair, satisfaction filling her more than the food. With darkness having fallen, the cabin glowed with lantern light and the stove's warmth.

"Sure is a good thing you got married, Pastor Abe," Will remarked from where he sat cross-legged with Violet snuggled on his lap.

"I cannot argue with you, Will." Abe settled his gaze upon Zoe and smiled with such contentment her breath snagged.

This. This was what it was like to have a family and a home. She had only a few memories of her own family together this way, when they'd been much younger, before Mum had delivered a stillborn babe and Father had turned to drinking to drown his sorrows.

She'd never imagined she'd have this all so soon after arriving at the colonies. It was everything she'd ever dreamed of having and more.

"I'm glad you chose Zoe and not Wanda," Will continued. "Zoe's sure a lot prettier. And nicer."

"I agree." Abe's gaze shifted to her cheek, to her ear, and then to her hair. His expression was as open and readable as always—filled with stark appreciation.

Even so, a prick of envy plagued Zoe as it had on the steamship. "Wanda's a fine-looking woman too. I'm sure any man would be happy to have her."

Abe's attention dropped to the table, and he rearranged himself in his chair.

More prickles lifted the fine hair on Zoe's neck. Maybe Abe wasn't as immune to Wanda's charms as Will claimed. What if he'd had a relationship with her in the past? Maybe he'd visited her when she'd been a madam?

She wanted to press him further, but at a knock at the door, Abe shot out of his chair. After opening the door and speaking with a man for several moments in low tones, Abe returned inside, grabbed his coat from where he'd tossed it over the end of the bed, and began to shrug into it.

"There was an accident today up in the canyon," he said gravely. "Several Royal Engineers were hurt in a collapse inside a tunnel they're blasting, and they think one of the injured might not last the night."

"What can I do?" Zoe paused in her cleanup of their dinner. She wanted to be of help to Abe in his ministry but felt suddenly ignorant of her duties. What did a minister's wife do in such situations? Surely she did something?

"There's nothing you can do right now." Abe stuffed his Bible and *Book of Common Prayer* into a sack, along with a few clothing items. She picked up his hat from the bed, and when he'd finished packing his bag, she handed it to him. "I don't know when I'll be back—maybe tomorrow or the day after. If you need anything, though, don't hesitate to ask Mr. Allard."

"I can help Zoe too." Will settled Violet on the bed amid the pillows and blankets.

"Thank you, Will." Abe situated his hat on his head. "I'd appreciate it if you'd swing by once in a while to check on Zoe and Violet."

"That'll be no trouble at all."

After Abe was gone and Will had left, Zoe hugged her arms to her chest and shivered against a chill that had crept into the cabin with the coming of night. The wind rattled the window-pane and the cedar roof shakes and whined down the stovepipe. With Violet asleep, the small cabin suddenly felt too dark and lonely.

Even though she hadn't been in Abe's home for very long, one thing was becoming clear—she may have married Abe, but he was in some ways already married to his work and the people he served. He loved them deeply and was committed to them—perhaps even above her.

That was to be expected, wasn't it? She certainly couldn't ask him to care more about her than his work, not when he hadn't asked for or wanted their marriage. And she certainly couldn't get upset at him for going away so soon after arriving in Yale.

Maybe she'd had a glimpse of what having a home and a family again could be like. But that's all it was—a glimpse. Not a reality. She had to remember she was only and always just a bride of convenience.

seventeen

At the sight of Wanda Washington exiting the general store with her little boy, Lyle, in tow, Zoe paused at the intersection of Main Street and the path that led up to the cabin. Clinging to a man's arm, Wanda was laughing about something, her pretty painted lips alluring and the tilt of her head inviting. Wearing an opulent green gown and low-cut bodice, she had no trouble attracting the attention of the man at her side, and that of every man she passed by.

For just an instant, Zoe wondered what it would be like to attract Abe's attention that way. Maybe if she were alluring, Abe would want to stay at home more. Since the night of the Royal Engineer accident up in the canyon two weeks ago, he'd been gone most of the time, showing up at odd times and only staying for a short while. She was beginning to wonder if they were even married.

But just as quickly as the thoughts came, she tossed them aside.

Abe was busy doing God's work, and she couldn't interfere with that. Hadn't she learned her lesson from when she'd interfered with Zeke and his work? Look at the trouble she'd caused

166

him. She'd do well to remember to stay out of Abe's business and attend to her own responsibilities, including getting Violet home for a feeding.

Violet released another disgruntled cry. Having fashioned a sling for the baby, Zoe peeked beneath the linen and repositioned Violet's thumb to help tide her over until they were back at the cabin and had a bottle.

"I'm sorry, wee one. We're almost home."

A glance overhead showed cloudy skies that were beginning to darken with the onset of night. She'd stayed too long in Shantytown that afternoon, and now Violet was protesting. When one of the Hurdy Gurdy girls had come to the cabin several days ago asking for the reverend to come and pray over one of her friends who was ill and near to dying, Zoe had gone in his stead.

As she'd entered the street lined with dilapidated shacks along the riverfront, the poverty and filth had taken her straight back to Manchester, reminding her of everything she'd left behind and how much her life had changed in a few short months. The biggest difference was that most of the residents of Shantytown were Chinese and natives and mostly women and children.

That first time she'd visited Shantytown, Zoe had prayed with the young woman, Mila. The second day and every day thereafter, she'd taken soup and biscuits along, to nourish not only Mila but also the three other women who lived in the tiny, cold shack. When Zoe had left a short while ago, Mila had been sitting up with color back in her thin face. Zoe could only pray the woman was through the worst of her illness, but she'd seen enough sickness and death in her life to know nothing was ever certain.

At another grunt from Violet, Zoe picked up her pace, trudging up the hill, the empty cedar-bark basket making her trek home easier. It also helped that a drop in temperature had frozen the ground so that she wasn't having to slog through mud anymore. Even so, her back and legs ached from the climb.

She tried to distract herself by praying for Zeke, that he'd return to the Lord, a prayer she'd uttered every day since he'd run away. She couldn't bear the thought that he'd rejected everything good and true he'd learned since childhood. The possibility that he'd die without making peace with Christ always made her prayers more desperate.

While she was anxious to travel to Williamsville and find out for herself if Jeremiah Hart was indeed Zeke, Abe had indicated that the roads and trails leading to the mountain town wouldn't be passable until late spring. The recent accidents on the road only confirmed the danger and that she'd have to wait to find out more about Zeke for a few more months—if she could force herself to wait that long.

"Mrs. Merivale," someone called, interrupting her heavenward pleas.

She raised her head to find that their middle-aged neighbor, Little Joe, was rushing out his cabin door toward her. "Let me help you with your basket."

"You needn't trouble yourself," she said with a smile. "The basket's empty."

The slip of a man with his wire glasses and dusty apron approached her anyway and lifted the basket from her arm.

A carpenter turned miner, Little Joe spent the winter months creating custom-ordered furniture in his tiny cabin, the pounding, sawing, and chiseling sounding at all hours of the day and night. Not that Zoe minded the noise. In fact, with Abe gone, the woodworking noises were a comforting reminder she wasn't alone.

As one of the rare women in town, she found that most men went out of their way to assist her, and Little Joe was especially helpful and talkative. Already in the short time she'd been in

Yale, she'd learned about the family he'd left behind in Dorches-
ter and that he was hoping to save enough to send for them.
He'd told her she reminded him of one of his daughters, who
was grown and married with a babe on the way.

She'd started knitting him mittens as a way to thank him
for his friendship.

"Don't know how you manage with the baby and the basket
the way you do," Little Joe said, falling into stride next to her.

"Violet hardly weighs more than a button." She used her free
arm to jiggle the babe, who was once again fussing.

"She seems to be filling out right nice enough."

"Aye. The goat's milk and pap are helping. . . ." At the sight
of the open door of the cabin ahead, her heart lurched. Was
Abe home?

Whenever Will visited, he closed the door behind him, conscious of allowing the cold air into the cabin. But Abe . . . well,
he was as heedless of the door as he was of being tidy.

At the distinct whistling of a hymn coming from inside,
Zoe picked up her pace. Abe was home, and her body suddenly thrummed with the need to see him. For just a moment,
she wondered at that need and then quickly rationalized that
he was a friend, like Jane. They shared easy conversation and
companionship, and being with him always made her ache for
Jane seem a little less painful.

A dozen paces away from the cabin, Little Joe handed her
back her basket. With a glance to the open door, he frowned.
"If I were Pastor Abe, I wouldn't be neglecting my new bride
so often."

She squeezed Little Joe's arm. "I can't complain. He's giving
me a very good home and everything I need."

It was the truth. She couldn't—wouldn't—complain. Especially after walking again through Shantytown and seeing the
kind of life she'd escaped.

As she approached the door, her steps lightened with the anticipation of seeing Abe, of sharing a smile, and of looking into his dazzling blue eyes. Maybe she'd throw caution aside and even hug him.

Her blood pumped faster at the thought. Did she dare do something so bold? Of course she would.

With a widening smile, she stepped inside only to stop short at the sight of not only Abe, but the kind-faced young reverend who'd married them, John Roberts. Abe was at the stove with his back to the door, and John Roberts was sitting at the table.

At the sight of her, John scooted back and stood.

She couldn't keep her smile from fading. Disappointment rose swiftly, although she wasn't sure why. She shouldn't expect Abe to be anxiously waiting to see her or longing to spend time with her after so many days apart. And maybe she shouldn't be so excited either.

"Good afternoon, Mrs. Merivale," John said.

At the mention of her name, Abe swiveled, a wooden spoon in hand. His whistling came to a halt, and he grinned. "There you are. I was about to serve John some of this delicious-smelling soup, but now that you're here, I'm sure you'd like to do the honors."

She paused for just a moment, wishing for a comment—even a tiny one—about how much he'd missed her and was glad to see her again. But as soon as the thought came, she stuffed it away. She couldn't allow herself to wish for what wasn't meant to be. Instead, she needed to remember just how blessed she was to be here and be his wife.

"'Course I'd like to do the honors." She forced a smile. "You go on and sit down, and I'll serve you both."

Abe's face registered relief as he crossed to the table. "I told you Zoe would be happy to have your company tonight, John. Right, Zoe?"

"Aye, indeed. Very happy."

John nodded his thanks, but at his raised brow, Zoe guessed she hadn't convinced him of her happiness.

Abe stood outside the cemetery gate and shook hands with the last of the Royal Engineers who'd attended the funeral service. Since the accident up in the canyon two weeks ago, he'd been ministering to those who'd been injured. One had died the first night. And now, another had finally succumbed to his injuries.

While the tragedy had been heartbreaking, Abe had seen God at work through it all, moving the men to seek after Him.

"Good sermon, Abraham." John Roberts reached out to shake his hand. His friend and fellow cleric had arrived yesterday on a steamship, having traveled upriver from Hope, where he oversaw a small parish. Though Abe had just returned home himself, he'd invited John to stay for the dinner Zoe had prepared. They'd talked well into the evening before John had insisted on taking his leave, saying he didn't want to impose any longer.

"Thank you for being here, John." Abe squeezed his friend's hand. "I appreciate the help officiating."

John glanced toward a sheltered boulder where Zoe huddled in her heavy cloak holding Violet. Will stood beside her talking animatedly, apparently having managed to sneak out of the livery and away from his duties there. He was wearing a snug winter hat Zoe had knitted for him, along with new mittens and thick socks. The moment Abe had returned to town, Will had made a point of finding him and showing him the gifts. He'd talked of nothing else but Zoe and Violet.

"It's been good to catch up," John replied, still watching Zoe interact with Will.

Her nose and cheeks were red from the cold, and guilt pricked Abe. Maybe he'd lingered too long with the fellows after the funeral. "I better walk Zoe home."

With January turning into February, winter had finally decided to visit, bringing arctic temperatures that had frozen the mud and the ground. A light layer of snow coated everything, hiding the gray and making the mountain town beautiful—at least until the next thaw.

"You're coming back to the cabin, aren't you, John?" he asked. "I'm sure Zoe will have plenty of whatever she's got cooking."

John stuck a finger into his clerical collar and attempted to loosen it. "Abraham, I know I'm hardly one to offer marital advice, since I'm still single, but I'd be remiss if I didn't caution you to take more care with your marriage."

"Take more care?" Abe watched Zoe tilt her head back and laugh at something Will said, likely teasing him the way she oft did. As far as he knew, everything in his marriage was going superbly, better than he'd ever expected. And he found that after being gone for days, he relished coming home like he never had before. He loved the warmth and womanly touch she'd brought to the cabin, the delicious meals she always had ready, and the companionship and conversations they shared.

"Yes," John said hesitantly. "As I said, I'm certainly no expert. . . ."

"Everything is great, John. Zoe's turning out to be a fine wife—"

"Of course you think she's fine," John rushed to speak, his face turning red. "She's taking very good care of you and your home."

Abe sensed the *but* without John having to say it. "She seems happy, doesn't she?" He'd assumed she'd been content with their arrangement. At least, she never complained about anything.

Now with a wife and child to take care of, he was thankful more than ever for his savings as well as his grandfather's inheritance. His parents had also been generous in supporting his missionary endeavors. Of course he still needed to write and inform them of his new marriage, and hopefully they would continue to support him, although he was sure they'd have plenty of questions about whom he'd married and why. In light of Lizzy's betrayal, surely they'd understand his choice to move on.

"She loves Violet. That's clear."

"But you don't think she likes me?" The cold nipped at Abe's ears, and a glance at the eastern mountains and the dark clouds obscuring the white peaks told him they would likely get another covering of snow before the day was over.

"From what I've witnessed, she seems more like a house-keeper than a wife."

Housekeeper? Abe hadn't set out to treat her like his house-keeper. But she had been doing a great deal, including laundering and ironing his clothing. "Should I hire a maid? Maybe one of the native women can come and help her."

"Perhaps. Or perhaps you ought to seek God and ask Him what kind of husband He would have you be."

The kind of husband God would have him be? Abe wanted to be a godly husband, had hoped he was doing everything right. But he'd also been trying to keep his ministry a priority and hadn't wanted to let his marriage interfere with his duties. What if, in his quest, he wasn't heeding God's instructions for husbands? What if he needed to give Zoe more attention?

"As I said, I'm no expert," John hurriedly added, "but I would be remiss not to share my concern with you."

"Thank you, John. I'll consider everything you've said." He waved at the snow-covered path leading away from the cemetery. "Shall we go warm ourselves and have supper?"

"Maybe Zoe would like to have you to herself this eve, especially since you just returned from a trip."

"We have visitors all the time. She never minds." At least, she'd never said anything. In fact, she'd taken to inviting Will to dinner almost every night. If she'd wanted more privacy, why would she have asked him for permission to feed and care for the boy? He'd been pleased with her desire to reach out to the child and had gladly given his blessing on her endeavor. He'd even approved of her sharing of her baked goods and her knitted items among their neighbors. He liked that she was thoughtful and generous.

"You're probably right. Please, disregard I said anything." John cupped his hands and blew into them.

"Then you'll come for dinner?"

"Very well."

eighteen

Crying woke Abe. He blinked and sat up to find daylight creeping into the cabin. His back and arms were stiff after the night upon his bed of blankets on the floor, and his feet and toes ached with the cold.

Another wail—Violet's crying—echoed in the cabin. And was followed by the sound of gagging and heaving.

Was Violet vomiting?

Abe tossed off his covers, the chill of the cabin hitting him. Though he slept in his clothing for additional warmth and to avoid awkwardness around Zoe, the morning air was especially cold.

He climbed to his feet and glanced to the chair where Zoe usually held and fed Violet in the morning. It was empty.

At more heaving and more crying, he pivoted to find Zoe on her knees on the bed, retching into the washbasin.

Concern ripped through him. "Zoe?" He crossed the short distance to the bed. She held her long hair back with her hand as the spasm racked her body.

"What ails you?" He hovered near the edge, unsure what he ought to do but knowing he needed to assist somehow.

Rising slightly, she lifted the bowl and moved to place it on the floor. Her hands trembled and her body shook. "My head," she rasped.

He took the basin and set it aside. "What's wrong with your head?"

She released her hold on her hair, and the waves spilled all around her. "I get headaches from time to time. It's nothing to worry about."

But even as she tried to console Violet, she gripped her head and moaned.

"What can I do to help you?" His worry was mounting with each passing moment.

"Would you get Violet's bottle ready?" she asked before collapsing.

While he'd only assembled the bottle once, the day Herman had left Violet with them, he'd watched Zoe do it oft enough now that he had no trouble putting it together. All the while he worked, Violet's cries swelled in intensity, and Zoe only groaned, holding her head and rocking back and forth.

He fetched the milk from the icebox, heated some in a pan, and then poured it into the glass container. When the bottle was ready, he held it out. "All set."

"Thank you," she whispered, taking the bottle with shaking hands. Her pupils were big, her face was pale, and her lips were pressed together with determination. Even as she tried to focus on Violet, she closed her eyes, her face taut with pain.

Although he'd never held Violet before, he'd watched Zoe and could surely feed Violet this morning, couldn't he? Doing so would give Zoe a chance to rest and recover from whatever was ailing her.

Hesitantly, he reached for the baby. Her face was scrunched with her wailing. What if she didn't like him? What if he made her cry more?

Lifting a silent prayer, he gingerly picked up the child and settled her in the crook of his arm just the way Zoe did. As Violet caught sight of his face, her crying tapered off. Her eyes widened, meeting his as if to question who he was and what business he had holding her.

He didn't quite know what to say to her. So again, he tried to imitate Zoe. "Hi there, little one." He spoke in his softest voice. "You're hungry, aren't you?"

Violet only stared.

Carefully, so that he didn't bump or bother the baby, he took the bottle out of Zoe's hand. She didn't resist, had already buried her head into the mattress and was moaning again. As soon as he was done feeding Violet, he'd fetch the doctor.

He lowered himself into Zoe's chair and then offered Violet the bottle. The baby quickly and eagerly began to feed. All the while she ate, her eyes never left his face. And he could only watch her with as much fascination as she did him. When she drained the last drop of milk and stopped sucking, she lifted one of her tiny hands up toward his face.

"Did you get enough?" he asked just as softly as before.

She gave a few last sucks and reached for him again.

Tentatively, he took hold of Violet's hand. The moment he did so, she curled her fingers around his thumb and made a gurgling happy noise. At least he hoped it was a happy noise and that she wasn't choking. Just in case, he propped her up higher into the crook of his arm.

She made another sound, this one almost like babbling, as if she were talking to him.

He glanced at Zoe as he'd been doing throughout the feeding. She'd stopped moaning, was curled up, and seemed to be sleeping. Even so, his worry hadn't abated, and he knew he wouldn't rest easy until the doctor came and examined her.

"I need to go, little one." He rose slowly from the chair, hoping he wouldn't jostle Violet. "I won't be gone long."

If only Will would stop by, then he could send the boy after the doctor so he wouldn't have to leave Zoe and Violet.

Abe paced to the window and tugged aside the new curtains Zoe had hung. Fresh snow blanketed the ground and trees and stumps. The thick layer on the neighbor's roof looked to be at least a foot high, if not more. Last evening, the snow had just started when John had left for his hotel room. Apparently it had snowed most of the night.

He'd need his snowshoes today. But the trek down the hill into town and back up would take longer than he wanted, especially if Zoe was asleep and unable to watch Violet. He couldn't leave either one of them.

With Zoe resting now, perhaps he ought not to have the doctor disturb her anyway. Surely Will would make his way up to the cabin soon enough. Violet cooed up at him as though agreeing.

"Very well, little one," he whispered. "I guess we're stuck here for now."

He crossed to the bed, pulled the covers over Zoe, and then stood and watched her sleep, the pain still tightening her features. Even so, she was utterly alluring and beautiful. Something stirred within him, something he couldn't explain, except that John's admonition from yesterday came back to him: *"Perhaps you ought to seek God and ask Him what kind of husband He would have you be."*

Abe thought he was being a good husband by purchasing everything she needed. He'd assumed she enjoyed the time together when he was home. And he'd believed she was content with the way of things between them.

Even if she was content, he needed to do more, just as John had urged. After all, in Ephesians God instructed husbands to love their wives the same way Christ loved the church. That kind of sacrificial love certainly moved beyond the realm of treating one's wife as a housekeeper.

If only he had some inkling of what to do as well as the courage to do it.

———✦———

Zoe stretched, waking slowly, praying the throbbing in her head was gone.

The first thing she felt was the cool cloth that stretched across her eyes to her temples. The second thing was the gentleness of fingers intertwined in her hair. The fingers were unmoving, but she recognized the tender pressure as Abe's.

She shifted to find that his arm was resting on the bed near her head, which meant he'd pulled up a chair as close to the bed as he could get.

Her heart fluttered, and at the same moment, the pounding in her head resumed—albeit not as strongly or as painfully as before.

How long had she been abed this time? Vaguely she remembered Abe taking the basin after the pain caused her to throw up. She also remembered he'd taken Violet's bottle. Did that mean he'd fed the babe?

Had a doctor come and examined her, or had she only imagined it? She vaguely recollected another male speaking in low tones with Abe as well as Will's voice ringing with worry. Was the boy still here? She needed to reassure him she would come through the ordeal just fine. She always did.

She pried open her eyes and at the same time lifted the cloth away. She winced against the daylight in the cabin, even though it was dim and gray.

"Will?" she whispered, her voice groggy.

A little foot jabbed into Zoe's ribs, and she rubbed a hand gently over Violet, who was snuggled against her, bundled loosely in a baby blanket. In the same moment, she took in Abe reclining, his head back, his eyes closed in slumber.

Zoe rolled to her side so that she had a better view of the two. Violet was sleeping contentedly, which meant somehow Abe had figured out how to feed her. *Bless him.* What would she have done without his help?

His expression was peaceful, his fair hair falling across his forehead, the unruly waves in need of taming. A scruffy layer of stubble covered his jaw and chin, shadowing his face. Even so, his features were well defined, etched in hardness, and yet somehow always tender. From the top of his messy head to his muscular shoulders and arms to his long lean legs stretched out in front of him, he was a handsome man. If he realized how appealing he was, he'd never allowed it to puff him up.

She studied his mouth. Even his lips were practically perfect. And 'course, his smile was always heart-stopping.

"How are you feeling?" he whispered.

She jerked her attention away from his mouth only to find that his eyes were wide open and that he was watching her watching him. "I'm better."

His expression relaxed, and his eyes softened with what could only be described as relief.

"Thank you for feeding Violet."

He smiled affectionately at the babe, which only made him all the more endearing. "She's a sweet baby."

"Aye."

The blue of his eyes was cloudless and pure and radiated warmth—a warmth that made a trail down her chest to her abdomen.

"I hope I did everything right," he whispered.

"I'm sure you did. Otherwise she'd be letting us know about it."

His smile widened. "I had no idea how to change her napkin. But Will coached me through the process."

"You changed her?"

"It was either that or endure an unbearable stench."

Zoe couldn't contain her smile, even if the motion made the thudding in her temples louder. "You're a saint."

"Not really. I did it for self-preservation."

She laughed but then regretted it, gripping her head.

Immediately his fingers were against her forehead, pushing her hand away and gently rubbing her throbbing veins. The coolness of his hands and the firm pressure eased the ache. "The doctor told me this might help."

She relaxed against her pillow, unable to protest, although a part of her warned that she should. "You needn't have called a doctor."

"I was worried."

She stilled at the censure in his voice. "I should have told you of my ailment sooner. I'm sorry I didn't."

"What if this would have happened while I was away?" He paused in his gentle massaging, his brows knitting.

"I make it through the worst. I always have."

"You needed help, Zoe. And so did Violet."

She wanted to think she could have managed. After all, she'd endured the headaches for many years. Sometimes they were short-lived, and she could function through them. Other times, she could do nothing but wait for the throbbing to go away.

"The doctor said laudanum could help relieve your pain." Abe resumed the pressure against her forehead.

"No. After what laudanum did to my sister, Meg, I'd rather suffer and die than take it."

Abe brushed a hand over her forehead and into her hair, something akin to what her mum had done when she'd been a wee girl. "What happened to Meg?"

Zoe pictured her wayward sister and wondered how she was faring, praying she was better but guessing things were the same as they had been for years. "After Mum got sick, Meg started to use Mum's laudanum. She liked it so much that she had to get the money for it one way or another." Zoe was too embarrassed to admit what Meg had become as a result of her need for the drug.

If he knew what she was referencing, he was too polite to say so. "The doctor mentioned one other treatment for your headache that might be beneficial." Abe combed her hair again, the motion soothing, more so than even his massage of her temples.

Zoe closed her eyes and relished Abe's tender touch. "I'm sure he can't recommend anything I haven't already tried."

"I doubt you've tried this." Abe's tone was mysterious.

She opened one eye. "What?"

"When Will comes, he'll watch Violet and I'll take you."

"Take me where?" She tried to sit up, only for Abe to gently push her back down.

"You'll have to wait and see."

She glanced at the window and tried to gauge the time. From the fading light, she guessed the afternoon was waning. "Have I been abed all day?"

He nodded.

"Then I've kept you from your work—"

"There's nothing urgent that needs my attention today."

"Are you sure? I can fend for myself now if you need to leave."

"I'm not leaving, Zoe," he said firmly. "Not until Will gets here, and then we're leaving together."

nineteen

At each bump of the sled, the hammer in Zoe's head pounded louder.

"It's not far now," Abe said from ahead. Outlined by the setting sun, he was a giant in his thick coat, hat, and snowshoes. With the reins wrapped over his shoulder and around his arm, he seemed to tug the sled effortlessly through the powdery snow. But the labored puffs of white he expelled told her the trek was difficult.

He'd cushioned her with blankets so that she was as comfortable as possible. Though the path was mostly smooth, the movement still hurt her head. Even so, she marveled at the view. The entrance of the Fraser River Canyon was spectacular with the river cutting through the mountains, forming high cliffs on both sides framed by evergreens, which had all looked the same to her until Abe showed her how to differentiate between lodgepole pine, white spruce, and Douglas fir. With the fresh coating of snow, the green was vibrant, especially with the reflection of the sun's last rays.

The trail wound above the river so that she could hear the rushing water below even when the thick forest obscured the view. With the stillness of the snow covering boulders and branches and only the swish of the sled and the soft thump of Abe's footsteps, she could almost believe the rest of civilization had disappeared.

"Here we are," Abe said as they came through a stand of white spruce to a rocky area of steeply cut cliffs. He dropped the reins and pushed aside more thick spruce growth to reveal the mouth of a cave.

She tossed aside the blankets and began to rise. Abe was at her side in an instant, assisting her to her feet. A wave of dizziness threw her off balance, but Abe took her arm and steadied her. "Hang in there." He led her to the dark opening. "It's just a short walk from here."

She held back. "We're going into the cave?"

"You've nothing to fear." He'd slung the blankets and his bag over his shoulder and held a lantern ahead of them.

"What about all the bears, coyotes, and wolves?" Over the past two weeks of her getting to know Will, the young boy had shared every gruesome story he'd ever heard about the predators that lived in the mountains.

"There aren't any here."

"How can you be sure?"

"This is a busy place, and the wild animals stay away."

"It doesn't look busy to me." In fact, it appeared deserted.

"That's because with all the new snow, everyone is hibernating away today." He ducked into the cave, his light illuminating a barren rock tunnel.

Still she hesitated.

He stretched out a hand, beckoning her. "Come on. I promise you'll love it." His eyes, his expression, everything about him was trustworthy.

She placed her mittened hand into his. Through the layers, his fingers folded around hers, strong and secure, and she allowed him to lead her deeper into the tunnel, the lantern revealing bumpy reddish rock all around. The cold air gave way to warm humidity until steam wafted ahead, obscuring the way.

"Where are we?" she asked as the warmth bathed her face.

"You'll see." A hint of excitement laced his voice.

A moment later, the tunnel opened into a wide cave with a steaming pool at the center. Water dripped from the roof and trickled from the walls into the dark glassy surface.

Abe released her hand and placed the blankets and his bag onto a dry ledge that held what appeared to be discarded or forgotten items of clothing and towels. He took off his mittens and hat, placing them on the ledge, nodding at her to do the same.

With the warmth of the cave, she needed no further prodding to divest not only her mittens, but her coat. As she took off the items, she stared at the strange pool, the rock formations above it, and a tunnel filled with water that branched off the opposite side.

"This is a hot spring," he said, answering her unasked question. "The mineral water is always seeping down into the pool with fresh hot water."

"How is that possible?"

"No one knows for sure. But apparently the natives who came up into the canyon to fish for salmon and pick huckleberries found the pool. They guided the first prospectors here. And we've been using it ever since."

She bent and swirled her hand in the water. The warmth was delicious and sent a tremor of longing through her. "Can I dip my toes in?" The request was bold, but she didn't care. She wanted to soak her feet in the pool.

"You can do more than dip your toes. You can sit in it."

She glanced down at her skirt. She would be cold on the ride home if she got her clothing wet. But perhaps the discomfort would be worth it.

"Doctor's orders." He cast aside his boots and began to tug off his socks. "He said the mineral waters can soothe all manner of aches and pains, might even be able to ease the ache in your head."

She followed his example and started taking off her boots. "Have you been in before?"

"A time or two." He shed his waistcoat, letting it fall to the cave floor with his socks. "But not oft enough."

She placed her boots neatly together on the shelf before attempting to roll her first stocking down without lifting her hem and exposing her legs. Abe was always asleep in the morning when she arose and dressed, and he stepped out every evening to allow her the privacy of donning her nightdress. She appreciated his courtesy and knew she couldn't be a prude now about showing her feet and ankles.

As she placed the first stocking into the boot for safekeeping, she flustered at the sight of him peeling off his shirt. She hadn't seen him shirtless since the first morning after their wedding. She turned away and busied herself with rolling off her next stocking. But her curiosity got the better of her, and she peeked sideways to find that he'd dropped his suspenders and was in the process of kicking his trousers off.

Her face flamed at the sight of his long bare legs and broad chest. He was practically naked, except for his drawers.

She averted her eyes and then froze. Did he expect her to take off her outer garments before getting into the hot spring? "I think I'll keep on my skirt and shirt."

"You can't." Splashing sounded behind her, the sign he was getting in.

"Sure I can."

"You can't ride home with wet clothes," he stated matter-of-factly. "It's too cold today, and you'll freeze even with the blankets covering you."

She waited to turn, hopefully giving him enough time to submerge.

"Don't worry, Zoe. If someone else decides to come, we'll hear them entering, and I'll be sure to have them wait until you're properly attired."

She wasn't worried about others so much as she was him. But she couldn't tell that to Abe.

"I packed an extra set of unmentionables for both of us to change into when we're done." His voice contained a hint of embarrassment at his admission.

At the splashing of more water, she guessed he'd lowered himself. If Abe was willing to bare himself, then why shouldn't she? After all, once she was in the pool, the water would cover her from view.

Tugging off her second stocking, she forced away her reservations. She wanted to get in and feel the warm water too much to let her anxiety over her state of undress hold her back. After all, Abe was her husband, and there was nothing indecent about stripping down to her undergarments in front of him. Certainly he could have asked her for more by now if he'd had any desire for her.

She'd come to the conclusion that he had no plans to take advantage of his marital rights. At first she'd been relieved. But another part of her was confused by his distance. Maybe he didn't find her desirable enough. Or was he still in love with Lizzy? Perhaps thoughts of the gentlewoman filled his dreams.

Whatever the case, he'd been chaste, even brotherly in all his interactions with her. And she had nothing to worry about now.

Straightening her shoulders with fresh resolve, she spun and faced him. He was reclining in the pool but wasn't completely covered. In fact, most of his chest was above water and drew her attention, every sculpted muscle and every hard contour.

Flustered again, she motioned at him. "Turn around."

His brows lifted.

"You must face the other way until I get in."

His eyes widened, and he scrambled to follow her instructions as if he'd only just thought about her need to undress. Once she was certain he was facing away and wouldn't turn around, she shed her skirt and blouse so that she stood in only her drawers and chemise.

The warm steam rising off the water touched her bare skin, beckoning her. She dipped her foot in, swished it, and smiled at the delight of the warmth. 'Course she'd washed in the tubs in public bathhouses. But she'd never had hot water.

"Are you in?" He still stared at the opposite cave wall.

"Almost."

She lowered herself to the edge and submerged both feet. The water went up to her knees and the lacy edge of her drawers. The warmth was so glorious that she pushed off and sank down into the pool, nearly moaning her pleasure.

"Ready?" Abe asked again.

She lowered herself even farther so the water covered her chemise and reached her shoulders. "Aye. I'm in."

He whirled around. At the sight of her along with her smile, he grinned. "It's heavenly, isn't it?"

"More than heavenly."

"And how is the aching in your head?"

"Almost gone already."

"Then it's a good thing you obeyed the doctor's orders."

"Aye, and it's a good thing I have a man strong enough to carry me out here."

"I've never thought of myself as particularly strong. But I guess my size is good for something after all."

"I suppose it is," she teased. She wanted to drop her gaze again to his broad shoulders and bare chest, but she didn't want him to think she was curious or interested in him as a man. Because she wasn't.

One little peek wouldn't hurt, would it? Her gaze darted, taking in the wide span from shoulder to shoulder. As she lifted her eyes, she realized he'd caught her looking. As if in response, his sights dropped to her chest. Thankfully it was underwater. But as she glanced down to make sure, she realized the water was translucent and that he could see her chemise well enough.

Strange warmth and embarrassment coursed through her. Before she could stop herself, she skimmed her hand along the surface and sent a spray his way.

He blinked through the droplets running down his face, surprise widening his eyes.

She was surprised at herself for splashing him, couldn't believe she'd done something so childish. She waited for a rebuke or at the very least a frown of displeasure. The last thing she expected was for him to grin and send a splash right back.

twenty

$\mathcal{A}$be was going mad. Bringing Zoe to the hot spring had seemed like such a good idea. He'd thought he was doing something nice, attempting to be kind and sacrificial like Christ. But now that they were in the pool, he knew he'd made a big mistake. The merest sight of her in her chemise and drawers was much too enticing.

Of course, he was trying his hardest not to let his gaze stray to her body, which was mostly shielded by the water. But he couldn't stop himself, especially every time her attention drifted to his chest.

Her curiosity only added fuel to his already overheated insides and burned through the wall of reserve he'd tried to build. Especially now that she was thoroughly soaked after their water fight.

He'd hoped the splashing would distract him and cool him off. But now with water dribbling from her hair, off her nose, and down her lips, she was even more beautiful than before, and he could think of little else but the fact that they were alone.

"Are you giving up?" she asked as she threatened to send another wave at him.

"I must." He wiped away the water that cascaded from his face. "I'm not nearly as fast and admit my defeat."

"Very well. Then as the winner, I should get a prize, shouldn't I?" She stretched back into the water, floating so that he caught a glimpse of her legs—exquisitely lovely legs, pale and slender with delicate feet.

With great difficulty, he tried to focus on what she was saying. "A prize? Of course. You may ask for anything you wish."

She sat up, her upper body surfacing. "Anything? Are you sure?"

"Anything."

She pushed away from the ledge and floated, growing more daring, clearly enjoying herself in the water. And clearly having no inkling of the effect she was having on him. "Then I make you responsible for changing Violet's napkin the next time she's smelly."

He glimpsed her feet again and her bare arms. Her skin was pale and smooth, and all he wanted to do was touch her. It was sweet torture to realize she might be his wife, and yet she wasn't his in heart and soul—the things that really mattered.

"Do you agree to my reward?" She reached the area diagonal from him and dipped back down, submerging her body.

He wrenched his attention back to his hands and began swishing water back and forth in front of him.

"Do you?" she persisted.

"Do I what?"

"Agree to changing Violet's napkin?"

"What?" His gaze was drawn back to her, irresistibly. She was smiling, the dimples in her cheeks making an appearance as they did whenever she jested.

"You weren't listening to me, were you?"

"I admit to being distracted. I'm not accustomed to soaking in the hot spring with a beautiful woman."

Her smile turned more impish. "Flattery won't work."

"It won't?" He still had no idea what she was talking about.

"Flattery only works if it's true."

"It is true. You're beautiful. More than anyone else." His voice came out more earnest than he'd intended.

She paused in the middle of kicking her feet to examine his face.

Embarrassment rushed through him, and he wanted to sink down into the water and hide himself. Why was he speaking to her so freely? Was he so enamored that he was losing all self-control?

It wasn't right that he should focus on her appearance and the wanting that came with it. Dwelling on those kinds of thoughts only led to lust. He knew that well enough from the lust he'd experienced with Wanda.

He swam to the opposite side of the pool, putting a safe distance between them, and attempted to shift the conversation. For a while, he told her of the legends that came with the hot spring, the stories of healing, and even the tales of people supposedly coming back from the dead. They talked about how such a natural wonder had formed and speculated over why God had created it, and he was amazed as he always was by how easy she was to talk to about such matters.

She released a contented sigh. "As much as I'd love to stay here all night, I promised Will we wouldn't be gone long."

The boy had eagerly agreed to watch Violet during the outing. But even though he was responsible enough at twelve years of age and had been practically living on his own the past couple of years, he didn't need to shoulder the care of the baby longer than necessary.

Using the last of his reserves of self-control, Abe kept himself turned around while Zoe got out, dried off, and changed back into her clothing. When she was done, she gave him the same courtesy, attempting to towel dry her hair while he dressed, although her efforts distracted and slowed him down so that she finally glanced at him over her shoulder.

"Aren't you finished yet?"

He'd already yanked up the dry pair of underdrawers and was in the process of tugging up his trousers. He jerked at the corduroy, but it stuck to his still-damp legs. "You're peeking."

"Just checking to see if you need my help."

The very notion of having her assistance sent a sizzle of anticipation skittering over his wet skin.

She smiled at him too innocently. "Especially since sometimes you get your trousers and shirts mixed up."

He looked down to double-check his attire and was relieved he wasn't making a fool of himself. "It appears I'm doing fine this time."

She twisted around and faced the cave wall again. "Just make sure to put your socks on before your shoes."

At the humor in her voice, he chuckled. "I can't help it. Your beauty distracts me." As soon as the words were out, he was tempted to pound his head with his hand. Why had he taken to gushing over her appearance? Again.

"Oh, I see. So your inability to dress yourself is my fault?"

Was she teasing him? He hoped so. "I could never blame you for anything."

"Not even for our marriage?" she asked lightly, but something in her tone told him she meant the question.

He finished tugging up his trousers and then reached for his shirt. Yes, even though he'd never anticipated that he'd return from Victoria with a wife and child, he didn't blame Zoe. If anything, he blamed himself. "I take full responsibility. I reacted to the letter from Lizzy telling me she'd gotten married. I suppose I wanted to prove to myself that it didn't matter."

"But it did. And it still does." She'd turned again and was watching him with solemn eyes.

He paused, one arm in his shirt. "I'm trying to forgive her. But I admit, it's not easy."

"What was she like?"

He wasn't sure he wanted to talk about Lizzy. Even if his wounds were healing, the rejection stung and made him feel inadequate, as if somehow he hadn't been enough, maybe still wasn't enough. And yet, Zoe deserved to know the truth about his past, didn't she?

As he finished dressing, he told her about his loneliness growing up, how his siblings had been so much older, how his parents had spared him little time, how Lizzy's father had been the rector and lived nearby. Her family had welcomed him into their midst, and Lizzy had become his closest friend. Her father and his sincere faith had influenced Abe's decision to become a rector himself.

"What about you?" Abe said as they left the cave and headed down the path. "Surely you had a sweetheart back home."

Darkness had settled and shrouded the woods, faintly lit by the lantern he used to guide their way. The beams of light touched Zoe bundled in the blankets on the sled but didn't reveal her expression.

"Jeremiah wanted to marry me," she admitted.

"Jeremiah?" Just hearing the name turned his insides. "What kind of fellow was he?"

"He was a good man, a hard worker, and he loved me."

Abe winced at the revelation that another man had loved Zoe. He shouldn't be surprised by the news. In fact, he wouldn't be surprised if a dozen men had loved her. Nevertheless, he didn't like the idea of her being with someone else, specifically a good man like Jeremiah. "Did you love him too?"

"I never gave him a chance."

Did her voice hold regret? "Do you wish you'd stayed to marry him?"

"No. I needed to leave. Needed to get away from Meg before she dragged me into her ways. And needed to get away from my father."

"Then you didn't get along with him?"

She was silent, and the swish of the sled in the snow along with the crunch of his footsteps echoed in the quiet of the night.

"I think he partly blamed me for Mum's death."

"How so?"

"One time he told me if I'd taken her place in the mill earlier, she wouldn't have gotten mill fever."

Abe had heard of the illness that afflicted mill workers. Some blamed the poor ventilation in the factories. Others believed the disease came about because of the long work hours. Many claimed it was just another form of consumption and could be cured with proper rest.

"Your father was wrong to put that burden on you."

"Aye. After Mum's death, he lost every ounce of kindness, and his drinking took a turn for the worse. And once he no longer had Zeke around to punish, he decided to take out his anger on me and Meg."

Abe stumbled to a halt in the snow and pivoted to give Zoe his full attention, his heart suddenly pounding hard. "Did he hurt you?"

"Not often. But I got tired of his bullying."

"So you decided to leave?"

"With my wee niece gone, I had no more reason to stay."

He nodded, finally beginning to understand the heartache lurking within her as well as her desire to protect Violet from Herman's neglect.

"I'm glad you came." He resumed his pulling, which was easier on the way back since they were moving gradually downhill.

"You don't have to say that. I know Violet and me are a burden you didn't ask for."

"I mean it. I'm glad you got away from your father." He was more than glad. In fact, he was surprised by the depth of his relief. "And maybe I didn't ask for all this, but I think we're getting along, don't you?"

"Aye. You're a good and kind man, Abe. I doubt there's anyone who wouldn't be able to get along with you."

When they reached the cabin, she stumbled in her effort to stand, the blankets tangling her legs. With a new courage he hadn't known he possessed, he scooped her up and carried her to the door. When she didn't protest his hold, he gathered more courage.

Her warm breath hovered near his neck, making him all too aware of her closeness and the softness of her body. His mind returned to the hot spring, to the picture of her dripping wet. And his pulse reacted by sputtering forward at double speed.

As he reached the door, he hesitated.

"Thank you for taking me to the hot spring," she whispered.

He was suddenly sharply aware of her mouth near his cheek, only inches away. All he had to do was turn his head just a little and he could kiss her.

Did he want to kiss her? He'd tried not to think about sharing such intimacies with her. Doing so only undermined his self-control. But at the moment, with her lips so near, he could think of little else but bending in and tasting her. Just one tiny taste. Surely it wouldn't hurt him. Or them.

Before he could make up his mind, she stretched up and pressed a gentle kiss against his cheek. Her lips were every bit as warm and soft as he'd imagined, but the briefness of the kiss was amiable and sweet, certainly not at all passionate or inviting of more.

Not that he wanted her to invite more—did he?

He hesitated a moment longer and was spared from answering his own question by Will's throwing the door open wide and greeting them with Violet cooing happily in his arms.

twenty-one

*V*iolet's giggles filled the air and Zoe's heart as she bounced
the infant on her lap.

With his feet propped on a crate near the stove, Abe paused
in reading aloud from *Pilgrim's Progress*, one of his few novels.
He turned his attention to the babe.

"She's happy you're home tonight," Zoe announced.

"Is that right?"

"Aye." Zoe held on to Violet's hands curled within hers. The
little girl had begun to gain strength and weight, rolling over,
pushing up on her arms, as well as sitting up with some support
from Zoe. The babe babbled as if in agreement.

"I should be home more oft this week ahead," Abe said, his
tone apologetic.

Zoe didn't respond. Instead, she clapped Violet's hands together, earning another giggle from the infant. In the month
Zoe had lived in Yale, she could count on two hands the number
of evenings Abe had been home. Between his travels to nearby
mining towns and his busyness when he was home, she'd learned
he took his calling as a minister very seriously.

She admired him for his dedication to his work and his love

for the people he served. She couldn't fault him. But she had to admit, she wished for more time with him, especially since their evening at the hot spring a week ago. The time together had been fun. He'd been sweet and attentive. And she craved more. More time like that. More of him.

With a rare evening home without any visitors, save Will, who was sprawled out on the bed listening to the story, Zoe didn't want to say anything that would ruin the mood or their time together, so she bit back her complaint.

"Don't you worry, Pastor Abe." Will curled his arms behind his head and settled in more comfortably. "I'm taking real good care of Zoe and Violet whenever you're gone."

"I know you are." Abe reached over and ruffled the boy's hair, which he'd finally allowed Zoe to cut. "I appreciate it."

Zoe appreciated Will's company too. He'd taken to sleeping in front of the stove whenever Abe was gone, keeping the wood burning, drawing water from the well, and even fetching more goat's milk from a nearby farm for Violet when the supply ran low.

"You know you can stay here anytime you want to," Zoe added. "And not just when Abe's away."

Will shrugged. "If'n I do, then Abe won't have no place to sleep."

The boy hadn't questioned her and Abe's sleeping arrangements, not even now that Violet was sleeping most of the night through in her own baby bed, which Little Joe had crafted and delivered earlier in the week. With the space available, she'd expected Will to ask why Abe didn't move up next to her.

As much as she tried to remind herself of her resolve to keep their marriage one of convenience, a part of her heart betrayed her with the desire for more. The longer she was with Abe and the better she got to know him, the more she liked him. There were so many things to like. And every time he was around, she discovered additional qualities to admire.

For instance, earlier in the evening when he returned from his trip downriver to the town of Hope, he'd not only greeted her with a welcoming smile, but he'd gone over to Violet, picked her up, and held her while Zoe finished preparing supper. She hadn't needed to ask for his assistance. He'd interacted with the babe as if he'd missed her during his absence.

She supposed some good had come out of her headache in that Abe had learned he was capable of holding and taking care of Violet and that he had nothing to fear from the infant. 'Course Zoe didn't expect him to tend to Violet, since she'd been the one to insist on keeping the babe. But she liked seeing a man being tender with children, the way her teacher Mr. Lightness had always been with his own children when they'd visited him.

"Yes." Abe settled back into his chair and repositioned the glasses he wore whenever he read. "You're always welcome to stay here, Will."

"There ain't enough room on the floor for two," Will said. "And no offense, Pastor Abe. But I can see why Zoe's making you sleep down there. You're too big and would kick her to pieces."

"I'm not *making* him sleep on the floor," Zoe blurted, but then immediately wished she could take back the words.

"You're not?" Will's question echoed with surprise.

"'Course not." She fumbled to find another excuse for why Abe bedded down on the floor at night. "He likes sleeping there."

"Oh." Will paused as if contemplating this new revelation. "Don't think it would be comfortable for a man like Pastor Abe. But acourse, I'm just a boy. What do I know?"

"Actually, it's not so comfortable," Abe remarked. "And I'm not particularly fond of it."

Will sat up. "Guess you're wrong, Zoe. Pastor Abe said he don't like sleeping on the floor after all."

"Aye, Will. I have two good ears. I heard him for myself."

The boy grinned with excitement. "If'n you're not making Pastor Abe sleep on the floor, and if'n he don't like sleeping there, then I guess he can jump on in the bed with you from now on and that'll leave me a spot."

Zoe opened her mouth to protest but realized anything she said would be entirely selfish. If Abe didn't like sleeping on the floor, then he deserved to enjoy the comfort of the bed, didn't he? And if Will wanted to move in with them rather than live in the lonely loft at the livery, how could she deny him the opportunity? Even if Mr. Barton was nice enough to give Will work and a place to sleep, the boy would benefit from a real home.

"That settles it," she said. "You can gather up your things and move in here."

"Really?" He perched on his knees and glanced at Abe. "I promise I won't be no trouble."

Belatedly Zoe realized she hadn't asked Abe before issuing the invitation. Thankfully, he was already nodding at the boy. "That's fine with me, Will. Maybe we can make you a mattress of sorts that you can put out at night."

"I have leftover material from the tablecloth," Zoe said. "I think I can come up with a pallet."

Will's grin spread, but before they could discuss the matter any further, a pounding on the door interrupted them. Abe answered the call and spoke to the visitor for only a minute before he turned back inside and began to don his coat, his expression grave.

"What's wrong?" Zoe stood and settled Violet on her hip. Over the past month, she'd gotten to know Abe's neighbors and others in the town. They'd been friendly to her, accepting her as the minister's wife and offering her the same respect that they showed him—even though she wasn't a gentlewoman.

"There's a fire over in Shantytown. I'm going to help keep it from spreading."

"I'll come."

Abe shook his head. "It's too dangerous."

"I'll stay away from the fire." She handed Violet to Will, who took the babe without question.

"No, Zoe." Abe thrust his foot into a boot. "It's dangerous in other ways besides the fire. I don't want you to go anywhere near that area."

"I've visited before and never had any problems."

He paused, the second boot halfway on. His brows came together in a rare scowl.

She jutted her chin. "It's not half as bad as where I lived in Manchester."

He watched her as if contemplating her revelation. Then he resumed wiggling his foot into his boot. "Thank the Lord you're safe now. And I plan to keep you that way—"

"I want to help." She didn't care that her tone was stubborn. He was always leaving her behind while he went off to take care of hurting people. Why shouldn't she go along? Why couldn't she help too? She was perfectly capable. In fact, she'd been waiting for God to show her the next thing He wanted her to do. Surely taking care of Violet wasn't all He had planned.

"Zoe . . ." Abe pleaded, his tone and eyes soft and asking her to accept his decision without arguing.

"I'll stay out of the way," she pleaded in return just as softly. "I just want to be there if any of the women and children need help."

His frown weakened, until finally he nodded. "Very well, but only if you promise to stay well away from the trouble."

"I promise."

Flames leapt into the night sky above several burning shanties. A line of people wound down to the river, and buckets of water passed between them in a race to douse the fire before it spread to surrounding structures.

Zoe approached a petite native woman who stood with a young boy on the fringes. Without cloaks or coats, they huddled together. From the sag of the woman's shoulders, Zoe guessed the fire was destroying everything she owned.

"Here." Zoe thrust a blanket into the woman's arms. "You can wrap up with this to keep warm."

The woman hesitated but then took the blanket, murmuring her thanks in stilted English.

Zoe glanced to where the Hurdy Gurdy girls stood on the fringes. They wore made-up faces and fancy gowns. Thankfully none of them had been in their shack when the fire had started, had instead been performing onstage when they'd gotten word of the disaster destroying their home. Zoe had already spoken with each of the women, including Mila.

A hunched man with a cane stood in the open doorway of a nearby pub. Behind him the warmth and brightness of the dining room seemed the only refuge on the cold night. Zoe guessed he was the proprietor of the business. From the gravity and concern lining his face, she could sense he was frustrated he couldn't lend a hand to the water brigade.

Perhaps he'd be able to help in another way. As ideas quickly formulated in Zoe's mind, she crossed the street toward him.

"I'm Mrs. Merivale, Pastor Abe's wife. I'm here to assist you with distributing cool drinks to those attempting to fight the fire."

She was relieved when the older man, who introduced himself as Mr. Hemming, set about to do everything she asked of him, eager to be of service rather than standing back and watching helplessly. He assembled pails of both water and ale and put together an assortment of rolls, cheese, and dried salmon. Zoe enlisted the help of the Hurdy Gurdy girls in distributing the drink and food among those battling the fire while she moved among the growing number of people who'd lost homes in the blaze.

Mr. Hemming offered more blankets for Zoe to give to anyone who needed warmth. And when she began to usher the injured into the dining room, he allowed them to push aside tables to make room for the physician to treat people.

Zoe made the rounds tending the needs of those who'd gathered in the dining room. Only when she caught sight of Abe out of the corner of her eye did she finally pause and realize that the flames had been completely extinguished.

As she wiped a sleeve across her perspiring forehead, her sights locked in on him, her heart pounding harder as she scanned him from his head to his feet. Other than the soot on his cheeks and forehead and a few singes in his coat, he was unscathed.

He was searching, almost frantically, around the room until his gaze landed on her. Ignoring those around him and the clamor for his attention, he crossed directly to her, scrutinizing her as if somehow he'd expected that she might be hurt. "You're unharmed?"

"Aye. I stayed away like you told me to."

"Good." His features relaxed only a little. "It's getting late. I'll walk you home and then come back."

"I'll stay too. Mr. Hemming still needs my assistance."

"Are you sure?" His brow furrowed as he surveyed her again. "I don't want you overtaxing yourself."

She laid a hand on his arm, wanting to reassure him. "I like being here and being useful, Abe. Please let me stay."

He nodded, then squeezed her arm in return before turning to answer a question from someone who'd approached him. As Abe began to mingle, Zoe's heart swelled with satisfaction.

Even though she was hot and tired, this serving with Abe had been energizing and fulfilling in a way she couldn't explain. As she looked around at all the people in the dining room, she realized this was where she wanted to be. With him, ministering alongside him.

If only he would realize that's where she ought to be too.

twenty-two

The northern lights put on a show for them as they walked back to the cabin. Brilliant stripes of green, yellow, and purple blazed across the sky against the backdrop of a million stars.

Even with so beautiful a display, Abe's attention kept returning to Zoe. Though she'd stayed far away from the flames, somehow she'd still managed to get soot on her cheek, and he was growing more tempted with each passing moment to wipe it off simply so he'd have an excuse to touch her.

He'd lost track of her during his efforts to extinguish the fire. Afterward when he hadn't been able to find her outside where he'd instructed her to wait, he'd started to panic . . . until one of the men had said he'd seen her inside Hemming's Pub helping with the relief efforts.

After he found her and assured himself that she was just fine, his admiration had expanded until his chest had swelled with it. She'd done more than help. She'd taken charge and made sure everyone was well taken care of during the ordeal. Several times when he'd noticed she was yawning, he'd mentioned leaving. But she'd insisted on staying until he was ready to go.

"It's incredible." She tilted her head back as she took in the expanse of sky overhead. "What causes northern lights?"

Abe tried to corral his runaway thoughts of Zoe and focus on her question. "I'm not entirely sure." He'd seen the magical display on several occasions since living in British Columbia, usually on clear, cold nights like this when he happened to be out much later than usual. "I've heard theories that the lights have to do with gas particles combining with magnetic fields."

"That doesn't sound very exciting."

"Scientific explanations usually aren't. The folklore is always more interesting. For example, the natives believe the lights are spirit guides holding torches in the sky to direct the departed to the next world."

"Maybe the lights belong to angels guiding people to heaven."

"I honestly don't know, so instead of trying to figure it all out, I just enjoy the beauty."

"I like your plan." She paused in the climb up the hill toward the cabin. With the display illuminating their way, he hadn't bothered to turn on the lantern, which made the heavenly lights even brighter. "Maybe we can check on Violet and Will, and if they're asleep, we could stay out for a little longer to enjoy the beauty."

At her suggestion, pleasure rolled through him, although he didn't quite know why. Was it because the sightseeing was exactly the kind of thing he would have done if she hadn't been along? Or was he pleased because he could prolong this brief time alone together?

Abe poked his head into the cabin to find Will and Violet slumbering soundly. He led Zoe a short distance farther up the hill to a clearing where the sky spread out endlessly. He brushed the snow from a log—the remnant from a cabin that had once stood on the spot—and they sat down to watch the spectacular whirling colors.

As they took in the view, they talked quietly about the fire, the people who'd lost homes, and what could be done for them.

"Zeke got blamed for starting a fire that burned down part of the mill where he worked."

Zoe's statement about her brother seemed to come out of nowhere, and she stared at the northern lights, her eyes sad.

He didn't say anything but instead waited patiently for her to continue when she was ready.

Finally, she heaved a sigh. "The fire killed several power-loom weavers who'd been kept on when everyone else had been let go."

"But Zeke didn't start the fire?"

She shook her head. "He'd had an argument with one of the supervisors earlier that day when he came in pleading to have his job back. Others had heard Zeke making threats, so when the news of the fire and deaths spread, everyone assumed Zeke was the one to blame."

"Surely they investigated before accusing him?"

"That's not the way of things where I come from. But fortunately, one of his friends warned him that the constables were coming for him, and he left town before they could arrest him."

"That's when he left his faith behind and sailed to British Columbia?"

"Aye." Her voice dropped. "And it's all my fault."

"How could it be your fault?"

She was silent for so long he'd almost decided she wouldn't say anything more, until she spoke softly. "The day of the fire, I begged him to go to the factory and ask for his job back. He didn't want to, and we argued about it. But I was afraid for him. Ever since he'd lost his job, he'd started getting in with the wrong crowd—union fellas who took to violent methods to solve problems. When I heard the mill might be hiring back weavers, I begged him to go, told him God wanted him to work honestly rather than side with violence and anger."

"Sounds like you did the right thing."

"But if not for my badgering him, he wouldn't have been there that day of the fire, and he wouldn't have gotten blamed."

"You couldn't have known that."

She stuck her hand into her pocket, and he suspected she was holding on to Zeke's pendant, the only part of him she had left. "After another identical fire at the mill a few months later, the culprits were caught. And it turns out Zeke's union companions were responsible for both incidents. They let him take the blame, but finally under pressure they admitted to the crimes."

"So you've come to tell Zeke he's been acquitted?"

"Aye, and to beg his forgiveness for my part in everything that happened. Only I'm afraid I might not be able to find him. And then if I do, what if he doesn't want to see me?"

Abe sensed the guilt she'd carried with her since Zeke's leaving. He offered a silent prayer for wisdom and then said, "Once the mountain roads are safe for traveling, we'll see if we can find Zeke. And then once we do, we'll go talk to him together."

"Really?" She lifted her beautiful eyes to him, so full of hope.

"Really."

She smiled. "What about you? Now that I've confided my deepest, darkest secrets, you must share yours."

His deepest, darkest secrets? A part of him resisted saying anything. But the other part of him knew it was only fair that he share the same way Zoe had. He sensed she'd be a good listener and offer him compassion.

Swallowing his pride, he began to share with her about his parish in Sheffield, the rising tensions between the laborers and their bosses, and the violence that had left people dead and disillusioned. He explained how his own frustrations and guilt for not being able to make changes had led him to come to the colonies, and how he hoped one day to become a bishop in order to advocate for the people better.

"Then you hope to one day return to England?" Her voice was laced with surprise.

"Yes." He hadn't thought about how that would affect her. "You don't mind, do you?"

She hesitated. "I don't know. I guess I thought this would be my new home."

He was silent for a long minute. Although he hadn't planned to stay in the colonies indefinitely, perhaps he could consider extending his five-year commitment. Regardless, if he hoped to become a bishop, he would need to return to England and start the process of applying for the position.

She shivered and hugged herself.

He'd kept her out long enough, and now they needed to head home for warmth. "Would you mind if I prayed before we go? I'd like to lift up your situation with Zeke before our heavenly Father."

"I don't mind."

He nodded and then bowed his head. Although he prayed with people everywhere he went, he suddenly felt shy about doing so with Zoe. Yes, he'd prayed with her after Jane had died. And he prayed before their shared mealtimes.

But out here, alone, with God's glory surrounding them, the moment was different, somehow more intimate. And yet, it was important. He'd always anticipated that he'd lead his wife in prayer, that together on their knees they'd face their challenges and grow stronger as a result.

He peeked at her sideways to gauge her reaction. But she'd already bowed her head and closed her eyes and was waiting for him without a trace of shyness or awkwardness. Taking a deep breath to quell his own discomfort, he began his prayer.

When he finished, he rose and offered her a hand up. As she took hold, she smiled so that her dimples made their appearance. The sight was nearly as breathtaking as the colorful lights in the sky. He circled his fingers around hers and didn't want to let go of the connection. Instead, he longed to hold on to the moment and to her for a few more minutes.

Thankfully, once she was standing, she didn't make an effort to pull away. Rather, she seemed content as they walked along to keep her hand within his—at least he hoped she was. "A hot spring. Northern lights. What other surprises await me here in British Columbia?"

"The beauty of the wilderness never ceases to amaze me."

"You'll have to introduce me to more. Perhaps another surprise?"

"What kind of surprise would you like next?"

"Surprise me with your surprise." Her answer was playful.

He was learning that when she was teasing him, she didn't expect a serious answer. Nevertheless, he wanted to reply with a witty response and said the only thing that came to mind. "I'll do my best."

She bumped her shoulder against his arm. "I like it when you're home."

"I like it too." The past few days while he'd been in Hope, he'd kept busy with making arrangements for all the supplies his new church would need when they started construction next month, particularly figuring out the number and sizes of windows— regular and stained glass. He'd also spent some time helping John Roberts install a new and bigger stove in his rectory.

All the while he'd been gone, thoughts of Zoe and Violet had been at the forefront of his mind. By the end of the second day, he'd been strangely restless. Even John had noticed it and had commented on his disposition. "Does this mean what I think it does?" John had asked.

"Something's wrong with me," Abe had admitted, "although I don't know what."

"I know what's ailing you."

"Then do not mince words and tell me straightaway."

"You miss your wife."

Abe had shaken his head in denial, unable to believe he could miss a woman he'd only met and married a month ago. But now that he was home with Zoe, he realized John had been right.

He loved being with Zoe, loved the time reading and talking with her in the evenings while she played with Violet or worked on her knitting, loved her teasing and her smiles, loved that she asked questions about everywhere he'd been and all the things he'd done while he was gone. He loved seeing her first thing when he awoke in the morning, loved sitting at the table across from her with a cup of tea, loved the brightness of her presence and beauty in his home.

As they all too rapidly reached the cabin, his footsteps slowed with the unwillingness to let the time together come to an end. And yet, he knew from experience he'd regret the late night and lack of sleep. Once daylight came, he'd have to drag himself out of bed. . . .

Bed.

He stopped abruptly in front of the door. With Will moving in, he and Zoe would have to share a bed tonight and every night.

As if remembering the same, she grew quiet and fumbled at the door nervously.

He released her hand and took a step back. "I think I'll take in a few more minutes of night air."

"'Course. I understand." She let herself in and closed the door quickly as if to block him from following.

He stuffed his hands into his pockets and stared at the vacant spot she'd just occupied. Even after a month of marriage, clearly she wasn't excited about his joining her in the bed. To some degree, he supposed he'd never really expected a wife would be excited about marital intimacies. From everything he'd ever learned, most women took little pleasure in such things.

When the time finally came, he couldn't fathom pushing himself on Zoe if she had no desire for him. At the very least, he wanted her to care about him, maybe even welcome his embrace—certainly not scuttle away from him as fast as she could. Was that too much to ask for?

The truth was that he needed to put forth more effort to win her affection. So far he hadn't exactly been doing a stellar job of that. He could blame his absence and busyness. But even when he was with her, was he more enamored with all she did for him than with what he was doing for her? He hung his head and chastised himself to do better, to be the kind of husband God wanted him to be.

Even if he won her heart, he couldn't expect more of the new sleeping arrangements. They still had many months left in the colonies, and he couldn't let their marriage progress yet and risk having children and additional responsibilities that would take him from his work. He might have to share the bed with her, but that's all it would be—sharing the bed.

The moment Zoe heard the door open and then close, she froze and held herself motionless. Having already moved to the far side of the bed, she stared at the wall, reminded all over again of the first awkward night she'd spent with Abe . . . except he was no longer a stranger.

She could hear him drop the latch to lock the door, kick off his boots, shed his coat, then tread quietly toward the bed. When he reached the side, he paused. She stiffened as she waited for him to slide in next to her.

Did he expect her to turn over and acknowledge his presence? To say something? Or was he as reluctant to share the bed with her as she was with him?

When he finally lowered himself, the mattress sank under his weight and seemed to pull her away from her side toward the middle. She clung to the edge to keep the distance. Once he was beside her, she held her breath, expecting him to roll over, hesitantly touch her back, and maybe whisper something.

But like that first night together, he held himself just as rigidly as she did. And he didn't move. Except for the steady rise and fall of his chest.

After a moment, she let herself relax. And then felt a tiny pang of disappointment, although she wasn't sure why. Had she hoped he would desire her more now that they'd been married awhile? Had she only imagined the attraction at the hot spring? Was she reading more into his desire to hold her hand tonight?

Whatever the case, his even breathing calmed her racing heart. And within minutes, her lashes fell and exhaustion claimed her so that when she awoke hours later, she was startled to realize she'd actually slept.

At the first moments of wakefulness, peace and warmth enveloped her, and she realized she'd had nothing to worry about with Abe. She should have known he'd treat her as respectfully and carefully as he always did.

But even as the peacefulness came, it drifted away, replaced instead by strange, tight longing. Would he never get over Lizzy and learn to like her instead?

At the shifting pressure against her, she was suddenly alert to the length of Abe's muscular body pressing against her back, his strong arm resting on her, and his long leg draped over hers.

For several heartbeats, all she could think about was his touch, his full, solid contours leaning into her. His head practically shared her pillow, and his chest rose and fell in the rhythm of heavy slumber. His hand was splayed across her hip with a familiarity that sent warmth into her face.

The quiet and darkness of the cabin told her morning hadn't yet dawned but that it wouldn't be long before Violet awoke, hungry for her first meal of the day. A part of her urged caution, warning her to slip out of bed now before Abe roused. From the care he'd taken earlier in the night, he'd likely be embarrassed to find himself wrapped around her and handling her so intimately.

But the other part of her wanted to stay right where she was for a few more minutes so she could relish the security of his hold along with the delicious sensations humming through her blood.

From the sagging of the mattress and the rope frame that held it, she supposed it was inevitable they'd end up together in the middle. In fact, noticing the way she'd rounded her body, she was embarrassed at her own brazenness in melting into his embrace.

At a deep exhalation, he shifted his head closer so she could feel his breath against her neck.

Tingles shimmied down her spine. And unexpected warmth unfurled in her stomach. She closed her eyes and let herself simply bask in his closeness, unwilling to bring the moment to an end. In some deep part of her, she knew this was what she wanted and where she wanted to be. But she also sensed the fragility of the hold, that one wrong move could snap the few threads binding them together.

Violet gave a soft squeak, the telltale sign she was beginning to awaken.

Abe shifted again, stirring with a soft, contented noise that made her melt even more. A second later, though, he stiffened and jerked his arm and leg off her, apparently no longer asleep. In the same motion, he rolled away, putting space between their bodies.

"Zoe?" he whispered.

"Hmmm?"

"You're awake?"

"Aye."

He groaned softly.

She rolled so she could see his outline next to her by the early light of dawn.

"I'm sorry," he whispered. "I didn't mean to—didn't intend to . . . well, you know."

"You didn't mean to snuggle with me?" She tried to keep her whisper light and teasing.

"The problem is with the bed," he whispered hurriedly. "I'll take a look at the frame today and see if I can fix it."

"It's alright, Abe." Once the words were out, a flush flooded her chest and cheeks. She sounded wanton. "What I mean is that without Violet to snuggle with, I appreciated having the warmth."

He didn't respond for a moment.

Violet squeaked again, this time louder. Zoe pushed herself up, letting the covers fall away, but Abe's touch against her arm stopped her. "I'll tend to her."

"She needs a bottle."

"I can get it ready."

"But I don't want to bother you."

"I want to do it." His voice was earnest.

She shivered against the chill of the cabin.

He tugged the covers back up. "Then you can stay in bed until I get the cabin heated."

"How can I argue with that?"

As Abe rose from bed, she wanted to reach for him and draw him back. Instead, she burrowed deeper under the covers, knowing she had to be more careful. She was starting to like Abe too much. And she suspected such feelings would only lead to heartache and trouble.

twenty-three

The level flooded land near the river provided a hockey rink, and Zoe stood with the other spectators along the side and cheered as the puck slid across the ice into the goal.

Abe raised his broomstick in a sign of victory and grinned at his teammates. His cheeks and nose were red from the cold and exertion of the game. With the afternoon sunshine glinting off his fair hair, he'd never looked more rugged and handsome, and Zoe's heart pattered faster with both pride and admiration.

Abe was the best player on either team. He was strong and fast and aggressive. And yet, he'd proven himself to be fair and kind not only to his teammates but also to the other players.

"Good game, Pastor Abe." One of the miners on the opposite team shook Abe's hand. "You won fair enough this time."

Abe traded compliments and wove among the men, back-slapping with his usual good-natured affection.

Violet babbled as though offering her congratulations, and Zoe made sure the knit hat still snugly covered the babe's ears.

"She gets bigger every day," Mr. Hemming said, patting Violet's cap as he passed by.

"Aye, she does." Zoe's shoulders ached under Violet's weight even though she held the babe in the sling.

"I'm still wearing the socks you knit for me." Mr. Hemming lifted one of his trouser legs and pointed with his cane to the thick stockings she'd delivered to him a few days after the fire in Shantytown as a way of thanking him for all the ways he'd worked with her and Abe to find temporary shelter for the people who'd been affected by the fire. "Haven't taken them off once."

"Not once?" She raised her brow. "Well, be careful. If you start losing diners, then you know it's time to give the socks a washing."

He laughed. "I'll keep that in mind. At least I'll be aware that it's not the food scaring them away, just my smelly socks."

"Guess I better get started knitting you another pair." She'd long since used up the yarn Mrs. Moresby had sent along with her, and she'd also purchased the last of what Mr. Allard had in his general store. Finally she'd asked Abe to look for more on one of his visits to another town.

Mr. Hemming squeezed her arm affectionately. "You're a mighty fine woman, Mrs. Merivale. Pastor Abe couldn't have picked a better wife." As he limped off, his kind words warmed Zoe all the way down to her bones, making her forget about her cold fingers and toes.

Though the sunshine made the day warmer, it hadn't penetrated the lingering cold. Now that March had come and spring was drawing nigh, Zoe expected warmer temperatures and melting snow, but winter clung to the hills and mountains with a tenacity that made the miners restless. The brawling and violence had escalated as the men took to drinking more while waiting for the thawing that would allow them to return to the mining camps and their claims.

'Course, the increasing problems meant Abe was busier than

usual. Since everyone respected him, they called upon him often to intervene in the disputes and problems. To combat the idleness and issues, Abe had started the hockey games as he'd apparently done last year.

On days that weren't too cold for Violet to be outside, Zoe liked going to the games—mainly to watch Abe, although she didn't tell him as much. Even now as he moved among the men, her sights lingered upon his chiseled profile that stood out among the others. He was not only taller and more muscular, but he was so handsome that her stomach flopped upside down, especially as her mind drifted back to the early morning hours when he'd nestled against her.

Over the past two weeks of sharing the bed when he was home, he'd made a valiant effort at staying on his side. But most mornings, she'd awoken with his body all too near. Even though he'd tightened the rope frame and attempted to stay in his spot, he ended up curved into her, his hand in her hair or on her hip.

Once he awoke, he was always embarrassed and scrambled away, even though she wasn't in a hurry for him to leave. In fact, just that morning when he'd shifted away from her, she'd started to reach for him and draw him back, only to catch herself.

She was trying to be careful not to like him any more than she already did, but he was making that awfully hard, especially since he continued to surprise her with his sensitivity. He prepared Violet's bottle every morning, and he'd also started changing her napkin rather than handing the babe back to her.

Not only were his efforts with Violet sweet, but he also surprised her from time to time with little gifts. After one trip, he returned with a small leather-bound Bible. Though it hadn't been new, she'd been thrilled to know he'd been thinking about her enough while he was away to bring her the gift. Another day, he'd brought her a pair of her own snowshoes and the next day had shown her how to use them. Since then, they'd gone on a couple of hikes in the snow, and he'd taught her how to identify animal tracks.

At a bump against her leg, Zoe glanced down to find Lyle smiling up at her. "Well, hello there, Little Man. How are you today?"

"O-ee," he said, botching her name, somehow unable to pronounce the Z. As usual his nose was runny and his face crusty. But thankfully, this time Wanda had the sense to put the boy in the warm hat and mittens Zoe had knitted for him and given to him at yesterday's game.

Wanda only came as the games were winding down, more interested in garnering the men's notice afterward than she was in watching them play. Zoe had taken to giving the boy some attention while Wanda flirted her way through both teams.

Lyle reached out his blue mitten and pointed at Violet. "Babee?"

Zoe crouched in front of him. "Would you like to see Violet?"

He nodded eagerly.

She pulled back the blanket to reveal Violet's face. At the sight of Lyle, she smiled and greeted him with a squeal of delight.

Lyle put his hands over his eyes and then said something that sounded vaguely like *peekaboo*, earning for himself another of Violet's squeals. Zoe couldn't contain her own smile at the sight of the boy imitating the game she'd shown him yesterday.

Nearby along the wharf, a steamer had docked and passengers were making their way down the gangplank. With each passing day, more and more miners were arriving in Yale and readying themselves for the hike up into the Fraser Canyon to the Cariboo region. The hotels and taverns were overflowing in readiness.

At the sight of a dark-haired man of medium build stepping off the gangplank, she took a second look. Something about the way he walked and held himself seemed familiar. Although his hat obscured his face, her heart pattered faster. *Zeke?*

At Abe's suggestion, she'd penned a short letter to the man named Jeremiah Hart up in Williamsville, asking if his true identity was Zeke. She'd also said that if he was her brother, then he was free from the accusation of the crime and she was sorry she'd driven him away. Abe had already given the letter to one of his trusted friends, who was departing soon for Williamsville, assuring her that his friend would do his best to deliver the letter to Mr. Hart.

She'd asked Abe when he was leaving to go on his circuit up into the mining camps of the Fraser Canyon, reminding him of his offer to take her and go to Zeke together. Abe had commented on how dangerous the path still was and his desire to wait until the road was firmer. He'd indicated that with the church building project, he wasn't free to ride his circuit for the time being anyway.

As the dark-haired man began walking in the opposite direction, Zoe stood, her heart suddenly pounding with the need to chase after the newcomer, spin him around, and see if he was Zeke.

With her hand sliding to the pendant in her pocket, she took several rapid steps, leaving Lyle behind. At a shout from someone on the gangplank, the dark-haired man looked over his shoulder. It was enough for Zoe to glimpse his face—the face of a stranger and not her brother.

Disappointment halted her steps, as did Lyle's call behind her. "O-ee, O-ee."

Silently she reminded herself to be patient, that she'd find Zeke sooner or later. She'd waited this long already, and a few more months wouldn't hurt her efforts.

"Ba-bee." Lyle toddled up next to her and tugged her hand.

She lowered herself to the boy's level again and let him play peekaboo with Violet to his heart's content before teaching him another clapping game.

"Lately all Little Man talks about is Ba-bee and O-ee" came Wanda's voice behind her.

Zoe stood and faced Wanda warily. Even though she was attired in her usual gaudy gown, it hung more loosely. Her painted face was thinner and her hair lusterless. The winter hadn't been kind to Wanda. Nevertheless, since the first meeting on the steamship to Yale, Zoe hadn't been able to shake the feeling she was competing with Wanda for Abe's affection. The envy was ridiculous. Especially since Abe never looked at Wanda, not even when the woman directly addressed him.

Or maybe that was why the unease plagued Zoe. If Wanda meant nothing to Abe, why was he so awkward every time she spoke to him? If he had no feelings for the beautiful woman, wouldn't he be able to view her as he did his other parishioners?

Maybe Wanda's show of flesh and wanton ways made him uncomfortable. Maybe he was simply trying to remain immune to her wiles, unlike the others who practically fell over themselves whenever she was near.

"Lyle really likes Violet." Zoe offered the boy a smile and a pat on his head.

"My invitation still stands." Wanda watched Zoe's interaction with Lyle and muffled a deep cough against her coat sleeve. "You and Pastor Abe must join me for a dinner party sometime."

Zoe bristled just as she had earlier in the week when Wanda had mentioned having them over. She didn't want Wanda anywhere near Abe, especially not in her home. Zoe's gaze flickered involuntarily to the mansion that sat a short distance away on the edge of town.

Set against the backdrop of the mountains, the blue clap-

board, three-story house with its multiple steep gables and turrets, along with yellow decorative bargeboard, was large enough
to fit Abe's cabin a dozen times over. With its bay window on the
ground floor, porch stretching across the front and overlooking
a grassy yard, and single-story rear wing, clearly no expense
had been spared in building the home.

"Abe's too busy for dinner parties," Zoe said. She wasn't
lying. He was busy. And when he wasn't out meeting the many
needs of the people he served, she wanted him to be home with
her and Violet and Will.

"Oh, I see." Wanda smiled but then coughed again. "You
don't like having to share him with the whole town."

Wanda's words hit too close to the truth, a truth Zoe tried
to avoid, the truth that she wanted more of Abe's time and
attention. "It's none of your business, Wanda."

"Maybe if you knew how to satisfy him, you wouldn't have
to share him."

Wanda's accusation landed with a sickening thud at the bottom of Zoe's stomach. The fact was, she wasn't Lizzy and never
would be. And even if Abe didn't talk about Lizzy, her picture
was still on the bookshelf, behind the pile of books. She might
be out of sight, but her presence was always there.

Wanda's attention shifted beyond Zoe, and her lips curved
up in welcome.

Zoe craned her neck to find that Abe was striding their way,
still in conversation with several teammates.

Wanda tossed her long ringlets over her shoulders and let
her cloak slip down, revealing, as usual, miles of bare skin.

A hot blade sliced into Zoe's chest. Even if she wasn't Lizzy,
she wouldn't stand back and allow Wanda to flaunt herself in
front of Abe and entice him away.

"I can satisfy my husband just fine," Zoe said. With her blood
pounding an angry tempo, she squared her shoulders. Then,

before Abe noticed Wanda, Zoe stalked toward him. She stopped directly in front of him, forcing him to a halt as well.

"Zoe?" He searched her face as though sensing something was amiss.

Before she lost her nerve and before Abe could step away, she reached both hands up to his face and cupped his cheeks.

His eyes widened, revealing questions and confusion.

She hesitated only a second before standing on her toes and at the same time guiding his head down so that her mouth met his. She wasn't entirely inexperienced with kissing. She'd once kissed a boy she liked when she'd been in school. And there had been another time, when a neighbor boy had stolen a kiss from her.

Even so, the moment her lips connected with Abe's, she knew her previous kisses couldn't begin to compare. There was something powerful, almost intoxicating about touching her lips to his. Without waiting for his response, she eagerly meshed her mouth more fully and pushed into him, giving him no choice but to kiss her in return.

He opened to her tentatively, exploring, tasting, and then returning the pressure. As though drawn in and wanting more, he settled one hand upon her hip and brought the other up to the back of her neck.

Breathless, she gave herself over to the kiss, letting the world and everyone else in it fall away from her consciousness so that all that mattered was him and the exquisite pleasure swelling with each passing moment.

Abe's hand upon her hip became tight, possessive, almost burning. His mouth moved urgently against hers so that she wanted to feel close to him the same way she did in the mornings. But as Violet's indignant squall rose between them, Zoe broke from Abe's kiss. Aye, somehow the kiss had become his and no longer hers.

She took a rapid step away. He let his hand fall from her neck but kept his hold on her hip and his attention riveted to her mouth. His pupils were wide and his blue irises cloudy with desire.

The sight of such blatant yearning sent sparks along every nerve ending so that she wanted to reach up to kiss him again and this time not stop.

Wanda's laughter cut through the haze of longing. "Pastor Abe's a good kisser, isn't he?"

At Wanda's words, Abe glanced up at her and winced. Wanda winked at him as though they shared a secret. And Zoe suspected that somehow they did.

twenty-four

*A*n avalanche of emotions crashed through Abe so that he couldn't think or talk on the way back to the cabin. He was confused over why Zoe kissed him in the first place. He was embarrassed he'd so hungrily kissed her back in front of everyone. And he was completely mortified Wanda had hinted at his indiscretion.

Zoe walked beside him without saying a word. Their footsteps crunched against the crusty snow, and Violet's baby talk filled the awkward silence that hovered between them.

Why had Zoe kissed him?

His mind replayed the moment she'd stalked up to him, her eyes blazing and her chin lifted with determination. He'd assumed something had happened, that someone had perhaps offended her. He'd never imagined she'd kiss him.

Then again, his relationship with Zoe had been full of surprises from the moment they'd met. She was unlike any woman he'd ever known. Just when he thought he was beginning to know and understand her, she did something to surprise him.

He shot her a sideways glance, his sights snagging on her mouth. Fire kindled in his blood and blazed through his veins.

Lord have mercy. He wanted to kiss her again. He wanted it so much that he had to look away lest she see the power of his ardor and be frightened by it.

After the past two weeks of lying next to her in bed and denying his flesh, his desires had been building to a dangerous level. And now he couldn't think of anything but kissing her again. Will was at work at the livery. They'd have the cabin to themselves. Could he do it when they stepped inside? Would that be too soon?

Although his mind warned him that doing so would only break the wall he'd built to help him focus on his ministry, his body protested waiting even that long. If he was bolder and more spontaneous like Zoe, he'd pull her into a nearby copse of trees and kiss her again until they were both breathless. But the fact was, he'd always been shy with women, never certain how to behave.

And besides, he couldn't kiss her again, not without admitting to her what had happened between him and Wanda. He owed her the truth.

A few minutes later as he followed her into the cabin, he closed the door and stood against it, watching her slip out of her cloak, set Violet on the bed, and then begin preparing a bottle.

Part of him wanted to ignore the nudge to share about Wanda. But the other part of him needed to finally confess. He cleared his throat and tried to formulate an admission. "Zoe, I apologize—" His voice broke, and he cleared his throat again.

She stopped abruptly and faced him with all the honesty and openness he'd come to expect from her. "Why did Wanda say you're a good kisser?"

He could feel a flush moving into his face and heating his ears. "We kissed once—and only once."

Zoe cocked her head, her expression more curious than angry. "She apparently isn't satisfied with just once."

Abe stuffed his hands into his pockets. "No, that's how she

interacts with all men. Sadly she doesn't know how to behave any other way."

"With the way she flaunts her body, I'm not surprised you kissed her."

He focused on his dirty boots. "After I received news of Mr. Washington's death, she asked me to call, said she needed me. So I visited to offer my condolences and to pray with her."

"Like you did at the hospital after Jane died?" She turned and continued readying Violet's bottle.

"Yes. But I should have known better than to call on Wanda alone. I should have brought someone along as a chaperone or visited with her in a more public place. As it was, we ended up in her sitting room, on her settee." He swallowed hard, his mortification slapping him full in the face again as it did whenever he thought about what had happened. "She was crying. In my effort to provide solace, I hugged her. Before I knew what was happening, she was kissing me. I should have stopped her. But I didn't."

"How could she even consider kissing another man right after her husband died?"

"Wanda married her husbands for their wealth. Not love."

Zoe was silent as though weighing his words.

He shuffled his feet, unable to meet her gaze and see her reaction. Even if Wanda had initiated the kiss, he could have cut her off the moment he'd realized what was happening. Not only did he have his integrity as a minister to uphold, but he'd been beholden to Lizzy and should have remained faithful.

Instead, he'd allowed the kiss with Wanda to become quite impassioned, until she'd started to unbutton his shirt. Her move had been a splash of cold water against his inflamed desires, dousing him and jolting him up from the settee.

He thanked the Lord every day for giving him the strength to walk away from the temptation. Even so, the kiss had awakened his desires before the time was right. And he'd had to struggle with his lust ever since.

Zoe finished preparing the bottle and gave it to Violet, who grasped it eagerly and began to feed herself. When Zoe straightened and faced him, he tried to meet her gaze directly.

"I never meant for it to happen and am ashamed that it did."

"Have you wanted to kiss her again?"

"I wouldn't be honest if I told you I've never struggled with my thoughts."

Zoe frowned and crossed her arms. "Then you still think about her?"

"Of course not. Not since I married you."

"Not even when she displays herself so wantonly?"

"No. You're the only one I think about." At his admission, the flush returned to his face, and he had the urge to slink outside to hide and cool off.

Zoe's frown faded, but the uncertainty remained. "What kinds of thoughts do you have about me?"

"All kinds."

"Good kinds or bad kinds?"

"Definitely good." Suddenly hot and near to perspiring, he shrugged out of his coat and tossed it over the chair. He was too embarrassed to admit even to himself some of the fantasies about her that filled his dreams.

Her brow furrowed as she moved toward his coat, lifted it from the chair, and then stepped next to him to hang it on the peg on the back of the door.

"Zoe, don't worry." He was tempted to reach for her but held himself at bay. "You're a kind and loving woman. And I hold you in the highest esteem."

She pressed her hands against her hips. "Are you more attracted to me than Wanda?"

Her hands emphasized her slender waist, which only served

to draw his attention first there, then up to her gentle curves, her graceful neck, and her determined chin, and finally her deep rose-colored lips. Lips he wanted to feel again.

When his eyes met hers, he hoped she could read the answer there. But just in case she couldn't, he pushed past his bashfulness and swallowed his reservations. "She can't compare to you, Zoe."

"You're sure?"

"You're the most beautiful woman I've ever known." He couldn't keep from admiring her features again.

Her lips pulled into the beginning of a smile. "And my kiss? Was it better than Wanda's?"

"By far," he whispered, his voice turning low and reflecting his desire.

Her smile rose and gave way to dimples. "You should have said you *think* it was better but that you need to try it again just to be sure."

At her suggestion, his insides tumbled wildly together. Did she want to kiss again?

She didn't move or take the initiative as she'd done outside. Instead, she peered up at him expectantly.

"You're right." He tried to make his voice light and teasing, when all he wanted to do was gather her up in his arms and kiss her the rest of the day. "I do think I need to try again. As long as you're agreeable."

She took a step closer. "Aye, perhaps a little practice will help make it better?"

He couldn't contain himself a moment longer. He reached for her waist and drew her toward him.

She didn't resist, her attention drawn to his mouth. The desire that flared in her eyes set his blood afire.

"Only a little practice?" He bent in and pressed his cheek to hers, relishing the softness of her skin, the warmth of her body, and the catch of her breath, which told him she was feeling every nuance of their encounter as much as he was.

"Perhaps we do need a good deal of practice." She brushed her lips along his jaw.

The touch was enough to drive him to insanity. He angled down and found her mouth, covering her and fusing them together with such force that he lost himself. For an endless moment, he kissed her, driven forward by her answering kisses, kisses filled with as much fervor as his own.

She didn't protest when he finally drew her body against his. At the sweet pressure, he would have moaned except he was too consumed with meeting her passionate kisses with his own.

All he could think about was heaven, that having Zoe in his arms and kissing her this way was as if he'd been given a piece of heaven on earth. He'd never imagined, not even in his dreams, that he'd experience such passion with his wife, such enjoyment, such pleasure. And this was only kissing. What would the rest be like?

He had a sudden pulsing need to sweep her off her feet, carry her to their bed, and let this passion take them where it would. But another part of him hesitated, reminding him of all the reasons he needed to wait. It was too soon, and he couldn't let himself be distracted by his physical desires. He couldn't chance having a baby. He couldn't compromise his ministry. He couldn't get distracted by other things, not after vowing to the bishop nothing would change.

He slid his hands up her arms to her neck, moving freely and boldly. Already he was locked away in the cabin kissing her when he should be out with his hockey team, ministering to them.

A knocking at the door made him jump and release her at the same time. She let go of him too and backed away, her chest rising and falling rapidly, her face flushed, her lips swollen.

He wanted to ignore whoever was on the other side of the

door, reach out and draw her back into his embrace, and continue kissing her. If they were quiet for a minute, whoever had come would eventually go away and they'd be left alone, except for Violet, who was content at the moment with her bottle.

He met Zoe's gaze. As if having the same idea, she pressed a finger against her lips, cautioning him to be quiet and wait for the visitor to depart. The knock sounded again, louder.

He shook his head, hoping Zoe would forgive him for this interruption. He couldn't pretend he wasn't home. What if someone was in dire need? What if he lost an opportunity to share the gospel?

He quickly combed his fingers through his hair and then lifted the handle. As he swung the door wide, Zoe started toward the bed and Violet.

"Mr. Merivale." At the sight of Bishop Hills's rotund figure and terse smile, Abe's heart dropped. The bishop was the last person Abe wanted to see. With the imminent approach of spring and the plans to start the construction of the church, Abe had hoped to get the project well underway before the bishop made a visit.

Apparently he was to have no such luck. The bishop must have been aboard one of the steamships that docked today.

The bishop peered past him into the cabin, taking in Zoe, who'd picked up Violet and was helping her drink the last of the milk in her bottle.

The bishop's attention returned to Abe, his eyes narrowing on Abe's shirt, which had somehow come untucked. Perhaps during the hockey game? Certainly not while he was kissing Zoe.

Heat saturated Abe's face, and he fumbled to stuff his shirt-tail back into his trousers.

"I do hope I'm not disturbing you, Mr. Merivale. With the late afternoon hour, I was rather surprised to hear you'd been engaged in a game of hockey. And I was even more surprised to learn that after the shenanigans you went directly home rather than attending to your duties as minister."

A fresh wave of guilt buffeted Abe. "The hockey is simply a way to build relationships with the men. And, of course, the healthy activity keeps them out of the taverns and out of trouble."

"Yes, Mr. Merivale." The bishop walked past Abe into the cabin. "So you've told me many times. But your methods are highly questionable as are the results."

Zoe cradled Violet. With her rosy cheeks and mussed hair, she looked as though she'd just been kissed. And Abe squirmed at the realization of how this all appeared to the bishop.

"Your Grace, may I introduce you to my wife, Zoe?" His mind scrambled to find a reasonable way to explain what he and Zoe had been doing before the bishop's arrival, but the more he thought about the passionate kissing, the more he squirmed.

"Perhaps you could have introduced me sooner, before you ran out of town."

"I'm sorry, Your Grace. Under the circumstances, I thought it best to leave Victoria as quickly as possible."

"Under the circumstances indeed." The bishop pursed his lips, letting Abe know he was well aware of his brawl with Dexter Dawson.

"Pleased to meet you, sir," Zoe interjected. "Would you like some tea?"

The bishop squinted at Zoe, scrutinizing her as though he was deciding whether she deserved the title of minister's wife. "Very well, Mrs. Merivale. I do require a generous dollop of honey in my tea, if you would."

The bishop pulled out a chair and sat down, giving Abe no choice but to close the door and face whatever might come his way.

twenty-five

Zoe placed a steaming cup of tea on the table for the bishop and one in front of Abe before returning to the bed and picking up Violet.

The bishop hadn't been in their home for more than five minutes and already Zoe was ready for him to leave. She didn't feel that way about too many other people who came to visit, not even some of the loud and brash miners who smelled as though they'd bathed in rum. At least those fellas accepted her.

The bishop, on the other hand, was watching her like she was a bug on the wall that he'd like to either squash or toss outside. He probably didn't think she was worthy of a man like Abe. Maybe Bishop Hills had known Lizzy and wished Abe had found someone more like her. Or maybe he was comparing her to his own wife and seeing nothing but shortcomings.

As the bishop sipped his tea, he questioned Abe about his endeavors in Yale. For all the many things that Abe did every day to love the people in the community, the bishop only seemed to point out Abe's faults.

The longer the two conversed, the lower Abe's shoulders sank, until Zoe wanted to step forward and speak her mind.

Before she could formulate the words to defend Abe, the bishop changed the subject to the church construction plans. But as before, the bishop found fault with Abe's ideas at every turn.

Finally, Zoe couldn't stand in the room's shadows any longer.

"Your Grace, pardon me for saying so"—she stepped up to the table and poured more tea in the bishop's cup—"but Abe's doing lots of good here in Yale. The people here love and respect him because of how much he cares for them."

Once the words were out, she realized she sounded unpolished and uneducated, much like the people who lived in the community. But she squared her shoulders and met the bishop's gaze anyway.

The older gentleman sat straighter, his cup poised halfway to his mouth.

"If anyone needs something, Abe's always there willing to lend a hand. Just yesterday he helped rebuild one of the homes damaged in the recent fire in—"

"Thank you for the kind words, Zoe," Abe said hurriedly. "But the bishop and I have different perspectives on how a minister should fill his spare time."

From the furrow in Abe's brow, Zoe sensed she wasn't helping matters. Even so, she felt as though she needed to defend him. "Abe fits right in with the people here, never putting on any airs, and they love him for it."

"Thank you, Mrs. Merivale." The bishop's voice contained annoyance rather than gratitude. "However, as this concerns matters far above your reasoning and understanding, you should stick with the tasks to which you are suited—taking care of your home. And, of course, the infant."

Violet, who was in the midst of gnawing her fist on the bed, stopped and babbled, as if voicing her concerns too. If the bishop hadn't been there, Zoe would have remarked on it to Abe, and they likely would have shared a laugh.

"Speaking of the native infant." Bishop Hills eyed the child with undisguised disdain. "Mr. Merivale, I hope you are making good efforts at locating a permanent home among the natives as I instructed you to do."

Zoe's spine stiffened. "Violet lives with us. She's our child now."

"This is only a temporary arrangement." The bishop waved his hand at the cabin interior. "I was quite clear about that during my last meeting with Mr. Merivale."

"You're mistaken, Your Grace. Abe and I are keeping Violet and raising her." After the past weeks of living in Yale, Zoe had almost begun to forget Violet wasn't her flesh and blood. She loved the little girl. And Abe had grown attached too. He couldn't deny it. Surely he wasn't planning to find a new home for Violet.

"Bishop Hills, I realize you consider our arrangement with the baby unnatural." Abe's expression was grave, which only made Zoe's heart pound harder. "However, as you can see, we're having no trouble caring for Violet. She fits right into our family. Moreover, the people here in Yale have been very accepting of her."

"The people here may be accepting, as they are mostly of a baser nature. What about your parish in Yorkshire? I doubt your parishioners there will be so indulgent."

"Surely they will love Violet as one of God's little children," Abe said, but his voice lacked confidence.

"You will not be able to take the child with you," the bishop insisted. "She might fit in here in the colony, but she most certainly will be an anomaly in England. Most people wouldn't be able to accept her as your child and would likely shun you as a result. The matter would most surely cause a great deal of scandal."

Zoe hugged Violet closer. "I don't care what people think."

"You may not care, Mrs. Merivale. But Mr. Merivale could very well bring disgrace to himself and the church. And as a result would find himself without a parish and ruin his chances for any advancement. If your husband's well-being isn't enough, then think of the child having to grow up in such an environment. She would be ostracized and ridiculed and would never fit into society."

The bishop's words cut off any further protest Zoe could offer. The bishop was right. Violet would be an oddity in England. Wherever she went, people would stop to stare or whisper. What kind of life would that be for Violet?

Abe watched Zoe with somber eyes.

"We'll stay here," Zoe stated. "We don't have to leave and go back to England." Even though Abe had informed her of his intentions, she'd secretly been hoping that when his assignment came to an end, he wouldn't want to leave, that he'd stay. Now, with the difficulty in taking Violet with them, this would make their decision easier, wouldn't it?

"Mr. Merivale most certainly cannot remain here in the colonies if he wishes to be chosen as a bishop. He knows his service here is merely a stepping stone for greater work within the church."

A stepping stone for greater work? Zoe couldn't contradict the bishop. Abe's compassion and energy were boundless. He was already doing great things for the Lord, and she had no doubt he would do even more once he became a bishop.

Abe bent his head and closed his eyes, and Zoe guessed he was either discouraged by the turn of the conversation or he was praying. Or perhaps both.

"That is precisely the point I have been attempting to emphasize, Mr. Merivale," the bishop continued sternly. "You must always consider future implications. Your hasty wedding and your poor choice of a marriage partner have already placed your chances at becoming a bishop in jeopardy. As such, you cannot afford to do anything else to stain your reputation, including keeping the native child."

"Pardon me, Your Grace. But Zoe is not a poor choice." Abe stood and shoved his chair back, his arms and shoulders rigid. "Nor is she a stain on my reputation."

Even with Abe's defense, the bishop's words chopped into Zoe's heart. *Poor choice of marriage partner? Stain on Abe's reputation?* Although she'd known Bishop Hills wasn't happy about the marriage, she hadn't realized exactly how displeased he was or the repercussions Abe would face as a result of marrying her.

The bishop pushed away from the table. "Let us be frank, Mr. Merivale. You know as well as I do that when you return to England, people will have a difficult time accepting a mill girl as your wife. You will already have enough obstacles to overcome, and bringing home a native infant will only make matters more difficult."

The muscles in Abe's jaw flexed as though he wanted to reply but was holding himself back.

"Since the two of you clearly have a great deal to discuss, I shall take my leave." The bishop took a final sip of tea, placed his cup on the table, and then rose from his chair.

"Do take care, Mr. Merivale," the bishop said as he crossed to the door. "It is rumored that Mr. Dawson is planning another altercation with you."

"Dexter Dawson?" Abe asked.

"The man you fought with before leaving Victoria." Bishop Hills's eyes filled with censure. "If he seeks you out, you must absolutely refrain from any more fighting. You know as well as I do that such interactions are not befitting your holy station and are a detriment to your aspirations of becoming a bishop."

"I realize that. And I have no intention of quarreling."

"Good. See that you refrain from all appearance of evil."

A moment later, when the door closed behind the bishop, Zoe collapsed into the nearest chair. She hugged Violet to her chest as if that was the answer to all their problems, but the infant released a cry of protest, wiggling so that she could resume playing with the buttons on Zoe's bodice.

Abe remained unmoving, staring at the door.

A mill girl. The bishop had spoken the words as if they were a curse.

She appreciated Abe's defense. He was a good man. But maybe she was no good for him. From the start of their marriage she'd realized she wasn't the typical genteel, well-bred pastor's wife. Now she understood even more starkly Abe's need for a woman who was his equal so that when he returned to England he could enter into a new parish without the condemnation he was sure to receive with his marriage to her—a mill girl.

Not only would their marriage make his work as a minister difficult, but it would diminish his opportunity of becoming a bishop. His dreams and future plans were in jeopardy because of her. Maybe he didn't recognize the issues now. But someday he'd realize she was to blame for the censure and missed opportunities. And no doubt, he'd come to resent her for being a blight on his promising future.

In addition to everything else, they also had to think about Violet's future.

Zoe pressed a kiss against the infant's downy hair, fighting back an ache at the prospect of losing the babe. "Why didn't you tell me the bishop wasn't planning to let you keep Violet?"

Abe expelled a long, weary sigh. "I didn't know until after we were already married, and then he gave me the ultimatum of returning her to the natives by spring."

"So all along you've been making plans to find another home for her?"

"No," he said quickly, his attention landing upon Violet. "I honestly haven't given the bishop's ultimatum much thought. Maybe at the back of my mind, I'd hoped the bishop would see how well she fit into our lives and put aside his demand. Or maybe I was hoping he'd forget all about it, and we could go on as we pleased."

"I think it's safe to say neither of those things happened."

"I'm sorry, Zoe." His shoulders drooped.

She could admit all of the bishop's reasons for finding Violet a home here in British Columbia made perfect sense. Violet wouldn't thrive in England. And Zoe knew she wouldn't like living there again either.

But here . . . here they were free, free to grow unhindered, free to live as they chose. Sure, there would still be people who judged and discriminated. But she'd learned the harsh wilderness of this new land put them all on more level ground.

Abe rubbed at the back of his neck. "Maybe I can make a trip up into the canyon and search again for my friend Sque-is. If he won't take Violet, maybe he'll know someone who can."

Violet had hold of one of Zoe's buttons and was trying to put it into her mouth. Under other circumstances, Zoe would have laughed at the infant's antics. But this time, tears stung at the back of her eyes. She bent and kissed Violet's head again.

"I don't think I can give her up, Abe." Zoe's throat was tight with unshed tears.

"I know," he whispered hoarsely in response. "But we have to do what's right for Violet."

She nodded and swiped at a tear that had escaped.

Maybe she had to do what was right for Abe too. With everything the bishop had revealed about how she would hurt his opportunities in England, maybe it was time to admit their marriage had been a mistake, give him an annulment, and stop holding him back.

With the coming of spring, she could find someone to take her and Violet up the Fraser Canyon to Williamsville. Once there, she'd track down Zeke, beg him to forgive her, and ask if she could live with him.

And if Zeke wasn't there . . . or if he refused to forgive her . . . then she'd have to figure out how to survive without him. She'd do it. She was strong enough.

The only trouble was whether she could survive leaving Abe. Because the truth was, whether she admitted it to herself or not, she didn't want to leave him. Just the thought of walking away was torture, and she couldn't imagine actually doing it.

But because she cared about him so much, she suspected the time was fast approaching when she'd have to do the impossible.

twenty-six

*A*be straddled the ceiling joist and hammered another nail into the rafter, relishing the sunshine on his head. Since the April day had dawned without rain, he'd joined the Royal Engineer construction crew at the work site.

He'd gathered as many other men as he could find to take advantage of the clear sunny day to finish the frame on the new church that they'd started several weeks ago when Bishop Hills had been visiting.

His superior had insisted on being a part of laying the foundation, no doubt to make sure the Royal Engineers followed his more ornate architectural plans rather than Abe's design, which better met the needs of the simple community folks.

The bishop had been adamant that his ideas were best, so Abe had conceded. He'd decided the fight for his way wasn't worth the additional tension and had resigned himself to the fact that God could use him anywhere and in any church building.

"Look who's coming!" shouted Mr. Hemming from below, where he was assisting as best he could. The stoop-shouldered man cocked his head in the direction of the livery down the street.

Zoe had just exited and was walking their way carrying a basket, bringing him a noon meal as she'd done on the couple of other occasions he'd helped with the church construction. No doubt she'd taken a portion of the fixings to Will first. She was thoughtful like that, and probably would have brought enough food for the whole construction crew if she'd had the means to do so.

Now that Violet was seven months old, the infant had grown too big and heavy for Zoe to comfortably hold in a sling. So Zoe had started carrying Violet in a cradleboard on her back. One of the native women in Shantytown had helped Zoe assemble the carrier and had demonstrated how to use it. Though it was heavy and at times cumbersome, Zoe never complained.

"Mrs. Merivale is a mighty fine woman," Mr. Hemming remarked, watching Zoe's approach through the open walls. "Never met a kinder woman. Or one as pretty."

With the sunshine warming the day, Zoe had tossed aside the usual scarf she wore over her head, revealing her dark, glossy hair, pale skin, and lovely features—features he dreamed about every single night without fail, features he wanted to caress and kiss.

He dropped from the rafter and landed among the debris of shavings and damp sawdust. His stomach chose that moment to growl loud enough that Mr. Hemming's brows shot up. Beneath his bushy gray beard, his lips cracked into a grin. "Guess you're hungry. From that expression, I'm guessing you're hungrier for your wife than food."

"Now, Mr. Hemming, that's not true." But even at his denial, warmth streamed into Abe's face, and he fumbled with his hammer in one hand and tried not to drop the nail from the other. Was his desire for Zoe that obvious to everyone?

It apparently wasn't obvious to her. Ever since the bishop's visit, she'd kept him at a distance. He understood that some of what the bishop had revealed had come as a surprise, especially the news that they must find a native family to take Violet. Zoe had a right to be angry and hurt that he hadn't told her about the bishop's decision. But she'd accepted his apology and had indicated she agreed Violet couldn't go to England and that it was best to find the baby a home now rather than in a year when the parting would be even more difficult.

Though Zoe seemed to understand, something was different between them, something Abe couldn't figure out. The camaraderie, the teasing, the laughter were gone. On the evenings he was home, the sweet fellowship and friendship they'd developed were no longer there.

Of course she was cordial and kind as always—like she was now by bringing him a noon meal. And yet, she had closed herself off to him and wouldn't open back up.

He had to admit, he hadn't tried too hard to get her to open up, had assumed a little time and persistent kindness on his part would be enough. When she'd had another one of her headaches the night after the bishop left, he'd thought by his tending her, she'd be able to see he still cared. But she'd pushed away his ministrations and turned down his offer to go to the hot spring.

"Go on out there and kiss her," Mr. Hemming teased with a nod toward the street. "You know you want to."

"I can't do that." Abe's face burned hotter. He hadn't realized that half the town had witnessed his kissing Zoe the day of the hockey game. But Mr. Hemming and plenty of others had seen the passionate display and now liked to jest with him every chance they got.

Abe wanted to kiss her again. He was embarrassed at how much he thought about the kisses they'd shared, about the pleasure he'd found in her embrace, and about the desire she'd shown in response. She'd enjoyed the kissing every bit as much as he had. Surely he hadn't been wrong about that.

Even so, he was biding his time and waiting for the right moment for another kiss. And now, with the strain lingering from the bishop's visit, he couldn't push her into more than she was ready to give.

As she strolled nearer to the construction site, she drew the attention of more workers, who paused to watch her approach. Even though most of the young Royal Engineers respected Abe enough not to flirt with Zoe or make suggestive remarks, they couldn't hide their interest in the town's prettiest woman. And Abe couldn't suppress his need to have Zoe to himself.

Amid good-natured teasing, he wound through the shell of the building until he stood outside on the plank sidewalk that the workers had already constructed to connect the church to the rest of town.

At his appearance, Zoe's steps slowed. He waited for a smile to light her face or for her eyes to brighten, but she watched his approach warily.

When he stopped in front of her, she held out the basket. "I thought you might be getting hungry."

"I am. Thank you." He stuffed his hands into his pockets, knowing if he took the basket, she'd leave and he'd lose the chance to be with her. Deep in his pocket, his fingers connected with the jade center of the ring he planned to give Zoe as a wedding band. Natives as well as miners dug up the gemstone in Lillooet, along the rivers, and in the surrounding mountains. And Abe had discovered a piece during one of his circuit rides last summer.

The vibrant green reminded him of Zoe's eyes. And shortly after their arrival in Yale back in January, he'd asked his friend to make a wedding band using the gem. The silversmith had delivered the finished product last week before he'd left for the goldfields. Abe had been carrying it around ever since, waiting for the perfect opportunity to give it to Zoe.

Maybe he needed to figure out another way to surprise her. He could take her someplace special and unique and give her the ring then. Maybe with such a gesture, he'd be able to bridge the gulf between them.

She looked behind him to the construction area. "You're making good progress."

"Having so many helping hands is a blessing." He drew in a breath of the crisp air that teased them with a warm breeze and hinted at the summer days that would soon be upon them. They were working on the roof so that during the next bout of rain, they'd have a measure of covering to allow the construction to continue.

"How long before everything is completed?"

"I'm hoping we'll finish by the end of the month."

Behind her in the cradleboard, Violet babbled something. Abe was tempted to step around Zoe to see the baby and perhaps earn one of her smiles. But he forced himself to remain where he was, determined not to allow himself to get closer to the child than he already was. Doing so would only make the parting all that much harder. And he needed to stay strong for Zoe's sake to support her during the loss.

She glanced toward the bend that took the river straight north. "So many fellas have already headed into the canyon and mountains. With the warm weather, I was hoping we could leave soon too." The brown waters rushed swiftly, flooded from the recent rains as well as the thawing snow in higher elevations. Fishermen dotted the riverbank, angling for the sturgeons that migrated into the Fraser River from the Pacific Ocean.

Abe had tried his hand at fishing for sturgeon in the spring and the salmon that were more plentiful in late summer. The fishing, like hockey, was another way he bonded with the men in the community. He only wished the bishop could see the benefits of building relationships. As a result of their trust, the men came to him when they had problems and listened when he shared God's truth. He'd witnessed numerous souls repent of wandering away from God and place their hope in Him.

"I'd like the chance to find Zeke." Zoe jutted her chin with a look that told him she was determined.

"If he's up in the Williamsville area, he's surely gotten your letter by now. Let's wait and see if he sends you a response."

"Maybe I shouldn't have sent him the letter. What if he doesn't want me to find him and decides to move away before I can get to him?"

"Or just maybe he'll be glad to see you."

"He might still hate me for what I did." She thrust the basket at him again.

Slowly he slid his hands from his pockets and took the offering. He peeked inside to discover bread, cheese, dried venison, and a crock of soup. "Thank you, Zoe. You're very thoughtful." Even as he said the words, somehow they didn't seem adequate to express his gratitude or feelings toward her.

He had a strange urge to give her the ring right then and there and tell her he cared about her. He wanted to reassure her that whatever the future brought, they'd handle it together with God's strength guiding them. But standing there holding the basket and watching her, his inadequacies reared up to taunt him.

Some part of him knew he needed to talk to her about the issues and about the future. But a strange fear pulsed underneath everything—the fear that perhaps she didn't want to be with him anymore, that she'd reject him just as Lizzy had, and that maybe she'd even leave.

It was easier to stay busy and pretend that everything was fine—or at least would be fine eventually.

"Will you promise to take me up to Williamsville by the end of the month?" she asked.

Abe was sorely tempted to agree to her request, not only to make her happy but because he wanted to do his own search for his friend Sque-is. He'd already sent out word with the miners that he was looking for the native, as well as a letter to his friend explaining the situation with Violet and the need to find her a home. But so much time had elapsed since he'd last heard from Sque-is that he couldn't count on any help. Even so, he clung to the hope his friend was alive somewhere.

As much as Abe wanted to go, he couldn't push past the inner warning telling him of the danger, not only on the roads but for his relationship with Zoe. What would happen if she found her brother and had a happy reunion? Would she decide to stay with Zeke so she could keep Violet? The very possibility sent his heart into a downward tumble that landed with a painful thud at the bottom of his chest.

He squared his shoulders. "I'm sorry, Zoe. I cannot make any promises. Even though the Royal Engineers are working hard on the road, it's not near completion. And with the wet conditions, I've been getting reports that the way up the canyon is treacherous. It's no place for you or Violet."

"Surely there are other women who've traveled to Williamsville already this spring. I wouldn't be the first woman to make such a dangerous trip."

His muscles tensed. "Please, Zoe. Put the trip from your mind for now."

"For now? Or forever?"

Before he could think of how to respond, someone down the street called his name. His relief was short-lived when he realized the diminutive, olive-skinned man rushing his way was Mr. Ping, Wanda Washington's Chinese servant.

"Pastor Abe, sir," he called, his clogs pattering hard against the planks. "The missee is asking for you, Pastor Abe, sir. She asks that you come visit her right away and says she needs you very much."

Zoe's brows rose as she took in Wanda's servant.

Abe squirmed. Was Zoe thinking of his admission over what had happened the last time he'd been in Wanda's house? When Wanda had insisted on needing him?

Mr. Ping arrived breathless, his straw hat askew over his short cropped hair. He bowed, and when he straightened, his normally placid façade was crinkled with obvious worry. "She is very sick. I never see her so sick before."

"I'm sorry to hear that."

"I think missee is afraid to die, Pastor Abe, sir."

"Surely she's not dying?" Zoe interjected.

"I'd heard she'd taken to her bed," Abe said. "But I didn't realize her condition was so serious."

Mr. Ping glanced away, but not before Abe saw the sadness in the man's eyes that told the truth. Wanda was sick, likely with one of the diseases that afflicted prostitutes. Perhaps she'd even been sick for a while, having caught something during her days as a madam before she'd gotten married—although Abe suspected Wanda hadn't honored her marriage vows either. And now she was succumbing to whatever had plagued her.

If she was near the point of death, Abe couldn't ignore the opportunity to lead her to the Savior. "Very well, Mr. Ping. Tell Mrs. Washington I'll be along shortly."

Mr. Ping rushed away, his clogs clattering again. As soon as the manservant was out of earshot, Zoe turned on Abe, her eyes flashing. "How could you fall for that? Unless you really do want to be with Wanda after all."

Quick denial formed on his lips but then stalled at the realization that Zoe was jealous. It was there in her eyes and her tone.

The tension eased from his shoulders. Certainly she wouldn't be upset if she didn't care about him and want him all for herself.

Summoning courage, he set the basket down and closed the distance between them. Before he changed his mind or she could retreat, he took hold of her arms and drew her almost flush. "Zoe." His voice came out low and husky, and he fought away his embarrassment, focusing instead on her. "You're the only one I want to be with."

Thankfully, she didn't wrench away and instead peered up at him, the green of her eyes as bright as the new buds on the aspens.

"Truly." It was the truth, and he hoped she could read it in his eyes.

"Kiss her!" came a teasing shout from the construction site.

Zoe's eyes rounded at the same time that mortification flooded Abe.

"Just kiss her!" called another of the workers.

Within seconds, the air was filled with the men chanting at him to kiss Zoe.

"I guess I need to kiss you," he said, trying to gauge her reaction.

Her lips quirked into the smile he loved, the one that showed her dimples. "I guess you do. You wouldn't want to disappoint them, would you?"

His pulse picked up speed. "No, I wouldn't."

She waited, unmoving.

This wasn't the romantic surprise or setting he'd wanted for their next kiss, but he couldn't turn down an opportunity to kiss her any more than he could resist breathing. Drawing her imperceptibly closer, he bent and touched her lips. With the construction crew providing an audience, he held his urges in check, brushing a soft kiss before tilting back.

Behind him the men began to boo and hiss.

"Give her a real kiss!" someone shouted.

"Do it like you mean it!" said another fellow.

Abe could feel his ears burning even as Zoe's smile widened and her eyes filled with mirth. A swell of emotion for her rose up within him, so unexplainable, so strong, so unlike anything he'd ever experienced before.

This time he couldn't hold back. With a swift pull, he brought her body against his and in the same motion seized her mouth with all the passion he'd been holding back. As her lips joined his with an equal fervor, his body only tightened with more need rather than less. Instead of the kiss being a release, it stirred him so that he wanted to dive deeper and never surface.

The cheers and whistles of his friends penetrated the haze of his desire. He gave himself over to the pleasure of kissing her a moment longer before breaking away. Rather than looking at her and being tempted to kiss her again, he spun and faced the men, giving them a bow and no doubt grinning like an idiot.

Amid laughter and more calls, he caught Zoe's hand. "Come with me to Wanda's? Be there with me?"

"Aye." She nibbled her bottom lip between her teeth, drawing his attention back to a place it didn't need to go.

He reached for the basket of food and made himself lead her away.

twenty-seven

One kiss.

Zoe glided her fingers over the mahogany bedstead and tried not to imagine she was running her fingers through Abe's hair, even though that's what she wanted to do. With his head bowed as he prayed with Wanda, his messy waves fell over his forehead, beckoning Zoe to comb them back.

She closed her eyes to ward off the urge. But the darkness brought back the swirl of longing their kiss had awakened.

One kiss. That's all it had taken to break down the walls she'd tried to build over the past weeks since Bishop Hills's visit. Just one kiss from Abe had undone everything . . . along with his declaration: "*You're the only one I want to be with.*"

The sincerity of his tone, the earnestness of his expression, the starkness of his desire. Surely those were all signs he wanted her to remain with him and be his wife. Surely those were all signs she ought to stop her plans to leave and put aside her notion to separate from him once they reached Williamsville.

His prayer for Wanda continued with the same tenderness he'd shown to Zoe the day Jane had died. Abe was at his best in these moments, praying, encouraging, and sharing the gospel.

And from the instant they'd walked into Wanda's room, Zoe had realized that this time Wanda wasn't seeking Abe out for pleasure. Rather, she was gravely ill and needed Abe to help her make peace with her Creator.

The heavy tapestries in the windows were pulled closed, shrouding the enormous bedroom and holding captive the heavy scent of the herbal remedies Mr. Ping had concocted. In the luxurious four-poster, Wanda was only a pale shell of her previous self. Her eyes were sunken, her skin shriveled, and her body wasted. Her decline and the change of her appearance in such a short time made Zoe ashamed she'd questioned Abe's motivation in coming.

"O-ee?" came a little voice from the doorway.

Zoe spun away from the bed to find Lyle standing with a tattered blanket in one hand and a toy bunny in the other. "Hi there, Little Man."

"Ba-bee?" He stepped into the room tentatively, his eyes wide, as though he didn't know what to make of the sight of his mother in bed.

Zoe had slipped out of the cradleboard after arriving and had propped it against the wall with Violet still inside napping contentedly. "Baby Violet's sleeping. Come. I'll show her to you."

Lyle accepted Zoe's outstretched hand and allowed her to guide him to the babe. Zoe gently brushed Violet's hair. Lyle followed her example, almost reverently stroking the babe's head.

As usual, Lyle was unkempt, stains dotting his smart little outfit, jam crusting his mouth and cheeks, and a sour odor indicating his need for a change of undergarments. If Wanda was incapacitated, who was watching the child? Mr. Ping?

With Violet sleeping and Abe praying, Zoe convinced Lyle to lead the way to his bedroom. The boy had no trouble taking her up a winding staircase to the third floor and about halfway down the hallway to a large nursery decorated lavishly with brightly papered walls, cheerful curtains, and a thick rug that was perfect for keeping an infant from having to sit or crawl on the cold floor.

Without a sign of Mr. Ping, Zoe helped Lyle change into clean garments, expecting some resistance from the precocious child, and was surprised when he cooperated completely. He even allowed her to wash his face and comb his hair.

"There." She sat back on her heels. "You look mighty handsome, Little Man."

He stuck his thumb in his mouth and laid his head against her shoulder.

That was all the invitation she needed to draw the boy into her arms. He melted into her further, as if he'd been waiting for someone—anyone—to hold him and give him some assurance he would be okay, even though everything in his world was changing.

She only had to think back to how lost she'd felt when her mum had died to know how scary and lonely the boy must be. At least she'd been old enough to understand. Lyle likely had no idea what was wrong with his mother.

For long minutes, Zoe sat on the rug and simply held the boy, rocking him and pressing kisses to his head.

Finally, she sat up. "Time to check on Baby Violet." She started to set Lyle on his feet, but he clung to her, wrapping his arms around her neck as though he had no intention of letting go. Zoe didn't attempt to pry him loose, deciding he must need the holding and loving a moment longer. Instead, she hefted him up and carried him through the mansion, back down to the second-floor master bedroom.

As she stepped into the room, she saw Abe had moved a safe distance from the bed, his expression guarded, even though

Wanda was clearly too weak to do any enticing. Nevertheless, the wrinkles in Abe's forehead smoothed out at the sight of Zoe.

"Lil' Man," Wanda croaked. "Where's Miss Bea?"

Lyle kept his head on Zoe's shoulder and sucked his thumb noisily, clearly not caring or knowing where Miss Bea was.

"Miss Bea takes good care of him," Wanda said.

Zoe stroked Lyle's hair even as his arms tightened around her neck. She had no idea who Miss Bea was, but clearly the woman wasn't doing enough for the boy. Even so, Zoe decided this was neither the time nor place to argue with Wanda.

"She's old," Wanda said as if reading Zoe's unspoken censure, "and doesn't always have the energy to keep up with Lil' Man."

"Little boys are certainly rambunctious." Zoe pressed another kiss against his head, wishing somehow she could spare the boy all the uncertainty and fear he was experiencing.

She could feel Wanda's scrutiny and prayed the woman wouldn't be upset at her for giving the boy a few more moments of love.

"You're not what I expected."

Zoe glanced up to meet Wanda's glassy gaze. Was Wanda talking about her?

"But you're exactly what Abe needs," Wanda continued breathlessly.

Zoe stepped closer. "Please, Wanda. Save your strength."

"You'll keep him from being too stuffy, that's for sure."

Zoe exchanged a glance with Abe. His expression was grim, confirming what she'd already guessed, that Wanda didn't have many days left.

The woman closed her eyes, and her features constricted, revealing the pain that racked her body. She seemed to be holding her breath until the painful spell subsided, then she expelled a long, heavy sigh. "You really do love Violet, don't you?"

"Aye. I do." Zoe avoided Abe's gaze and the caution sure

to be there. She didn't want to think about losing Violet. Not today. Not at this moment.

"You're good with infants."

"I suppose so."

Again Wanda was silent so that Lyle's noisy thumb-sucking filled the air. *Poor boy. Poor, poor boy.*

"Zoe?" Wanda held out a trembling hand.

Zoe guessed Wanda wanted her to draw closer, but she was wary of doing so. At Abe's nod of encouragement, she crossed to the bed and took Wanda's hand. It continued to shake within Zoe's.

"Zoe," she said more faintly. "Will you take Lil' Man as your own when I'm gone?"

"'Course I will—"

"Wanda," Abe said hurriedly, the protest all too evident in his tone. "We want to help, but that's a big step."

"We can make it work." Zoe tucked Lyle's head into the crook of her neck.

"Do you have family somewhere who could take the boy?" Abe asked. "Or perhaps Mr. Washington's relatives?"

Wanda released a hoarse laugh. "None of them want anything to do with me or my child. As far as they're concerned, I'm dead already and have been for years."

Zoe understood the pain of broken family relationships all too well. "He's a precious child, and we'll do what we can."

Wanda eased back into her pillows.

"Zoe," Abe replied, his tone low, "you know we can't just take on another child."

"If it's the right thing, then why can't we?"

Abe stared at Lyle, his forehead furrowing. "Why don't we think and pray about this before making the decision?"

"I don't have much time, Pastor Abe," Wanda croaked, "and you know it."

Abe nodded solemnly. "I know. And hopefully we can figure out something for Lyle."

"Please, Pastor Abe." Wanda's voice was growing weaker. "I haven't been a good mother to Lil' Man. Giving him to you and Zoe might be the only decent thing I ever do for him."

"That's not true," Abe protested.

Wanda closed her eyes, exhaustion settling over her gaunt features. "Please let me do this."

"Can you give us some time to pray about it?"

She nodded but didn't open her eyes again.

A few minutes later, after finding Miss Bea and handing Lyle over to the older woman, Zoe followed Abe from the mansion. With Violet in the cradleboard upon her back again, Zoe's shoulders ached from the heavy load, and she honestly wasn't sure how she'd be able to care for Lyle too. But her heart swelled with the longing to keep the boy and give him the love he so desperately needed.

Her feet dragged as she left the enormous three-story house behind with its sprawling grassy yard. It was as opulent inside as it was on the outside. And certainly no place for a boy to live alone once Wanda was gone.

"He needs us, Abe." She broke the strained silence between them.

"Zoe," he said sadly, resignedly. "We're already needing to find a home for Violet. We'd eventually have to find one for Lyle too."

"We can keep them both."

Abe stopped and stuffed his hands into his pockets. "You heard what the bishop said. We can't give Violet the kind of life she deserves in England. And Lyle will suffer there too once people learn about Wanda's nature and background."

"We'll give the children lots of love to make up for anything they might face."

"Perhaps. But what if it's not enough?"

"Then let's stay here where they won't have to face so much prejudice."

"I haven't shared the nature of my financial situation with you, Zoe. But I see that I can no longer hold it back."

Zoe hadn't ever really considered Abe's money other than the fact that he seemed to have an endless supply, which allowed her to purchase anything she needed at Allard's General Store.

"I'm not receiving an income for my missionary work here in the colonies." His words came out in a rush. "None of us missionaries are."

"You're not? Then how can we afford everything?"

He took a deep breath as if to fortify himself. "I'm drawing from my personal savings, the money I earned from the vicar position I held before I came here, as well as a small inheritance I received from my mother's father."

"It must not be too small if you can support yourself on it all this time."

"It is significant enough that I can live comfortably." He paused and cleared his throat. "But I cannot rely upon it forever, especially with a growing family to support. I must return to England and resume my work there as a vicar and possibly one day as a bishop."

She tried to make sense of what he was leaving unsaid. "The church won't pay you to be a minister here?"

"Maybe someday when the colony is larger and the financial contributions are more significant. But at present, that isn't the case."

Disappointment sifted over her.

"I'm sorry, Zoe," he said as if reading the regret in her face. "You came here wanting to make this your new home, and so I'll understand if you don't want to go back to England."

She couldn't formulate a response.

"Everything happened between us too quickly. And I wasn't thinking about the long-term consequences."

Her heart sank even more. "Consequences because you have a mill girl for a wife? That I'm a stain on your reputation? That maybe you won't be able to become a bishop now because of me?" Bishop Hills's accusations came rushing out, as did the hurt she'd tried to ignore.

Her rising voice drew the attention of a group of men passing by with several packhorses so heavily loaded with mounds of supplies that their hooves sank deeply into the mud, making their progress slow.

She inhaled and tried to calm herself. Thankfully, Wanda's mansion was set on the edge of town, away from the majority of the activity, away from the prying eyes and listening ears. Even so, she held her tongue as the miners headed out of town on the canyon road.

When they were well out of earshot, Abe spoke again in a low tone. "Everything will be fine, Zoe. You'll see."

"You mean everything will be fine as long as you do exactly what the bishop asks?" Again, she couldn't keep the hurt from lacing her words.

"The bishop and I have already had enough conflict, and I cannot afford any more."

"So you're willing to compromise your convictions and grovel at his feet in order to become a bishop someday? If that's how it's done, then what kind of bishop will you be?"

"It's not just about me becoming a bishop." Frustration radiated from Abe's eyes, more so than she'd ever seen there before. "Bishop Hills has the power to take away my ministry completely. He could make sure I'm not allowed to serve anywhere ever again."

Zoe studied Abe's handsome features. She'd never met a

man as sincere, godly, or kind as Abe. She understood he had plans for the future and that he didn't want to jeopardize his work in the church. But surely he shouldn't have to live in fear of displeasing the bishop. Surely his first priority ought to be obeying God and living to please Him.

"I'm just an ignorant mill girl and don't know much." He opened his mouth to protest, but she continued before he could respond. "But what if God's the one who calls us? What if He's the one who gives us our ministry?"

She thought of the words Mrs. Moresby had spoken to her that afternoon in the Marine Barracks in Victoria when she'd encouraged Zoe to pay attention to what God was asking of her and to follow His leading one step at a time.

"If God gives us our ministry," she continued, "then no one else has the power to take it away. Not even the bishop."

Abe just shook his head. "You don't understand. It's not that simple."

"Maybe it can be."

Behind her, Violet released an unhappy grunt, one that told Zoe the infant was ready for a break from the cradleboard and likely in need of a bottle. Besides, Zoe sensed the conversation with Abe was over, that they'd both said all they could.

"I need to take Violet home."

As she walked away, he didn't try to stop her. With each step, her heart sank lower with the growing realization that while Abe might like her and might even enjoy kissing her, he'd always see her the same way he viewed Violet—as an obstacle. Of course, he'd deny it. But by giving in to the bishop's demands, he was agreeing with the bishop's position.

"Mrs. Merivale!" At a call from the open door of the general store, Zoe forced a smile for Mr. Allard as he waited for her to draw nigh. She made small talk with him for a few moments before he gave her a parcel from Mrs. Moresby. At the light weight and softness of the bundle, Zoe guessed the dear woman had sent her more yarn.

"And I have here a packet for the reverend." Mr. Allard handed her a bundle of letters tied together with brown twine. "Now that he's married, I sure didn't expect him to get any more mail from that gal back in Yorkshire."

Gal in Yorkshire? As in Lizzy?

Zoe followed Mr. Allard's gaze to the top letter, to the lovely, gently flowing penmanship and the name Elizabeth Northrop.

"'Course, it's just a friendly letter, is all." Zoe tucked the packet into her pocket.

"'Course," Mr. Allard replied. "I suspect it's perfectly natural for some men to carry on correspondences with former sweethearts after marriage. Perfectly natural."

The concern in Mr. Allard's eyes was anything but perfectly natural, and Zoe's pulse sped erratically.

As she started up the hillside path toward home, the letters burned ever hotter in her pocket until they were near to searing her skirt by the time she stepped inside the cabin, where she threw the packet onto the table.

All the while she fed Violet and changed her napkin, the top letter seemed to stare at her and mock her. Why was Lizzy writing to Abe? Mr. Allard was right to be concerned. And maybe Zoe needed to be concerned too.

Sitting on the edge of the bed with Violet in her lap, Zoe stood so suddenly that Violet squealed. "She's trying to steal him away from me. That's what."

Zoe set Violet on a blanket with several of the wooden blocks Will had carved for her, then stalked to the table, tugged the letter out from the twine, and tore it open. She had no intention of hiding the fact that she was opening Abe's personal correspondence with Lizzy. He may as well know that she didn't plan to sneak around. If he wanted to get letters from his former love interest, then he'd need to resign himself to Zoe reading every word.

Her fingers trembled as she opened the sheet. It didn't want to unfold, and she had to give it a violent shake before it straightened. She scanned the neat flowing print inside before settling on the first line.

My dearest Abraham, I cannot begin to express the joy I felt upon receiving your last letter containing your marriage proposal asking me to sail to the colony so that we might be together for the duration of your missionary service. Your invitation came at a moment of great trial and unhappiness at the dissolution of my engagement to Daniel Patterson.

Zoe sucked in a sharp breath and then scrambled to keep reading, skimming over the part about how Lizzy had learned of Daniel's unfaithfulness, how she'd been heartbroken, how Abe's letter had come just when she'd needed it.

At the end, Zoe read each word carefully. *All that to say, yes, darling. I accept your proposal of marriage and have made plans to sail to British Columbia on the* Falmouth, *leaving before the New Year. By the time you receive this letter, I hope to arrive shortly thereafter. I will be forever and always your faithful friend. Lizzy.*

Zoe reread the closing and then let the letter fall to the table.

Lizzy was coming to British Columbia. And she planned to marry Abe.

twenty-eight

For an endless moment, Zoe stared at the letter, unable to move or think.

Finally Violet's disgruntled cry over being ignored forced Zoe out of her stupor. She hoisted the babe to her hip, then crossed to the bookshelf, dug behind the stack of books, and retrieved the gilded frame. From beneath a film of dust, Lizzy's serious and yet elegant face peered back at her.

The woman Abe loved was sailing here to marry him. In fact, she could arrive any day and at any moment.

Violet tried to grab the frame at the same time Zoe glanced to the door and tensed for the woman's knock.

After a few seconds of silence, Zoe released a laugh that came out much too shaky and high-pitched.

"This is ridiculous," she said to Violet. "Lizzy isn't gonna come up to Yale. She'll stop in Victoria first. Most likely she'll seek out Bishop Hills. And she'll learn Abe's already married and unavailable."

But was he unavailable?

The question made her knees weak so that she groped for the nearest chair and lowered herself onto it with Violet in her lap. She sat back and closed her eyes against the certainty of what she knew she had to do.

Since the bishop's visit, the pressure had been building—the pressure to separate from Abe and give him freedom.

Today, after calling on Wanda and the disagreement over what to do with Lyle, their differences had become even clearer. And now Lizzy's letter seemed like the final confirmation. There was no more doubt about it. Zoe needed to leave Abe. Today. Now. Before he came home and tried to stop her.

And he would try. Because that's the kind of man he was . . . honorable to his own detriment. He'd never agree to do anything that might harm her reputation or put her at risk. And he'd likely insist on staying together though no good could come of it—even to the point that he would deny himself the opportunity of having Lizzy, who now clearly wanted him and was coming to be with him.

With Lizzy, Abe would be able to realize his potential. He'd please the bishop. He'd be able to return to England without blemish. And he could pursue becoming a bishop, unhindered by a mill girl. Or by lowly children.

Meanwhile, she'd travel to Williamsville and attempt to make a new life for herself there, hopefully with Zeke's help. Once she was settled, she'd send for Lyle. And maybe she'd even convince Will to come live with her so she could be the mum he needed. She'd continue to follow God's leading in caring for the children He brought to her.

The realization of what she needed to do nudged her, yet she couldn't make herself rise from the chair. All she could do was let her gaze drift over the cabin, seeing Abe everywhere— the way he sat with his legs outstretched in front of the stove, one of his books in his lap and his reading glasses perched on his nose, his adoring smile as he tickled Violet's stomach, the peaceful look on his handsome face on the pillow next to hers, the eager glimmer in his eyes whenever he opened the door to one of his parishioners, the kindness in his expression as he patiently explained truths to Will while they ate supper.

Zoe's throat tightened, and tears welled in her eyes. At the thought of endless days and nights without him, her future stretched out before her, bleak, almost unbearable. Was it possible she'd fallen in love with her husband?

The pain in her heart swelled up so that the tears spilled over and started to run down her cheeks. She pressed a fist against her mouth to keep from crying out, and she fought hard against her need for him.

"This is exactly what you told yourself not to do," she chided herself harshly. "You weren't supposed to fall in love with him."

As if hearing the turmoil in Zoe's voice, Violet twisted around, reached up, and touched the tears. Her beautiful eyes widened, and then she pressed her hand against Zoe's cheek as if to say that together they'd be okay.

Zoe inhaled a shaky breath. "Aye, my sweet one. God gave you to me, and I won't let you go. Not unless He makes it very clear He has better plans for you with someone else."

Violet lifted her chin and scrunched her face into a smile that revealed her gums and made her utterly adorable. Zoe bent in and hugged the babe, breathing in the clean scent of lavender soap. Violet leaned in and seemed to hug Zoe back, but then just as quickly began to wiggle, ready to play and move about.

Zoe forced herself up from the chair and positioned Violet back on the blanket on the floor with her toys. Then she set to work packing her bag.

She had a great deal more now than when she'd left Manchester, more even than after she'd departed from Victoria. In fact, with all Violet's clothes, blankets, toys, and necessities, she found she needed a second bag, one she hoped Abe wouldn't mind her taking.

When she'd gathered everything they needed for the journey, she bundled Violet and returned her to the cradleboard. Bags in hand, she stepped out of the cabin, peeking toward Little Joe's cabin to make sure he wasn't watching. Assured her doting neighbor wasn't in view, she closed the door and hurried down the path toward town, praying she wouldn't run into Abe or anyone else who might ask her questions about where she was going.

With caravans of miners leaving all the time, she suspected she'd have no trouble finding a group willing to let her tag along and share their food provisions with her, since she only had enough room for Violet's supplies. At least that's what she was counting on.

As she made her way along the riverfront, pesky doubts swarmed after her. Abe had warned her about the difficulty of the road. Was she taking too great a risk? The heavy rains of recent days made the new sprouts of grass soggy beneath Zoe's boots so that by the time she reached the opposite edge of town, her boots and socks were damp and her toes cold.

A dozen or more mules were already loaded, packs of supplies tied upon their backs. Men milled about, many with new bags, awaiting their first venture up into the canyons in search of gold.

As the prospectors caught sight of her, they ceased their interactions, and silence descended so that blasts of an approaching steamer echoed in the air from the river behind them. Although Yale had grown busier in recent weeks, she hadn't realized exactly how many steamboats and miners were arriving from downriver every day.

Zoe surveyed the group that was readying to leave, trying to figure out which person might be the leader and the one she should speak to about joining the caravan.

"Can I help you, miss?" A tall man with a bushy beard stepped out from behind a mule with a mountain-high mound on its back. From the stains on his trousers, his dusty coat, and his well-worn hat, she guessed he was an old-timer of the goldfields.

"I'm looking for a caravan to ride with." She straightened her shoulders and attempted to make herself look bigger and stronger so that he wouldn't have any reason for turning her away.

He studied her, his expression revealing nothing of what he was thinking. "You bringing the babe?"

"Aye."

"It'll be hard going at times even without the extra load."

"I'm stronger than I look." At least she hoped she was.

His gaze shot behind her, then flickered with apprehension.

Before Zoe could turn and find out what had gained his attention, someone spoke. "I'll take care of her."

She spun to find Dexter Dawson striding her way. "Well, if it isn't Zoe Hart herself. You're looking as pretty as always."

He was walking from the direction of the wharf where several of his companions lounged against their gunnysacks, likely having arrived on one of the steamers still tied along the quay. She hadn't thought much about Dexter since Abe's black eye had faded. But she should have guessed the miner would eventually arrive in Yale before heading up to the goldfields.

"What do you want?" she asked, remembering Bishop Hills's warning that Dexter was planning to fight Abe. She prayed by now he'd given up his need for a brawl.

His brown hair and beard were longer than they'd been the last time she'd seen him. Even so, he was handsome in a self-assured kind of way. "Nice to see you too."

"I'm not interested in talking to you." She lowered her bags, her arms already tired from holding them, and then returned her attention to the bushy-bearded miner.

"You might be interested," Dexter continued, "when I tell you I can take you all the way up to Williamsville to your brother."

She paused in working the kinks out of her arms.

"Thought so." He laughed. "I guess things didn't work out with the holy man?"

"My business isn't any of your concern." She huffed with irritation that Dexter already had figured out her dire straits. "I'm sure I can get to Williamsville just fine without your help. These nice fellas were about to let me join up with them."

"These *nice fellas* don't have any room for you." Dexter's voice took on a hard edge. "Ain't that right, McLean?"

The bushy-bearded man gave a curt nod without meeting Zoe's gaze. "That's right."

"See?" Dexter was close enough now that she could smell the rum on his breath. "And I'm guessing if you ask around, no one else is gonna have room for you either."

"You're planning to make sure of that, aren't you?"

"Yep." Though he grinned, something about it was hard, even dangerous. "Since you want to go, I'm your best option."

"My only option," she groused as she picked up her bags.

He started to take them from her, but she clung to the handles. "Listen, Zoe." Dexter lowered his voice. "I can help you. So let me. Okay?"

She hesitated. She didn't want to give Dexter the idea that she was interested in him. Maybe she'd been willing to marry him once. But after the past few months of being with Abe, she couldn't see herself marrying anyone else, at least not anytime soon. Even just thinking about Abe brought a wave of sadness and loneliness she didn't want to feel.

"I'm not planning to marry you, Dexter."

"Maybe not. But I can still help you find your brother."

She'd known enough fellas like Dexter, and they never did anything for nothing. "What's in it for you?"

His answering grin was slow. "There's plenty in it for me. Don't you worry about that."

268

She scowled. "Just because I'm leaving Abe doesn't mean I'm a loose woman."

He laughed.

She jerked her bags in an attempt to wrest them from his grasp.

"I'm not a brute, Zoe." His expression turned serious. "I prefer a willing woman."

She understood exactly what he was talking about. When Abe had kissed her earlier, she'd been all too willing to fall into his arms, all too willing to kiss him back, all too willing to press nearer. She'd never felt that way with anyone before and doubted she ever would again.

"I need to leave soon." She glanced toward town, hoping to see Abe racing along the river toward her, while another part of her prayed she wouldn't have to face him again. Doing so would make her second-guess her decision, and she couldn't do that.

"He doesn't know you're leaving?"

"No."

"Well, aren't you a sweetheart?"

She hung her head. What she was doing to Abe was downright lousy. But what other choice did she have? "I don't want him to try to change my mind."

"He won't." Dexter's voice contained too much confidence for Zoe's taste. "Besides, we'll be on our way once my men are back with the horses."

She released her bags, and Dexter easily hefted them up to his shoulders. As he started toward his supplies, she followed behind, telling herself she was lucky to find Dexter today, that riding with him was better than tagging along with a group of strangers.

But even with the reassurances, she couldn't keep from thinking she'd made her worst decision yet.

Zoe sat atop her bags with Violet on her lap. The sunshine blanketed them with surprising warmth so that she'd shed her headscarf and shawl.

Violet didn't seem to be in any discomfort. She was bent over and too distracted by digging her fingers into the soft growth of new grass.

Dexter and his four companions readied their horses, talking among themselves and casting her glances. She supposed Dexter had to give them some explanation for why he was helping her, and she still couldn't figure out what that might be.

But with the other caravan well on their way without her, she had little choice but to stay with Dexter.

Unless she waited for Abe to take her up to Williamsville. He'd said he would once he was done with the church-building project.

Violet lifted a fist to her mouth, opened wide, and shoved in the grass she'd managed to pluck.

"No, no, wee one." Zoe pulled Violet's hand away but was too late. Violet was already gumming the tiny green blades. She chewed only for a moment before her face contorted and she began to spit them out.

At the disgust in the infant's expression, Zoe burst out laughing. But as soon as she allowed herself the moment of mirth, grief swelled to replace it. Abe would have laughed too. And Zoe loved his laughter, the way his blue eyes danced, and the peace that settled over his features.

"Oh, Violet, what have I done?" She wiped the grass away from Violet's mouth, and anguish ripped at her heart. She couldn't leave Abe. She loved him too much to simply walk away.

Aye, she'd be selfish to stay, but how could she live without him? And the truth was, he seemed happy with her. They enjoyed being together, talked as friends, and made a good team in serving his parishioners.

Surely they could work out their differences regarding Violet and Lyle. Maybe Abe didn't ever have to know about the letter from Lizzy. . . .

At the thought, Zoe rose so suddenly she nearly stumbled backward over the bags. At her movement, Dexter's attention jerked to her, his brows rising.

All she needed to do was go directly home and toss Lizzy's letter into the stove. She could destroy it within seconds, and Abe would never be the wiser. Unless Mr. Allard asked him about it. Or until Lizzy showed up in Yale.

Zoe paced forward and then back, her mind racing with possibilities. Maybe she could warn Mr. Allard not to say anything. And maybe Lizzy would turn around and sail home after learning of Abe's marriage. Or maybe the gentlewoman would still embark on the journey to Yale, in which case maybe they'd be gone upriver. Whatever happened, Zoe couldn't allow Lizzy to have Abe, could she?

Possessiveness swelled within Zoe. Abe was hers. Aye, he might have married her only because he'd believed he'd lost Lizzy forever. But he was still her husband, and now they needed to make the best of their situation.

With a final finger swipe inside Violet's mouth to dislodge any more grass, Zoe reached for the cradleboard, situated Violet inside, and worked to slip it on over her shoulders. Once Violet was secure, she hefted her bags from the ground and then turned to let Dexter know.

He'd been tying the last of the saddlebags onto a mare, his gaze half on her and half on what he was doing.

"I've decided not to go to Williamsville right now after all."

At her declaration, he cursed under his breath and started toward her.

"I don't want to leave Abe."

"That lover's spat didn't last long." Dexter's tone was loaded with derision.

"It wasn't a lover's spat." Aye, she and Abe didn't see eye to eye on what they needed to do about Violet or Lyle or even about the future. But surely if they prayed together, God would direct them. Maybe God would help them find loving homes for both of the children. And even though she didn't want to return to England, she'd work hard to become the proper wife Abe needed so she wouldn't harm his ministry there. Being with Abe was all that mattered. Together, they could face whatever came their way.

"I don't care what happened," Dexter said. "You know as well as I do you're not Abraham Merivale's type."

She fought against the truth of his words. "We're happy together."

"If you're so happy, then why are you here?"

"You wouldn't understand."

"What I understand is that you were never meant to marry him in the first place. And now you finally realize your mistake."

Was it a mistake? Doubts once again rolled in to cloud Zoe's thoughts.

Dexter took hold of her arm and tugged her forward. "Come on. It's time to go."

For several steps she couldn't find the will to resist him. He'd voiced her fears and maybe even the truth. How could she stay? But how could she leave? She pulled back from Dexter. "I need to go talk to him." It was the least she could do before going.

Dexter's fingers tightened around her upper arm. "We ain't got time for that. Daylight's burning."

She dug her feet into the ground and jerked against Dexter's hold. "I'm gonna return to Abe."

"No, you're not." Dexter yanked her, giving her no choice but to stumble forward.

She twisted, trying to free herself. "Let me go."

He didn't respond except to drag her.

"I've changed my mind," she said louder, fighting his hold. "I'm not going with you."

When he still didn't answer or lessen his grip, worry pricked her, and she thrashed against him. Finally she screamed. She hadn't wanted to draw attention, hadn't wanted any of the townspeople to question where she was going or why and then run back to Abe and tell him. But now that was exactly what she hoped for. She needed someone to see her and come to her aid.

She only had the chance to release one scream before Dexter cupped a hand over her mouth. In the same movement, he wrenched her up so that she had no choice but to fall against him.

"Listen here, Zoe," he growled, his face only inches from hers. "You can come with me nice-like and things'll be easy for you. But if you fight me, then you'll force me to make this difficult."

His hand smothered her mouth. Even so, she attempted another scream. Why was Dexter making her go with him?

As if seeing the question in her eyes, he pressed closer, his voice low. "Once good ole Jeremiah Hart learns I've got his sister, I won't have to steal his gold. He'll hand it right over, especially if he wants to see you alive."

It took a moment for Dexter's threat to register, but when it did, she attempted to protest. Apparently Dexter was kidnapping her and holding her for ransom. Too bad he didn't realize that if Jeremiah Hart really was Zeke, her brother probably wouldn't want to see her, that he'd said he didn't want to have anything to do with her ever again.

'Course, sometimes people said things in anger that they didn't mean—and that's what she was hoping for. But in all the time Zeke had been gone, he hadn't written once or reached out to her. And while she'd clung to the hope that he'd see her, that she'd be able to apologize, and that maybe he'd even forgive her, she doubted her brother would hand over gold to ransom her.

She tried to speak, but Dexter's hand clamped harder, and his scowl deepened. She struggled, anger and panic mingling together to give her a burst of strength that helped her to break out of his grasp, but only for a few seconds. He caught her arm and bent it at a painful angle, one that made her cry out only to have him slap her mouth.

At Violet's wail in the cradleboard behind her, Zoe held herself motionless even as her thoughts rioted.

Dexter's eyes blazed. "You try to break free again, and I'll go find your holy man just like I'd originally planned, and I'll teach him the lesson he has coming. Believe me, he won't walk away from the fight this time."

Dexter wasn't threatening to kill Abe, was he?

At the deadly gleam in the miner's eyes, Zoe let her protest fade. Whether Dexter intended to kill Abe or just hurt him, Zoe couldn't take any chances. She had to do whatever she could to keep Abe safe . . . even if that meant cutting herself off from him and leaving him behind.

twenty-nine

The evening chill nipped Abe as he climbed the path toward home. He whistled as he usually did, but somehow the melody of praise to the Lord fell flat and his mind kept replaying his conversation with Zoe from earlier in the day when they'd left Wanda's house.

"So you're willing to compromise your convictions and grovel at his feet in order to become a bishop someday? If that's how it's done, then what kind of bishop will you be?"

What kind of bishop indeed? Abe let his whistling fade away and instead lifted his face to the cloudless sky overhead. Within the dark violet, the first few stars winked at him as though asking him why he cared about being a bishop anyway.

Certainly he wasn't pursuing the position for the prestige, was he? Maybe his parents and Lizzy had supported his decision because of the power and status it would bring. But he hadn't considered that, had only been drawn to the leadership role because it would afford him more opportunities to do good.

Ever since the deaths of his parishioners in Sheffield, he'd wanted to push for reforms within the church. With so many regulations and traditions holding rectors above the people, he longed to break down barriers so ministers could shepherd their flocks more effectively and compassionately.

But if he went along with everything Bishop Hills required him to do, then Zoe was right. He'd compromise one conviction at a time until eventually he was the kind of rector and bishop he hoped to change.

As he passed Little Joe's cabin, his footsteps slowed. Even though he'd had all afternoon while hammering away on the new church's roof to think about his argument with Zoe, his thoughts were still too full and he wasn't sure he was ready to face her quite yet. She'd probably ask him if he'd made a decision regarding Lyle.

On the one hand, he loved that she was so compassionate. He wanted to have an open home and open heart to anyone in need, and he'd discovered Zoe operated in the same way. She never turned people away and always helped wherever she could.

But opening their home to every orphan who came along? Wasn't that taking things too far?

Even as he wanted to find fault with her, he couldn't find fault with God's Word, which commanded His people to take care of widows and orphans. Hadn't he recently read in the Psalms the verse that said, "Defend the poor and fatherless: do justice to the afflicted and needy"?

She'd been right when she'd told him that because God gave them their ministry, no one else had the power to take it away. While the bishop might be able to revoke titles and positions with the Church of England, he couldn't revoke God's calling to minister.

In his heart, Abe knew it was better to obey God rather than man. But he still couldn't keep from fearing what would happen if he pushed onward in following God's leading rather than listening to the bishop. There was the very real chance he could lose everything—not only his work in the colonies, but all future opportunities in England. In fact, maybe he'd have no reason to return to England at all.

Without a church to serve in British Columbia or in England, what would he do? He could continue to preach and serve the miners the same as always, except without the support of Bishop Hills. He loved living in Yale, and it would be an ideal place to raise both Violet and Lyle.

But how would he provide for Zoe and the children? Especially long term, after he depleted his funds? His parents wouldn't continue to support him—not if the bishop suspended his license to preach and administer sacraments. They'd likely want nothing more to do with him.

He stopped, his heart thudding with the same nervousness that came over him whenever the bishop threatened him. "Lord," he whispered, "do I have enough faith to believe that if you called me to minister in new and different ways, you'll provide the means for my ministry?"

His pulse sped with the worries of an unsettled future, one without all the answers, one in which he would truly have to walk by faith and not by sight.

Could he do it?

"Lord, give me the courage and strength to seek your kingdom and righteousness first. For you promise that when I do, you'll provide all else."

He prayed for a short while longer before resuming his trek. At the sight of the cabin ahead, peace rushed over him. He picked up his pace, ready to talk to Zoe. The light emanating from the window welcomed him and filled him with the need to draw her into his arms.

Of course, he had some explaining to do before he earned the right to hold her again. But his heart pattered with anticipation anyway. Whistling for the last few steps, he pushed open the door and searched for her. At the sight of a barren stove without the usual scent of a meal, his gaze swung to the bed. Did she have one of her headaches?

The bed was empty, the covers pulled up neatly.

Will sat at the table, carving another block for Violet. He looked up expectantly with the beginning of a smile, but it quickly faded as he took in Abe. "Where are Zoe and Violet?"

"I don't know." Abe closed the door behind him and tried to think of where she might have gone this late in the day. Had she returned to visit Wanda and Lyle? Or maybe she'd walked down to Shantytown as she did whenever she wanted to check on the women and children who'd lost so much during the fire.

Even as he sorted through the possibilities, a strange uneasiness sifted through him. Zoe was always home by dusk, even on those days he was returning from an out-of-town trip. Almost always—except for the rare times she had a headache—she greeted him with one of her lovely smiles and offered him a cup of tea to tide him over until she finished making supper.

What had happened to keep her away?

"Did you see her this afternoon?" he asked Will.

"Nope. Didn't see her a lick after she left the livery."

Abe rested a hand on the door handle. Maybe one of his parishioners had come seeking his help. Maybe she'd gone out in his stead. "Were there any emergencies around town today that you heard about?"

"Nope. Nothing unusual." Will peered closely at the outline of the dog he was carving.

"Maybe I'll head back down to Wanda's and see if she went back there."

Will stuck his tongue out in concentration, his knife working magic on the wood. The boy was talented, and Abe never hesitated to let him know.

"If she comes back before I do, let her know I'm looking for her."

"Sure thing."

Abe turned and lifted the latch.

"Oh, I forgot," Will said quickly. "Dexter Dawson's in town. His men came into the livery for horses."

Abe froze, an icy cold trickling into his veins. Abe had expected Dex would eventually show up. He'd even expected another confrontation, especially after the bishop's warning.

But surely it was a coincidence Zoe had disappeared on the day Dexter arrived. Surely Zoe hadn't sought out Dex. Why would she? Not when she was happy with their marriage.

Even as Abe tried to reassure himself, doubts wafted in. She hadn't been happy earlier in the day when they'd parted ways. In fact, she hadn't been all that happy over the past few weeks since the bishop's visit.

"You don't think Dex got ahold of her, do you?" Will's brow furrowed as he set aside his knife and the block, well informed of all that had transpired with Dex when they'd been in Victoria.

A burst of anxiety hit Abe. Maybe Zoe hadn't gone to Dex. Maybe Dex had sought her out instead.

Will shoved back from the table, his freckled face etched with worry. "Are her things here? I don't see Violet's blocks." The boy got up and began to rummage around.

Abe watched Will, ashamed to admit he didn't normally pay attention to where Zoe kept her or Violet's clothing and other belongings. He had a hard enough time keeping track of his own stuff, much less anyone else's.

His cabin had never been neater or more organized since Zoe had come, and he hadn't expressed his appreciation oft enough for all she did—the laundering, mending, cooking, cleaning, and probably a dozen other things he wasn't aware of. When he next saw her, he'd have to be sure to thank her.

"I don't see anything of Violet's." Will's eyes rounded and brimmed with panic. "What if Dex took Zoe and Violet?"

"Let's not jump to conclusions." But already Abe's own panic had spiked. He stalked to the bed and glanced underneath. Her bag was gone.

He crossed to the chest, threw open the lid, and rummaged inside. The only items there were his neatly folded clothes. He didn't see a stitch of women's or baby clothing anywhere. Dropping the lid, he charged across the room toward the kitchen supplies Zoe had lined up neatly on the shelves. He skimmed them, searching for Violet's bottle parts to no avail.

With his heart thudding hard and fast, he spun and scanned the cabin, praying, hoping for any sign of what had happened. The only items out of place were a bundle of letters on the table and a sheet of paper on Zoe's chair by the stove.

He stepped over to the chair, grabbed the paper, and unfolded it. At the sight of Lizzy's penmanship, Abe's wildly beating pulse slammed to a halt. Was this a new letter from Lizzy? Or had Zoe found this among the stack of old ones he kept with his books?

Smoothing out the sheet, he found the date at the top. *December 1862.*

She'd written it over four months ago, which meant it had just arrived.

He frowned. Why did Zoe have his letter? He supposed Mr. Allard could have given it to her to bring home. Even so, why would she have opened something addressed to him? Especially so personal a correspondence?

"What did you find?" Will asked. "A note from Zoe?"

"No. This is . . . from someone else." How could he explain to Will who Lizzy was and what she'd meant to him?

Abe glanced again to Zoe's chair. What if their situations had been reversed and Zoe had received a letter from a former fiancé? Abe had no doubt he'd want to know the contents. He couldn't be upset at Zoe for being curious.

Besides, he had nothing to hide from Zoe. Lizzy had likely written in response to his letter belatedly asking her to travel to British Columbia and marry him. She'd probably described how sorry she was for him but how happy she was with Daniel Patterson.

Rather than subject himself to further humiliation, Abe had half a mind to burn the letter without reading it. But against his better judgment, his attention dropped to the greeting: *My dearest Abraham.*

She'd always opened her letters with that salutation. But wasn't such familiarity inappropriate for a married woman?

"Who's it from?" Will asked.

Abe couldn't answer. Instead, he continued reading and immediately sat down, the shock of Lizzy's news draining the strength from his body. Lizzy hadn't married Daniel after all. Moreover, she had accepted Abe's invitation to sail to the colonies and marry him.

He skimmed over the paragraphs detailing the items she planned to bring for their home as well as gifts sent by his parents. *I do hope you will have your maid make all the necessary arrangements at your house before my arrival. Perhaps the new rectory will even be completed by the time I reach Yale so that we might start our new life together there. Whatever the case, I am certain I shall soon be happy again once I am away from the scandal here and happily ensconced in a marriage of my own.*

Will stood at Abe's side. From his scrunched-up forehead and his attempts at sounding out words, he was attempting to read the letter.

Abe folded it back up before the boy could piece anything together. Will wouldn't understand why another woman was coming and might even get angry. He adored Zoe and Violet. Zoe was like the mother he'd never known, and he saw Violet as his little sister. Yes, Will would be angry at him for inviting Lizzy.

Angry. A vise clamped around Abe's heart. Had Zoe read the letter and gotten angry? Maybe she'd misunderstood and believed he'd written the invitation to Lizzy recently. Maybe she thought he didn't want her anymore and was planning to set her aside for Lizzy.

With elbows propped on his knees, he dropped his head into his hands and groaned.

"What?" Will's voice rang with worry.

"I made a mess of things."

"I just figured you might."

Abe lifted his head to find Will standing before him, his eyes narrowed with condemnation.

"I don't know much about women, but any ole fool could see you made everyone else more of a priority than her. You're always rushing around to help others, which is good. But maybe she don't think she matters."

The boy's words sounded vaguely like John Roberts's admonition to take care with his marriage and work at becoming the kind of husband God wanted him to be. He'd attempted to do some little things for Zoe to show he cared. But maybe Will was right. Maybe he'd neglected the most important thing of all—making her a priority.

In an effort to prove to Bishop Hills—and himself—that he wouldn't let his marriage and family interfere with his work, he'd obviously put his work first. Was that one more way he'd let his fear of the bishop and the future dictate how he behaved in the present?

In making his ministry his top priority, he'd expected Zoe to adjust to his schedule and lifestyle but hadn't given any thought to how such selfishness would affect her. He wasn't a single missionary any longer, and he had to stop acting like he was.

He had a wife . . . and a child. And they deserved more from him than the leftovers of his life.

He scooted farther back into the chair only to bump into something and cause it to fall to the floor with a clatter. He reached down and picked it up. At the sight of the framed picture he'd kept of Lizzy, the clamp around his heart pinched tighter. Although he'd forgotten the portrait, Zoe must have found it when she'd tidied up. Where had he left it? Perhaps on the bookshelf?

It didn't matter now where he'd kept it, only that he had.

What must Zoe think of him hanging on to Lizzy's picture and never throwing it away? Why hadn't he?

Will leaned in and studied the picture. "Who's that?"

Abe couldn't hide the truth from the boy any longer. "This is Lizzy, my former fiancée, the woman I planned to wed before I met Zoe. And now she's on her way here, assuming I want to marry her."

Will gave a low whistle. "Guess that's why Zoe left you. She figured you must still love Lizzy, what with getting a letter and having her picture and all."

Abe had the urge to bury his face in his hands and block everything out. But there was no escaping his mistakes.

"Do you?" Will's brow furrowed and his expression turned fierce.

"Do I what?"

"Still love Lizzy?"

He studied Lizzy's familiar face. He'd always believed she'd make the perfect minister's wife. Of course, he'd once been the perfect minister, doing everything right, following the traditions handed down to him, and never questioning the way of things. At one time, they had been right for each other.

Over the past three years, he'd recognized he was going a new direction, but hadn't given it much thought except during the times he came into conflict with the bishop. However, since marrying Zoe, he'd begun to see more clearly the path where God was leading him.

If God was calling him to a new way of ministering, then perhaps God had orchestrated his marriage to the kind of helpmate he needed. Zoe and Lizzy were as different as any two women could be. But Zoe was exactly right for him and for the work God was giving him—giving *them*.

He couldn't imagine Lizzy, with all her proper ways, living here in Yale—in this tiny cabin or a rectory—not the way Zoe did. Lizzy wouldn't open the door and feed strangers, not even a scraggly orphan boy like Will. Lizzy wouldn't reach out to the neighbors with food and handmade mittens. She wouldn't have gone down to the fire at Shantytown and never would have mingled with foreigners or the women of ill repute. Even if she'd involved herself in the relief efforts, Lizzy wouldn't have returned to the displaced people to check on their welfare on numerous occasions. Certainly Lizzy wouldn't have visited Wanda's home. While she might have shown some concern over Lyle, she wouldn't have insisted on caring for the boy.

"Then I take it you still love Lizzy?" Will asked, an edge to his tone.

Abe turned the frame over and met the boy's gaze. "I love Zoe." The moment he admitted his feelings, tears sprang to his eyes.

Will studied his face. "You're sure?"

Abe blinked hard to fight away the rush of emotion. "I love her more than I ever thought possible to love any woman."

Will's shoulders relaxed and a grin tugged at the corners of his mouth. "Good. Cuz I was gonna have to punch you if you didn't."

Abe's love for Zoe was suddenly so clear that his previous feelings for Lizzy couldn't begin to compare. They'd had friendship and companionship. But his relationship with Zoe was all that and more. It was vibrant and alive, and their connection was deep.

And now he'd lost her.

"I've really botched things, haven't I?"

Will folded his arms across his chest, his expression once again serious. "Aye, but the good thing is that Zoe's real forgiving and kind. If you tell her you're sorry and you aim to do better, she won't hold it against you."

Abe did "aim" to do better. It had taken Zoe's leaving and the words of an orphan boy for him to finally recognize his need to prioritize his marriage over his ministry and to see Zoe as the gift from the Lord that she truly was. "I need to figure out a way to get her back."

"Where do you think she went?"

"She might try to make her way to Zeke up in Williamsville." For all he knew, she could have gone anywhere, even back to Victoria. But since she'd wanted to find Zeke all along, he suspected that was her destination. If only he'd been more sensitive to her need to find her brother instead of putting his church work and fears first.

"So you don't think she went off with Dex?"

"It's possible." Abe's chest squeezed painfully at the thought of her willingly going to Dex. She probably figured if the man had offered to take her to Zeke once before, he might still be willing. And perhaps Dex had accepted, guessing he could pay Abe back for stealing Zoe away from him.

Will crossed to the door and unhooked his coat. "Well, whatcha waiting for? Let's go on after her before she gets too far away."

Abe stood, his senses and muscles coming to life at the prospect of chasing after Zoe, finding her, and declaring his love. If Zoe really had left with Dex and his men, they wouldn't have gone far. The town of Boston Bar was twenty-six miles up the canyon, north of Yale. With its few taverns and hotels, it was a popular stopping area after a busy day of traveling. However, if Dex had left in the afternoon, Abe doubted he'd be able to travel the full distance to Boston Bar, not with a woman and child slowing him down.

It was possible that if Abe left now, he might reach Zoe before daybreak. Maybe he'd even be able to sneak her away in the dark before Dex or his men were the wiser. All the better to avoid another confrontation like the one in Victoria.

Hopefully she'd come with him willingly. He'd get down on his knees and beg her if he had to. In fact, he'd do or say anything to win her back.

As Will donned his coat, Abe removed his rifle from the rack above the door. While he used the gun primarily for hunting purposes, he'd learned to carry it with him during his travels. He'd never had to use it to fight a man, and he prayed this time would be no different.

thirty

*A*be slowed his steps in front of the livery. "Saddle up two horses," he instructed Will. "And meet me down at Hemming's Pub just as soon as you can."

Will nodded and bounded off inside to take care of their mounts. The darkness of night had fully descended. Without street lanterns, the light from the taverns and hotels provided the only guidance to the busy thoroughfare.

Nightlife was just beginning with the sounds of piano music, laughter, and shouts wafting into the street as Abe lengthened his stride and made his way to the far side of town close to the riverfront and Shantytown.

He didn't halt until he reached the front door of Hemming's Pub. As he stepped inside the dimly lit eating house, the scent of baked sturgeon overpowered him. Many of the tables were still full, while the rest were littered with plates and mugs from those who'd had their fill and gone their way.

Abe glanced around for Mr. Hemming only to find a dozen pairs of eyes upon him. Everyone had stopped eating and talking to stare. The clatter of a fork and knife against a plate echoed in the silence.

He removed his hat, smoothed back his hair, and then took another step into the room. "I'm looking for Mr. Hemming."

At the ensuing silence and intense scrutiny, Abe squirmed with the need to retreat into the coolness of the night. What was going on? Where were the warm greetings that usually met him everywhere he went?

"Pastor Abe. I thought I heard your voice." Mr. Hemming limped out of the kitchen, one towel draped over his shoulder and another between his hands.

At the sight of the stoop-shouldered older man, Abe released a tense breath.

"What can I do for you?" Mr. Hemming asked.

Abe lowered his voice. "May I speak with you in private?"

"You may as well speak your piece in front of everyone." Mr. Hemming's usual smile was gone, replaced by a deep groove between his brows.

"My piece?"

"Everyone knows you've been carrying on with another woman and that Mrs. Merivale up and left you today because of it."

"What?" Abe bristled, straightening to his full height. "That's not true."

Mr. Hemming crossed his arms and scowled. Abe glanced around the dining room to find that almost everyone else was scowling at him too.

"It's true I received a letter today from the woman I once intended to marry. But I haven't been 'carrying on' with her. Not in the least. I haven't written to her or received mail from her since I got married."

"Then can you tell us why Mrs. Merivale was so upset and determined to leave town?"

Again, every gaze fixed upon him. The wariness and mistrust in their eyes was more confirmation that he hadn't been the kind of husband Zoe deserved.

"Unfortunately, this friend from Yorkshire is on her way to the colony to marry me. She doesn't realize I already have a wife."

Murmurs erupted around the room.

"Rest assured, I have no intention of abandoning Mrs. Merivale." After today's letter incident, he apparently needed to have a talk with Mr. Allard about the danger of spreading rumors.

"Then you're not divorcing your wife?" came a call from across the room.

"Of course not," he said adamantly. Although he'd briefly considered annulling their marriage the morning after the wedding, he hadn't contemplated the idea again, not even once. And he still had no intention of it.

"I confess when I brought Mrs. Merivale here to Yale as my bride, I didn't realize the treasure I'd been given. But over these past weeks, the Lord has shown me just what a precious gift she is. I couldn't ask for a better wife—" His voice surprised him by filling with emotion and breaking off. He quickly cleared his throat. "I love her more than my own life. And I don't want to lose her—" Again his voice cut out.

Thankfully, his confession seemed to soothe away the hostility, and the eyes peering at him filled with compassion instead.

"Glad to hear it, Pastor Abe." Mr. Hemming approached, the usual friendly smile in place. "I was telling everyone I didn't see how anyone could kiss his wife the way you did and not love her."

Abe fidgeted again, this time with embarrassment. "I'm actually heading out right now to go after Mrs. Merivale to explain the misunderstanding, and I hope to bring her home."

The nods around the room bolstered Abe's determination. Everyone seemed to approve of his efforts except a lone stranger at a corner table who shook his head curtly. With the brim of his hat pulled low over his face, his features were too shadowed for Abe to distinguish. Nevertheless, the man's censure radiated like a beacon in the dead of night.

"That's why I stopped by." Abe focused on the rest of the patrons. "While I have my suspicions she may have headed up into the canyon, it's possible she might have gone downriver toward Victoria. I was hoping someone saw her earlier and can give me more information on her whereabouts."

He didn't want to start on the canyon route only to later discover she'd gone somewhere else entirely. If anyone could help him, Mr. Hemming was the man. Since his pub was near the waterfront as well as the trailhead, surely someone had come in with news not only of Zoe's leaving but of where she'd gone.

Sure enough, one of the patrons called out, "Heard someone say she was talking with McLean."

Hope flickered inside Abe. McLean was a rough-looking fellow, but he was decent and would look out for Zoe.

"Nah," said another man from a table close by. "She took off with Dexter Dawson. Saw her riding out with him."

Abe's hope quickly snuffed out. "You saw her with your own eyes?"

The man hesitated. "Couldn't be sure, since I just arrived and never saw Mrs. Merivale before. But she were a real purty lady with a babe on her back."

"That's her." Mr. Hemming nodded his head vigorously. "With Violet."

Abe replaced his hat. "Then I guess I'll be heading out tonight to chase her down."

"You won't be getting her back," said the stranger in the corner. "At least not tonight. And not by yourself."

The certainty in the man's voice stopped Abe.

The stranger pushed away from the table and rose. When he tipped up his hat, the shadows fell away to reveal dark hair and a handsome face with features that seemed vaguely familiar.

He wasn't a particularly large man, but something about his presence was overpowering, and the other patrons fell silent again.

He wound through the maze of tables and outstretched legs until he stood in front of Abe. He hooked his thumbs in his belt and studied Abe like a sheriff would a criminal. When he finally looked Abe in the eyes, the green was bright and keen and curious.

Abe pressed a hand against his pocket and the wedding band waiting for Zoe's finger. The man's eyes were the color of jade. The same as Zoe's.

Abe's pulse sped up. "Zeke?"

The man had long, dark lashes that were the same as Zoe's. "The name's Jeremiah. Jeremiah Hart."

He had to be Zoe's brother. Determined to find out, Abe leaned in and lowered his voice. "Your real name is Zeke, isn't it?"

The man hesitated, wariness creasing his features.

"You're Zoe's twin brother."

"Aye."

Abe nodded, relieved that Jeremiah and Zeke were the same person. Zoe would be glad to know it. "She's talked about you. And you share similar features."

"So you're the minister she married?"

"Yes, I'm Abe." He reached out for a handshake, trying to comprehend the fact that Zeke was here in Yale.

Zeke gripped Abe's hand solidly.

"Then you received Zoe's letter?" Abe asked. "She got word that you might be in Williamsville, and she's been waiting anxiously to find you."

"Aye. I got her letter. That's why I'm here." Zeke spoke quietly, somberly. Was that regret in his green eyes? Maybe Zeke was as anxious to see Zoe as she was him. "Arrived in town early this afternoon. By the time I asked around and found out where she was living, no one was home. I went back several times, but she was never there."

"She'll be happy to see you and is hoping to make things right with you."

Zeke stared at his boots a moment before meeting Abe's gaze again, despair clouding his eyes. "With the way I left, I'm the one who needs to make things right with her."

"Zoe came to tell you that you're a free man. The real culprits were caught, and you've been exonerated."

"Really?" Zeke's head lifted and eyes widened. The expression reminded Abe so much of Zoe that his chest hurt.

"Yes. Really. I'll let Zoe tell you all the details once we find her." Abe clamped Zeke on the shoulder. "You'll come along and help me bring her back, won't you?"

"'Course. Wouldn't consider doing anything else." Zeke finally let his sights trail over the others in the pub, who'd mostly gone back to eating. "But I have to warn you that if Zoe's with Dex, then she's in a lot of danger."

Fear pricked the back of Abe's neck. "He's a dangerous man. But I don't think he'll harm Zoe. He wanted to marry her and planned on it until I stepped in and married her first."

"So he's angry at you too?"

"Too?"

Zeke rubbed a hand across the back of his neck as if he had the same fear pricking him. "Dex blames me for stealing a claim from him. Says he got to the land first and that it's his. But he knows as well as I do that it's mine."

"So you're doing well for yourself?"

"Aye." Zeke nodded. "I struck pay dirt nigh to the surface last spring and am still pulling out two to three thousand dollars' worth a day."

"Then you're doing more than well." At that amount, Zeke

was a very wealthy man, maybe one of the richest in British Columbia.

From the way Zeke dressed and carried himself, he clearly hadn't let his riches turn him into a proud man as Abe had seen the rapid rise to wealth do to other miners who landed upon profitable claims.

"Unfortunately, Dex wants my gold," Zeke said. "He's been trying to figure out a way to steal it away from me. And he may have just succeeded."

"We won't let him get away with it."

Zeke leveled a look at Abe that sent a chill up his backbone. "No doubt the minute Dex figured out Zoe was my sister, he started plotting how he could use her to get my gold."

Was that why Dex had offered to marry Zoe in the first place and why he'd been so angry when Abe had beaten him to it? So he could use her in his battle to take possession of Zeke's gold?

"He won't hurt her," Abe said more to assure himself than Zeke. Even so, his insides twisted hard. If only he'd been a better husband, Zoe wouldn't have run away. She would have wanted to stay with him.

Even as the guilt assaulted Abe, he realized he needed to find Zoe and get her away from Dex as soon as possible. "Can you be ready to go soon? We need to leave right away."

Zeke hooked his thumbs back into his belt. "Dex always has at least four to five men with him wherever he goes. We'll have a better chance of rescuing Zoe if we form a posse so we have the same number or more."

"Will we have to fight them for Zoe?"

"I have no doubt we will."

The gravity in Zeke's tone only stirred the urgency in Abe, and he silently lifted a prayer for Zoe's safety. He couldn't bear the thought that Dex might hurt or use her in any way. The prospect nearly made him ill. "I can't let anything happen to her," he whispered, his voice suddenly hoarse. "I love her."

"I can see that." Zeke cracked a faint smile. "But you should know that once we free Zoe, if she doesn't want to be with you, I'm taking her with me back to Williamsville."

"I understand." Abe swallowed the fear that kept pushing up. "But you'll give me the chance to win her first, won't you? I can't let her go without trying."

Finally Zeke's smile spread, showing dimples identical to Zoe's. "Good answer. I think I might like you after all."

thirty-one

Zoe shifted on her bedroll, unable to sleep, her body aching from so many hours on the horse. Even with the pine boughs the men had cut and laid out several inches deep, the earth was damp and cold. She hadn't been warm since she'd started the journey hours ago.

Dexter had pushed them onward relentlessly, even after darkness had fallen and they'd had only their lanterns to guide them. Finally, they'd reached a low area along the bank of the Fraser River, a place where other travelers were making camp, apparently one of the few level areas in the canyon that allowed for stopping.

Abe had been right about the trail. It was muddy, slick, and narrow. In some places the road wound on cliffs so high above the river that the drop would have been deadly. When she'd asked if anyone had ever fallen, the men had laughed and proceeded to tell her one horror story after another about miners and mules plummeting to their deaths on the rocks below. She'd clung more tightly to Dexter after that, praying she'd make it to Williamsville alive and resolving never to question Abe's judgment again.

She snuggled Violet closer, giving the babe every bit of body heat she could. Though the temperatures had dropped as they'd reached the higher elevation, the campfire blazed, putting out a measure of warmth. Two of Dexter's friends sat close to it, feeding it fuel they'd cut from the endless supply of pine all around.

Dexter and two others were stretched out on bedrolls near Zoe. From the minute they'd lain down, their instant snoring told her just how accustomed they were to sleeping out in the wilderness. Neither the cold, nor the blackness of the night, nor the strange animal noises bothered any of them.

Even though Zoe had closed her eyes and attempted to sleep, each eerie howl, croak, and hoot had made her shiver. Dexter had warned her of the wolves and coyotes that were especially hungry after the long winter. He'd likely done it to scare her from trying to escape.

But he needn't have worried. She had no plans to leave, wild animals or not. While she considered herself a fairly brave and determined woman, she wasn't stupid enough to navigate the trail in the dark by herself. It was hard enough by daylight and would be deadly at night.

Besides, how could she travel in ankle-deep mud while weighted down with Violet and make any progress? Dexter would catch up to her and then carry through on his threat to harm Abe.

And there was no telling what he'd do to her. While he'd been considerate of her needs thus far, she was only a pawn in a bigger game he was playing with Zeke, and when he no longer needed her, he wouldn't think twice about disposing of her.

She shuddered. Aye, the best course of action for now was to cooperate. Then once she got to Williamsville, she'd write to Abe and tell him where she was.

A vision of Lizzy's face sifted through Zoe's mind. What if Lizzy arrived during her absence? What if the young gentlewoman made a claim on Abe before Zoe could tell him how she really felt?

With fresh worry pounding through her body, Zoe decided to give up on sleep altogether. She opened her eyes, rolled to her back, and peered up at the sky. Only a few wispy clouds blocked the view of the thousands upon thousands of stars. She breathed in deeply, taking in the aroma of pine mingled with the thick smoke of the damp burning wood.

The canyon was beautiful, even if it was ruggedly dangerous. Maybe the grandeur of the place was worth treasuring even more because of the danger involved in getting there.

Wasn't that a reflection of life? Beautiful things usually co-existed with pain and danger. The two walked hand in hand on the same path, and the contrast only made the beauty and joy all the greater.

She'd thought she needed to cut herself off from loving and investing in relationships because of the pain of loss. But whenever she considered her friendship with Jane and all the wonderful times they'd had together, she couldn't imagine giving that up just so she didn't have to feel the sorrow of losing her friend. She would have missed out on so much joy.

Wasn't that the way it was with Abe too? She didn't know how long she'd have him. There weren't any guarantees. But she didn't want to hold herself back from loving him and miss out on the joy and beauty because she was too focused on the dangers.

As she took in the stars, she remembered the sky the way it had been on the night they'd watched the northern lights, the easy way they could talk, the pleasure she had in his company, the way his smile made her insides tumble. She wanted more times like that for as long as God would give them to her.

She sighed her regret at reacting so rashly earlier and running away, and her eyelids drooped in weariness.

A hand covered Zoe's mouth and startled her awake. For an instant, Zoe fought to understand where she was and what was happening.

At the sight of the starry sky overhead, everything came rushing back. Dexter had forced her to leave Yale with him. After riding up into the mountains, they'd camped for the night. And now someone was taking advantage of her, the lone woman in the group.

As her attacker pulled her off her bedroll, she thrashed wildly and attempted to break free. She couldn't see her captor, but he was exceptionally strong and pinned her hands behind her back with his free hand.

She tried to make a noise, to scream, even to grunt. But the hand over her mouth and nose stifled the sound. A glance in the direction of the fire told her the two who'd been feeding the flames wouldn't be of much help in protecting her anyway. Though sitting, they'd rested their heads and closed their eyes, shirking their duties.

Whoever was assaulting her had apparently been watching for this opportunity when no one was awake to defend her—maybe one of the fellas from a nearby camp. He crept with such stealth that no one would be able to hear him above the rushing of the river nearby. He half carried, half dragged her toward the forested area behind them.

Her mind screamed at her to figure out a way to free herself or alert Dexter of her danger before she was out of sight and out of range for anyone to rescue her.

She kicked and twisted and even tried to bite the hand that was across her mouth. But the hold was too immovable and strong. From the corner of her eye, she caught sight of another intruder slinking close-by, but only the outline.

Did more than one man intend to assault her?

As the darkness of the forest closed in around her and branches scraped her, she expected that any moment he'd drop her to the ground. She tensed in readiness, determined to hit, claw, and kick, even if she was outnumbered.

The blackness of the wild thick pines and night combined so that she couldn't see anything, not even the sky. Her captor moved with surprising swiftness and agility. And he hardly made a sound. She couldn't hear the other person either. But the frightened cry of a babe came from not far away.

Violet? Had the men taken Violet too?

Anger and fear erupted inside Zoe. How dare they harm an innocent babe? Zoe flailed again and managed to wrench one of her arms free. She pounded it against her captor, desperate to free herself and rescue Violet.

The man grabbed her hand again and this time picked her up into his arms so that he was no longer dragging her. She bucked against him and wrestled to free herself, suddenly sensing that this wasn't a man from another camp.

The leather clothing was strange and his movements too certain to belong to a miner. As he stepped into a thinning area of forest, the canopy of branches overhead opened enough for her to see his bronzed face. His dark hair was smoothed back into braids, and his expression was fierce.

"No more fight," he said in broken English. "Must be quiet."

But Zoe had already stopped fighting, too frightened to do anything but stare. During the voyage from England to the colonies, the women had liked to tell one another stories. Some of their favorites had been about natives kidnapping English colonists and forcing them to become their slaves. Many of the abducted were never seen again, but a few were later recovered hardly recognizable, as they'd become part of the tribe with whom they'd lived for so many years.

As the native carried her deeper into the forest, Zoe closed her eyes to block out what was happening. She'd thought being kidnapped by Dexter Dawson was bad enough. But this was worse. Much worse.

thirty-two

The rocks beneath Abe dug into his ribs and thighs where he lay unmoving on the ridge with Zeke on one side and Will on the other. His finger against the trigger was stiff, and his arm ached from holding the rifle in one position for so long.

But the light of dawn was finally beginning to make its way above the canyon walls and the towering pine and fir trees. It wouldn't be long before the men in the camp below began to stir. And then the fight would begin.

He squinted through the darkness again, trying to figure out exactly where Zoe was bedded down. Against the low blaze of firelight, they'd counted six people in Dex's camp—two keeping watch by the fire and four on pallets nearby. A couple smaller campfires revealed half a dozen other prospectors camping in the level area next to the river. Abe could only pray they wouldn't join Dex in the conflict.

He glanced around the ridge. Thankfully, the men in the posse were staying well hidden, just as Zeke had instructed. During the past hour of tense waiting, Abe had been praying

God would protect all who had ridden with him for long hours that night to rescue Zoe.

And he'd been praying Zoe, with Violet, would scramble to safety the second the first gunshot was fired. Zeke had assured him Zoe was smart, that she'd take cover, especially when she realized they'd come after her. While Abe agreed Zoe was a strong woman and could handle anything that came her way, his uneasiness had swelled.

Maybe he shouldn't have brought so many innocent men with him—men who had become like brothers to him. Of course, the moment he'd stepped into Happy's Tavern and voiced his need to form the posse, his friends had eagerly come forward, wanting to help him the same way he'd always helped them. Abe could only pray none of them would come to harm, especially Will.

"How are you doing?" he whispered to the boy as he already had a dozen times since they'd left Yale.

"Stop worrying about me, Pastor Abe." With his head resting on his arms, which were crossed in front of him, Will didn't seem in the least perturbed by the fact that they were about to engage in a gunfight with a dangerous group of outlaws.

"You just make sure you stay up here and out of the way."

"I lost count of how many times you told me that."

"I should have made you stay home."

"And you know I'da just followed you up here anyway."

Zeke pressed his finger against his lips, warning them to silence.

Abe nodded, adjusted his arm, and sighted down his rifle, which he'd fixed square upon Dex. He'd never shot at a man before, but if Dex had hurt Zoe in any way . . .

He quickly cut off the thought before he got worked up again. He wouldn't do Zoe any good if he panicked. He had to stay composed. Like Zeke.

Abe eyed Zoe's brother again. His low, lean profile was intense, his gaze focused, his muscles taut. Over the past hours of riding and working together, Abe had grown to admire the man's leadership skills. With his commanding and yet calm attitude, Zeke had taken charge of the posse, planning out their method of attack and assigning each person specific tasks. When he'd given Mr. Hemming the job of standing guard down trail and watching their back, Abe had wanted to hug him for his sensitivity to the older man. Abe suspected Zeke had positioned himself in the same area as Will so he could keep his eye on the boy just as Abe was doing.

He saw a great deal of Zoe in Zeke, not just in his physical appearance, but in his mannerisms, the easy way he smiled and teased, the inner strength of purpose, and his consideration for everyone he met.

They'd talked most of the ride up the canyon, and Zeke had been open about his life since running away from Manchester, how he'd struggled the first months up in the goldfields and had almost given up.

Abe had asked him if he'd made peace with God over all that had happened, and Zeke had closed up. The silence had been all the answer Abe needed to realize that while Zeke might be willing to reconcile with Zoe, he wasn't willing to do so with the Lord.

Abe lifted up a silent prayer for Zeke as he had throughout the night, a prayer that God's Spirit would break through the barriers holding Zeke back. Then he prayed again for Zoe, that the Lord would graciously give him another chance with his wife so this time he could show her just how much she meant to him.

The light over the eastern range took on a golden quality, illuminating a distant mountain in color while everything else around it was like a black-and-white photograph. With the glow, the sleeping forms below took better shape.

"Five more minutes," Zeke whispered, "and I'll fire the first shot to wake them up."

Abe nodded. The element of surprise was on their side, as well as the fact that they surrounded Dex and his group, having the higher ground and the cover of the cliffs.

"Will?" Zeke angled his head at the boy. "You're my messenger. I need you to crawl around to each of the men and tell them to be ready in five minutes. Then hightail it right back here. Think you can do that?"

"Acourse I can," he whispered before wriggling backward like a snake and disappearing into the brush.

Zeke waited a moment as if making sure the boy was gone and then leaned toward Abe. "If things go wrong, I want you to grab Zoe, gather up the men, and get on out of here as fast as you can."

The seriousness in Zeke's eyes told Abe that anything could happen. That even with their element of surprise, there weren't any guarantees. Abe also knew what Zeke wasn't saying—that if needed, he'd hand himself over to Dex in order to gain Zoe's freedom.

"I'm not leaving you behind at the mercy of Dex," Abe whispered back. "I could never do that. And you know as well as I do Zoe wouldn't either."

"That's why you have to make her leave. Throw her over your shoulder and ride off with her if that's what it's gonna take."

Abe started to shake his head, but the gleam in Zeke's eyes stopped him. "I'll never forgive myself for leaving her behind at the mercy of our father's fists. Now with the chance to save her, I have to do it."

"I should be the one to hand myself over to Dex. My ignorance got us into this mess in the first place."

"No. She needs you. She needs someone who'll love her the way she deserves."

"She needs you too—"

"Promise you'll keep her safe?"

The urgency in Zeke's voice told Abe he had no other choice but to agree. "I promise."

Zeke nodded, then focused down the barrel of his rifle.

Zoe had ceased struggling now that she was holding Violet.

Earlier, the other native had handed Violet over to her when the babe's cries had grown too loud.

"Keep baby quiet!" he'd demanded.

Zoe had snuggled Violet against her chest, kissed the little girl's cheeks, and then whispered endearments until the cries had silenced.

They walked for a short while before they reached a cave. Her captor set her down and forced her to enter ahead of him. He kept a tight grip on her arm so she had no chance of slipping away—not that she considered trying it, not in the middle of a forest. She had no way of knowing which way to go and would only get hopelessly lost. Her best chance of escaping was waiting until daylight and finding a marked trail she could follow.

More voices speaking the native language greeted her captor, but in the darkness, Zoe couldn't distinguish how many more there were. Without any light, Violet went back to sleep, and Zoe nearly did too.

She guessed an hour or two passed by the time her captor prodded her back up and ushered her into the forest. The sky overhead had begun to lighten, showing the first signs of dawn. The native picked her up again, and they resumed their hike through the woods, this time with more Indians creeping along soundlessly behind them.

Violet snuggled against Zoe, sucking her thumb, eyes wide open, and frightened of the stranger holding them both. Zoe kissed the little girl's nose to reassure her and to keep her from crying again, thankful her captors had allowed her to keep Violet and hadn't left the infant behind at the mercy of Dexter and his men.

She shuddered to think of Violet alone with Dexter. Yesterday he'd threatened to toss Violet over the side of the canyon if she caused too much trouble. Even though he'd said it with a grin, Zoe had sensed an undercurrent of threat, one warning her not to cause any trouble either.

Maybe her new kidnappers would show more compassion toward Violet since she was a native child.

Even as her entire being protested the idea of having to give the sweet babe up, Zoe realized she loved Abe enough to do anything for him, even if that meant letting go of Violet. If she ever made it back to Abe, she'd work hard at locating a good family for Violet, one that would love the child as their own.

When her captors finally stopped again, the man holding her was breathing hard. While she was a fairly thin woman, she guessed that carrying her was no easy feat, especially at the pace he'd kept and with the added burden of holding Violet.

Around them, the light of dawn revealed that the forest had given way to craggy cliffs rising steeply upward. The other men moved into the open and stared at her and Violet. Their faces were painted with black streaks. Many were adorned with feathers, beads, or shells wound with leather strips around their long braids. Others had shells in their ears similar to the Indian guide she'd met in Victoria. Some wore English shirts and trousers, but others had leggings and bare chests covered by hand-woven capes.

Though they appeared fierce and warlike, Zoe quelled her fear and tried not to think about what these men were capable of doing to her or where they might take her. Instead, she stared back defiantly, ready to defend herself and Violet if anyone tried to harm them.

Her captor spoke quietly, almost urgently, in a language Zoe didn't understand. And the others glanced up the cliff and around. From the way he held himself and the respect he commanded, she sensed he was the leader.

The question was, What did he want from her? Did he plan to make her and Violet his slaves? If so, why would he carry her rather than tying her up and making her walk?

A gunshot came from a short distance away, but higher up. The bang echoed off the rocks and jarred Zoe down to her bones. Violet paused in sucking her thumb only to start up again more quickly.

Her captor issued sharp words to his comrades, and they scurried off in different directions, carrying an assortment of weapons—bows and arrows, long knives, and even rifles. Who were they fighting and why?

Only her captor remained. As he lowered her, she wobbled, her legs stiff from disuse. He reached out a strong hand to steady her, and she saw his features clearly for the first time. Violet stared at the Indian, her eyes growing wide again. While his face was as fierce and painted as the others, his eyes regarded her kindly, almost gently.

"You stay here," he said. "Here you will be safe."

He spoke better English than she'd realized. "Safe from what?"

"From man who steals Pastor Abe's wife."

Zoe stared into his dark eyes, her heartbeat speeding at the mention of Abe's name. "Do you know Abe?"

He nodded curtly. "Pastor Abe save my life. Now I save his."

"Save his?" Was Abe in danger? If so, how?

Another gunshot cracked in the early morning air. The native glanced to the cliffs above him and then frowned. "I go now."

"Where are you going?"

He started away from her, and she followed. She needed to know what was happening and if Abe was here. But before she could walk more than two steps, the native turned and glowered at her with a dangerous look, one that made her stop.

"Pastor Abe's wife stay here," he said louder, as if that would make her understand his instructions better. "Stay safe."

She stood still, guessing if she attempted to follow again, he wouldn't hesitate to tie her up. With a final warning glare, he spun and sped toward a section of crumbling rock, his steps as silent and stealthy as they'd been all along. She forced herself to remain motionless and watched his every move as he made his way along the rocks until he disappeared behind a boulder.

After he was gone, the reality of what had happened hit her. She'd been rescued—not kidnapped—by one of Abe's native friends. And now the natives were spreading out and intending to join in a fight against Dexter and his men, a fight that apparently Abe was leading.

Her pulse pounded a new rhythm, one of thrill that Abe had cared enough to come after her. He hadn't known Dexter had forced her to leave Yale. For all Abe knew, she was running away from him willingly.

But he'd come anyway. She'd been gone less than twenty-four hours, and he was already here fighting for her.

Just as quickly as the thrill came, a burst of cold dread replaced it. Abe was in danger. He was clearly planning to take part in a gun battle with Dexter and his men.

She glanced around for signs of the native who'd rescued her. Even though he'd ordered her to stay hidden, she couldn't just sit down and do nothing. Her heart demanded she find a way to help Abe. Before it was too late.

thirty-three

W e've got you surrounded," Zeke shouted to the camp below. "No sense in fighting us."

A bullet pinged against the cliff above them, sending a spray of rocks onto their backs.

Abe kept his head down as Zeke had instructed, hunkering behind the ledge away from the returning gunfire.

"I guess Dex isn't planning to give Zoe up easily," Abe whispered.

"Didn't expect him to," Zeke whispered back as he prepared his rifle for another shot.

"What do we do now?"

"We start aiming for the men."

Abe shuddered. "I'd prefer not to take any lives."

"I'd prefer it that way too, but I guarantee Dex'll be shooting to kill." Zeke positioned his gun on the ledge.

At the movement, another shot fired above his head, and Abe yanked him down. "Careful. Zoe won't be happy if you die today."

Zeke lay low for a moment before belly-crawling away. "I have to move to another place and distract them. Will, you get around to the others and tell them to start picking off Dex and his men one at a time while I keep them focused on me."

"No," Abe said. "I'll go around to the men." Will had returned unscathed from his last mission, but Abe didn't want to chance the boy being out in the open again.

"I can do it." Will's freckled face was earnest.

"Zoe won't be happy if anything happens to you either." Of everyone, Abe could take a bullet. He was the most dispensable, the one Zoe would mourn for the least.

"Zoe still loves you, Pastor Abe." As if he'd read Abe's mind, the boy clasped Abe's arm and squeezed. "Don't you be worrying none about that."

Abe couldn't keep from worrying. The longer Zoe was away, the more Abe beat himself up for being a fool and not cherishing her the way he should have. "I still want you to wait here."

"I'm smaller and can keep out of sight better."

"And he'll be faster," Zeke added from his position farther up the cliff.

Abe counted all the reasons why Will should be back in Yale but finally shook his head in defeat. "Fine."

Will grinned and began to wriggle away.

"Stay low and hurry back."

The boy nodded and was gone before Abe could change his mind.

Zeke crept slowly along until he disappeared too.

Once he was alone, Abe dropped his head, all pretense of courage gone. "Oh, Lord God, I'm a peace-loving man, not a fighter. But I'm out here fighting for the woman I love. You gave her to me. She's the only one I want. Please. I'm begging you. Protect her."

At a soft crush of rocks next to him, Abe tried to gather his emotions into control so Will wouldn't see him in such despair. "You're back quicker than I expected."

When Will didn't answer, Abe cast him a glance and then swung around fully, surprise rushing through him at the sight of a native sprawled on his belly beside him. "Sque-is?"

His friend pressed a finger to his lips, his face taut, his eyes intense. The black paint on his face indicated he was ready to go into battle.

"What are you doing here?" Abe hissed the question. He hadn't received a reply to the letter he'd sent, hadn't seen his friend in months, hadn't even known if the native and his tribe had survived the smallpox epidemic. And now here Sque-is was, as alive and fierce as always. Was his Indian friend fighting with another tribe? Would they soon find themselves in the midst of two wars?

"I help get Pastor Abe's wife away from that lowlife Dex."

"You're here to help?"

"Hand Zoe over to us." Zeke's shout echoed in the canyon, cutting off Abe's reunion with his friend. "Then we can end this without anyone dying."

Another gunshot came from Dex's camp and ricocheted against the cliff wall near Zeke's new position.

"Maybe you should hand yourself over to us," Dex called out in his cocky voice. "And we can end this without hurting Zoe."

Abe drew in a sharp breath and closed his eyes. Dex was threatening Zoe. His stomach churned. He couldn't—wouldn't let anything happen to Zoe. He pushed himself up. He'd give himself over to Dex before he let Zeke do it.

Sque-is jerked him down so hard that Abe's shoulder landed against the rocks painfully. "What are you doing?" The Indian's eyes blazed with anger.

He tried to yank himself free. "I won't let them hurt Zoe."

"I have Pastor Abe's wife. I helped get her away."

This time his friend's words penetrated his despair. "You

have her? Now? Where?" He glanced to the rocky ledge beyond his friend and started to sit up.

Sque-is dragged him down again. "She is safe. We put bundle of branches in her bedroll so Dex does not know she is gone."

Overwhelming emotion welled up within Abe, and for a moment he struggled to breathe past his gratitude. *Lord.* He couldn't manage any more than the one-word prayer, but somehow he sensed it was enough for his heavenly Father.

"Give me your gun." Sque-is reached for the rifle, and Abe, weak with relief, relinquished it all too willingly. "I shoot the bedroll. It will surprise them. Then my warriors attack the camp."

"What if my friends start shooting your warriors? What if they don't understand you're helping?"

"You tell them not to shoot."

Abe nodded. The plan was dangerous, especially for Sque-is and his tribe mates. Now that Will was moving among the men and instructing them to shoot to kill, Abe was afraid they wouldn't understand who was friend and who was foe. What if they didn't hear his warning above the commotion and the gunshots?

Zeke's voice rang out again. "If I hand myself over, what guarantee will you give me that you'll set Zoe free?"

Urgency prodded Abe. They had to act now before Zeke gave himself up. "Hurry," he whispered to Sque-is. "Make the shot before Zeke ends up hurt."

Zoe paused in her climb up the rocky path, hefting Violet in her aching arms and trying to catch her breath. She'd discovered the stairsteps that Abe's native friend had just used to climb up the sloping cliff.

Even so, it was steep, and the closer she got to the top, the more exposed she was. She crouched lower until she was practically on her knees to keep herself hidden from Dexter and his men.

After the traveling she'd done with the natives earlier, she realized they'd circled wide and had taken her south of the camp, perhaps in an effort to join up with Abe.

Now, as a man attempted to bargain with Dexter for her life, Zoe tried to place the familiar voice.

"Free my sister, and I'll give you all the gold you want." The voice rang out again, the desperation within it tugging at Zoe.

Zeke?

"I want your gold and the claim," Dexter called back.

In a fraction of a second, Zoe put everything together—the reason Dexter Dawson had decided to marry her in the first place, the reason he'd forced her to come along, and the reason why he hadn't yet hurt her. All along he'd hoped to manipulate Zeke's compassion in order to get his gold.

And in a fraction of a second she also understood what Zeke was doing—he was sacrificing himself to save her. He didn't hate her anymore. In fact, he cared enough about her that he was giving himself up for her.

Tears rushed to Zoe's eyes. Heedless of the tense battle that was about to ensue, she shouted out. "Zeke? Is that you, Zeke?"

"Zoe" came Abe's worried voice from a short distance away. "What are you doing up here?"

She lifted her head carefully and searched for him, but the rocks ahead blocked everything. "Abe? Your native friends set me free. You don't have to fight."

At her call, confusion erupted in Dexter's camp. She raised herself up until she was peering down at the river's edge. The men rushed to her bedroll, threw back the covers, and found pine boughs. As they began to argue with each other, Indians charged out of the woods, their warlike cries filling the air and sending chills down Zoe's spine.

Dexter and his men had no time to react before the warriors with their black-painted faces were upon them. When one of Dexter's companions lifted a knife to attack, a gun sounded from Abe's direction, and a second later, the man screamed, dropped his knife, and grasped his hand, blood oozing from his fingers.

For several moments, chaos ensued as Dexter and his men tried to fight the natives and exchanged gunfire with the men hiding in the rocky cliffs. But the battle didn't last long before the Indians captured and subdued Dexter and his men.

"Zoe." Abe's call was closer.

She glanced up to find him scrambling down the stone path toward her. His hat was crooked, revealing tight worry in his features. Though he was dusty and dirty from the ordeal, he'd never looked more handsome.

When he reached her, he hesitated, his blue eyes reflecting the ever-brightening morning sky overhead. "Are you hurt?" He examined her up and down before doing the same to Violet.

"I'm not hurt and neither is Violet." Only then did she feel the twinge of an ache forming behind her eyes, the beginning of one of her headaches. With all the goings-on, she wasn't surprised to have the start of a headache and was grateful she didn't have to be at the mercy of Dexter and his men while battling the pain.

"You're sure?" Abe reached up as though he'd touch her cheek or hair. But then he dropped his hand and tucked it into his trouser pocket.

"Just a little tired, is all." There was so much she wanted to say to him, so many things she needed to explain. But where did she begin?

"Violet?" Abe's forehead still wrinkled with concern.

At her name, Violet kicked her legs and held out her arms toward Abe. A beautiful smile filled the girl's face, one that would have melted the hardest of hearts.

The worry in Abe's face smoothed away and was replaced by a smile. He reached for the babe, and she went into his arms with a delighted gurgle. Zoe only wished she could go to Abe as easily and that he'd welcome her as willingly.

Abe pulled Violet against his chest and pressed a kiss to her head. The sight of the two together made Zoe's heart ache with such longing she wasn't sure she could bear it. Even if Abe had come after her and Violet, she couldn't assume everything would be better between them. After all, there was still that letter from Lizzy along with the uncertainty of the future. If only she could make him understand she wanted to be with him anyway, no matter what happened.

"Thank you for coming after me," she finally said.

"Then, you didn't leave with Dexter on your own accord?" He cuddled Violet against his chest and studied Zoe's face, the anxiousness returning. "I thought after reading Lizzy's letter you decided you didn't want to be with me anymore."

Shame pressed hard against her chest. "I set out to run off. But once I got down to the trail, I knew I couldn't."

His eyes were expectant, dare she even say hopeful.

"Before I could get away, Dexter forced me to join his group."

"Then, he kidnapped you?"

"Aye, in a manner of speaking, using threats . . . threats to find and kill you."

Once again, Abe's expression grew serious. "We might not be able to put him in jail for stealing gold from miners coming down out of the goldfields, but surely we can convict him for kidnapping."

"I hope so." She wanted so much to throw her arms around Abe and hug him and never let him go. She wanted to shout out she loved him and that she'd never leave him again. But seeing him so real before her overwhelmed her—his presence, kindness, and good looks reminded her of how different they were. No matter her personal feelings for Abe or even how much he might care about her, she didn't want to trap him into a relationship he might come to regret.

As though he sensed the inner turmoil rising inside her, Abe's eyes softened. "Zoe . . ."

Before he could say anything more, Will called out behind her. "Zoe!" An instant later he barreled into her, throwing his arms around her and sobbing her name again. She closed him into her embrace and held him tight, letting her tears mingle with his.

"I thought I lost you," he said after a minute.

"You can't get rid of me that easily." She sniffled, realizing just how much her presence meant to Will. Having no memory of his mum and having lost his pa, he was as much in need of her love and attention as a starving child was of nourishment. She supposed now that he'd had a taste of a real family, he was desperate to keep it.

She hugged him closer and met Abe's gaze over the boy's head. Abe nodded, as though to agree with her silent assessment. Oh, how she wanted to continue to give a home to Will, and Violet, and even little Lyle.

But she had to trust that if God had plans for her to take care of the children He put in her path, He'd provide a way, and if not, then He'd give each of the orphans new homes.

At the approach of a man coming down the rocky path behind Abe, Zoe sucked in a breath.

Will pulled away from her, and Abe stepped aside, giving her full view of the man she'd come halfway around the world to find. Zeke.

thirty-four

The young man climbing toward Zoe didn't take his eyes from her—eyes she'd recognize anywhere.

Beneath the brim of his hat, his expression was sad, almost haunted. But otherwise, from what she could tell, he was robust, strong, and unharmed. His skin was tan, his muscles well defined against his tightly rolled-up shirtsleeves, and his movements as sure and confident as always.

From all appearances, his life in British Columbia suited him. He'd never looked more handsome or healthy, certainly not the pale, half-starved young man he'd been in Manchester in the long days following his unemployment from the mill.

"Zoe," he said as he drew near. "Are you alright?"

"Aye. Other than tired and hungry, I'm just fine."

He stopped in front of her and swiped his hat from his head, revealing thick, dark hair so like hers in color and texture. The morning sunlight revealed the dark circles under his eyes and the pain in their green depths.

"I left Williamsville the day I got your letter."

Hope blossomed to life inside her once again. "You did?"

"I couldn't believe you were here, so close. I had to come see you."

"I've been waiting for spring to travel to see you too. I have so much to tell you." Abe stepped to her side, his shoulder brushing hers, and his eyes filled with encouragement, almost as if he were reminding her that he would stand beside her no matter what happened. With Violet in one arm, he reached for her hand and squeezed it. When he made a motion to let go, she clung to him, needing him now more than ever. In response he laced his fingers through hers, holding her hand even closer.

"I need to speak my piece first." Zeke swallowed hard and then spoke in a rush. "I shouldn't have left you behind the way I did. And I loathe myself for it."

"I'm sorry too, Zeke—"

"No, Zoe. I left you with Father. And no matter what would have happened to me, I shouldn't have run off like a coward."

"It's my fault you had to run off in the first place. If I wouldn't have pushed you to go to the mill that day, you wouldn't have gotten blamed for the fire."

"But you were right to be concerned about me and the union men. They weren't a good influence, and I'd have gotten into trouble with them sooner or later. They weren't the kind of friends I needed. Real friends wouldn't have set me up to take the blame that day."

"The culprits were caught." Zoe leaned against Abe, his strength and support giving her the courage she needed to push forward as she told Zeke about the second, identical fire and the union admitting to being responsible for both.

They talked for a while until Violet started to fuss with hunger. Someone had recovered her bags, and she set to work putting together a bottle of pap for Violet. While the watery bread mixture wasn't as filling as the sweet goat's milk Violet had enjoyed in Yale, the infant was hungry enough not to turn it down.

While she tended to Violet, she and Zeke sat on a quiet ledge away from the group. Zeke told her about the past year in British Columbia, the friendships he'd made and the riches he'd found. Zoe shared about her last months in Manchester, about Meg's continued drug addiction, promiscuity, and giving birth to Eve, and then about the babe's sudden death. She explained her reasoning for joining the bride ship and how she'd ended up with Violet and married to Abe.

Zeke glanced down to the camp where Dex and his men were tied up and guarded by the natives. His gaze landed on Abe, who was talking with the native who'd rescued her, the one called Sque-is.

"Pastor Abe's a good man, Zoe."

Zoe watched Abe, admiring his sturdy frame and the strength emanating from him. "I won't argue with you about that. Abe's been good to me."

"Then you want to stay with him?"

"If he wants me to."

"He says he loves you."

"Loves?" Her heart fluttered.

"Aye. Said it more than once."

She wanted to take hope in Zeke's assurance. Yet, even if Abe thought he loved her, that didn't necessarily mean he'd want her once Lizzy showed up.

Violet squeaked as though to agree, and Zoe handed the babe a piece of hard biscuit to gnaw.

Zeke patted the babe's head. "I want you to know you can always count on me for anything. If Pastor Abe ends up not loving you the way you deserve, then write to me, and I'll come get you as fast as I can."

Zoe nodded, ignoring the pounding in her head that was throbbing louder behind her eyes. "I hope it doesn't come to that. But Abe rushed to marry me, and I fear he may realize he made a mistake."

"You're not a mistake. Any man would be real lucky to have you."

Zoe wanted to push aside her insecurities, wanted to rest assured of Abe's love, not only because of what Zeke had told her, but because Abe had come after her and rescued her from Dexter. Surely that meant he wanted her back and longed to make a life together somehow.

"What about you?" she asked Zeke, needing to take the focus off herself. "Is there anyone special for you?" He'd left plenty of broken hearts behind when he'd sailed away from Manchester. And he was still the kind of man who could make women's heads turn whenever he walked past.

Zeke snorted. "Women are as rare as dry ground in these parts."

"That bad?"

"That's just fine by me. I'm too busy anyway. Don't have time for those kinds of shenanigans."

"Maybe so. But eventually you'll need a wife."

Zeke shrugged, but the wistfulness in his eyes told her his longing was greater than he was admitting.

She laid a hand on his arm. "I'll be praying for you, that God will bring you the right woman."

"Don't bother praying for me, Zoe. God won't hear it."

Zoe wanted to protest. Instead, she dug into her pocket and let her fingers close around Zeke's pendant, the one Mr. Lightness had given him the day he'd professed his faith and his desire to live for God.

"This is yours." She tugged out the bronze circle and handed it to him.

He started to reach for it, then seeing what it was, he dropped his hand.

"Take it. You might still be running away from God. But He's never left you, and He's waiting for you to seek Him again."

From all she'd experienced, she'd learned that when it seemed God was distant, she had to trust Him, even when she didn't understand how He would work things out.

"I don't need God," Zeke said. "I'm getting along just fine without Him."

Zoe didn't know what to say and wished Abe were still by her side to offer wisdom. The only thing she could think to do was thrust the pendant into Zeke's hand and force his fingers to close around it.

"I'll be fine," he said again, but thankfully this time he stuck the pendant into his pocket.

"I love you, Zeke." She reached for him and squeezed him into the hug she'd wanted to give him for the past year and a half. And as she did so, she whispered a silent prayer that he'd make his peace with God—a petition she knew she'd be praying over and over.

Abe urged his horse faster as they rounded the bend and started down the last stretch of the trail leading into Yale. In the saddle in front of him, Zoe moaned, barely conscious.

She'd ridden the first half of the journey behind Will, the two of them together hardly weighing as much as a grown man. Even though Abe had wanted Zoe with him, he'd known their mounts would travel faster and longer if Zoe and Violet shared a horse with Will.

But by midafternoon, Zoe had started vomiting, the sure sign she had one of her headaches. For a while, she'd insisted on continuing with Will. But eventually, the pain had become so unbearable she hadn't been able to hang on to the boy and had almost slipped off. Abe had been so frightened that he'd stopped, put Violet in her cradleboard on Will's back, and then moved Zoe to his horse in front of him.

"We're almost home now," he whispered against her head, the loose silky strands of her hair brushing his cheek. She huddled against him, hopefully asleep so that she could forget about her pain for a short while.

Ahead, the glowing windows of taverns and hotels guided them through the darkness of the coming night. The friends who'd so graciously formed a posse with him rode behind with Dexter Dawson and his men. Sque-is and his tribe mates had accompanied them, helping to guard the prisoners.

Abe had hoped to have more time with Sque-is, but his friend only planned to finish trading before returning to his isolated mountain camp. Sque-is had successfully administered the vaccination Pete had managed to sneak to him last autumn. And thankfully he'd returned to his tribe in time to prevent them from contracting the disease that had decimated the native population.

Sque-is had apparently just arrived in Yale when he witnessed Dex forcing Zoe to join his group. Because of Abe's letter asking him to help find a home for the native baby that Zoe had taken in, Sque-is had discovered that the white woman with the native baby was Abe's wife. He'd made the quick decision to follow Dex. Although they'd already walked for hours to get to Yale, intending to trade as well as visit Abe, Sque-is had taken all but two of his men, who'd remained behind with the game and furs, and they'd started after Dex in an attempt to rescue Pastor Abe's wife.

Abe didn't want to think of the outcome if Sque-is hadn't helped. Zoe might have been hurt. And Zeke most certainly wouldn't have been free. As it was, the peace on Zoe's face after she reconciled with Zeke had made the entire trip worth it.

With a prayer of thanksgiving for the Lord's mercy and protection, Abe laid a kiss against Zoe's head.

She moaned softly, still oblivious to the world.

He had so much he wanted to say to her, so many apologies

to make. While he wished he could have spoken to her of his feelings right away, he couldn't begrudge her the time with Zeke. And he took encouragement from the fact that she hadn't insisted on going to Williamsville with her brother. Instead, she'd said good-bye to Zeke, wished him well, and told him she would visit in the summer.

Abe had corrected her and informed her he planned to take her up to Williamsville just as soon as Dex and his men were safely in jail and prosecuted, even if that meant he had to leave the church construction unfinished.

Zoe had smiled and told him the next time she left, they'd be doing it together. Even with the reassurance, Abe knew they still desperately needed to talk. He had to convince her of how much he loved her and never wanted her to leave again.

"I love you, Zoe," he whispered. "I just wish you were awake for me to tell you."

She didn't stir, except for her head to loll and her body to slacken into unconsciousness.

thirty-five

*Z*oe groaned and pried one eye open. At the bright daylight that accosted her, she retreated behind closed lids. For a moment, she used her other senses to take in her surroundings. The warmth of coverlets surrounding her, the strong odor of an onion poultice, a waft of mint, and bubbly kisses followed by baby giggles.

She was home. *Home.*

When she'd walked out the door, she'd never believed she'd be back. But here she was, in her bed, in her cozy house, with all the delightful memories greeting her.

Another playful sound caused more baby laughter.

"Will?" she croaked.

"Mama's awake!" Will's voice rang out nearby with eagerness.

An instant later, the mattress sank under his weight and Violet's.

Mama? Will had called her Mama. The ache in Zoe's head seemed to fall away into a dull throb.

"Say it, Vi-Vi," Will crooned in his baby-talk voice. "Say Ma-ma again."

"Ma-ma," Violet chorused.

Zoe's eyes flew open, and she found herself peering up at the most beautiful sight in the world—Will's lopsided grin and Violet's wide eyes and smile. Joy welled deep in Zoe's chest and pulsed into her throat. "You both called me Mama."

Perched on the edge of the bed, Will glanced down and bunched the blanket in his fist, his expression shy but chagrined. "I know you ain't really my ma—"

"I want to be your ma, if you'll let me."

His eyes turned shiny and he nodded. "I'd like that right well."

"Good, then you'll need to call me Ma or Mama."

"Mama," Violet chirped, clapping her hands together.

Zoe laughed and Will joined her. Violet bent low and puckered up for the kiss she was apparently growing accustomed to getting from Zoe. With another laugh, Zoe obliged the babe, even though the girl's kiss was sloppy and full of drool.

Squinting against the brightness of the cabin, Zoe glanced to the window and attempted to gauge the time. From what she could tell, it was midday or perhaps early afternoon. How long had she been asleep?

"I hope you're not getting in trouble with Mr. Barton for missing work."

"Nah, he told Pastor Abe I could miss for a little bit if'n I was looking after you."

"That was mighty nice of him."

"Guess giving him those mittens and sending along those piping hot biscuits sure did make him like you an awful lot."

She hoped Will understood she hadn't been kind to Mr. Barton so that he'd be nice back. That wasn't her way.

Before she could voice the correction, Will hurried on, as talkative as always. "I'm only staying until Pastor Abe gets back from his visit with Wanda Washington."

"Wanda?"

"She sent for you and Pastor Abe. Guess what they say is true, that she's really dyin'."

If Wanda had sent for her, then Will was right. The woman must be nearing the end. What would she do about Lyle?

Zoe pushed up to her elbows and blinked away the dizziness. "I need to go to Wanda's too, Will."

"Pastor Abe didn't want to bother you. Said he'd go on his own. He ain't been gone long and will be back real soon. 'Sides, he's been sitting here by your side ever since we got back last night. Ain't gone out except to pass along word to someone to fetch me."

Zoe raised herself until she was sitting, noting that she was still in the same clothing she'd been in for the past couple of days. Her skirt, namely her hem, was caked with mud. Her stockings were splattered and dirty, and even her bodice hadn't been able to withstand the dirty trip.

"I need to change first." She dragged her legs over the edge of the bed and fought another wave of pain—this one farther back in her head.

"Abe'll tan my hide if'n I let you out of my sight." They both knew Abe would never tan anyone's hide. Even so, Will's thin face was wreathed with worry, most likely that he'd disappoint Abe.

"I'm feeling much better." She placed first one foot on the floor and then the other. Even though she silently reminded herself of her resolve to trust God's plan for the children, she couldn't keep her anxiety for Lyle at bay and wouldn't rest until she knew he would be well taken care of.

Zoe pushed past the lingering haze of pain and knocked on the front door of Wanda's mansion. She wrapped her shawl tighter, even though the early afternoon contained the warmth and sunshine of spring.

She'd encountered numerous townspeople on her way, all of whom had greeted her cheerfully and welcomed her back. Though she'd worried that her escapade might have repercussions for either her or Abe's reputation in the community, everyone put her at ease, as accepting as always.

Hearing no sounds coming from inside the house, Zoe raised her fist to knock again, only to find the door opening and Mr. Ping standing there. Before she could remind him who she was and explain her presence, he bowed at the waist and then waved her inside.

Zoe hesitated. Should she bow back? What was the proper etiquette?

"Missee will be glad to see you," he said as he closed the door.

Zoe followed Mr. Ping through the grand entryway, her footsteps echoing against the glossy white tiles to the wide spiraling staircase with an enormous chandelier hanging above it.

"How is Lyle?" She peered around, hoping for a glimpse of the little boy.

"Lil' Man needs a mother." Mr. Ping spoke gravely from several steps ahead of her. "You will take the boy and be mother to him."

Zoe wasn't sure if Mr. Ping was telling or asking her. As much as she wanted to agree, she had to think of Abe and what he needed. "I don't think my husband is in favor of the idea."

"You convince him."

This time Zoe had no doubt Mr. Ping was ordering, and she couldn't formulate a response, so she said nothing as they reached the second floor and he led her into Wanda's bedchamber. Abe knelt beside the bed on one side, and another man sat in a chair on the opposite side—a man Zoe didn't recognize.

"Zoe," Wanda croaked from the shadows of her dark canopy bed.

At the mention of her name, Abe's head jerked up, and his attention flew to her. "Zoe, what are you doing here?" He jumped to his feet and started toward her, his brow furrowing. "You should be home in bed."

"I'm doing fine." Though her head pounded a little, the pain was bearable compared to what it had been like yesterday riding home.

Eyes filled with worry, Abe reached for her, slipping his arm around her waist and supporting her. "Come on. I'll take you home."

He was right. She probably shouldn't have rushed to get out of bed. Nevertheless, now that she was here she could support him and be of help to Wanda, couldn't she? After all, Wanda had wanted her to come too.

"I want to help." Zoe broke free of Abe and strode to the bedside. "What do you need, Wanda? Tell me what I can do for you."

Though thick window tapestries held out the sunlight, there was still enough daylight in the room for Zoe to see that Wanda had deteriorated even further. Her body was wasting away, her skin a sickly yellow. She lifted her hand toward Zoe, but could hardly raise it from the bed.

Though Zoe had never liked this woman, she reached for Wanda's hand and circled it in her own. Whatever Wanda's past mistakes, Zoe couldn't hold on to them and had to forgive.

"Please, ple-ase, take Lyle," Wanda whispered, her grip surprisingly strong. "Raise him as your own."

Zoe swallowed the words of agreement that pushed for release. She had to do what was right for Abe, for their future together. "I can't promise you I'll raise him, Wanda. But I can promise I'll try to find him a good home."

"No, she'll raise him," Abe said.

Zoe turned to find Abe by her side.

"*We* will raise him." Once again, Abe wrapped his arm around her waist, the solidness of his hold drawing her into the crook of his arm.

"We?"

His eyes were gentle and earnest. "Yes, we will raise him as our child. And we'll do the same with Violet."

"What about your chances of becoming a bishop?"

"I don't need to be a bishop to become the leader God wants me to be."

"Are you sure?"

He nodded. "And I'm fairly certain God isn't finished with me yet in the colonies, that He has more work for me to do here."

The man across from the bed coughed lightly as if to remind them they weren't alone. But Zoe's heartbeat was racing too hard and her thoughts whirling too fast for her to slow them down, much less stop them. "But won't the bishop cut you off from your ministry? And how will you be able to support yourself?"

Abe's arm only tightened around her. "Someone wise once told me that if God's the one who gives us our ministry, then He's the only one who can take it away."

"That's right." She couldn't hold back a smile.

"He's put us here together, Zoe. He's given us work to do. And now we have to trust that He'll provide the means, no matter what happens with the bishop."

"Then you'll take Lyle?" Wanda cut in, her voice weak and winded.

Abe glanced first at Wanda and then at the man across the bed. "If you'd like, you can have your lawyer draft adoption papers. We'll make him our little boy."

Tears sprang into Zoe's eyes. "Really?"

"Really." He squeezed her as if to reassure her.

"Draw up the papers right away, Langston." Tears started streaming down Wanda's cheeks.

The man stood. "Certainly, Mrs. Washington. I'll get to work on it."

"No, now, this instant," she insisted. "I've signed everything else, and I want this signed before I go."

A timid knock on the door drew their attention to Mr. Ping standing in the hallway. "Sorry to interrupt, Pastor Abe, sir. But someone is here and insists to speak to you."

"Would you please tell them I'm detained at present?"

Mr. Ping hesitated. "She said to tell Pastor Abe, sir, that she is your fiancée."

thirty-six

*H*is fiancée? Abe's stomach dropped. Did that mean Lizzy was at the door? Wanting to speak with him? Next to him, Zoe stiffened and started to pull away.

"Wait, Zoe." He drew her near. "Let's go together."

She studied his face warily before nodding.

They followed Mr. Ping down the stairs. As they waited for him to open the door to the front entryway, Zoe stepped back as though to put distance between them. But Abe reached for her hand. "Please, Zoe," he whispered, intertwining his fingers with hers and tugging her closer. "Please. I need you."

Her green eyes met his, as though testing the sincerity of his words. The truth was, he did need her. He always had and just hadn't known it. Thankfully, the Lord knew his needs better than he did.

Zoe returned to his side.

He wanted to say more, but Mr. Ping swung the door wide to reveal Bishop Hills as well as his friend John Roberts. He took in their serious expressions in only a glance before his attention shifted to the woman—to Lizzy.

She wasn't looking at him but was instead examining Zoe and noticing their clasped hands.

"Lizzy, welcome." Abe knew he had to do the right thing by welcoming her as well as explaining all that had happened, even though he'd much rather close the door and pretend she wasn't there.

"Hello, Abraham." Her attention shifted to him, giving him full view of her face, of the features that hadn't changed a bit in the years they'd been apart. She didn't have Zoe's stunning beauty, but she was still pretty in her own way, with a gentle expression, kind eyes, and a gracefulness in how she held herself.

"The boy at your cabin said we could find you here." Bishop Hills pulled himself up as if to make his presence known.

"Bishop Hills." Abe nodded at his superior and then also at his friend. "John."

"Abraham. Good to see you." John's cheeks reddened, and he didn't look Abe in the eyes.

Why had both John and the bishop come with Lizzy?

"Bishop Hills and Lizzy—Miss Northrup—stayed with me in Hope last night," John offered quickly as though sensing Abe's question. "I decided to accompany them today since I haven't visited you in a while."

"I couldn't allow Miss Northrup to travel here by herself," the bishop added. "Since I needed to return and check on the progress of the church construction, I offered to act as her chaperone."

"That's very kind of you both," Abe replied, although he was tempted to tell them that neither of them should have made the trip, that bringing Lizzy here was pointless. What did they hope to accomplish by it?

"May we step inside to talk?" the bishop asked.

Abe glanced behind him, to Mr. Ping and then to Miss Bea, the heavyset older housekeeper, who was attempting to hold

Lyle. The child was wiggling and trying to get loose. With an exasperated sigh, Miss Bea set the boy down.

In an instant he toddled as fast as his little legs would carry him to Zoe. "O-ee! O-ee!"

Zoe let go of Abe's hand, knelt, and held out her arms to the boy. With a big smile, she scooped him up and hugged him tight. "How are you, Lil' Man?"

Abe's chest tightened at the beauty of the sight of the two together. Zoe had such a gift with children, whether she realized it yet or not. And he knew with certainty he'd made the right decision in telling Wanda they'd adopt Lyle.

"And who is the child?" Lizzy watched the interaction between Zoe and Lyle with interest.

Abe started to answer, but Bishop Hills cut in. "He's the child of the woman who lives here, a woman of ill repute."

Lizzy took an immediate step back, her eyes widening with mortification.

Zoe stood up with Lyle, and the boy laid his head on her shoulder as if that's where he belonged. Abe brushed his hand over the boy's head, hoping to show Lizzy she had nothing to fear, that the child was perfectly adorable.

"Mrs. Washington is very ill," Abe explained. "She's asked Zoe and me to take care of Lyle after her passing, and we've just told her we would adopt him."

"Adopt?" Bishop Hills crossed his arms behind his back, his expression severe. "You plan to adopt the child of a harlot?"

At the obscene word, Lizzy blushed and averted her eyes.

Suddenly Abe understood more than ever that this wild colony was his home and the place where God had called him to love the sinners and outcasts the same way the Savior had during His walk on earth.

He met the bishop's gaze directly. "Your Grace, not only do I intend to adopt Lyle, but I'm also planning to adopt Violet."

At his declaration, Zoe reached for his hand again, laced her fingers through his, and leaned her head against his arm. At her quiet show of support, overwhelming love for her welled up so that he wanted to draw her into his embrace and tell her how much she meant to him.

"We've already discussed this, Mr. Merivale." The terseness of the bishop's voice prevented Abe from making the open display of affection for his wife. "If you disregard my instructions regarding the native child and now with this—this boy, then you'll have no chance at all of becoming a bishop."

"I realize that. And I'm prepared to give up those aspirations."

"Are you also willing to give up your position as a minister of the Church of England?"

The red had drained from John's face. "Your Grace, you cannot take away Abraham's position. The people here love him—"

"I did not ask for your opinion on the matter, Mr. Roberts. Please kindly refrain from interrupting my conversation."

John's expression had grown distraught. He opened his mouth to speak again, but Abe cut him off. "I'll be fine, John. Whether I'm connected with the Church of England or not, God gives me my ministry and no man can take that away from me."

Zoe's hand squeezed his, giving him a burst of confidence to press on. "I'm sorry, Your Grace. But I must do the work God gives me whether you approve of it or not."

"Very well, Mr. Merivale." The bishop's nostrils flared with his barely restrained anger. "You leave me with no choice but to send you back to England in disgrace—"

"I'm staying here and continuing my work—"

"Not in one of my churches as one of my ministers."

The air filled with tense silence.

Lizzy took another step back and stood next to John. She kept her focus on her hands clasped tightly in front of her.

"Very well, Bishop Hills." Abe weighed his words, hoping he could remain loving and kind even though his worst fears were coming true. He hadn't wanted to leave his church, hadn't wanted to cut himself off from the bishop. But he could no longer deny the need to make changes right where he was. He didn't have to wait until he was a bishop someday. He had to start here and now.

"While I had hoped you could see the validity of what I'm trying to do here in Yale, I also understand if you cannot. I am most certainly falling away from tradition in many areas. It has been my hope that by meeting the people on their level, I might be able to present the gospel to them in a way they can understand."

The bishop only shook his head in disapproval. "We do not change our practices based on the whims of people. We adhere to the truth and traditions that have held our church in high regard and in good stead for hundreds of years. If you cannot abide the way of things, then it is most certainly time for you to be cut loose."

Abe silently acquiesced.

"Your Grace." John spoke again, his voice urgent. "Surely we should take some time to think and pray on this before making a decision."

"No, Mr. Roberts." The bishop rocked on the balls of his feet. "I've made my decision and will begin the process of finding a replacement for Mr. Merivale just as soon as I return to Victoria."

"Abe's a true man of God," Zoe interjected, as bold as always. "It's just too bad you can't see it."

The bishop's expression soured. "What's too bad, Mrs. Merivale, is that I no longer wish to persuade Mr. Merivale to set you aside and declare an annulment so that he might resume his relationship with Miss Northrup. I'm only sorry I gave Miss

Northrup false hope about such a possibility and inconvenienced her by bringing her all this way."

"I'm sorry you came all this way too." This time Abe looked directly at Lizzy. Thankfully, she met his gaze, albeit somewhat reservedly after all she'd just witnessed. If she'd hoped to re-institute a relationship with him, she likely was having second thoughts now that he'd all but ruined his career with the Church of England.

"When I wrote and invited you to come and marry me," he continued, "I was still very much committed to you. But after I received your letter regarding your impending marriage to someone else, I admit I was shocked and hurt. I couldn't believe you'd cast me aside so easily."

"I'm sorry, Abraham." Lizzy's shoulders drooped. "I was foolish and rushed into the new relationship. I have regretted my decision these many months."

"I regret I confused matters and now have caused you more pain. Nevertheless, I could never annul my marriage. I took marriage vows and plan to honor them. Even if the bishop could still recommend me to you, I cannot recommend myself, not when I'm deeply in love with someone else."

At his declaration, Zoe lifted her head away from his arm, and he could feel her studying him.

He hadn't planned to tell her of his love this way, in front of everyone. But now that he'd started, he couldn't stop. He twisted so he was facing her. "Zoe, I love you more than I ever knew was possible to love a woman. I thank the Lord for bringing us together and pray for many opportunities in the days and years to come to show you just how much I love and cherish you."

Zoe's beautiful features lit, and her lips curved into a smile that revealed her dimples. "I love you too."

His heart welled with more joy than it could contain and

overflowed into a wide grin. Even though he'd just lost everything he'd been holding on to for so long, he'd gained the love of his bride. And that was all he needed.

Zoe's chest ached with sweet pressure. With the bishop already having stormed away, leaving John and Lizzy behind, Abe took his time reassuring John that he'd find a way to continue his ministry in Yale and that John needn't worry about him.

Finally, Abe said good-bye to both John and Lizzy and now stood in the door with Zoe, watching them walk away. Zoe felt only pity for the elegant young woman, pity that Lizzy had come all this way to win Abe back and had failed.

"Do you think perhaps there's a future for John and Lizzy?" Abe's sights trained on John's hand at the small of Lizzy's back as they strolled along the plank sidewalk.

"I noticed the way he was admiring her," Zoe replied. "Perhaps he can persuade her."

"I'd like for John to have a wife. And if Lizzy came all this way, maybe she would stay with him."

"You should give John some tips on how to win a woman."

At the low teasing in her voice, Abe's attention immediately jumped to her. "What kinds of tips do you suggest?"

As usual, Abe's seriousness in response to her lightheartedness made her want to laugh. Instead, she continued to tease him. "Maybe you can suggest that John take Lizzy to the hot spring while they're here. Undressing in front of each other always works wonders."

One of Abe's brows quirked. "Are you saying you like watching me undress?"

She pretended to be occupied with smoothing down Lyle's tangled hair.

"It certainly wasn't me," Abe continued. "I never peeked at you."

"'Course not." She smiled at him coyly. "Maybe you can tell John to go shopping with Lizzy and pick out her undergarments."

Abe grinned, finally catching on to her teasing. "I didn't pick out your unmentionables."

"Take that up with Mr. Allard. He saw the silky drawers and corset the same as I did."

Abe chuckled and started to pull her near, but she was still holding Lyle. Even so, his eyes darkened, and his attention dropped to her mouth. His smile fell away and was replaced by a hunger that sent pleasure dancing along her nerve endings.

Suddenly all she wanted to do was be with him, in his arms, and kissing him. He was a fabulous kisser. Even though that qualification for a husband had always been just a silly fantasy, she couldn't deny her desire for it or her delight that Abe was quite a natural.

As he studied her, he drew in a breath, and she knew he'd seen her desire, that it was evident all over her face. And she didn't care.

He loved her and wanted to stay with her forever. He'd said it in front of everyone, including Lizzy and the bishop.

He leaned in, his sights trained on her mouth.

Her body rose up to meet him, her entire being keening for his touch.

"Pastor Abe, sir?" came Mr. Ping's voice in the hallway behind them.

Abe hastily straightened and cleared his throat. "Yes, Mr. Ping?"

"The missee and Mr. Langston need you to sign papers."

As she and Abe walked back up the spiraling staircase, her body was suddenly attuned to every move he made behind her—the brush of his fingers against her back, the thud of his footsteps, the soft exhalation he made when they ascended to the top.

When they reached the room, Miss Bea stood outside, her eyes red rimmed from crying. Zoe guessed the older woman had gone to Wanda and said her good-byes. Although Lyle didn't want to leave Zoe to go into Bea's care, the housekeeper finally managed to peel the boy away with the promise of a cookie.

With Lyle taken care of, Zoe followed Abe into the room and approached Wanda's bed. Her lawyer had spread out several papers on the bedside table.

"Sign each of these, if you will, please." Langston held an inkpot and handed Abe a pen.

"Very well." Abe bent to look at the first sheet. With the pen poised above it, he stood abruptly and looked first at the lawyer and then at Wanda. "What is this?"

Wanda gave him the ghost of a smile. "What does it look like?"

"The deed to your house."

"It is."

Abe thrust the pen back at the lawyer. "I cannot sign for it."

"Then let Zoe."

"We're not taking your house, Wanda." Abe's expression radiated distress.

"You're not taking it. I'm giving it to you." Wanda paused, took a deep breath, and then pressed on as though every word cost her. "I want you to have everything—the house, everything in it, and my fortune."

"No, absolutely not—"

"Yes!" Wanda's voice grew stronger. "You'll take it and use it not only for Lyle, but for all the other children who will ever need a home and family."

Her impassioned declaration silenced Abe and left Zoe in a

state of shock. Abe met Zoe's gaze, and they could only stare at each other. Abe had just sacrificed his job, his future, and even his financial security to stay true to God's calling. Was this then God's next step for them? His provision? So soon?

As Abe's eyes filled with wonder, Zoe's heart swelled with the same. When he smiled at her, she smiled back and nodded her encouragement.

Quickly Abe signed the papers, and then before the ink was dry, he turned, captured Zoe, and drew her against him. In the same motion, he dropped his lips upon hers and sealed their future with a kiss . . . a kiss that sent light and heat through her body in more brilliant colors than the northern lights.

thirty-seven

THREE MONTHS LATER

Zoe stood in front of the gilded mirror and smoothed a hand over the blue silk brocade. She'd never imagined she'd ever own a gown so lovely. Or that they'd reach a milestone like today.

At a tapping against the bedroom door, she spun to see Abe's handsome face peeking in.

"Are you ready?" he asked with an excited smile.

"Not yet." She pretended to fiddle with her gown. "I can't get my bodice to fit quite right."

He glanced behind him, stepped inside, and then closed the door soundlessly, clearly not wanting to alert anyone to their presence together alone.

Someone in the massive house was usually in need of either her or Abe's attention. Even with Mr. Ping, Miss Bea, and the native women Zoe had hired from Shantytown, she and Abe were always busy. Zoe had her hands full with Lyle and Violet. And Abe had been enjoying the small school he'd started in the sitting room with Will as his first pupil along with several other orphan boys in the community.

"I might be able to help you." Abe tiptoed toward her. In his best suit coat, matching waistcoat and trousers, and shiny black boots, he made a dashing picture, especially with his failed attempt to smooth down his hair.

She intended to help him with his hair every bit as much as he intended to help her with her gown. Ducking her head, she stifled a smile. She loved all the sneaking around they did, the stolen moments, the secret kisses, the touching, and the playfulness.

"Where do you need help?" He came up behind her and circled his arms around her, then leaned into the bare spot at her neck and pressed a breathy kiss there before dropping another kiss onto her exposed collarbone.

She relaxed back into him, relishing the hardness of his body.

"Do you need help here?" His hands skimmed her hips.

"No." She angled so she could kiss his jaw.

"What about here?" His hands began to roam.

His touch, as always, brought her to life. And if they weren't careful, they'd grow distracted—and disheveled—and end up walking out late, causing everyone to whisper about them again.

"I need your help here." She placed her hands over his and guided them toward her abdomen. The jade jewel at the center of her wedding band glistened, reminding her of the special afternoon when Abe had surprised her with a picnic by a nearby waterfall. Against the backdrop of the spectacular view, he'd gotten down on one knee, slipped the ring on her finger, and professed his undying love.

When his hands were firmly in place, she held them there.

"Here?" The confusion in his voice made her smile again.

"Aye."

He brushed several more kisses against her neck before growing motionless. "What does this mean?" His question wavered with emotion.

She turned in his arms so that she was facing him. She wound her arms around his neck and lifted her face up to him. "It means we're having a babe."

"Are you sure?" His blue eyes filled with hope.

"I'm positive." All the signs had been there for days, but she'd waited long enough to make sure.

He searched her face for a moment before he bent in and took her lips in a kiss that rose and fell with all the love they shared. But his passion was gentler, almost as if he were afraid of hurting her.

She pressed against him. "Kiss me again, just like you always do, and never stop."

At her demand, he kissed her hungrily, this time his mouth taking possession of her down to her very soul, so that she could hardly hold herself upright when he finished.

"There," he whispered. "Will that do?"

"Aye. But I'll need another one like that again soon."

His lips curled into a smile. "I might be able to arrange it."

"Do you remember when we first met that day at the hospital after Jane's death?"

"How could I ever forget the best day of my life?"

"You prayed with me and asked God to help me find a husband. Did you ever think that He'd answer your prayer the way He did, by making you my husband?"

"I'm heartily glad He did. I can't imagine my life without you."

She hugged him, letting the joy of this moment waft over her. She was grateful for the new life growing inside her as well as the children God had already given them. Hopefully this was only the beginning of many more.

At a knock, Abe rapidly released her and began to straighten his shirt and collar.

"Ma?" Will's voice came from outside the door. "Pastor Abe? I know you're in there smooching."

Abe froze, his eyes widening with chagrin.

Zoe smiled. "Tell everyone we'll be right out."

"Sure thing."

As the boy's footsteps faded, Zoe drew Abe back, smoothed out his hair, and then pressed a tender kiss against his cheek before they exited the room. Hand in hand, they descended the spiraling staircase, crossed through the wide entryway, and then stood before the closed door.

Abe took a deep breath. "Ready?"

"Ready."

Together they nodded at Mr. Ping, who swung open the door. As they crossed the threshold, the gathered crowd erupted into cheers. People stood all around the front yard and even in the street. Zoe clutched Abe's hand tighter, not having expected so many to come out for the dedication.

Among the sea of well-wishers, she caught sight of Zeke's handsome face. He'd traveled down from Williamsville to join them for the occasion. She'd loved being able to visit with him for longer periods over the past few days. He'd told her only that morning he was making a sizeable donation to her and Abe's new ministry. When she told him God had already provided far more than they needed, he'd still insisted that she take his gift and use it any way she saw fit.

Her heart swelled with gratefulness at the sight of so many other familiar friends—Mr. Allard from the store, Mr. Hemming from the pub, their previous neighbor Little Joe, the native women and their children, the Hurdy Gurdy girls, Mr. Barton from the livery, the Royal Engineers who'd helped build the church, and all of the different people Abe had ministered to who lived in and around Yale.

Even John Roberts had come up from Hope for the day with his new bride, Lizzy. Zoe had decided the two were perfect for each other, since they were both quiet and reserved. John had continued to protest the bishop's decision to take the Yale parish away from Abe. But Abe had been at peace with the change and had remained involved among the miners anyway.

The only difference was that Abe didn't leave her for days at a time anymore. He'd told her their marriage was his first priority, next was his family, then his parish. He was rarely gone for more than a few hours before returning to her and eagerly seeking her out.

Besides, together they had a new ministry. God had used Violet to bring them together, and the child would always be special because of that. But now that the house was finally ready, they'd put out word that their doors were open. Zoe liked to think Wanda would have been pleased with their accomplishments and plans.

Together they walked down the front steps. Zoe stopped to kiss Violet, who was content in Will's arms. Then she reached over and kissed Lyle, who was wiggling against Miss Bea to get loose. He reached for Zoe, and Miss Bea gratefully relinquished the bundle of energy.

With Abe at her side and Lyle on her hip, she stopped in front of the new sign draped with a sheet. Abe offered a prayer, and then, sharing a smile, they tugged the covering away. It fell into the grass and revealed the sign: *Merivale Home for Foundlings*.

Another cheer rose into the air, and with it Zoe let her praise rise to God. She'd given Him her willing heart and trusted Him. And He'd led her one step at a time into so much more than she ever could have asked for or imagined.

Author's Note

*W*hen I first heard of the concept of bride ships I was utterly horrified and fascinated by the idea that women would actually willingly board ships, leave everything they'd ever known behind, and sail to a strange land, all for the purpose of marrying complete strangers. I couldn't help but ask myself what kind of woman would do such a thing and why.

In the 1860s several bride ships left England's shores with the destination of Victoria on Vancouver Island (which was at that time still a colony of England and not yet part of Canada). As I researched these ships and the women who took the voyages, I searched frantically for the answer to a question, namely, What sort of desperation did these women face that would drive them to board one of the bride ships?

In this third book in THE BRIDE SHIPS series, my hope is to show the perspective of one of the brides who came on the second bride ship that sailed to Victoria. This ship, called the *Robert Lowe*, left approximately four months after the *Tynemouth* (the bride ship highlighted in the first two books in the series).

While the women aboard the *Robert Lowe* were sponsored by the Columbia Emigration Society the same as the *Tynemouth* women, a distinct difference exists between the two groups. The group on the first ship came largely from the London area and consisted of wealthy middle-class women as well as the poor plucked from orphanages and slums.

The *Robert Lowe* women, however, were from the cotton manufacturing districts in Manchester, England. The calamity in the midlands was widespread, with tens of thousands of cotton-mill workers suffering from unemployment as a result of the cotton shortage brought about by the American Civil War. The women chosen to immigrate aboard the *Robert Lowe* were among the many who'd lost their jobs. In light of the bleak conditions in their homeland, the three dozen Manchester mill girls were happy to be offered the chance at a better life in the colonies where work and husbands awaited them.

As I portrayed in the book, this bride ship arrived in January after three months without any stops. After spending a weekend of rest and quarantine aboard the *Robert Lowe*, the women were ferried to Victoria aboard a steamship. Before they could go to shore, however, two ill women were taken to the hospital with what was believed to be consumption or mill fever, illnesses common among mill workers. Since the lung ailments can lie dormant, the women may have already had the disease, and the damp sea voyage may have allowed it to progress. Whatever the case, the two women died shortly after arriving in Victoria.

The rest of the brides came ashore much the way I portrayed. With the arrival of another bride ship, the excitement of the men in the colonies was out of control. With not nearly enough women for all the eager men, the women (similar to the *Tynemouth* women) had to run a gauntlet through the mobs hoping to find brides. While Zoe isn't based on any real person in particular, I did hope to portray her bride-ship experience through the eyes of a mill woman.

Finally, in developing Abraham Merivale as a minister, I was inspired by the story of a pastor who lived in the colonies during this time period. The Anglican Church really did send missionaries to the mining towns and camps with the intention of spreading the gospel as well as maintaining order and civility among the miners. One such missionary was a tall, well-liked preacher by the name of John Sheepshanks, a highly educated man and the son of an upper-class family, who'd chosen to volunteer for a period of five years in the colonies without a salary.

John Sheepshanks was a cheerful and resourceful minister whose compassion made him popular among both the miners and natives. He spent time building relationships by playing ice hockey, spearfishing for salmon, and teaching reading. I modeled Abe around this beloved missionary who showed God's love wherever he was within the mining districts of British Columbia.

I hope you've enjoyed taking this bride-ship journey with Zoe as she learned to seek after God's will for her life and follow His direction, even when the whole plan wasn't clear to her. I pray that as you seek after God's will and leading in your life, you never forget He's able to do exceedingly more than you can ask or imagine. If you allow Him to guide you, He might just surprise you with what He does!

Jody Hedlund is the bestselling author of over twenty historical novels for both adults and teens and is the winner of numerous awards, including the Christy, Carol, and Christian Book Awards. Jody lives in Michigan with her husband, five busy teens, and five spoiled cats. Visit her at jodyhedlund.com.

Sign Up for Jody's Newsletter!

Keep up to date with Jody's news on book releases and events by signing up for her email list at jodyhedlund.com.

More from Jody Hedlund

When three orphaned sisters are left nearly destitute, they must journey from New York to the west where they strive through tragedy and loss for the hope of a better life—but they find that the promise of the orphan trains is not all that it seems. Along the way, they encounter the true meaning of family, friendship, and love.

ORPHAN TRAIN: *With You Always, Together Forever, Searching for You*

You May Also Like . . .

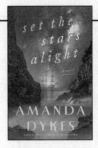

Reeling from the loss of her parents, Lucie Clairmont discovers an artifact under the floorboards of their London flat, leading her to an old seaside estate. Aided by her childhood friend Dashel, a renowned forensic astronomer, they start to unravel a history of heartbreak, sacrifice, and love begun 200 years prior—one that may offer the healing each seeks.

Set the Stars Alight by Amanda Dykes
amandadykes.com

Years of hard work enabled Douglas Shaw to escape a life of desperate poverty—and now he's determined to marry into high society to prevent reliving his old circumstances. But when Alice McNeil, an unconventional telegrapher at his firm, raises the ire of a vindictive co-worker, he must choose between rescuing her reputation and the future he's always planned.

Line by Line by Jennifer Delamere
LOVE ALONG THE WIRES #1
jenniferdelamere.com

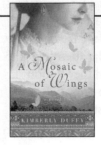

Determined to uphold her father's legacy, newly graduated Nora Shipley joins an entomology research expedition to India to prove herself in the field. In this spellbinding new land, Nora is faced with impossible choices—between saving a young Indian girl and saving her career, and between what she's always thought she wanted and the man she's come to love.

A Mosaic of Wings by Kimberly Duffy
kimberlyduffy.com

BETHANYHOUSE

More from Bethany House

Wanting to do her part in the Civil War effort, Clara McBride goes to work in the cartridge room at the Washington Arsenal. Her supervisor, Lieutenant Joseph Brady, is drawn to Clara but must focus on preventing explosions in the factory. When multiple shipments of cartridges fail to fire and everyone is suspect, can the spark of love between them survive?

A Single Spark by Judith Miller
judithmccoymiller.com

Ex-cavalry officer Matthew Hanger leads a band of mercenaries who defend the innocent, but when a rustler's bullet leaves one of them at death's door, they seek out help from Dr. Josephine Burkett. When Josephine's brother is abducted and she is caught in the crossfire, Matthew may have to sacrifice everything— even his team—to save her.

At Love's Command by Karen Witemeyer
HANGER'S HORSEMEN #1
karenwitemeyer.com

When Beatrix Waterbury's train is disrupted by a heist, scientist Norman Nesbit comes to her aid. After another encounter, he is swept up in the havoc she always seems to attr   he
men trying to steal h
discover the curious
two very different pe

Storing Up Trouble by Jen
AMERICAN HEIRESSES #3
jenturano.com